BY KIRKMAN & AZACETA

VOLUME 8: THE MERGED

OUTCAST BY KIRKMAN & AZACETA
VOL. 8: THE MERGED
May 2021
First printing

ISBN: 978-1-5343-1604-1

Published by Image Comics, Inc.

Office of publication: PO BOX 14457, Portland, OR 97293.

IMAGE COMICS, INC.
Todd McFarlane—President
Jim Valentino—Vice President
Marc Silvestri—Chief Executive Officer
Erik Larsen—Chief Financial Officer
Robert Kirkman—Chief Operating Officer
Eric Stephenson—Publisher / Chief Creative Officer
Nicole Lapalme—Controller
Leanna Caunter—Accounting Analyst
Sue Korpela—Accounting & HR Manager
Marla Eizik—Talent Liaison
Jeff Boison—Director of Sales & Publishing Planning
Dirk Wood—Director of International Sales & Licensing
Alex Cox—Director of Direct Market Sales

Chloe Ramos—Book Market & Library Sales Manager
Emilio Bautista—Digital Sales Coordinator
Jon Schlaffman—Specialty Sales Coordinator
Kat Salazar—Director of PR & Marketing
Drew Fitzgerald—Marketing Content Associate
Heather Doornink—Production Director
Drew Gill—Art Director
Hilary DiLoreto—Print Manager
Tricia Ramos—Traffic Manager
Melissa Gifford—Content Manager
Erika Schnatz—Senior Production Artist
Ryan Brewer—Production Artist
Deanna Phelps—Production Artist
IMAGECOMICS.COM

For SKYBOUND ENTERTAINMENT

Robert Kirkman - Chairman
David Alpert - CEO
Sean Mackiewicz - SVP, Editor-in-Chief
Shawn Kirkham - SVP, Business Development
Brian Huntington - VP, Online Content
Shauna Wynne - Sr. Director, Corporate Communications
Andres Juarez - Art Director
Arune Singh - Director of Brand, Editorial
Alex Antone - Senior Editor
Jon Moisan - Editor
Carina Taylor - Graphic Designer
Johnny O'Dell - Social Media Manager
Dan Petersen - Sr. Director, Operations & Events

Foreign Rights & Licensing Inquiries: contact@skybound.com

WWW.SKYBOUND.COM

Robert Kirkman
Creator, Writer

Paul Azaceta
Artist

Elizabeth Breitweiser
Colorist

Rus Wooton
Letterer

Paul Azaceta
Elizabeth Breitweiser
Cover

Jon Moisan
Editor

Rian Hughes
Logo Design

Carina Taylor
Production

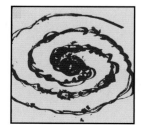

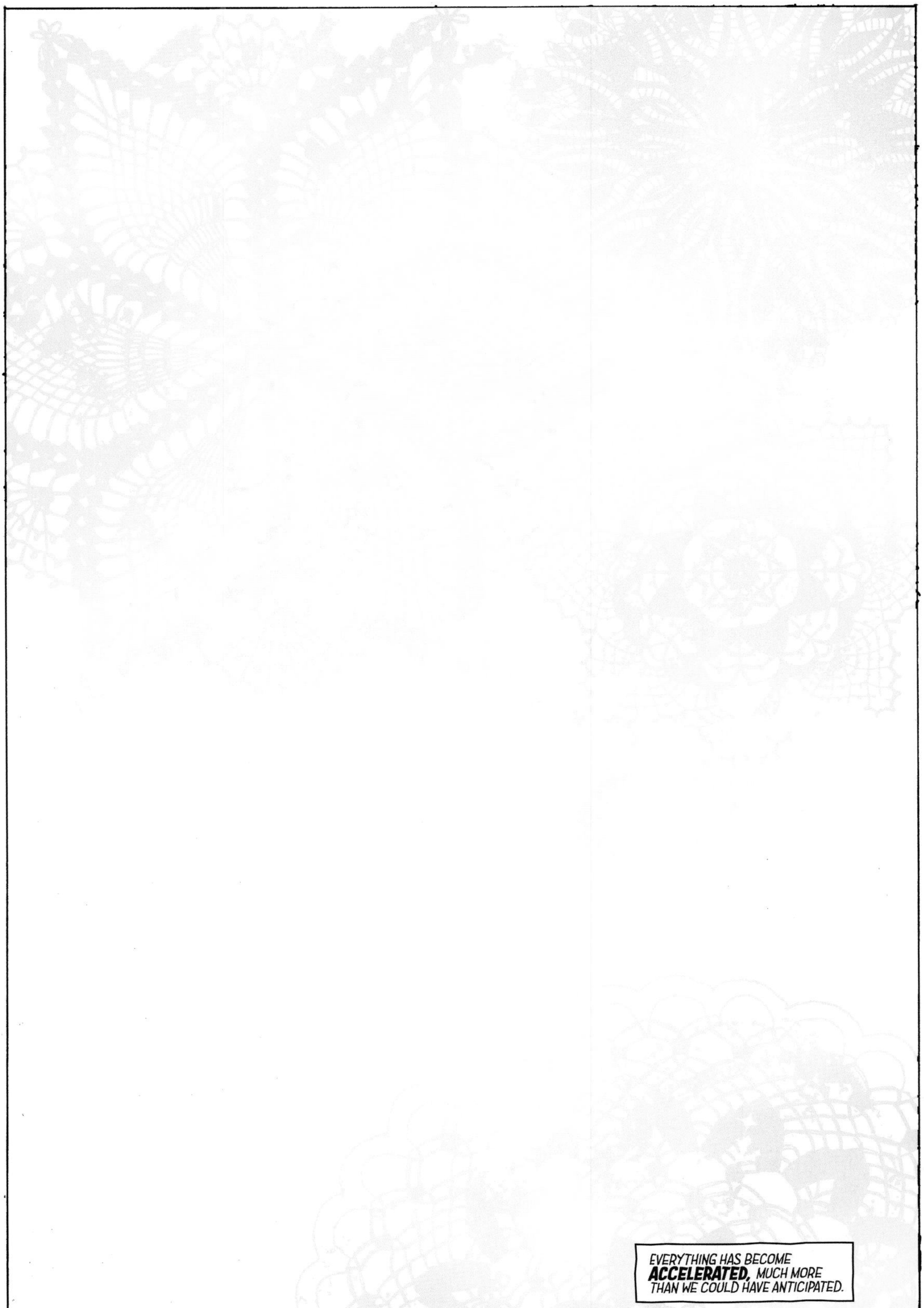
EVERYTHING HAS BECOME ACCELERATED, MUCH MORE THAN WE COULD HAVE ANTICIPATED.

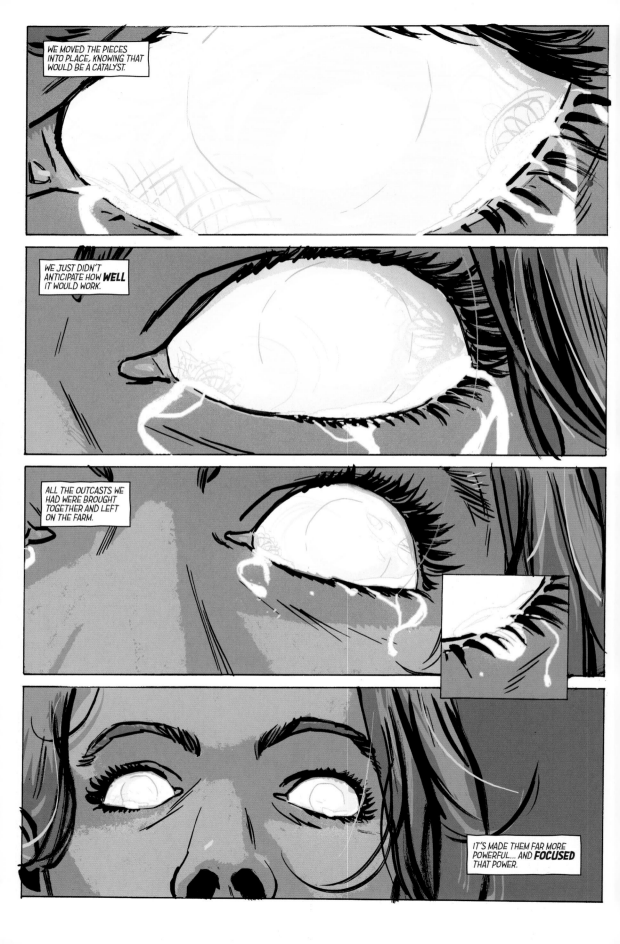

WE MOVED THE PIECES INTO PLACE, KNOWING THAT WOULD BE A CATALYST.

WE JUST DIDN'T ANTICIPATE HOW **WELL** IT WOULD WORK.

ALL THE OUTCASTS WE HAD WERE BROUGHT TOGETHER AND LEFT ON THE FARM.

IT'S MADE THEM FAR MORE POWERFUL... AND **FOCUSED** THAT POWER.

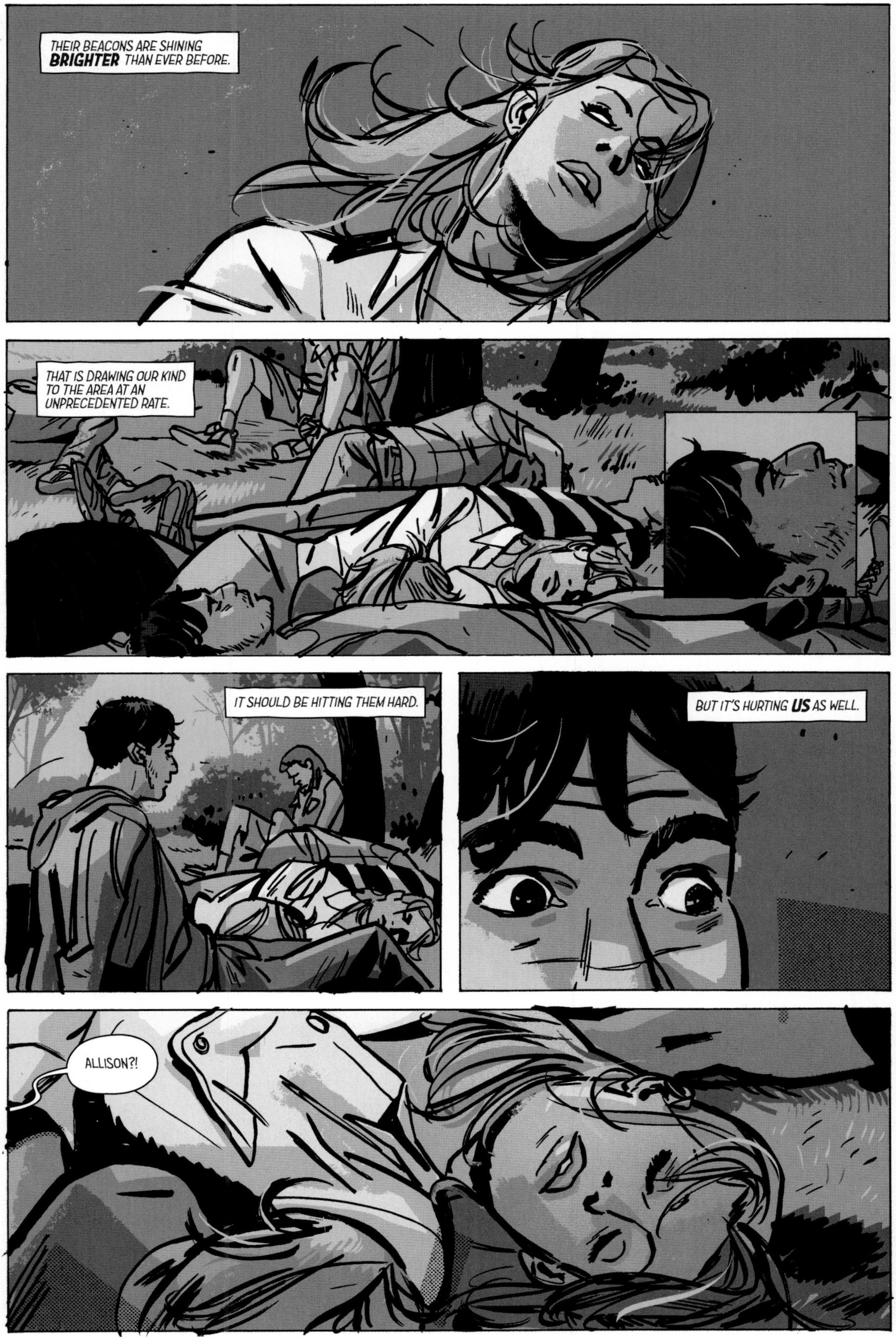
THEIR BEACONS ARE SHINING BRIGHTER THAN EVER BEFORE.
THAT IS DRAWING OUR KIND TO THE AREA AT AN UNPRECEDENTED RATE.
IT SHOULD BE HITTING THEM HARD.
BUT IT'S HURTING US AS WELL.
ALLISON?!

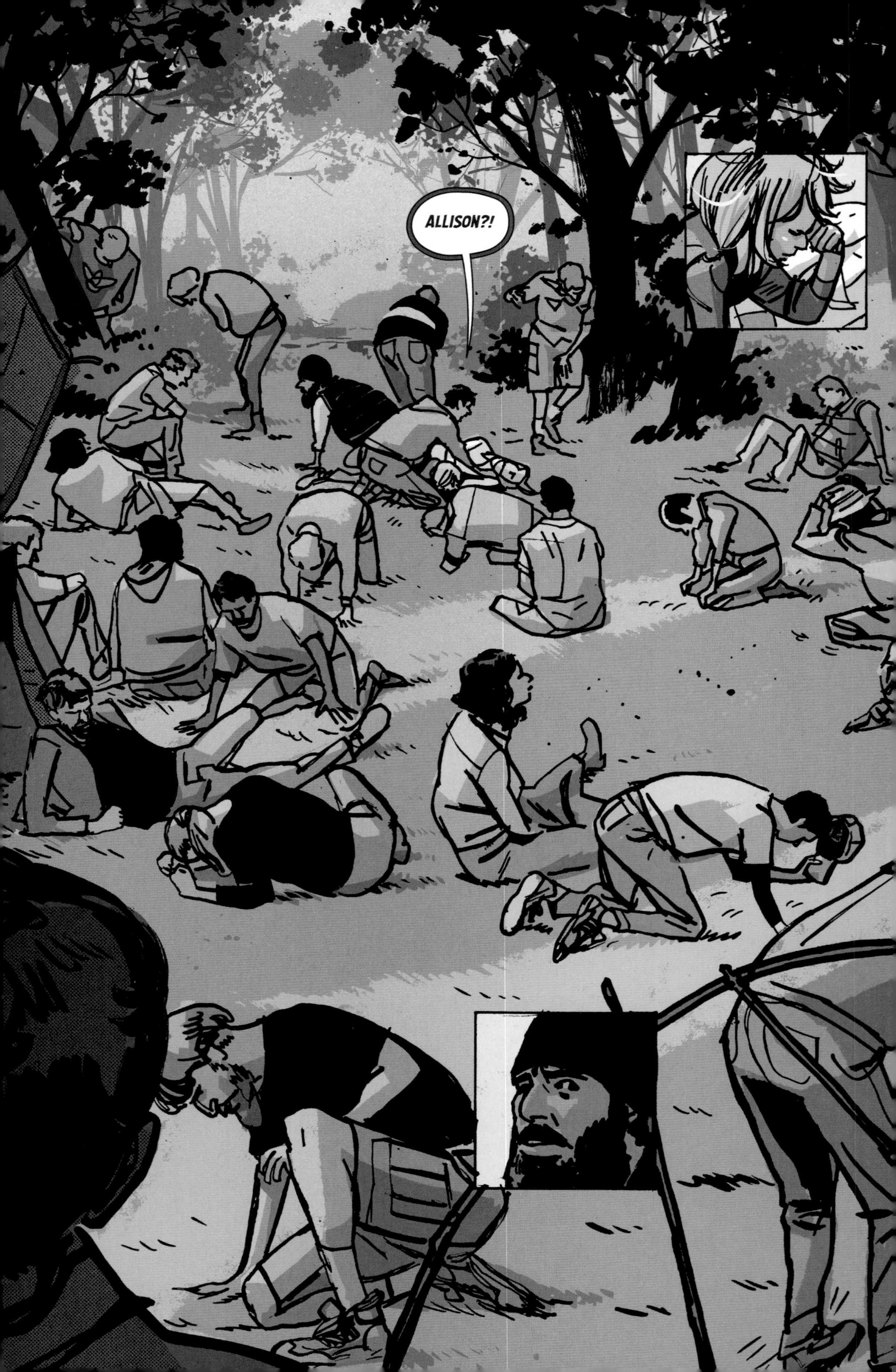
ALLISON?!

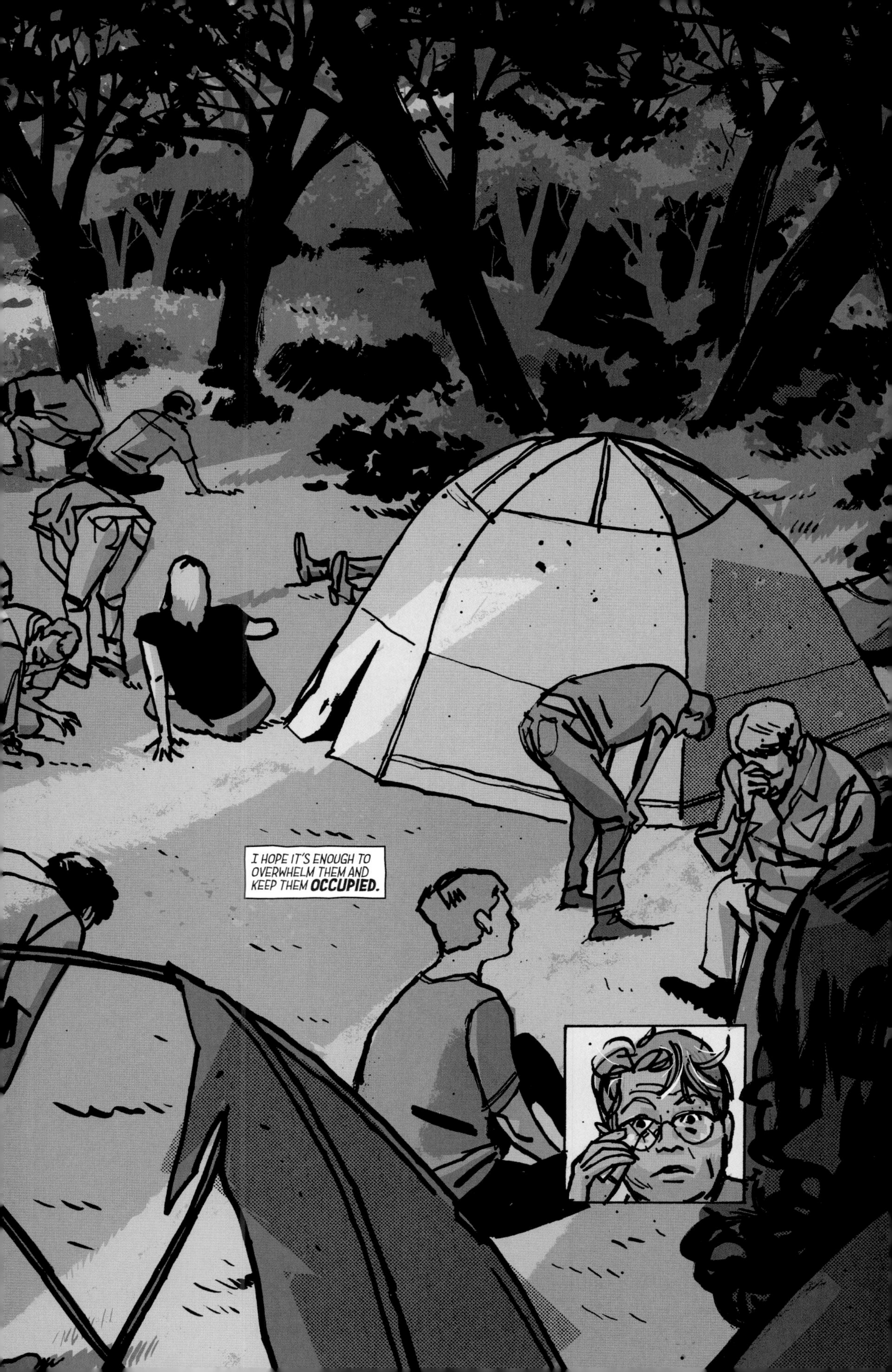
I HOPE IT'S ENOUGH TO OVERWHELM THEM AND KEEP THEM OCCUPIED.

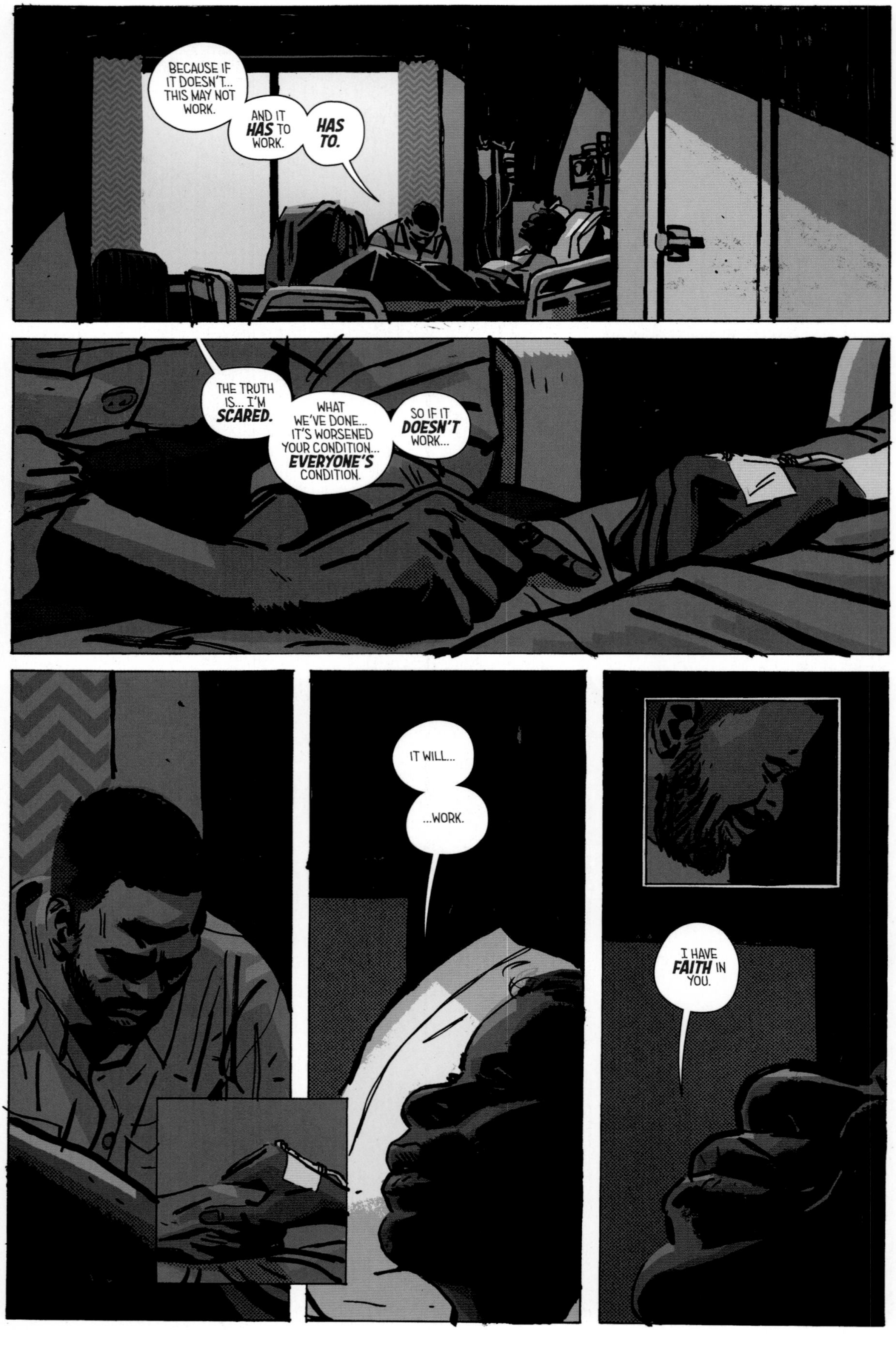
BECAUSE IF IT DOESN'T... THIS MAY NOT WORK.
AND IT **HAS** TO WORK.
HAS TO.
THE TRUTH IS... I'M **SCARED.**
WHAT WE'VE DONE... IT'S WORSENED YOUR CONDITION... **EVERYONE'S** CONDITION.
SO IF IT **DOESN'T** WORK...
IT WILL...
...WORK.
I HAVE **FAITH** IN YOU.

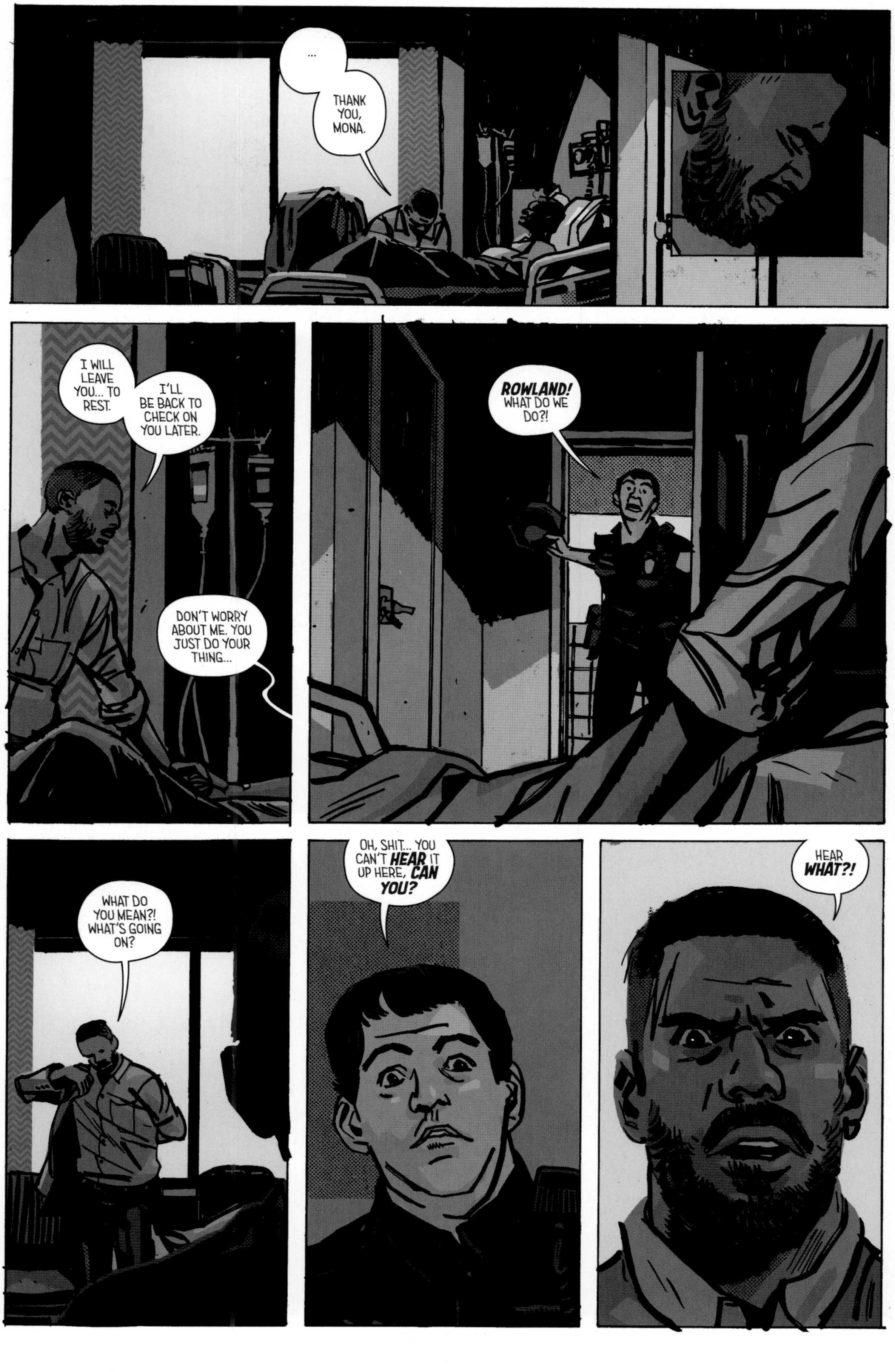
...
THANK YOU, MONA.
I WILL LEAVE YOU... TO REST.
I'LL BE BACK TO CHECK ON YOU LATER.
DON'T WORRY ABOUT ME. YOU JUST DO YOUR THING...
ROWLAND! WHAT DO WE DO?!
WHAT DO YOU MEAN?! WHAT'S GOING ON?
OH, SHIT... YOU CAN'T HEAR IT UP HERE, CAN YOU?
HEAR WHAT?!

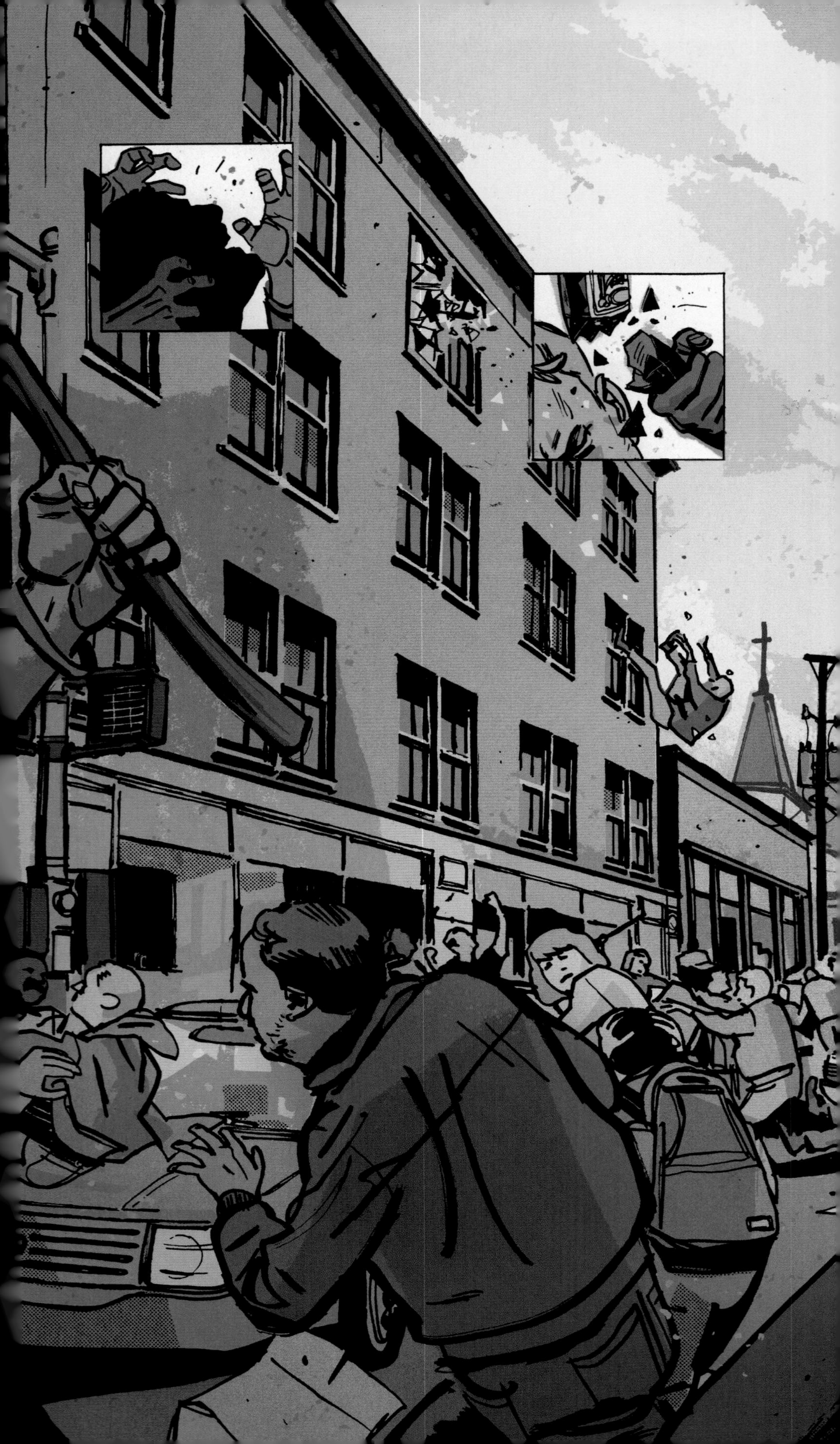

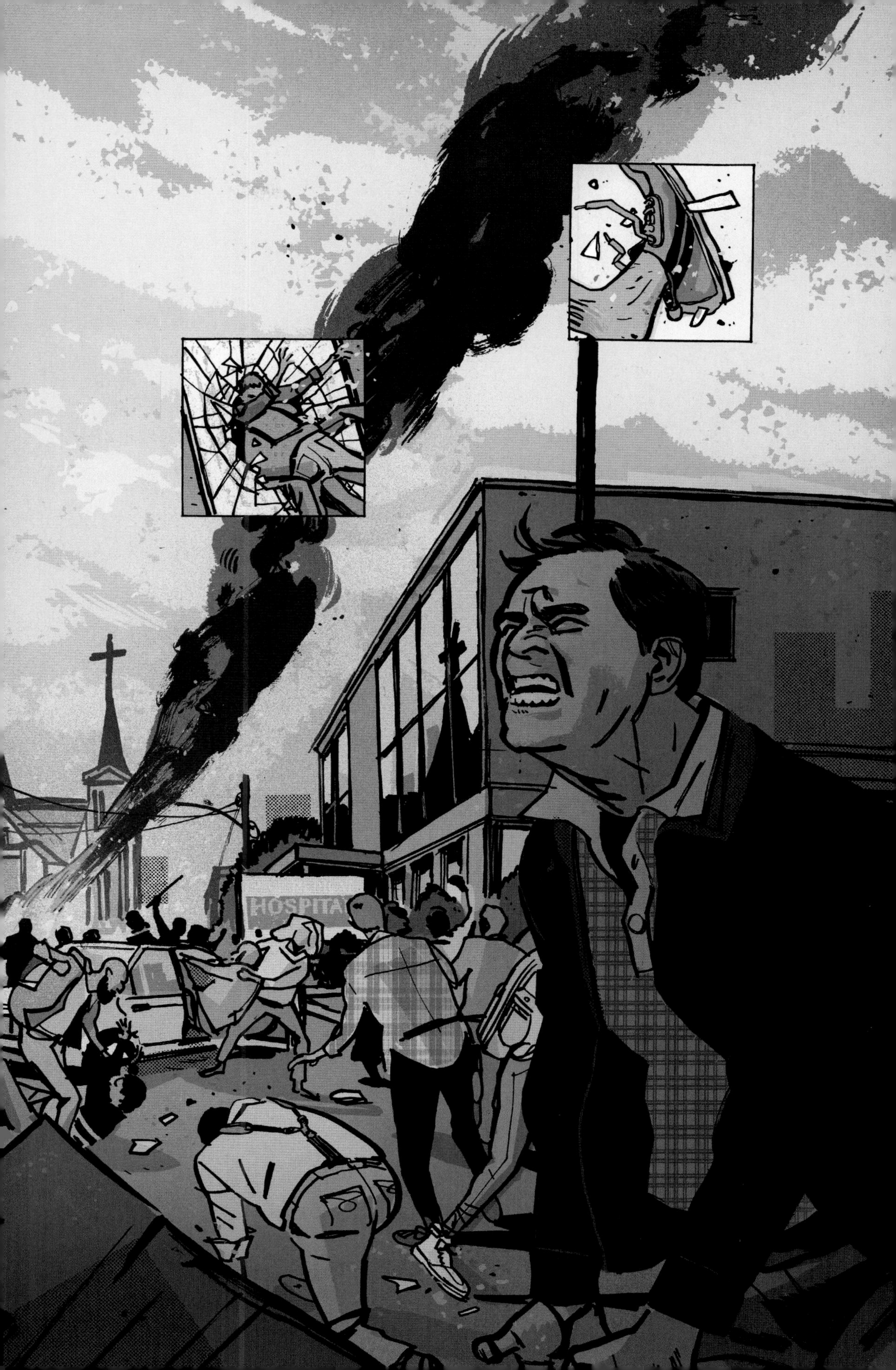
HOSPITA

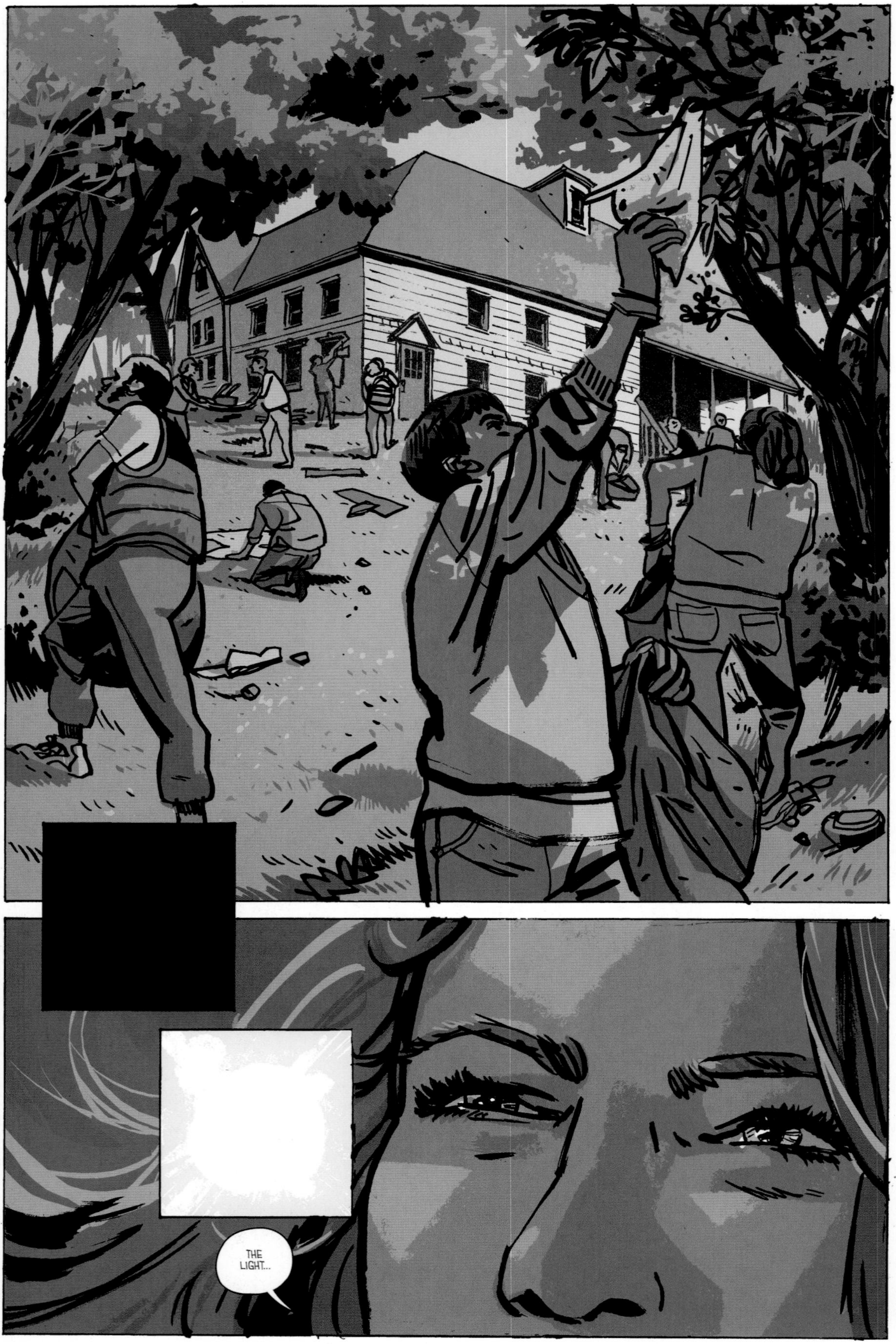
THE LIGHT...

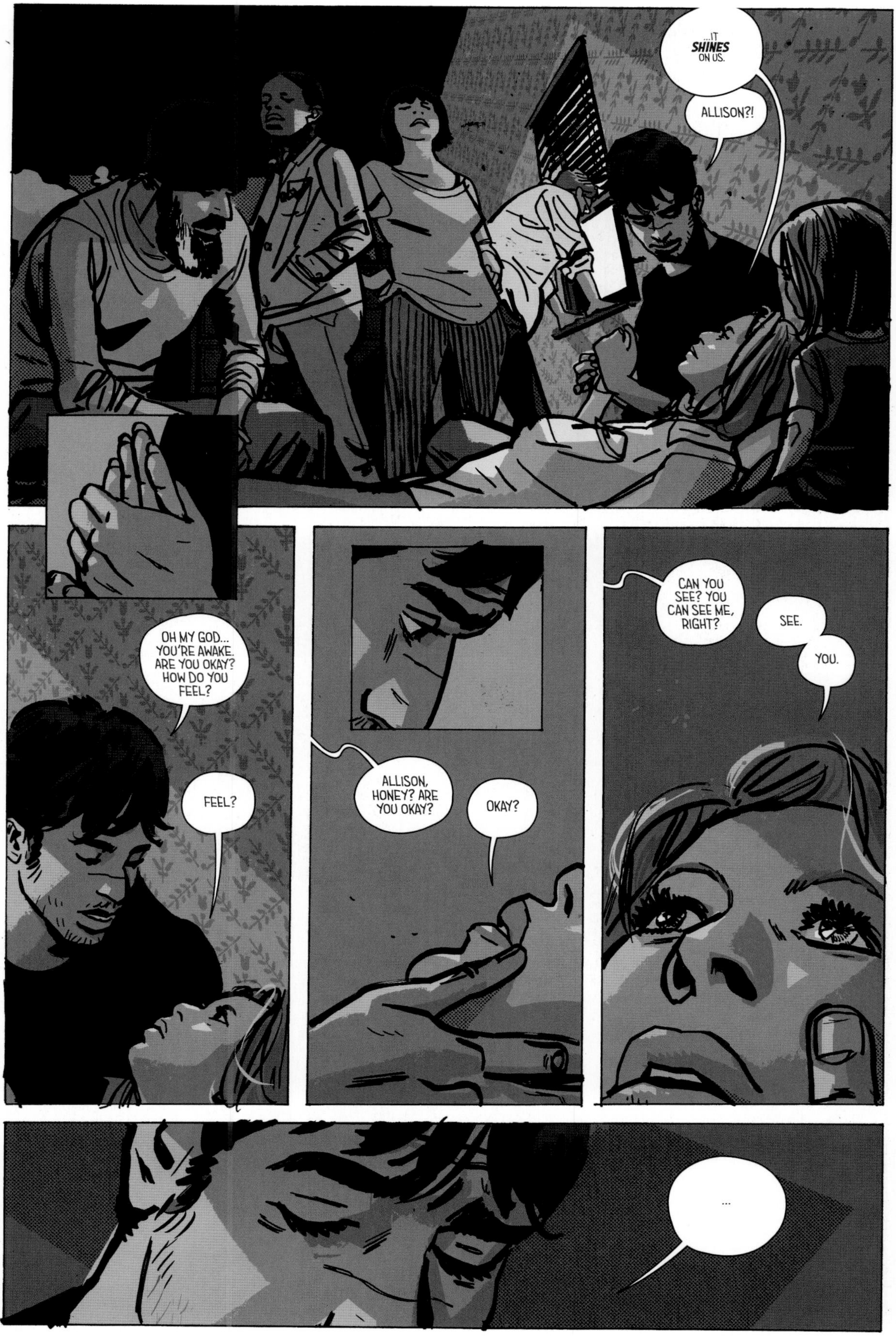
...IT **SHINES** ON US.
ALLISON?!
OH MY GOD... YOU'RE AWAKE. ARE YOU OKAY? HOW DO YOU FEEL?
FEEL?
ALLISON, HONEY? ARE YOU OKAY?
OKAY?
CAN YOU SEE? YOU CAN SEE ME, RIGHT?
SEE.
YOU.
...

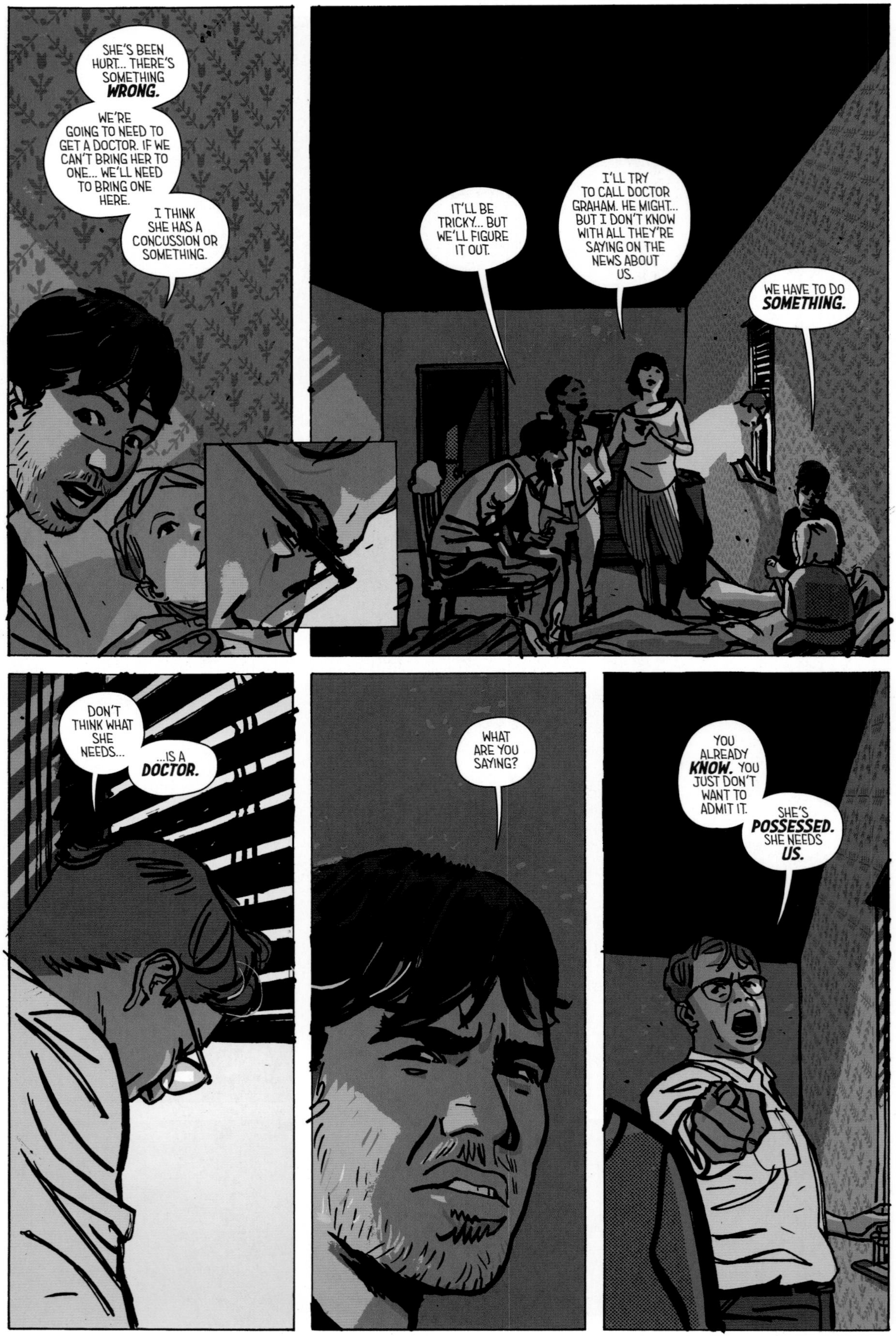
SHE'S BEEN HURT... THERE'S SOMETHING WRONG.
WE'RE GOING TO NEED TO GET A DOCTOR. IF WE CAN'T BRING HER TO ONE... WE'LL NEED TO BRING ONE HERE.
I THINK SHE HAS A CONCUSSION OR SOMETHING.
IT'LL BE TRICKY... BUT WE'LL FIGURE IT OUT.
I'LL TRY TO CALL DOCTOR GRAHAM. HE MIGHT... BUT I DON'T KNOW WITH ALL THEY'RE SAYING ON THE NEWS ABOUT US.
WE HAVE TO DO SOMETHING.
DON'T THINK WHAT SHE NEEDS...
...IS A DOCTOR.
WHAT ARE YOU SAYING?
YOU ALREADY KNOW. YOU JUST DON'T WANT TO ADMIT IT.
SHE'S POSSESSED. SHE NEEDS US.

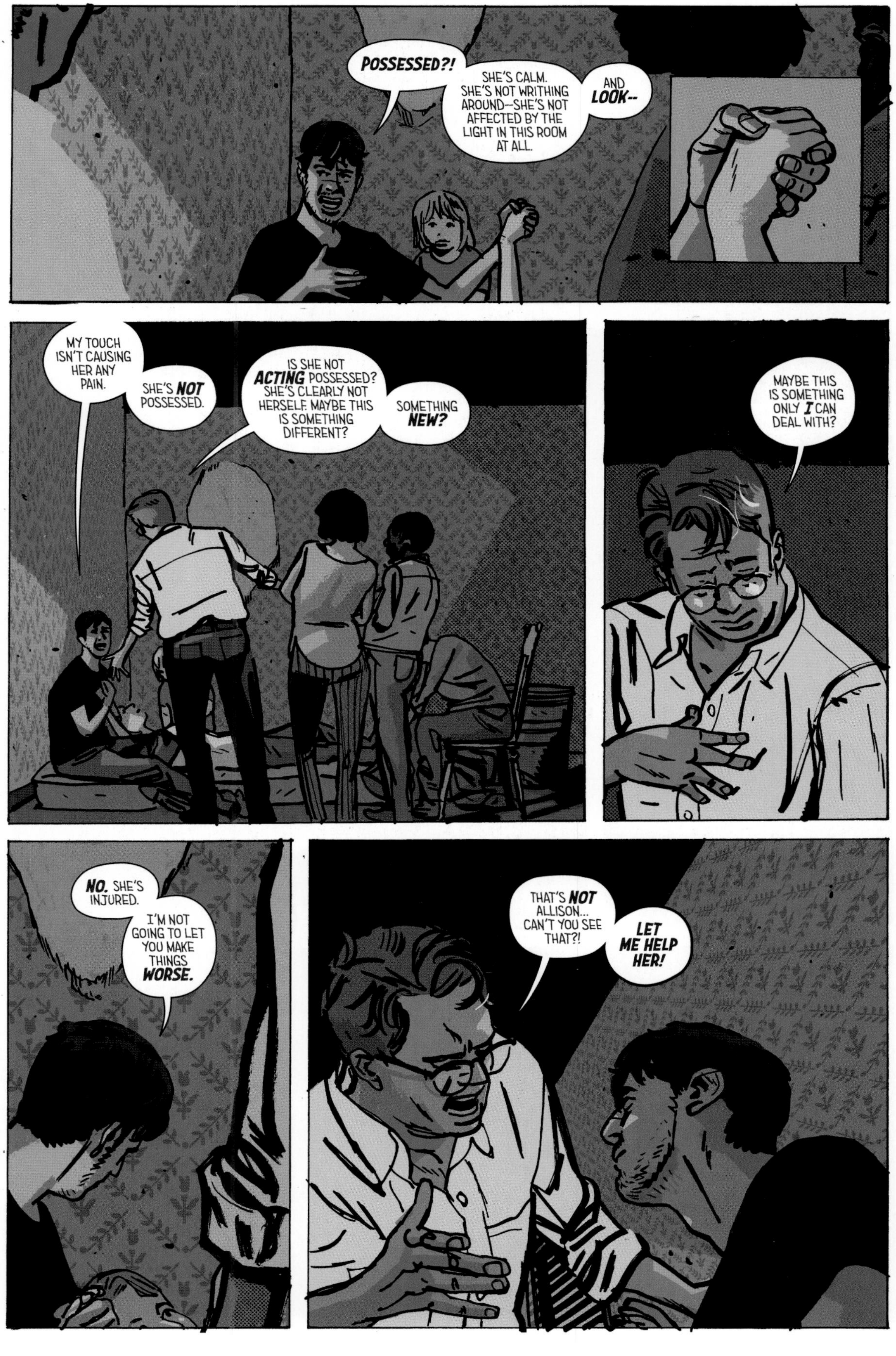
POSSESSED?!
SHE'S CALM. SHE'S NOT WRITHING AROUND--SHE'S NOT AFFECTED BY THE LIGHT IN THIS ROOM AT ALL.
AND LOOK--
MY TOUCH ISN'T CAUSING HER ANY PAIN.
SHE'S NOT POSSESSED.
IS SHE NOT ACTING POSSESSED? SHE'S CLEARLY NOT HERSELF. MAYBE THIS IS SOMETHING DIFFERENT?
SOMETHING NEW?
MAYBE THIS IS SOMETHING ONLY I CAN DEAL WITH?
NO. SHE'S INJURED.
I'M NOT GOING TO LET YOU MAKE THINGS WORSE.
THAT'S NOT ALLISON... CAN'T YOU SEE THAT?!
LET ME HELP HER!

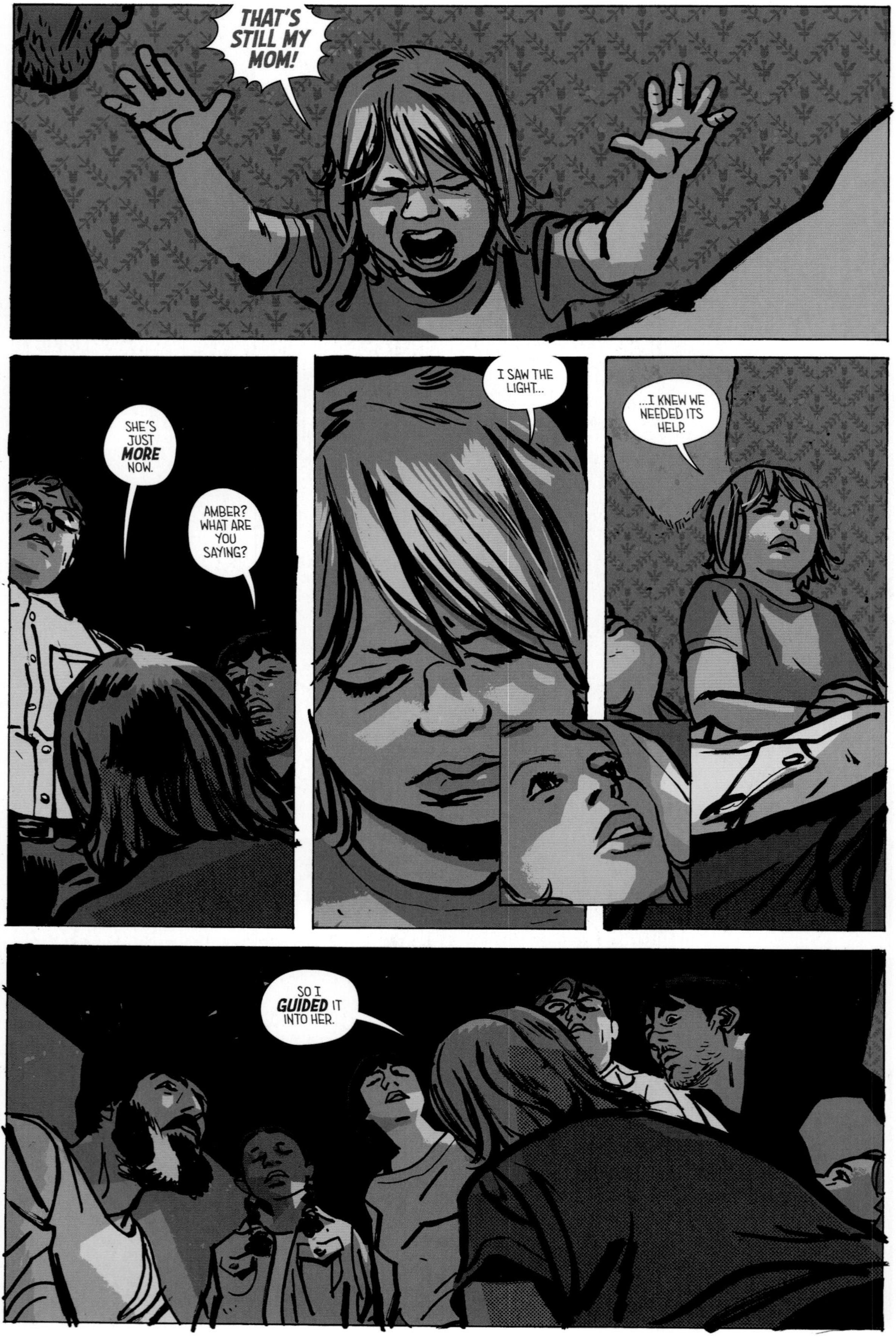
THAT'S STILL MY MOM!
SHE'S JUST MORE NOW.
AMBER? WHAT ARE YOU SAYING?
I SAW THE LIGHT...
...I KNEW WE NEEDED ITS HELP.
SO I GUIDED IT INTO HER.

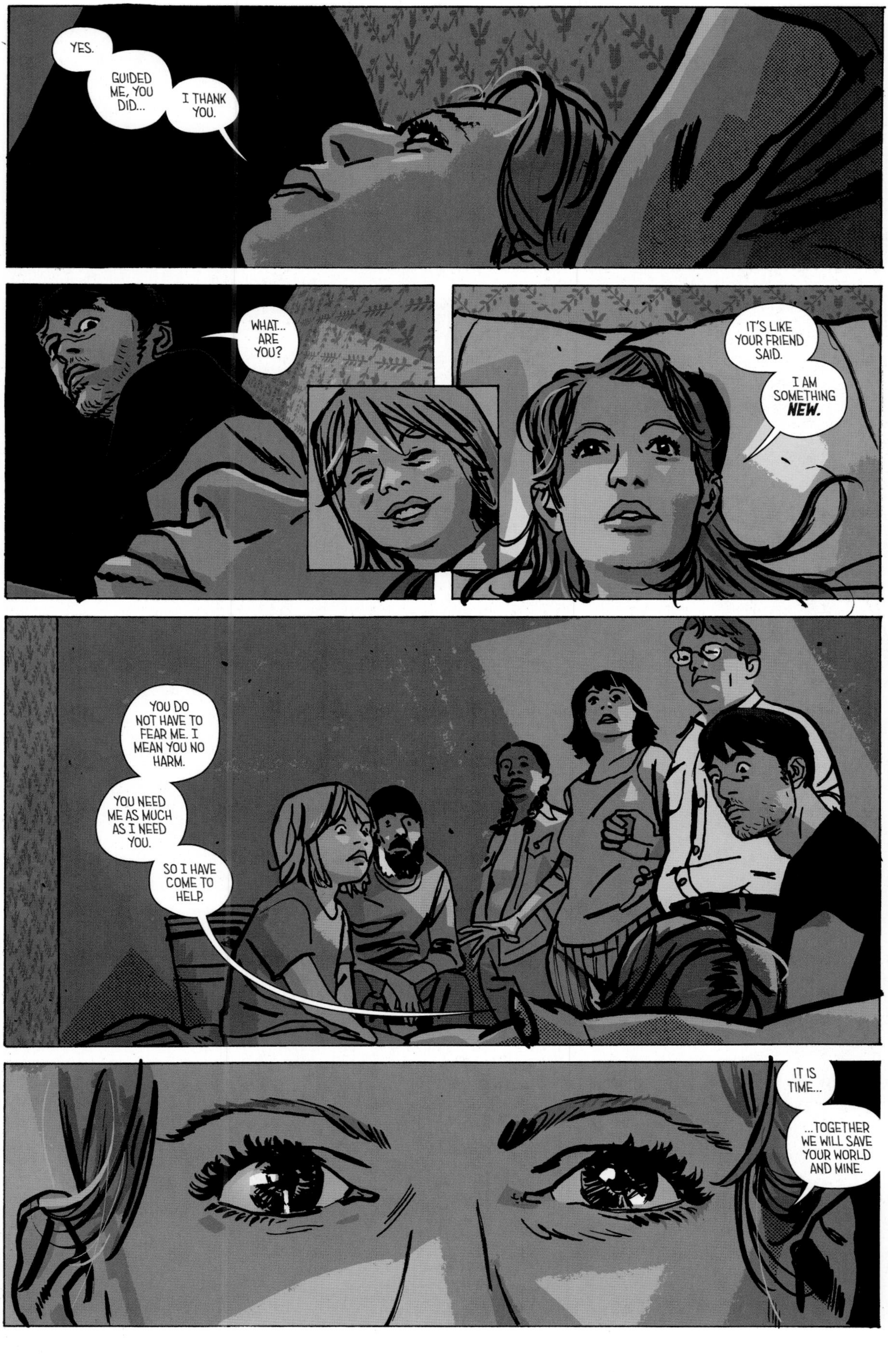
YES.
GUIDED ME, YOU DID...
I THANK YOU.
WHAT... ARE YOU?
IT'S LIKE YOUR FRIEND SAID.
I AM SOMETHING ***NEW.***
YOU DO NOT HAVE TO FEAR ME. I MEAN YOU NO HARM.
YOU NEED ME AS MUCH AS I NEED YOU.
SO I HAVE COME TO HELP.
IT IS TIME...
...TOGETHER WE WILL SAVE YOUR WORLD AND MINE.

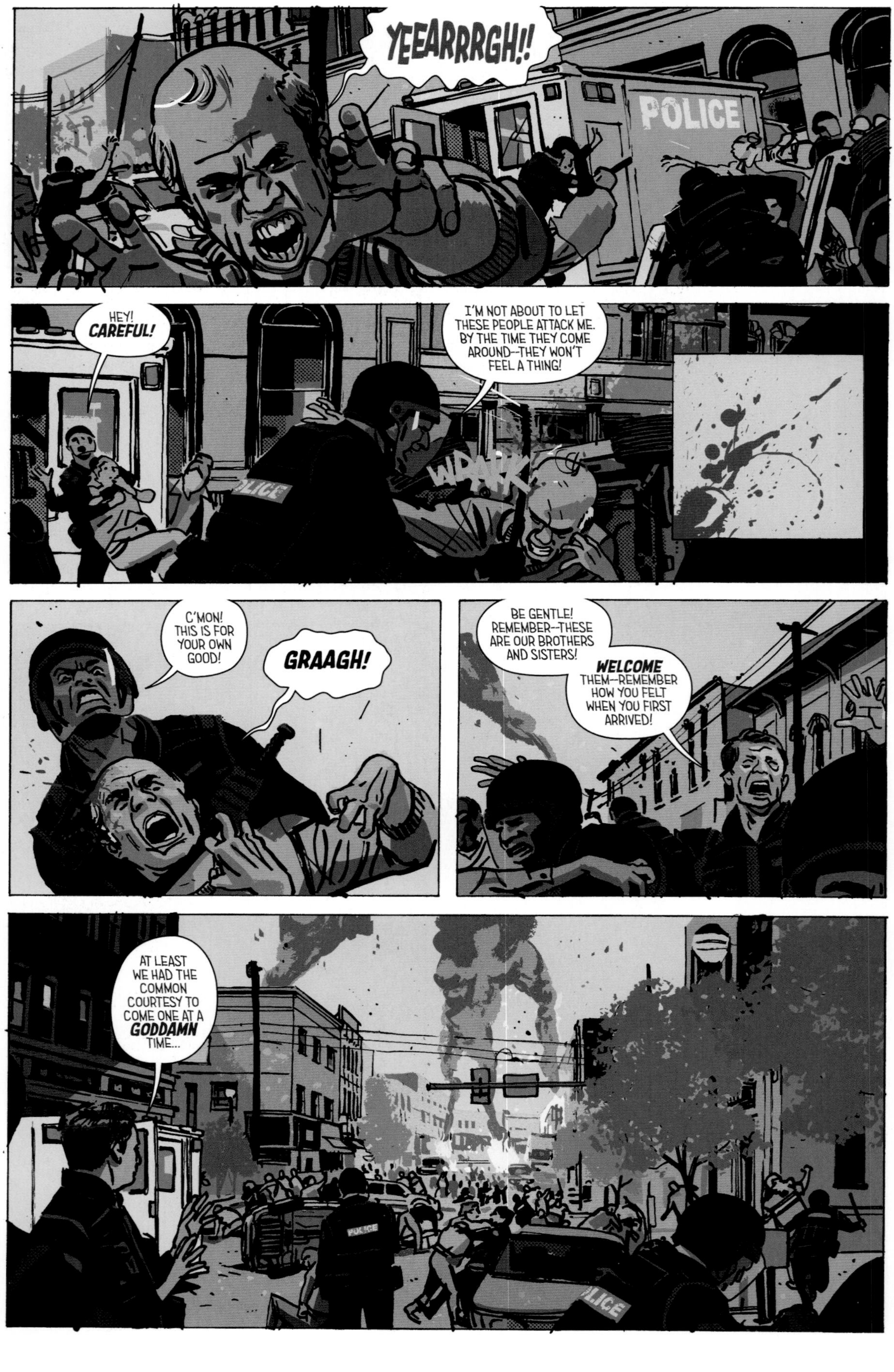
YEEARRRGH!!
POLICE
HEY! CAREFUL!
I'M NOT ABOUT TO LET THESE PEOPLE ATTACK ME. BY THE TIME THEY COME AROUND--THEY WON'T FEEL A THING!
POLICE
WPAKK
C'MON! THIS IS FOR YOUR OWN GOOD!
GRAAGH!
BE GENTLE! REMEMBER--THESE ARE OUR BROTHERS AND SISTERS!
WELCOME THEM--REMEMBER HOW YOU FELT WHEN YOU FIRST ARRIVED!
AT LEAST WE HAD THE COMMON COURTESY TO COME ONE AT A GODDAMN TIME...
POLICE
POLICE

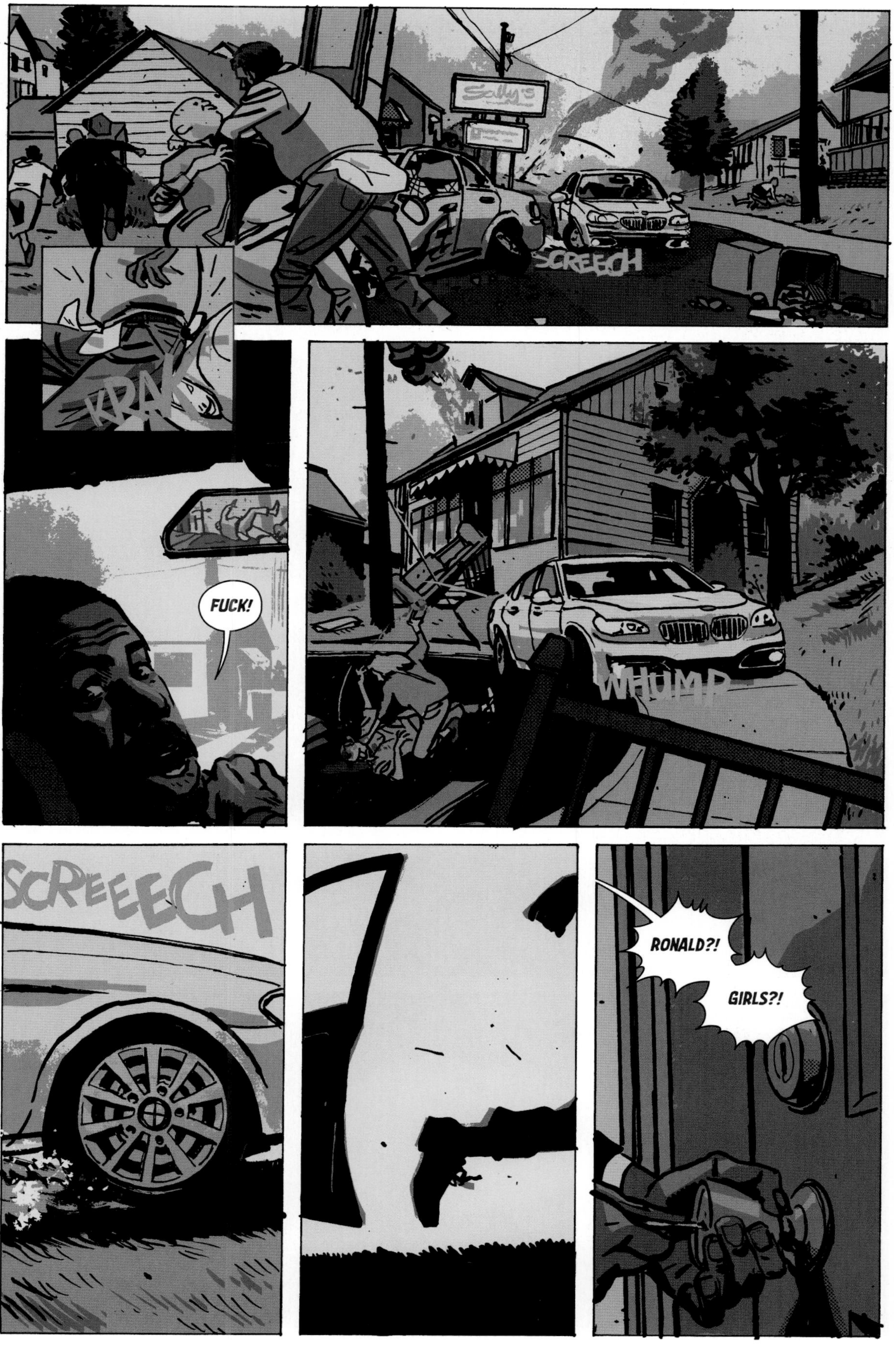

SCREECH
KRAK
FUCK!
WHUMP
SCREEECH
RONALD?!
GIRLS?!

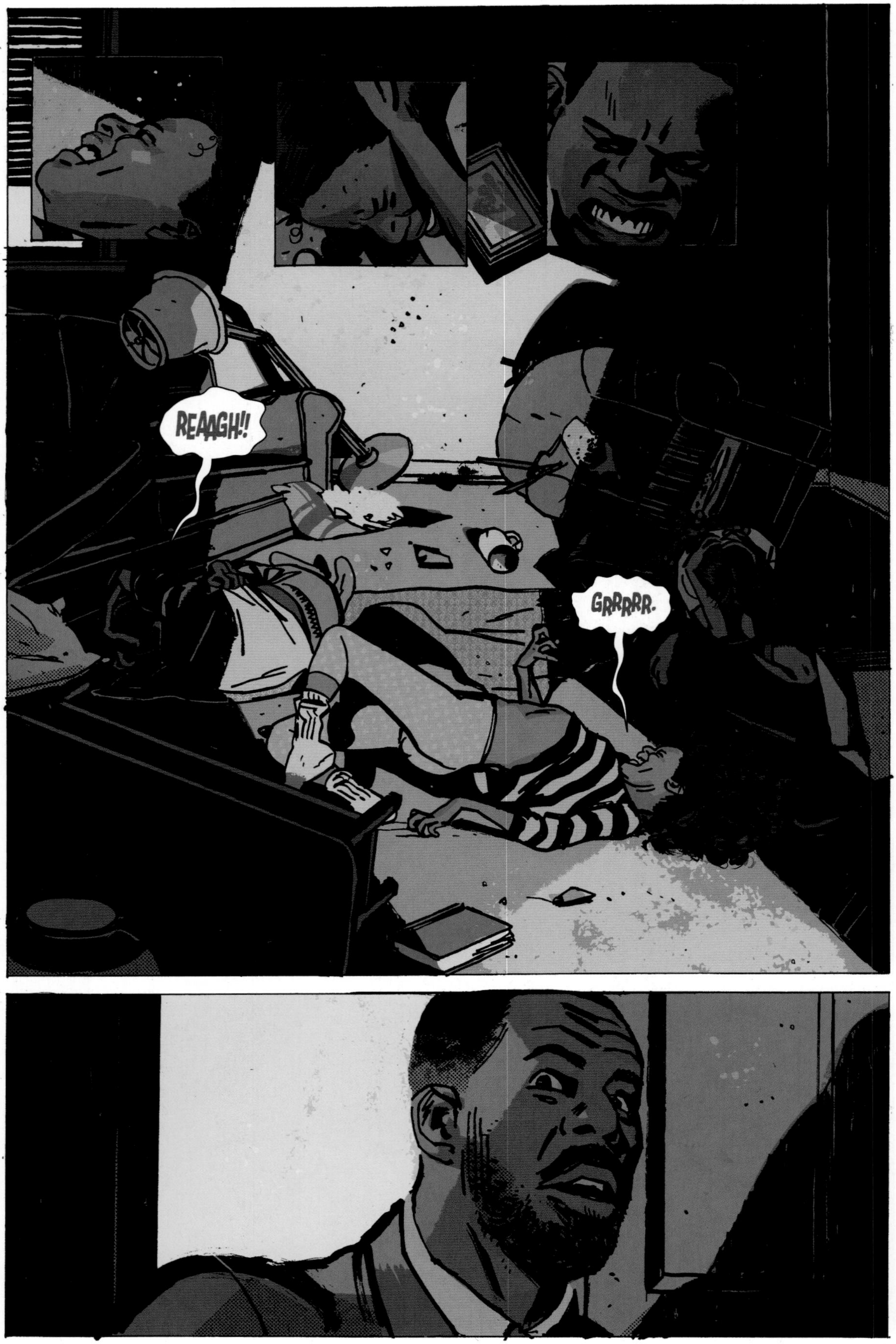
REAAGH!!
GRRRRR.

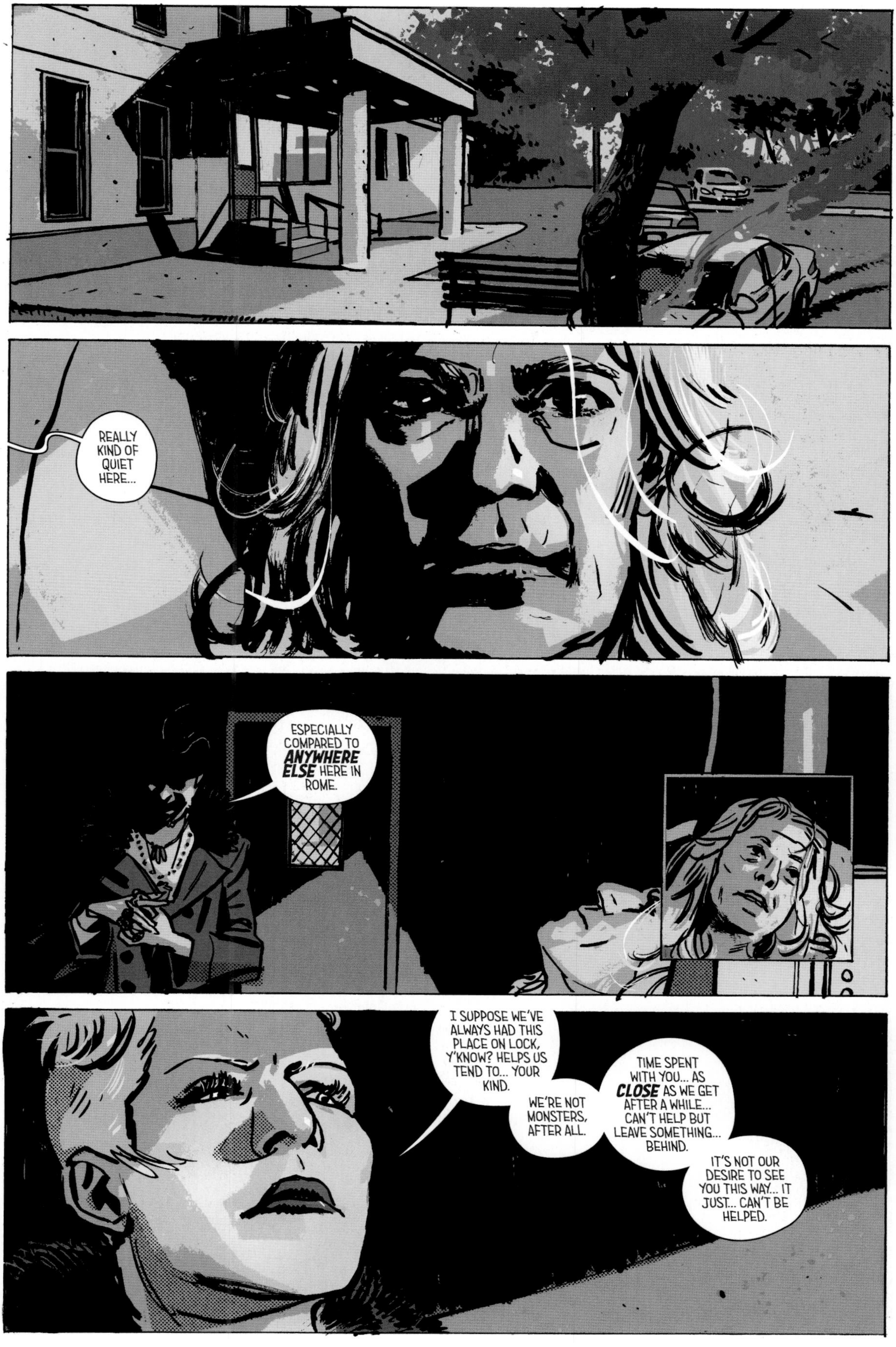
REALLY KIND OF QUIET HERE...
ESPECIALLY COMPARED TO **ANYWHERE ELSE** HERE IN ROME.
I SUPPOSE WE'VE ALWAYS HAD THIS PLACE ON LOCK, Y'KNOW? HELPS US TEND TO... YOUR KIND.
WE'RE NOT MONSTERS, AFTER ALL.
TIME SPENT WITH YOU... AS **CLOSE** AS WE GET AFTER A WHILE... CAN'T HELP BUT LEAVE SOMETHING... BEHIND.
IT'S NOT OUR DESIRE TO SEE YOU THIS WAY... IT JUST... CAN'T BE HELPED.

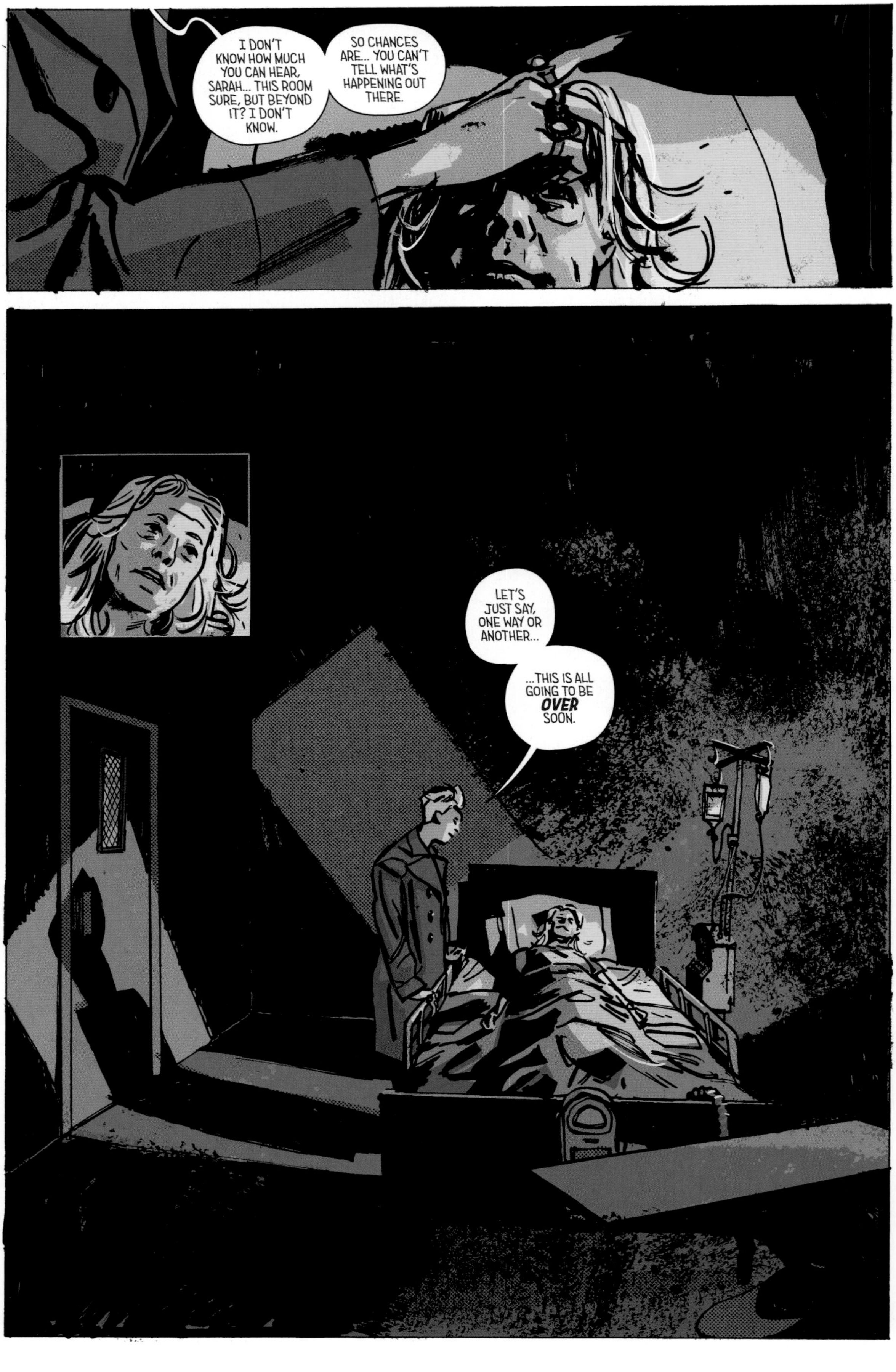
I DON'T KNOW HOW MUCH YOU CAN HEAR, SARAH... THIS ROOM SURE, BUT BEYOND IT? I DON'T KNOW.
SO CHANCES ARE... YOU CAN'T TELL WHAT'S HAPPENING OUT THERE.
LET'S JUST SAY, ONE WAY OR ANOTHER...
...THIS IS ALL GOING TO BE OVER SOON.

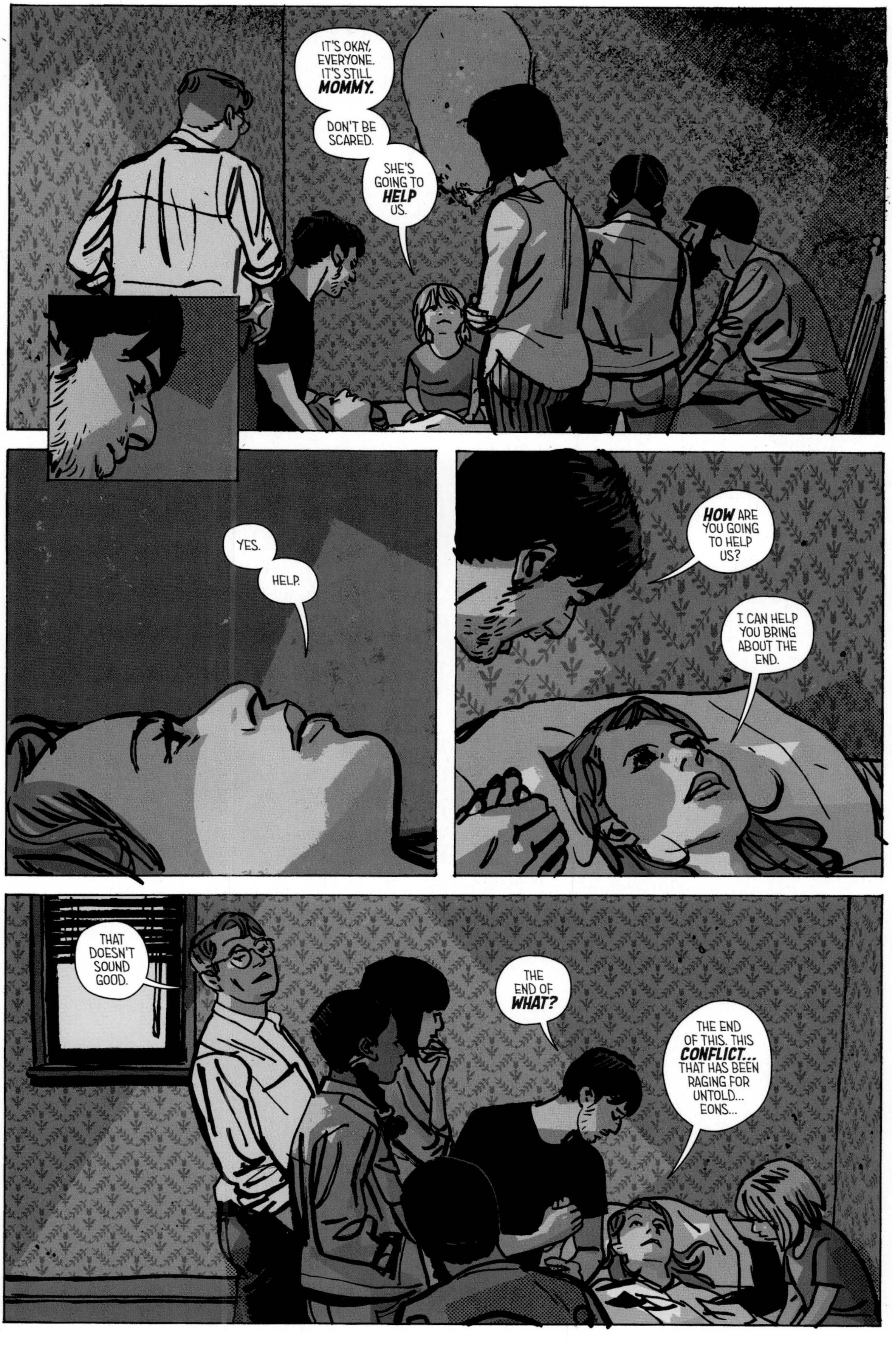
IT'S OKAY, EVERYONE. IT'S STILL **MOMMY.**
DON'T BE SCARED.
SHE'S GOING TO **HELP** US.
YES.
HELP.
HOW ARE YOU GOING TO HELP US?
I CAN HELP YOU BRING ABOUT THE END.
THAT DOESN'T SOUND GOOD.
THE END OF **WHAT?**
THE END OF THIS. THIS **CONFLICT...** THAT HAS BEEN RAGING FOR UNTOLD... EONS...

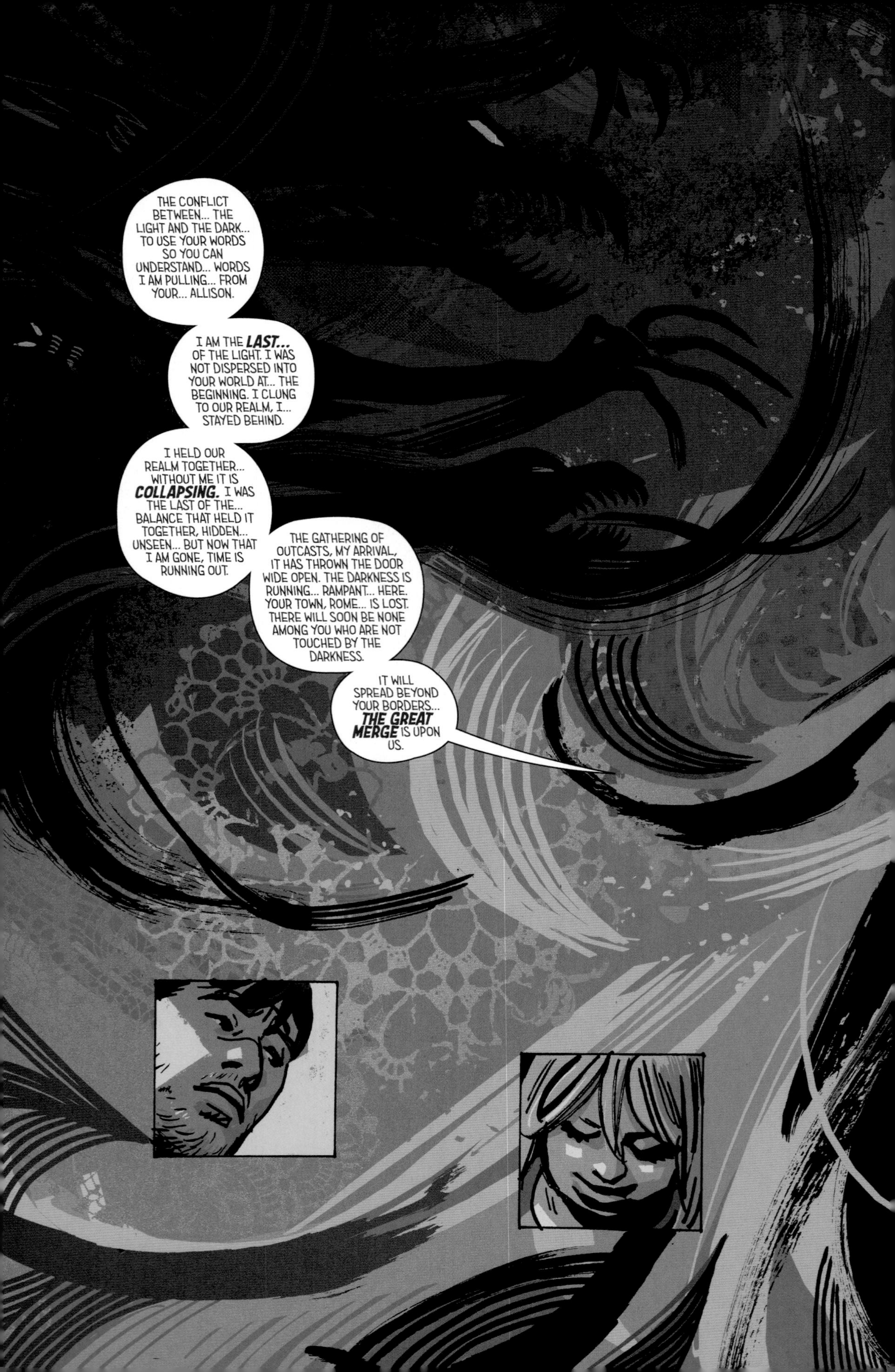
THE CONFLICT BETWEEN... THE LIGHT AND THE DARK... TO USE YOUR WORDS SO YOU CAN UNDERSTAND... WORDS I AM PULLING... FROM YOUR... ALLISON.
I AM THE ***LAST...*** OF THE LIGHT. I WAS NOT DISPERSED INTO YOUR WORLD AT... THE BEGINNING. I CLUNG TO OUR REALM, I... STAYED BEHIND.
I HELD OUR REALM TOGETHER... WITHOUT ME IT IS ***COLLAPSING.*** I WAS THE LAST OF THE... BALANCE THAT HELD IT TOGETHER, HIDDEN... UNSEEN... BUT NOW THAT I AM GONE, TIME IS RUNNING OUT.
THE GATHERING OF OUTCASTS, MY ARRIVAL, IT HAS THROWN THE DOOR WIDE OPEN. THE DARKNESS IS RUNNING... RAMPANT... HERE. YOUR TOWN, ROME... IS LOST. THERE WILL SOON BE NONE AMONG YOU WHO ARE NOT TOUCHED BY THE DARKNESS.
IT WILL SPREAD BEYOND YOUR BORDERS... ***THE GREAT MERGE*** IS UPON US.

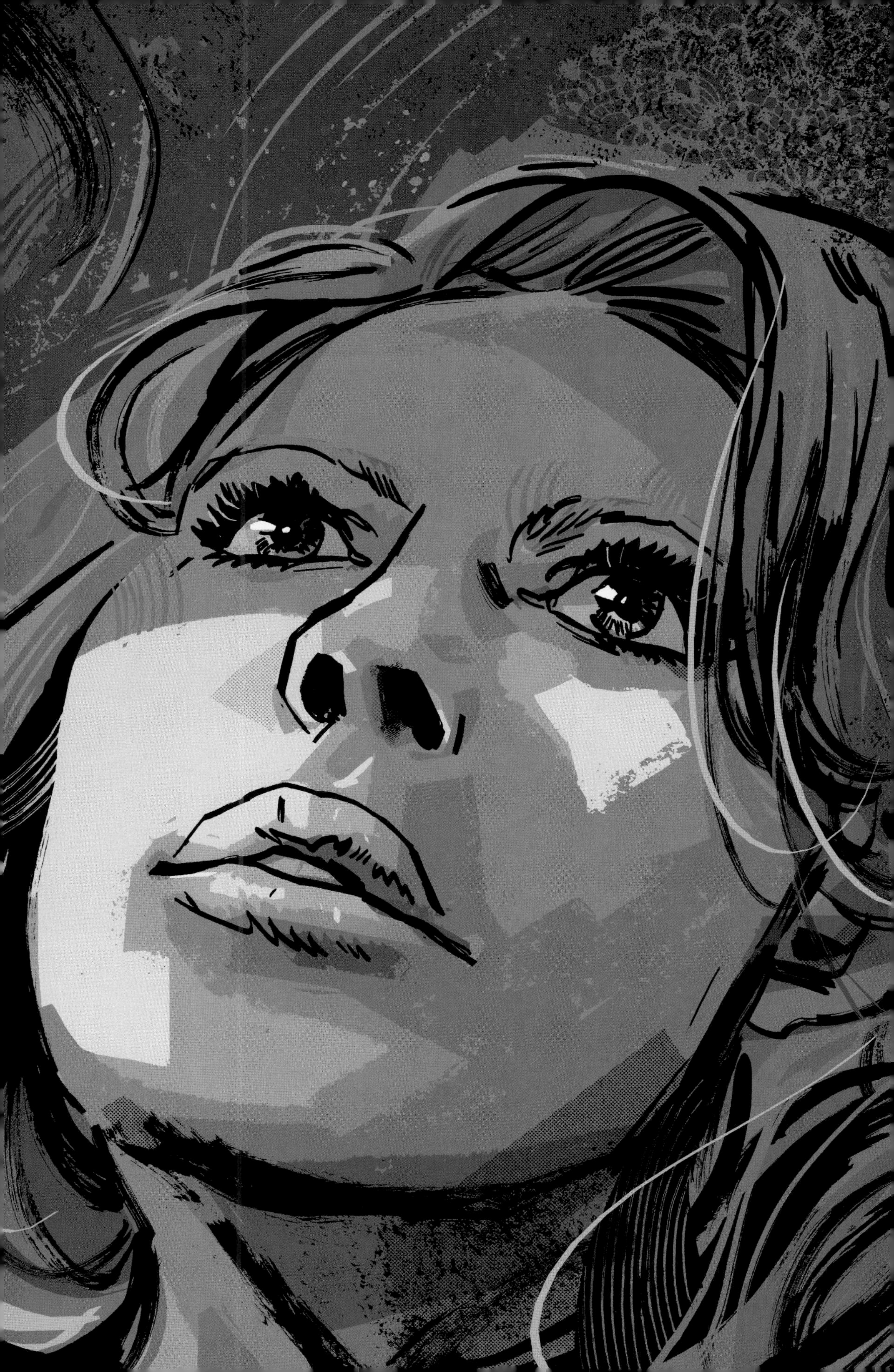

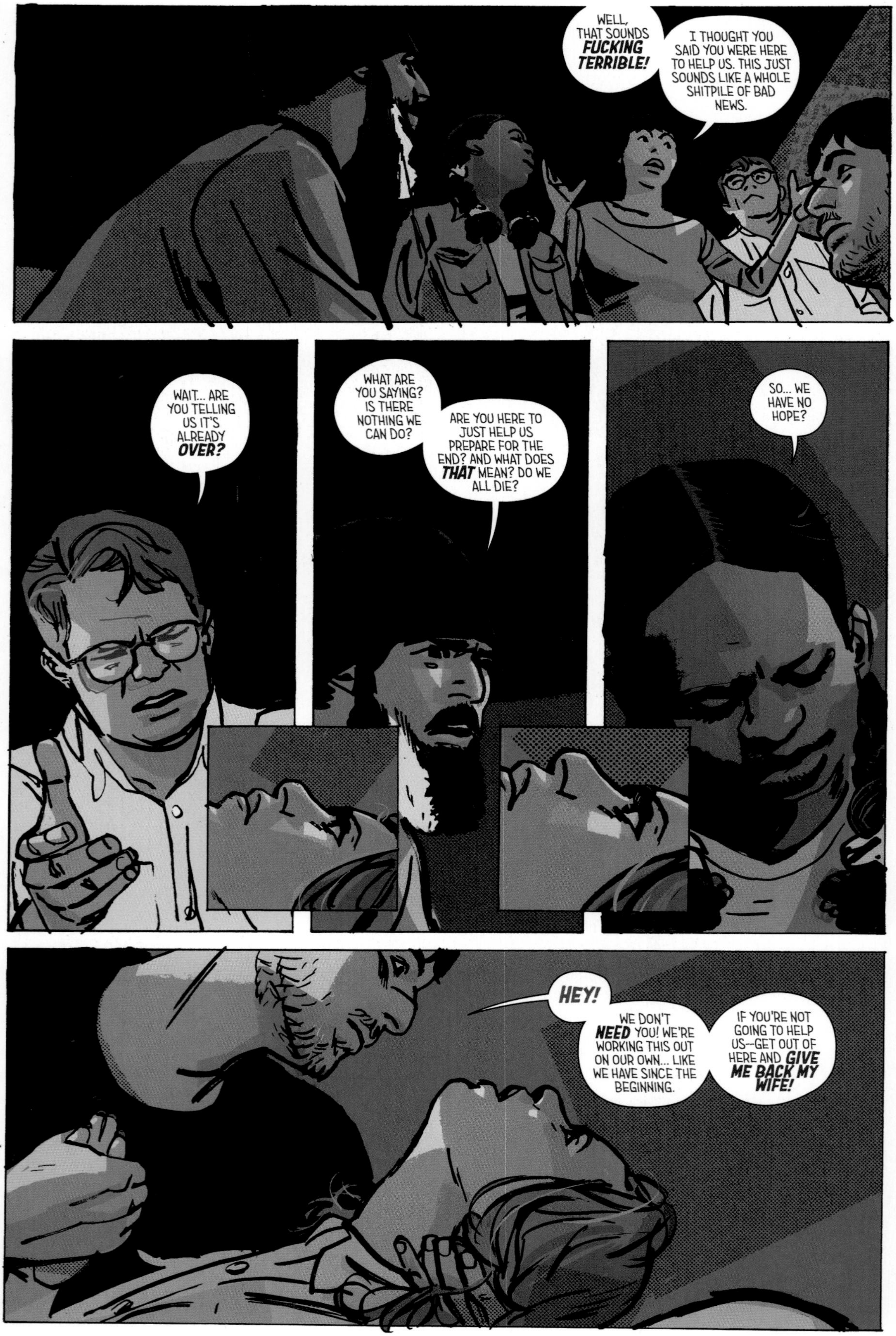
WELL, THAT SOUNDS FUCKING TERRIBLE!
I THOUGHT YOU SAID YOU WERE HERE TO HELP US. THIS JUST SOUNDS LIKE A WHOLE SHITPILE OF BAD NEWS.
WAIT... ARE YOU TELLING US IT'S ALREADY OVER?
WHAT ARE YOU SAYING? IS THERE NOTHING WE CAN DO?
ARE YOU HERE TO JUST HELP US PREPARE FOR THE END? AND WHAT DOES THAT MEAN? DO WE ALL DIE?
SO... WE HAVE NO HOPE?
HEY!
WE DON'T NEED YOU! WE'RE WORKING THIS OUT ON OUR OWN... LIKE WE HAVE SINCE THE BEGINNING.
IF YOU'RE NOT GOING TO HELP US--GET OUT OF HERE AND GIVE ME BACK MY WIFE!

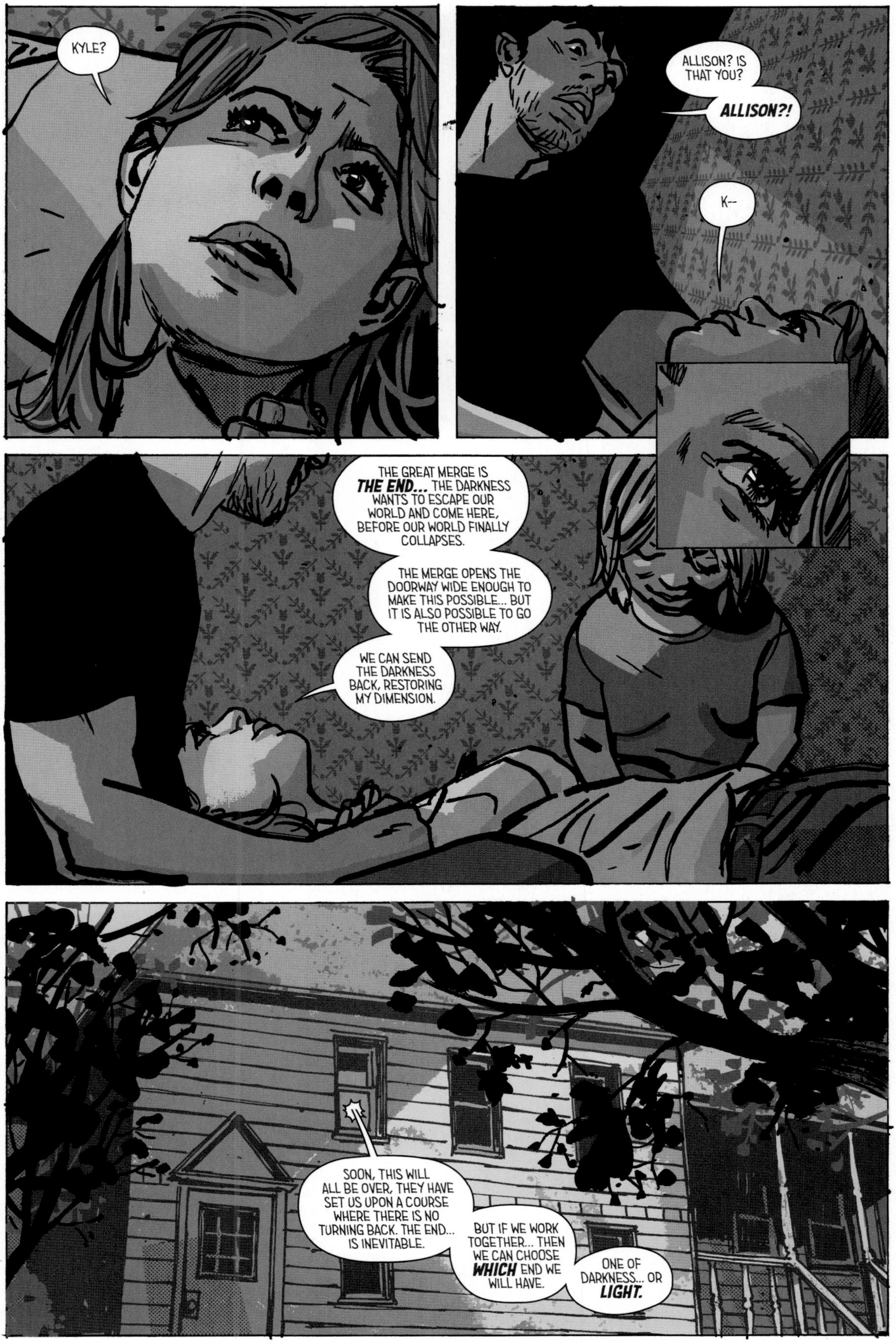
KYLE?
ALLISON? IS THAT YOU?
ALLISON?!
K--
THE GREAT MERGE IS THE END... THE DARKNESS WANTS TO ESCAPE OUR WORLD AND COME HERE, BEFORE OUR WORLD FINALLY COLLAPSES.
THE MERGE OPENS THE DOORWAY WIDE ENOUGH TO MAKE THIS POSSIBLE... BUT IT IS ALSO POSSIBLE TO GO THE OTHER WAY.
WE CAN SEND THE DARKNESS BACK, RESTORING MY DIMENSION.
SOON, THIS WILL ALL BE OVER, THEY HAVE SET US UPON A COURSE WHERE THERE IS NO TURNING BACK. THE END... IS INEVITABLE.
BUT IF WE WORK TOGETHER... THEN WE CAN CHOOSE WHICH END WE WILL HAVE.
ONE OF DARKNESS... OR LIGHT.

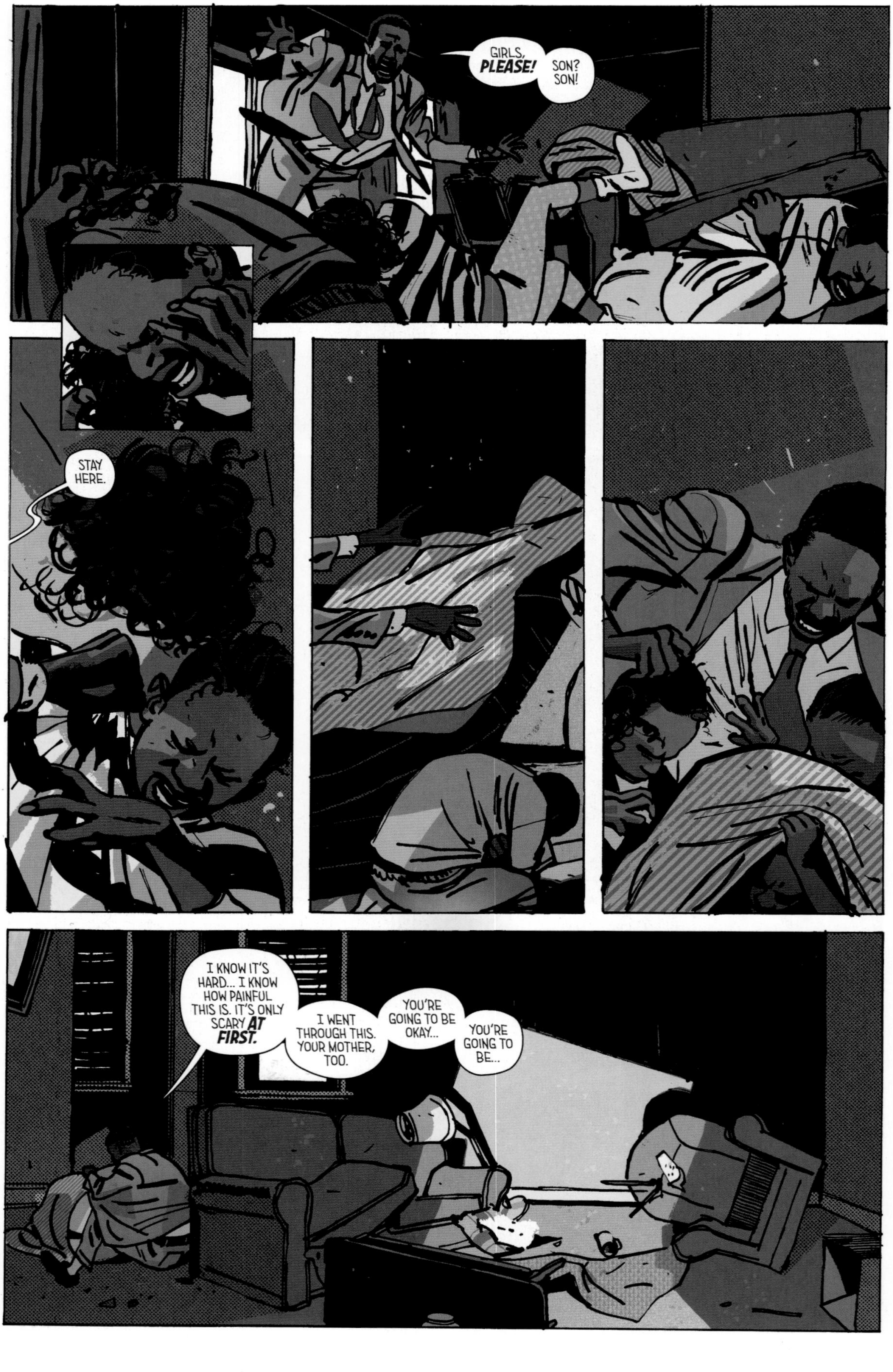
GIRLS, PLEASE!
SON? SON!
STAY HERE.
I KNOW IT'S HARD... I KNOW HOW PAINFUL THIS IS. IT'S ONLY SCARY AT FIRST.
I WENT THROUGH THIS. YOUR MOTHER, TOO.
YOU'RE GOING TO BE OKAY...
YOU'RE GOING TO BE...

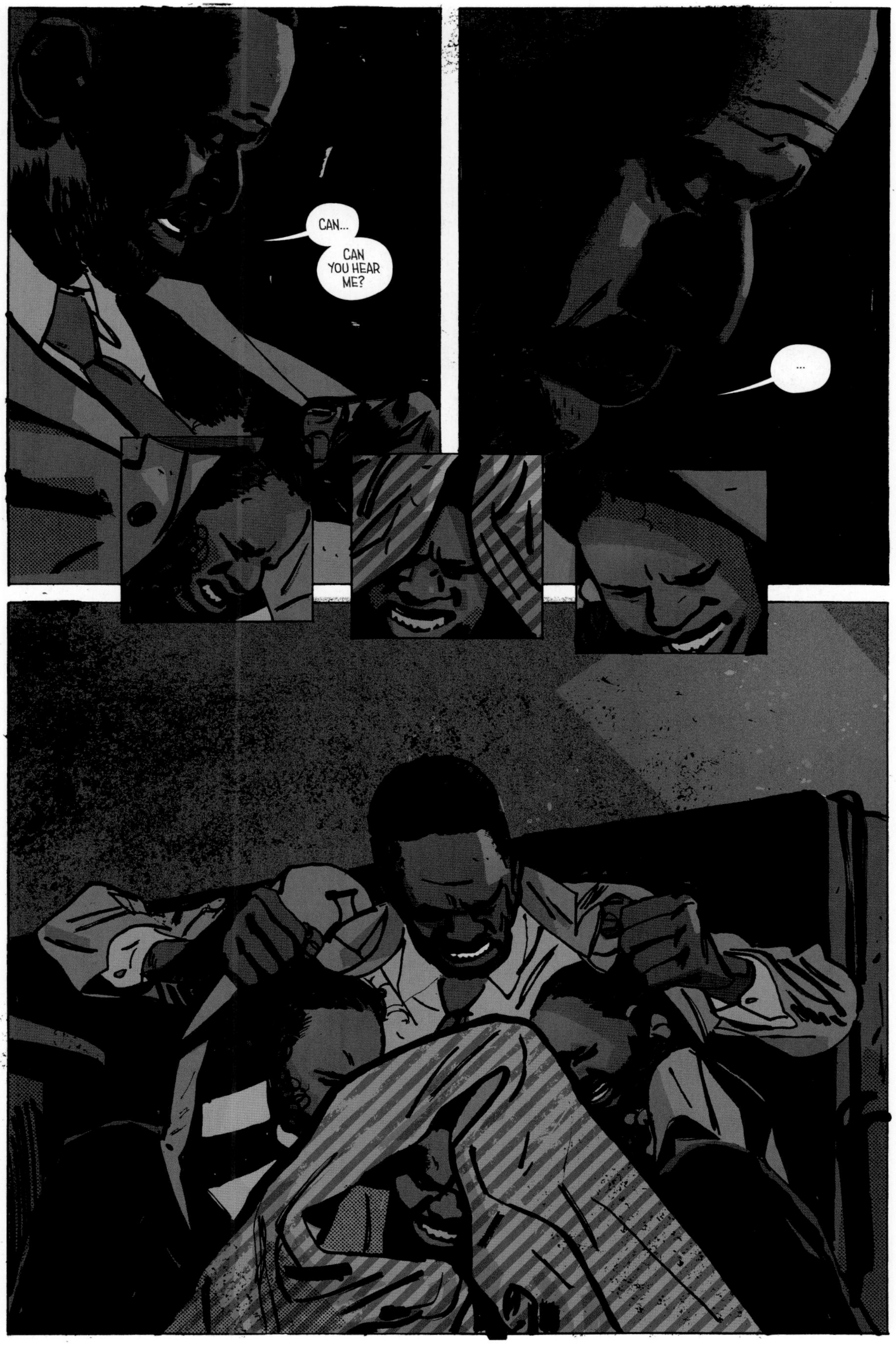
CAN...
CAN YOU HEAR ME?
...

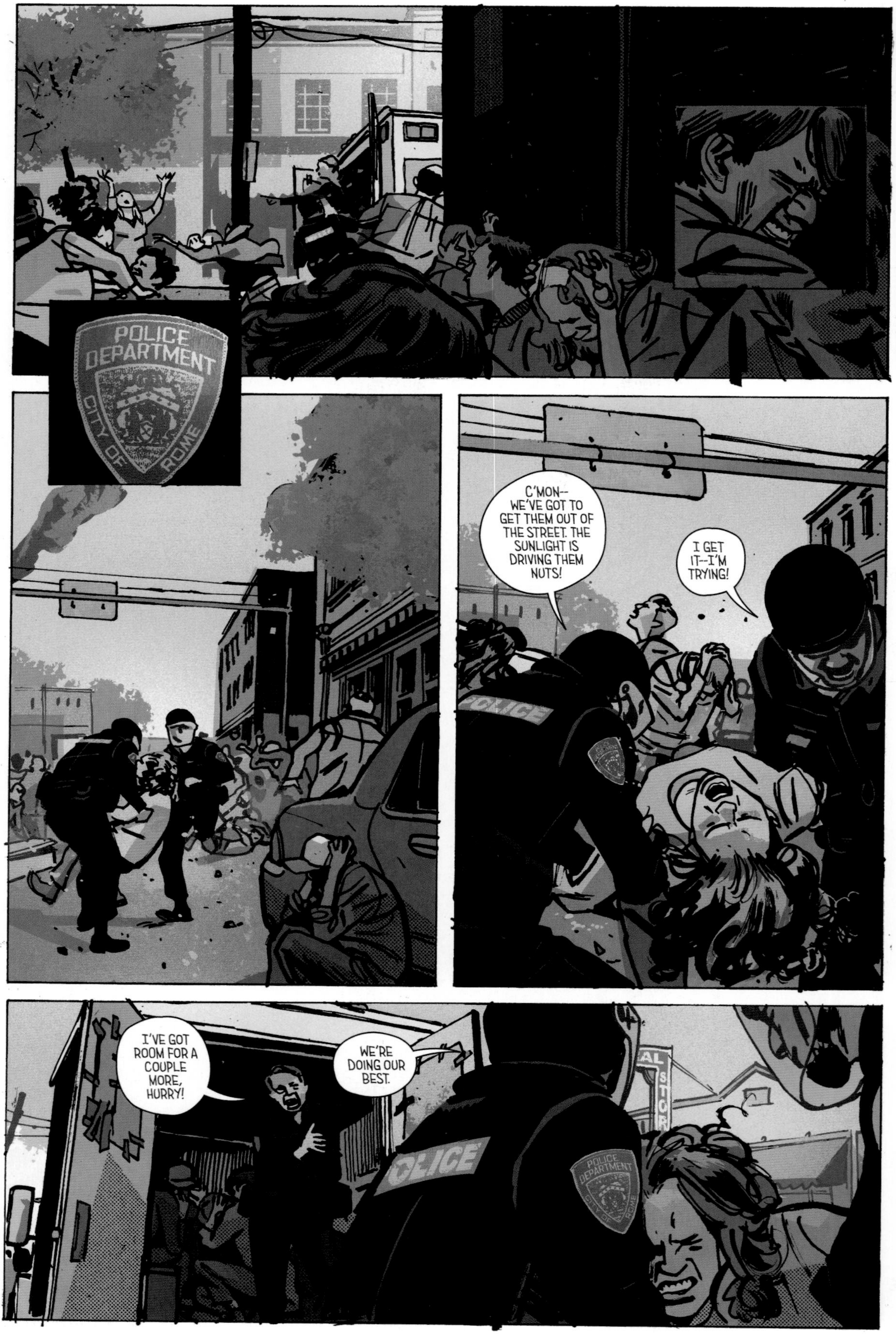
POLICE DEPARTMENT
CITY OF ROME
C'MON-- WE'VE GOT TO GET THEM OUT OF THE STREET. THE SUNLIGHT IS DRIVING THEM NUTS!
I GET IT--I'M TRYING!
POLICE
I'VE GOT ROOM FOR A COUPLE MORE, HURRY!
WE'RE DOING OUR BEST.
POLICE
POLICE DEPARTMENT

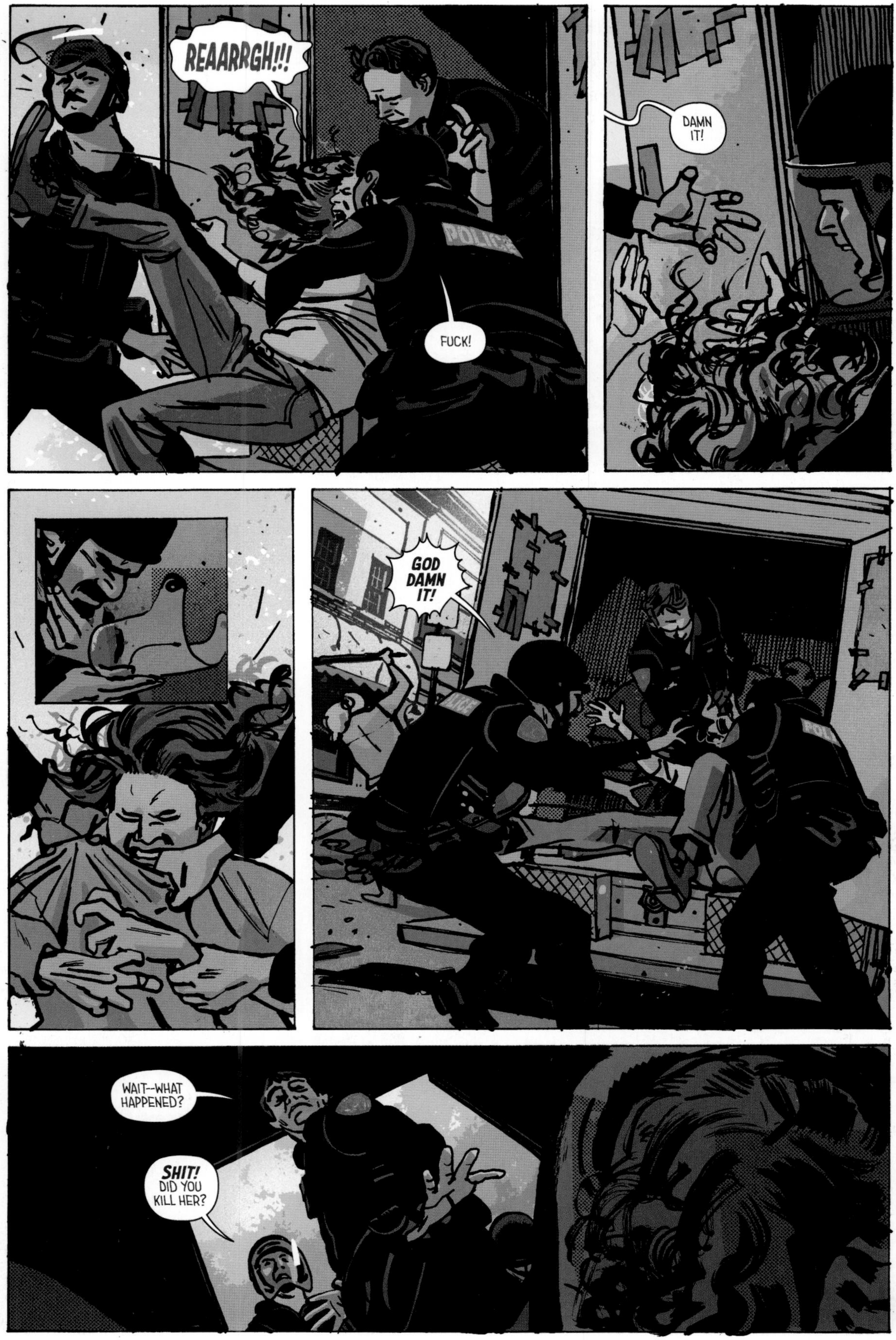
REAARRGH!!!
FUCK!
DAMN IT!
GOD DAMN IT!
WAIT--WHAT HAPPENED?
SHIT! DID YOU KILL HER?

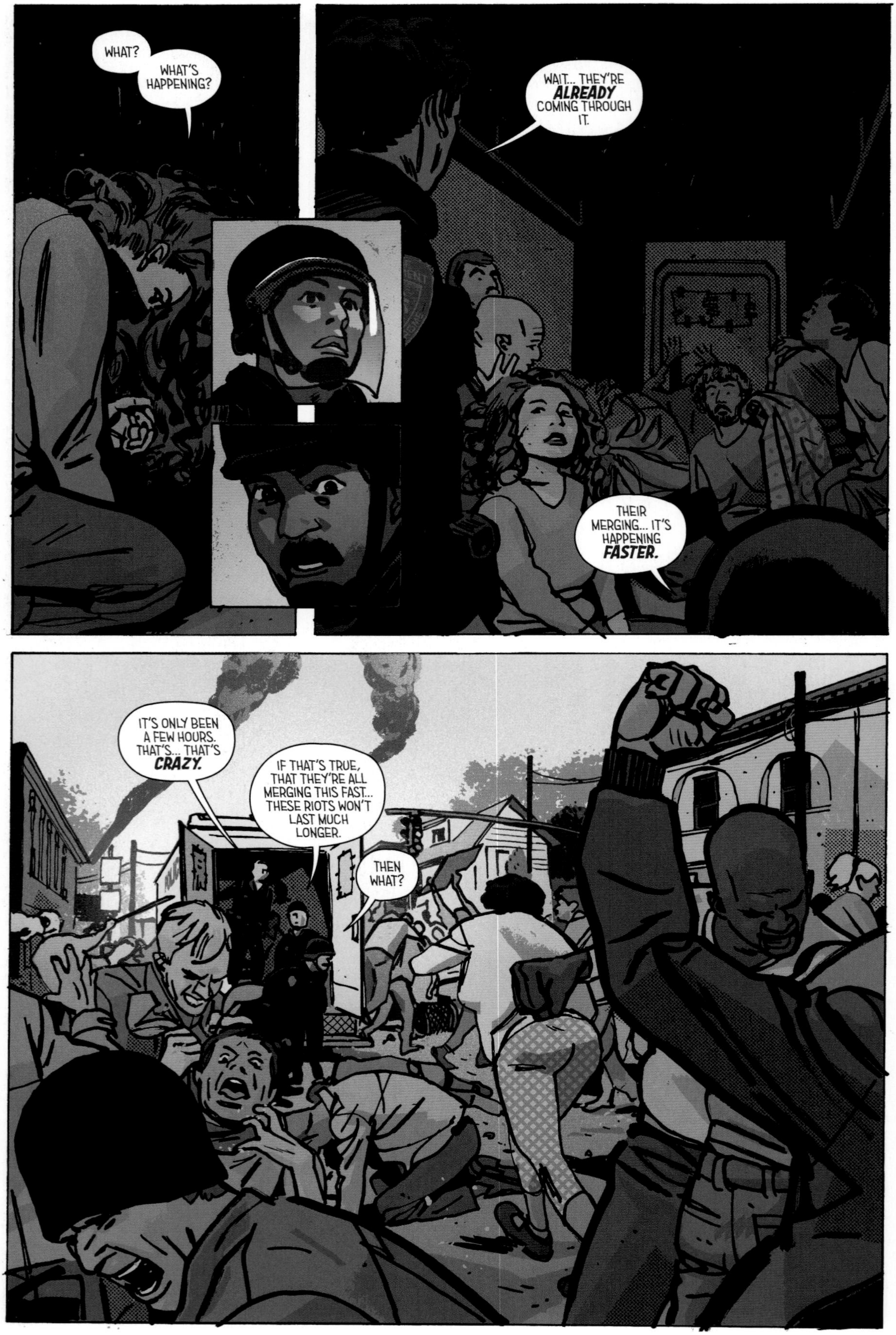
WHAT?
WHAT'S HAPPENING?
WAIT... THEY'RE **ALREADY** COMING THROUGH IT.
THEIR MERGING... IT'S HAPPENING **FASTER.**
IT'S ONLY BEEN A FEW HOURS. THAT'S... THAT'S **CRAZY.**
IF THAT'S TRUE, THAT THEY'RE ALL MERGING THIS FAST... THESE RIOTS WON'T LAST MUCH LONGER.
THEN WHAT?

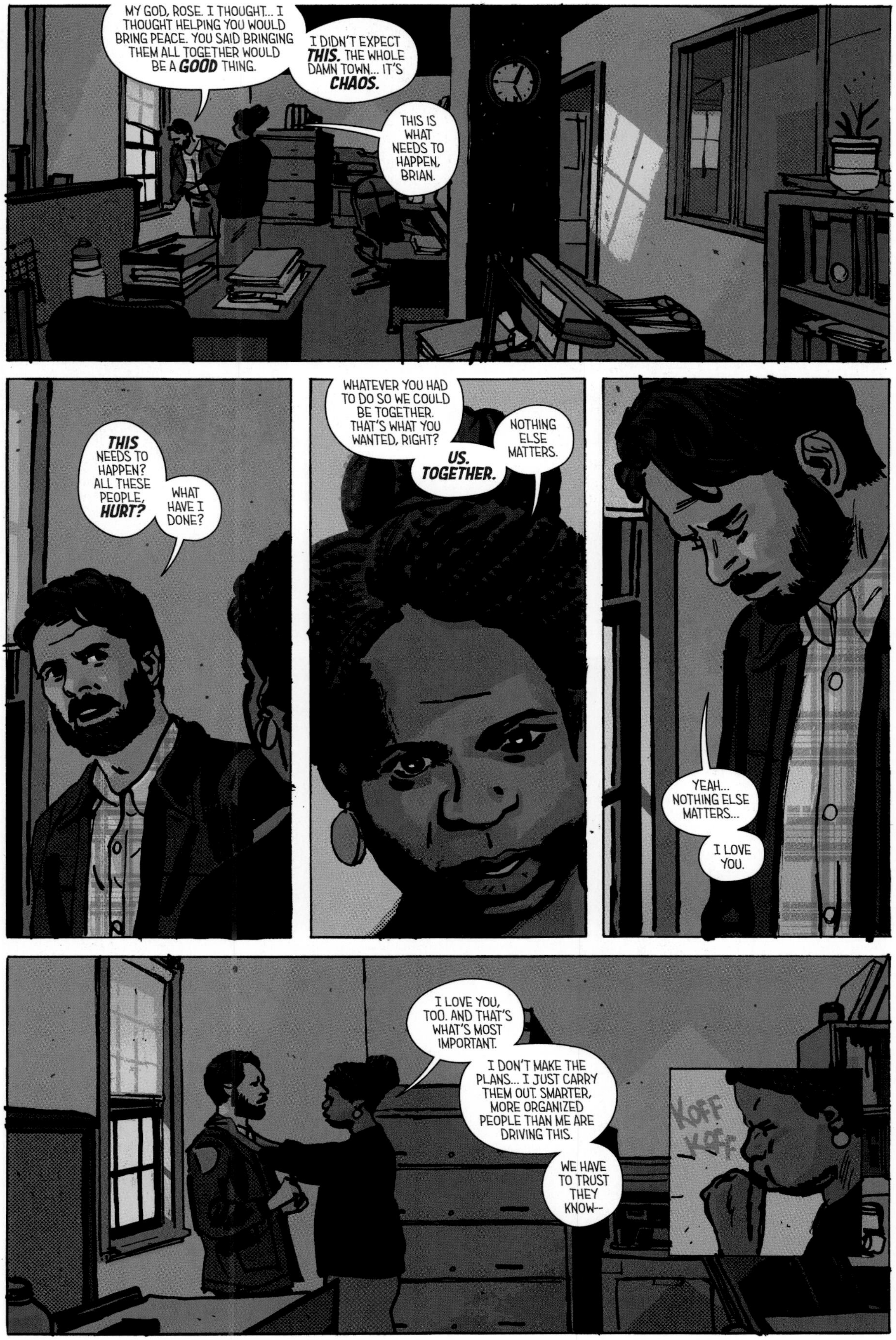
MY GOD, ROSE. I THOUGHT... I THOUGHT HELPING YOU WOULD BRING PEACE. YOU SAID BRINGING THEM ALL TOGETHER WOULD BE A GOOD THING.
I DIDN'T EXPECT THIS. THE WHOLE DAMN TOWN... IT'S CHAOS.
THIS IS WHAT NEEDS TO HAPPEN, BRIAN.
THIS NEEDS TO HAPPEN? ALL THESE PEOPLE, HURT?
WHAT HAVE I DONE?
WHATEVER YOU HAD TO DO SO WE COULD BE TOGETHER. THAT'S WHAT YOU WANTED, RIGHT?
US. TOGETHER.
NOTHING ELSE MATTERS.
YEAH... NOTHING ELSE MATTERS...
I LOVE YOU.
I LOVE YOU, TOO. AND THAT'S WHAT'S MOST IMPORTANT.
I DON'T MAKE THE PLANS... I JUST CARRY THEM OUT. SMARTER, MORE ORGANIZED PEOPLE THAN ME ARE DRIVING THIS.
WE HAVE TO TRUST THEY KNOW--
KOFF KOFF

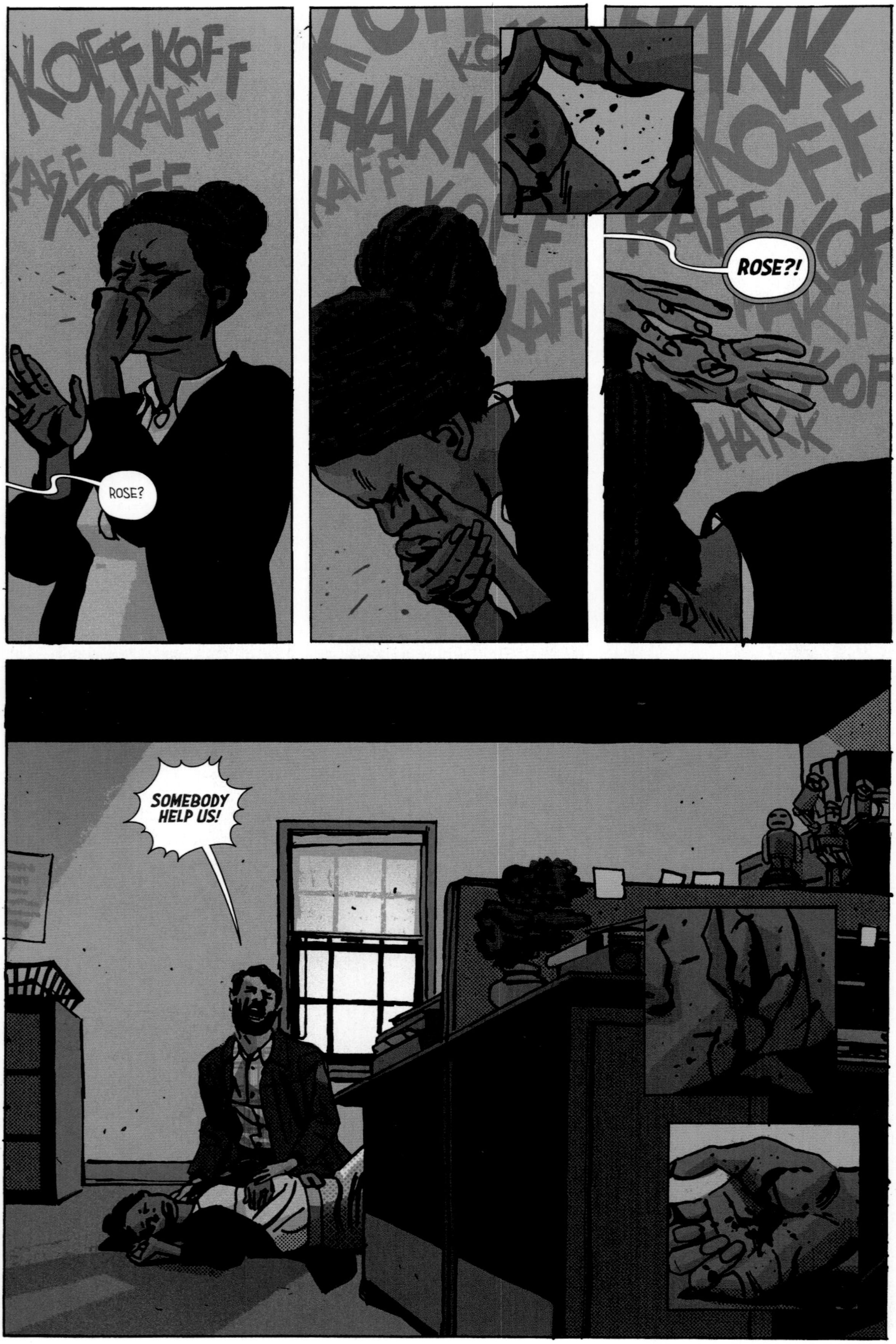
KOFF KOFF
KAFF
KAFF
KOFF
ROSE?
KOFF
HAK
KAFF
KOFF
HAKK
KOFF
ROSE?!
KAFF KOFF
HAKK
KOFF
HAKK
SOMEBODY HELP US!

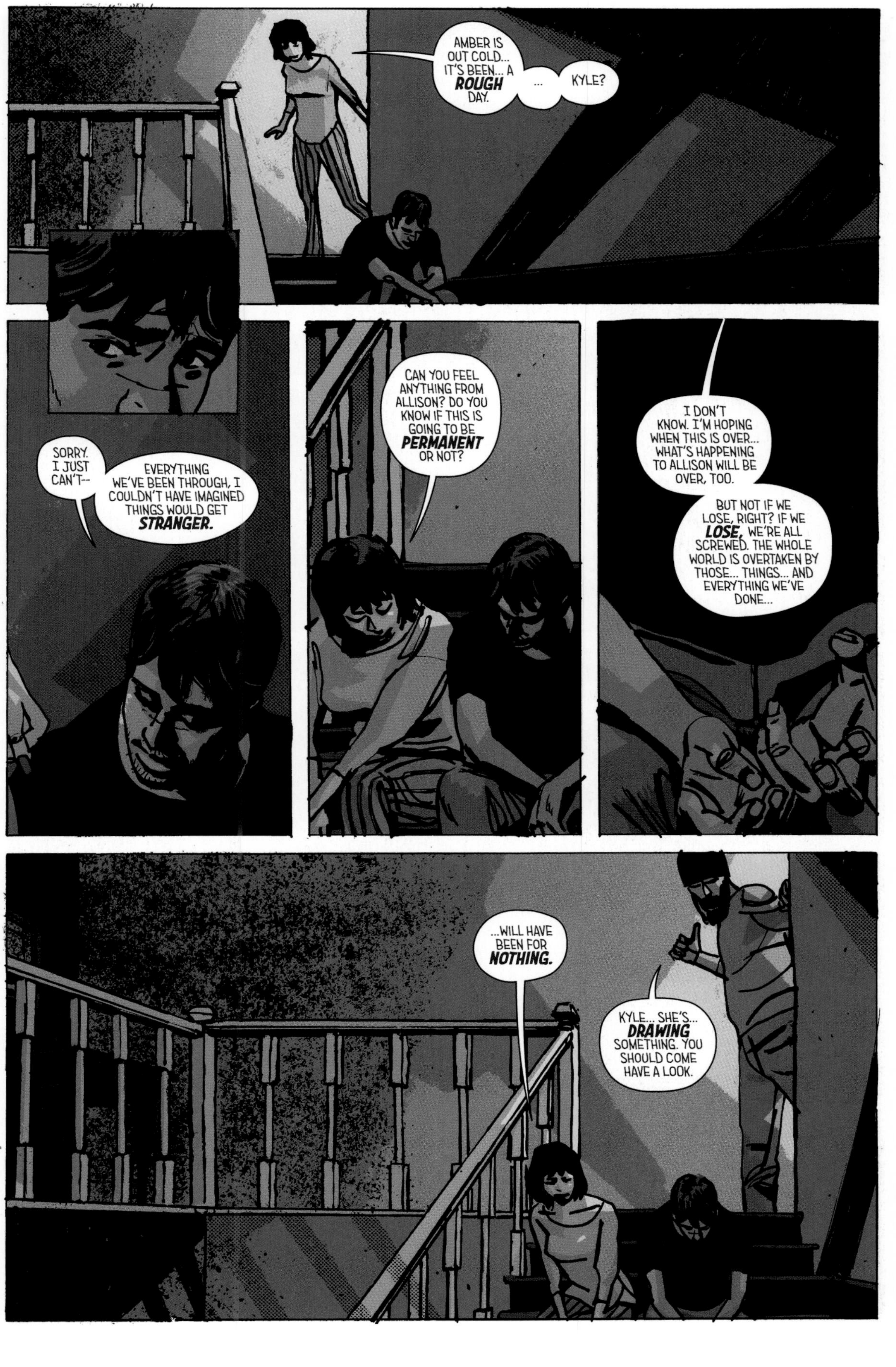
AMBER IS OUT COLD... IT'S BEEN... A ROUGH DAY.
...
KYLE?
SORRY. I JUST CAN'T--
EVERYTHING WE'VE BEEN THROUGH, I COULDN'T HAVE IMAGINED THINGS WOULD GET STRANGER.
CAN YOU FEEL ANYTHING FROM ALLISON? DO YOU KNOW IF THIS IS GOING TO BE PERMANENT OR NOT?
I DON'T KNOW. I'M HOPING WHEN THIS IS OVER... WHAT'S HAPPENING TO ALLISON WILL BE OVER, TOO.
BUT NOT IF WE LOSE, RIGHT? IF WE LOSE, WE'RE ALL SCREWED. THE WHOLE WORLD IS OVERTAKEN BY THOSE... THINGS... AND EVERYTHING WE'VE DONE...
...WILL HAVE BEEN FOR NOTHING.
KYLE... SHE'S... DRAWING SOMETHING. YOU SHOULD COME HAVE A LOOK.

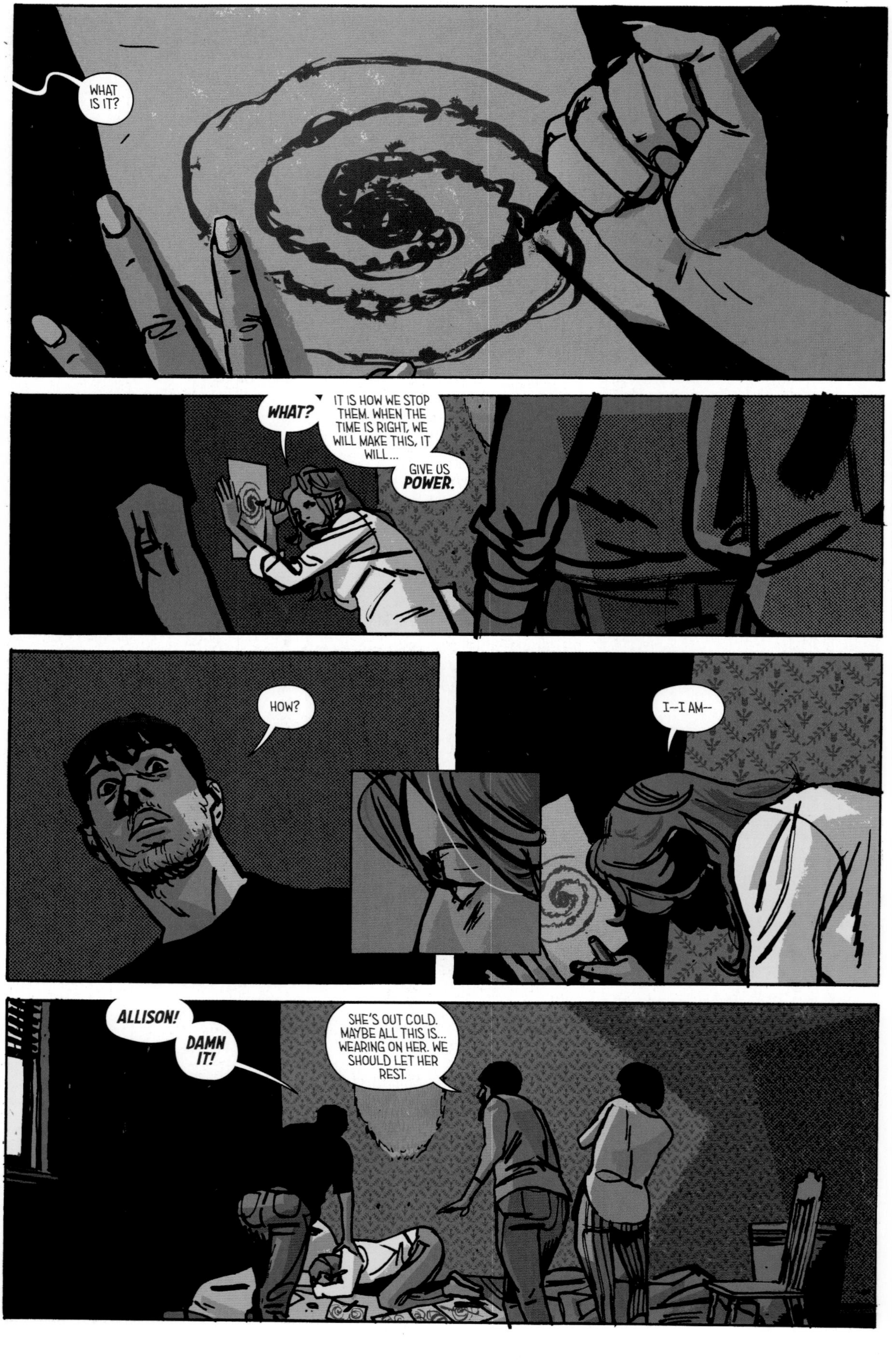
WHAT IS IT?
WHAT?
IT IS HOW WE STOP THEM. WHEN THE TIME IS RIGHT, WE WILL MAKE THIS, IT WILL...
GIVE US POWER.
HOW?
I--I AM--
ALLISON!
DAMN IT!
SHE'S OUT COLD. MAYBE ALL THIS IS... WEARING ON HER. WE SHOULD LET HER REST.

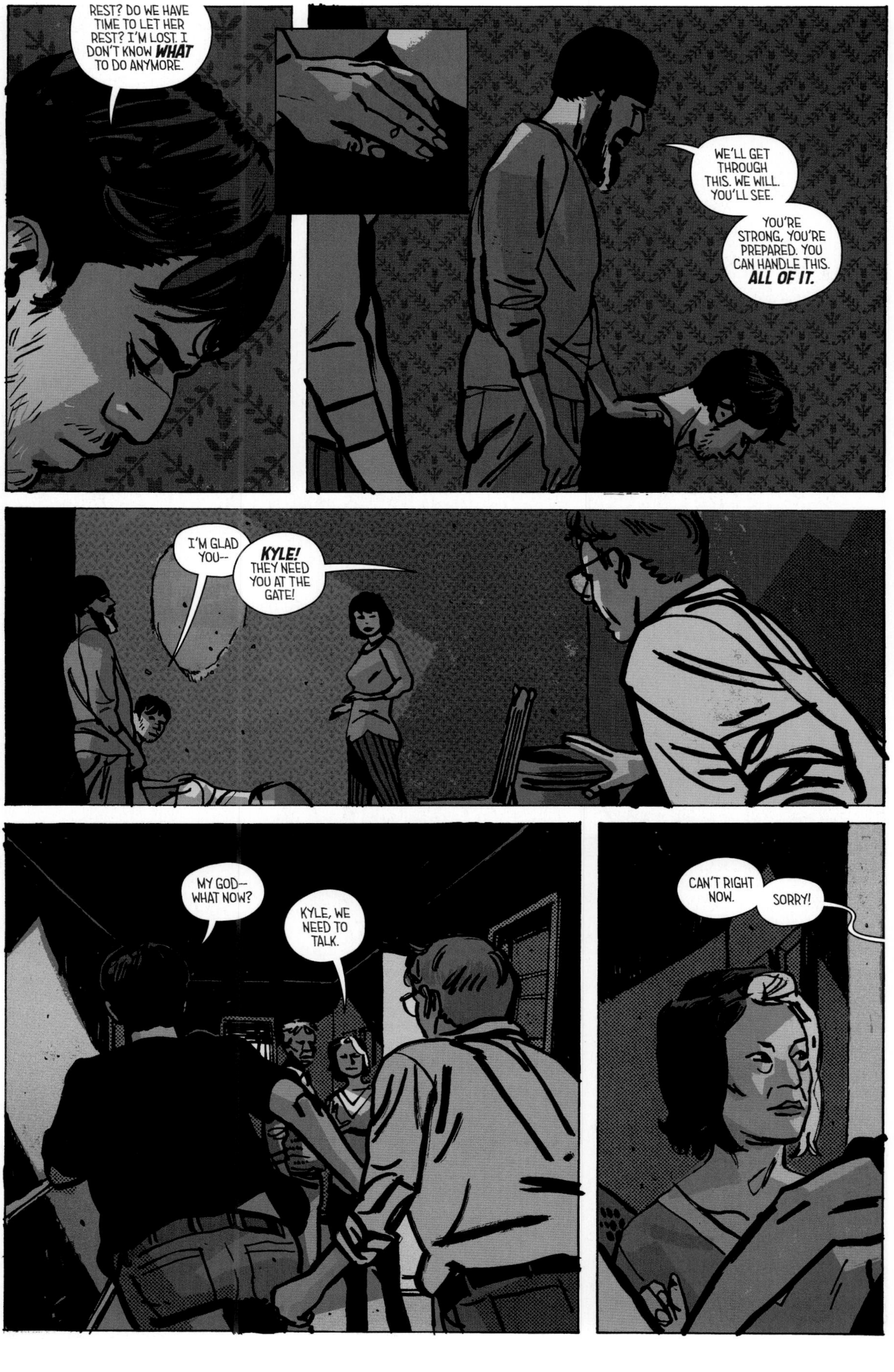

REST? DO WE HAVE TIME TO LET HER REST? I'M LOST. I DON'T KNOW **WHAT** TO DO ANYMORE.
WE'LL GET THROUGH THIS. WE WILL. YOU'LL SEE.
YOU'RE STRONG, YOU'RE PREPARED. YOU CAN HANDLE THIS. **ALL OF IT.**
I'M GLAD YOU--
KYLE! THEY NEED YOU AT THE GATE!
MY GOD-- WHAT NOW?
KYLE, WE NEED TO TALK.
CAN'T RIGHT NOW.
SORRY!

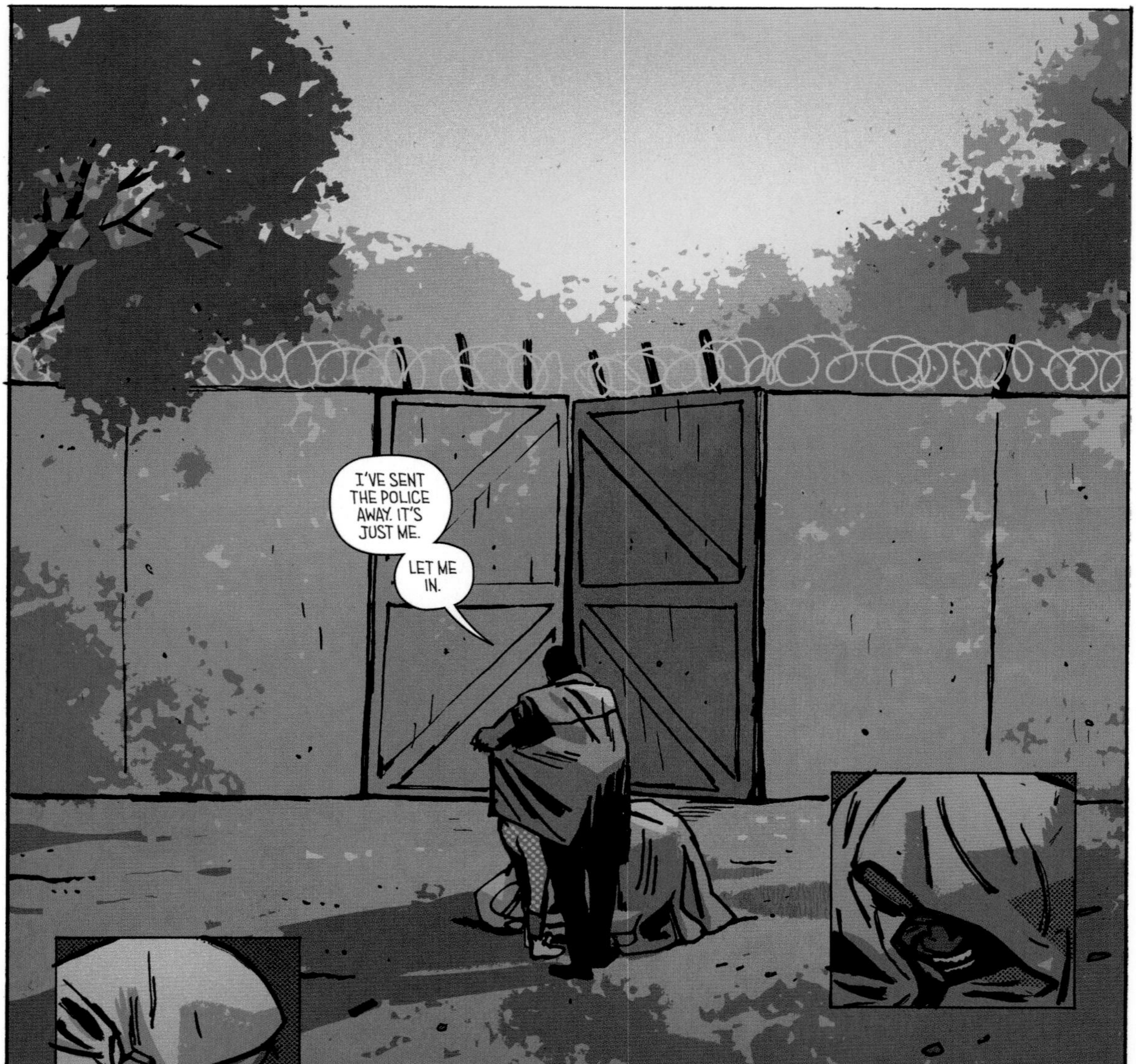
I'VE SENT THE POLICE AWAY. IT'S JUST ME.
LET ME IN.

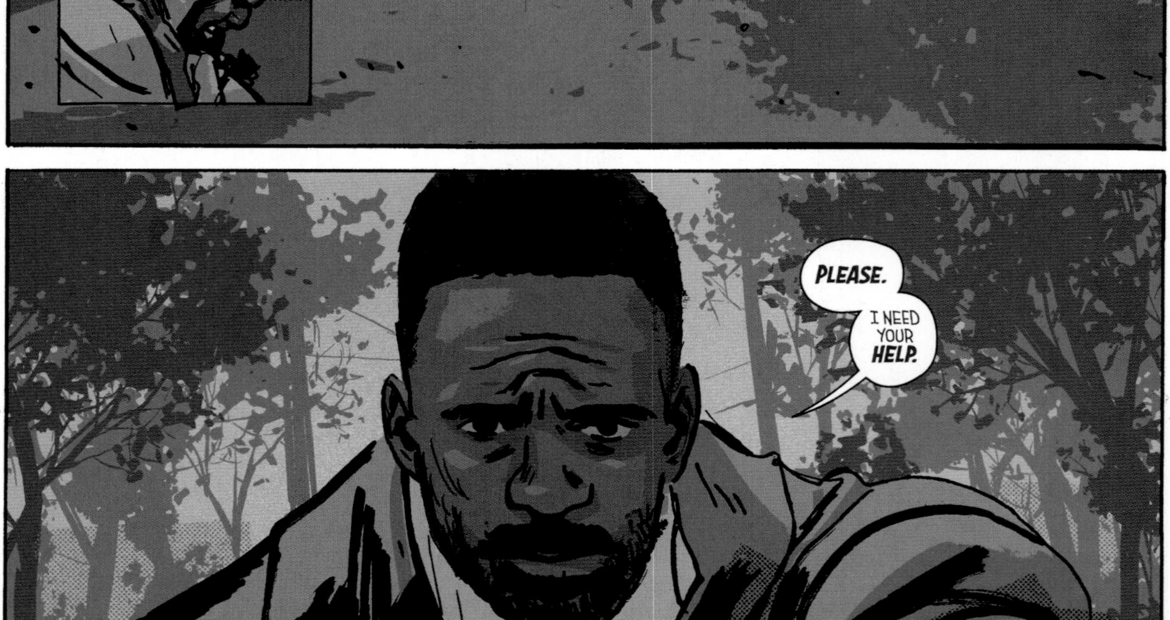
PLEASE.
I NEED YOUR HELP.

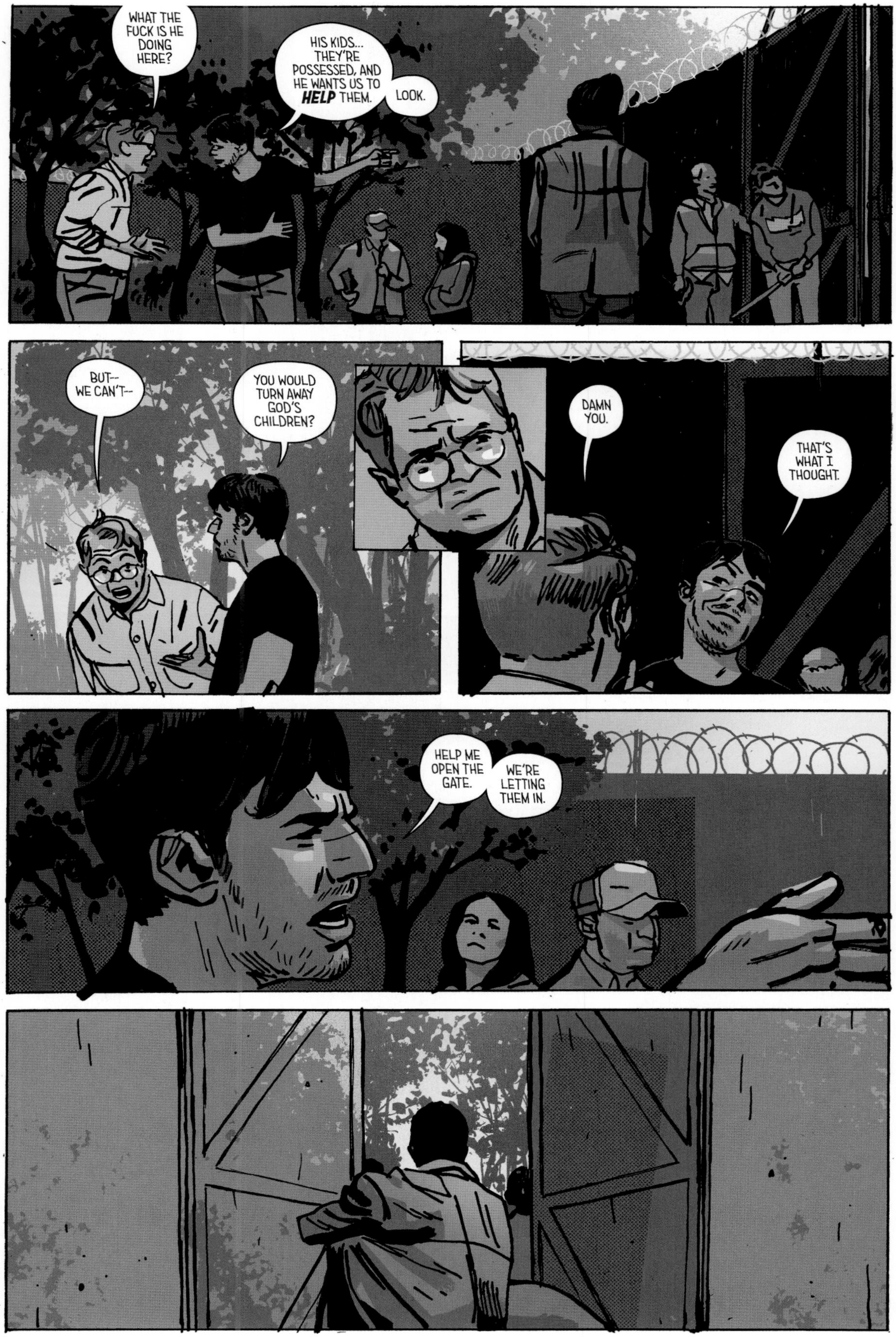
WHAT THE FUCK IS HE DOING HERE?
HIS KIDS... THEY'RE POSSESSED, AND HE WANTS US TO **HELP** THEM.
LOOK.
BUT-- WE CAN'T--
YOU WOULD TURN AWAY GOD'S CHILDREN?
DAMN YOU.
THAT'S WHAT I THOUGHT.
HELP ME OPEN THE GATE.
WE'RE LETTING THEM IN.

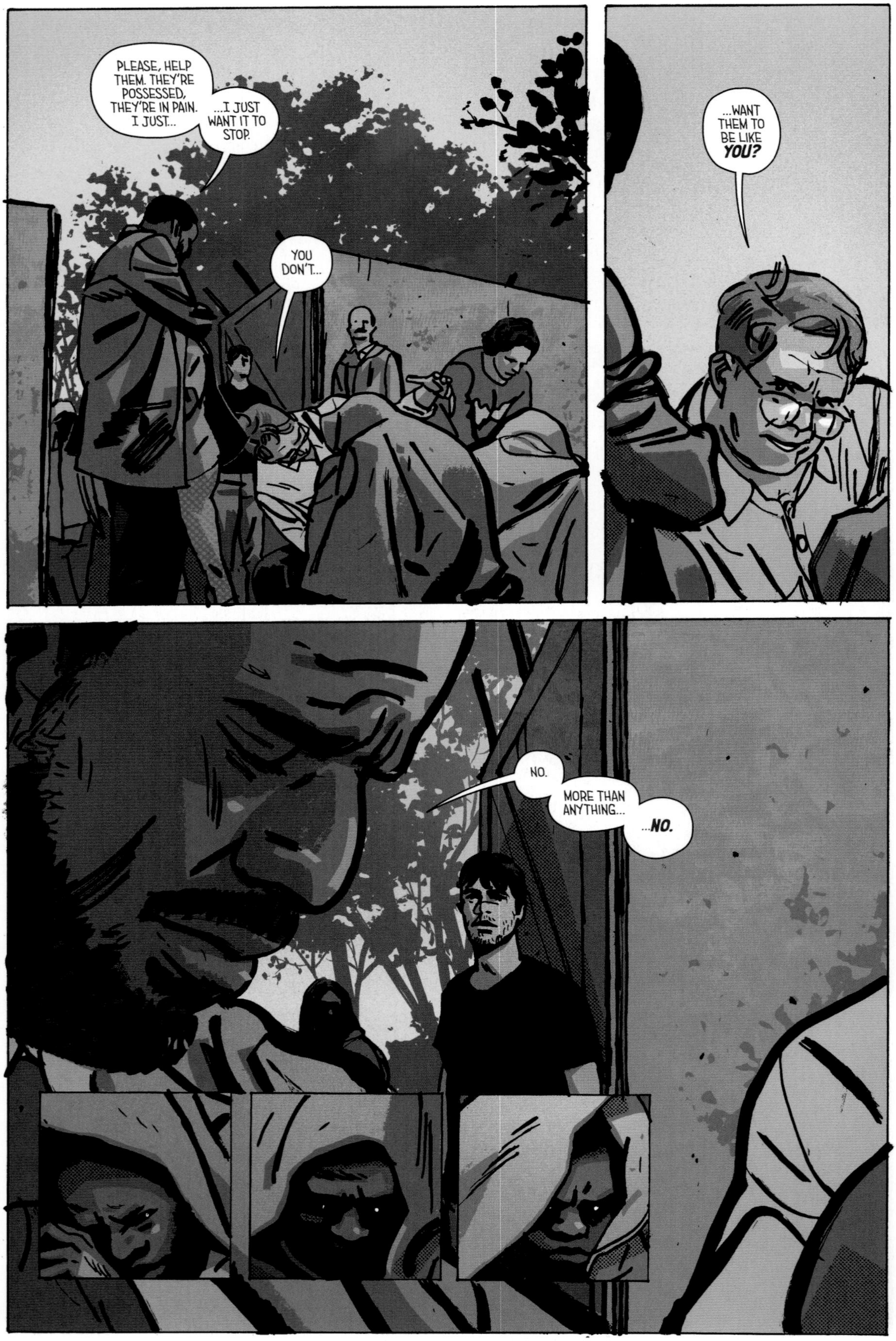
PLEASE, HELP THEM. THEY'RE POSSESSED, THEY'RE IN PAIN. I JUST...
...I JUST WANT IT TO STOP.
YOU DON'T...
...WANT THEM TO BE LIKE **YOU?**
NO.
MORE THAN ANYTHING...
...**NO.**

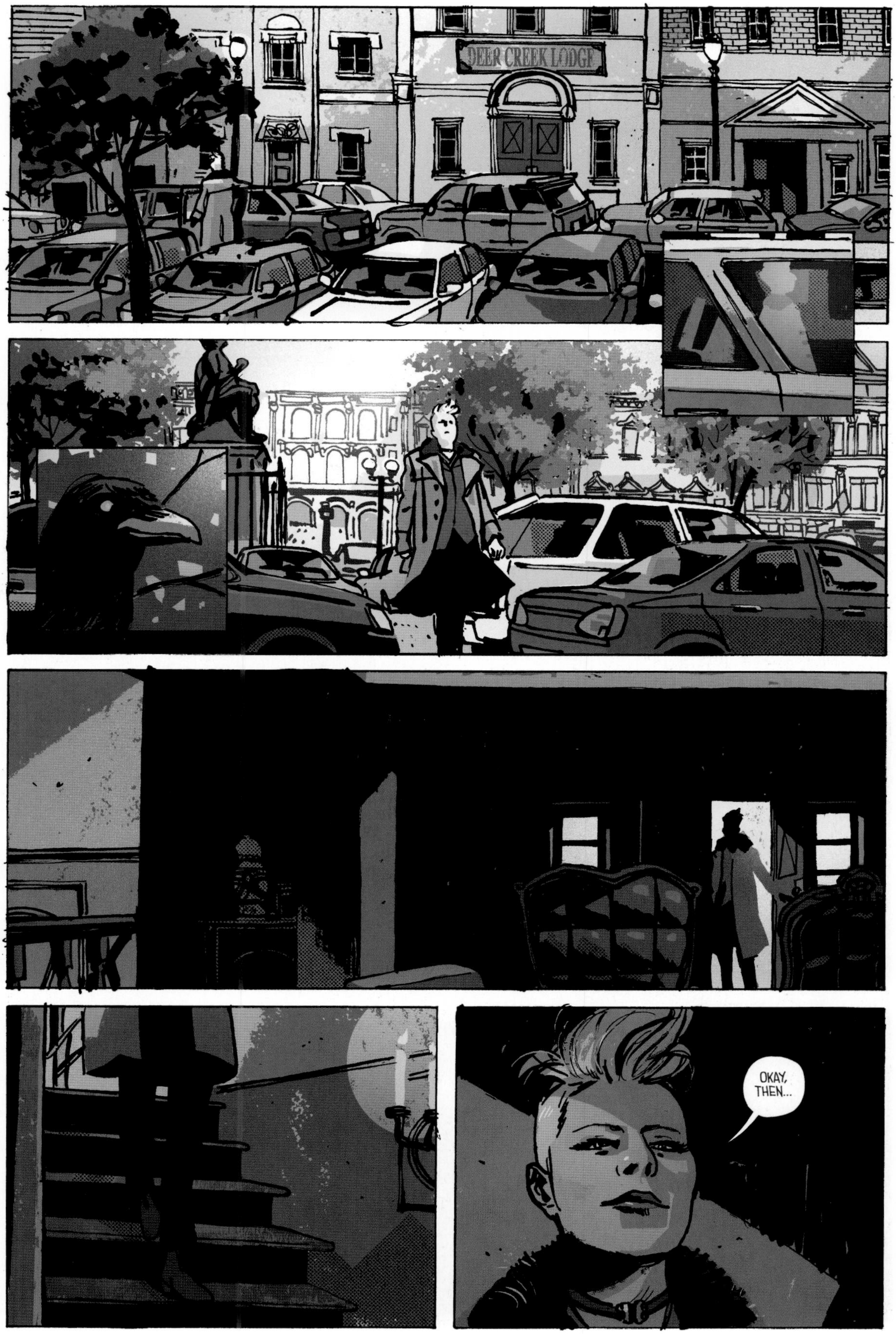
DEER CREEK LODGE
OKAY, THEN...

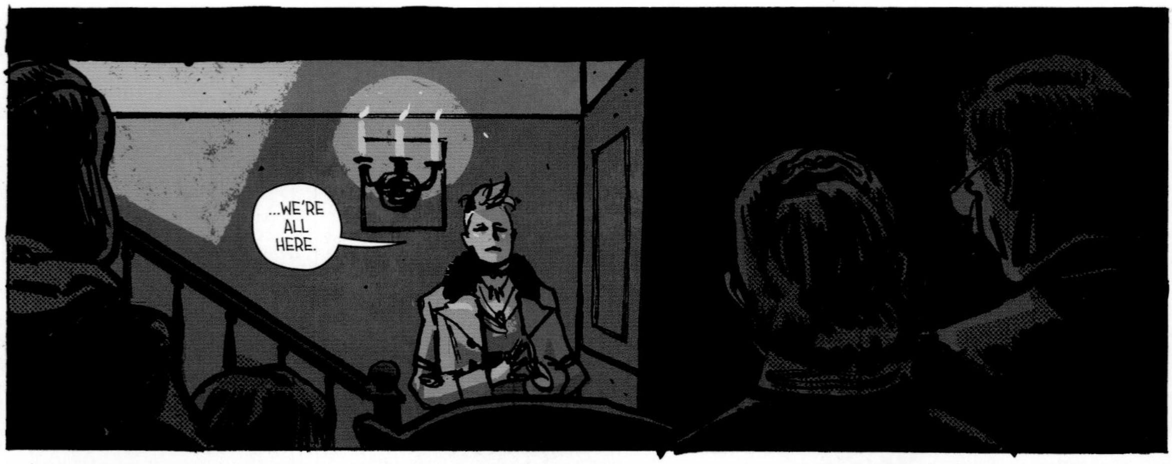
...WE'RE ALL HERE.

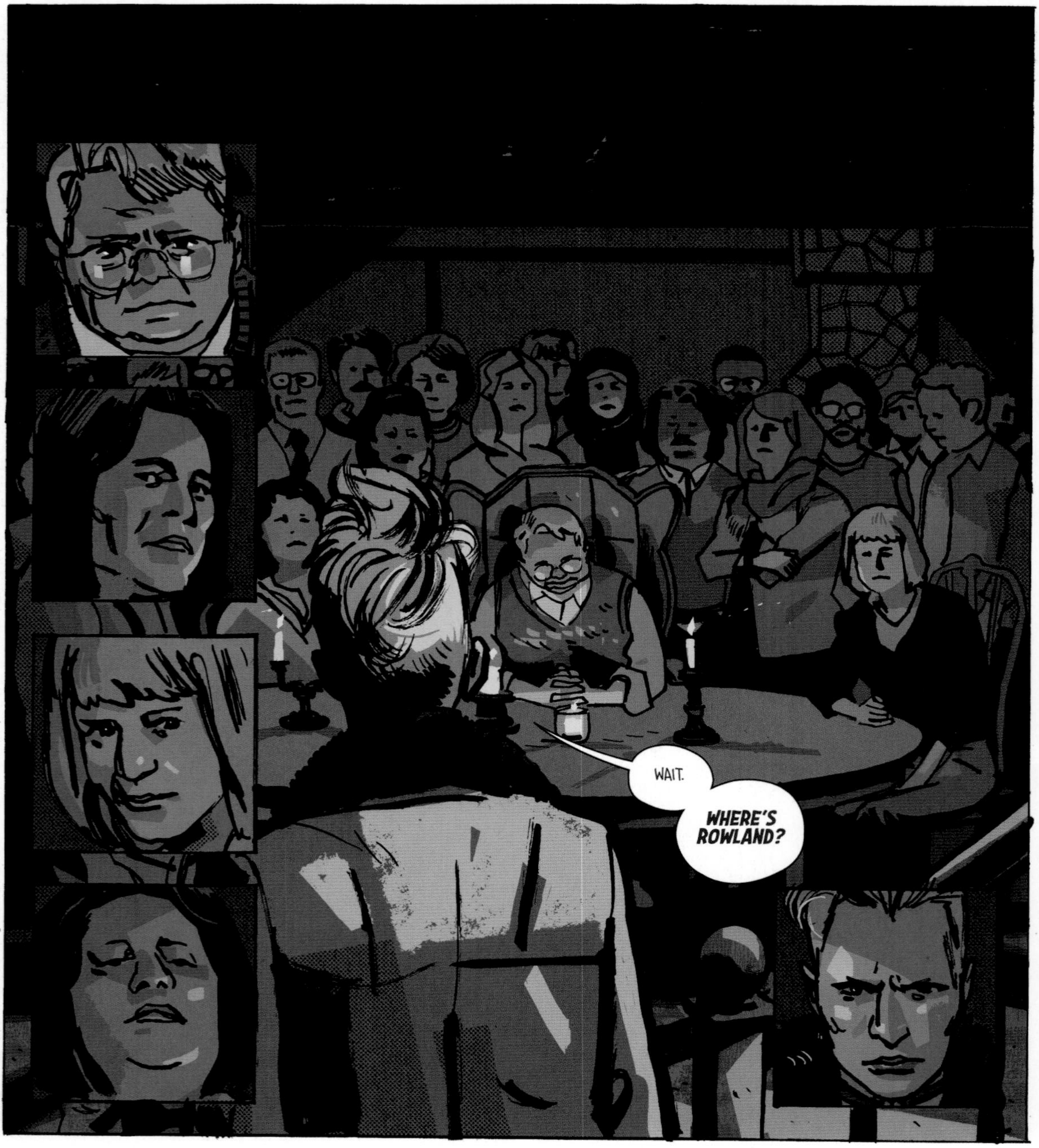
WAIT.
WHERE'S ROWLAND?

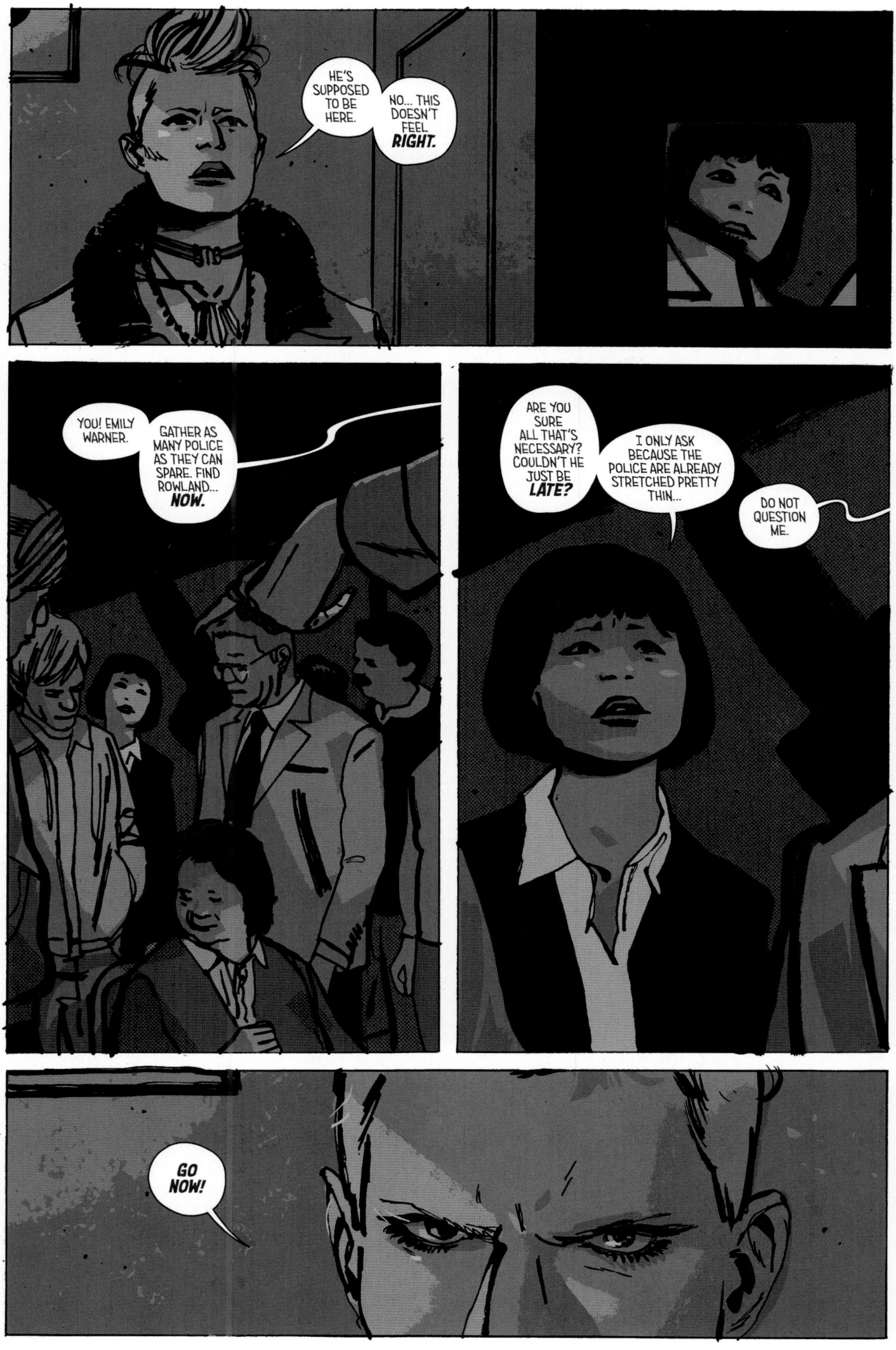
HE'S SUPPOSED TO BE HERE.
NO... THIS DOESN'T FEEL **RIGHT.**
YOU! EMILY WARNER.
GATHER AS MANY POLICE AS THEY CAN SPARE. FIND ROWLAND... **NOW.**
ARE YOU SURE ALL THAT'S NECESSARY? COULDN'T HE JUST BE **LATE?**
I ONLY ASK BECAUSE THE POLICE ARE ALREADY STRETCHED PRETTY THIN...
DO NOT QUESTION ME.
GO NOW!

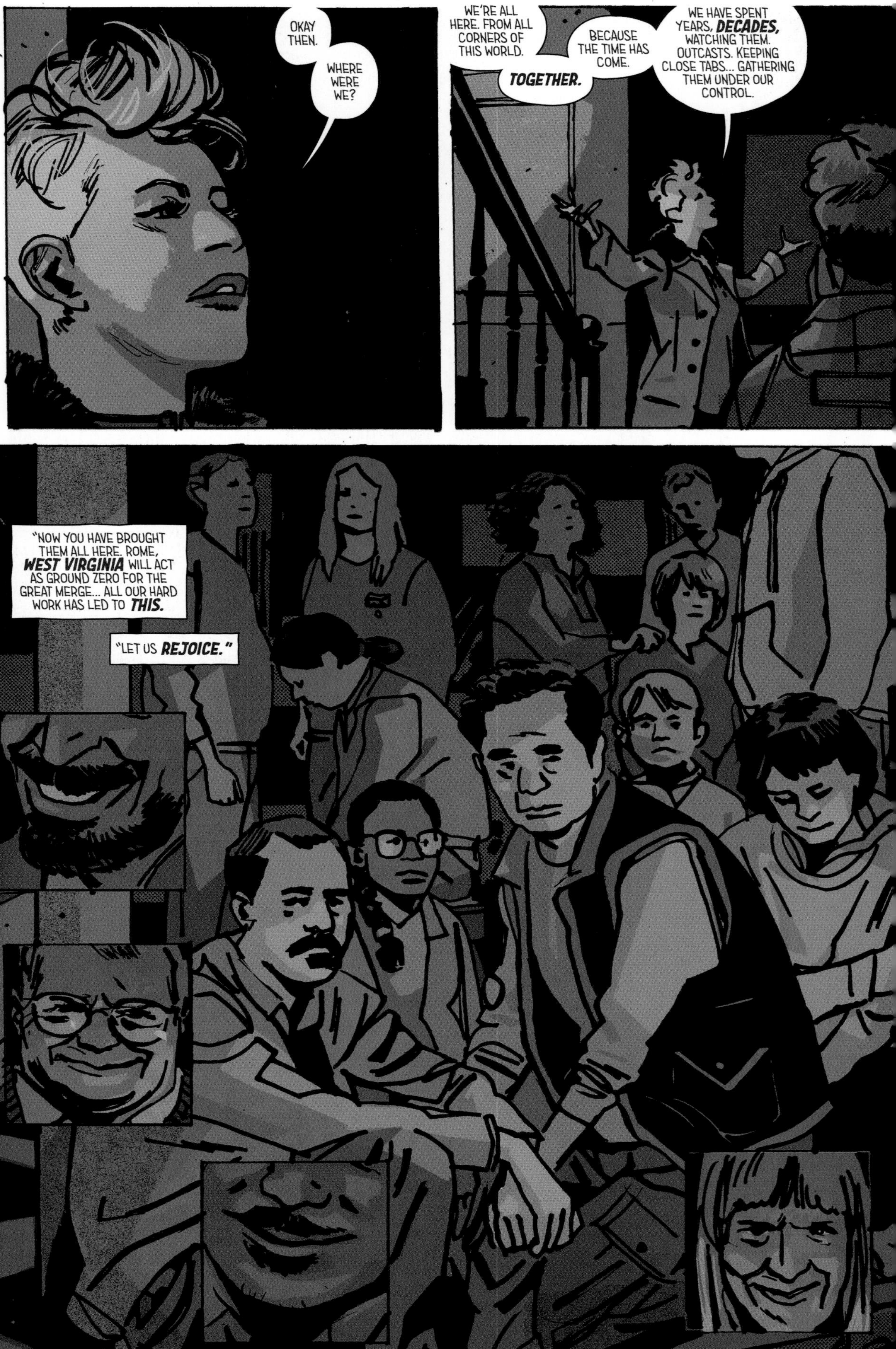
OKAY THEN.
WHERE WERE WE?
WE'RE ALL HERE. FROM ALL CORNERS OF THIS WORLD.
TOGETHER.
BECAUSE THE TIME HAS COME.
WE HAVE SPENT YEARS, DECADES, WATCHING THEM. OUTCASTS. KEEPING CLOSE TABS... GATHERING THEM UNDER OUR CONTROL.
"NOW YOU HAVE BROUGHT THEM ALL HERE. ROME, WEST VIRGINIA WILL ACT AS GROUND ZERO FOR THE GREAT MERGE... ALL OUR HARD WORK HAS LED TO THIS.
"LET US REJOICE."

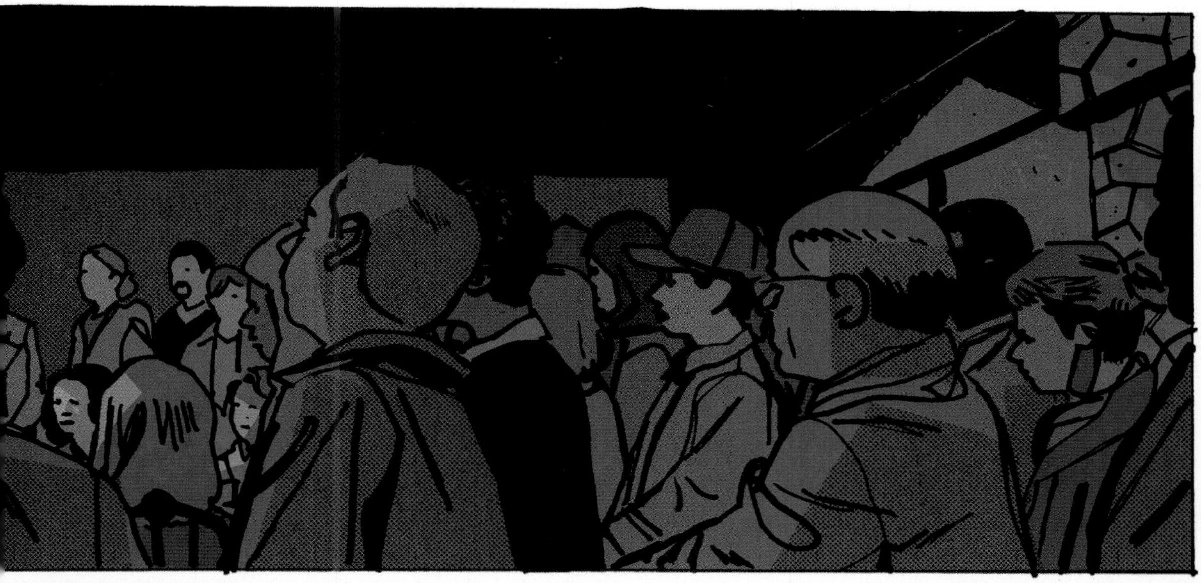
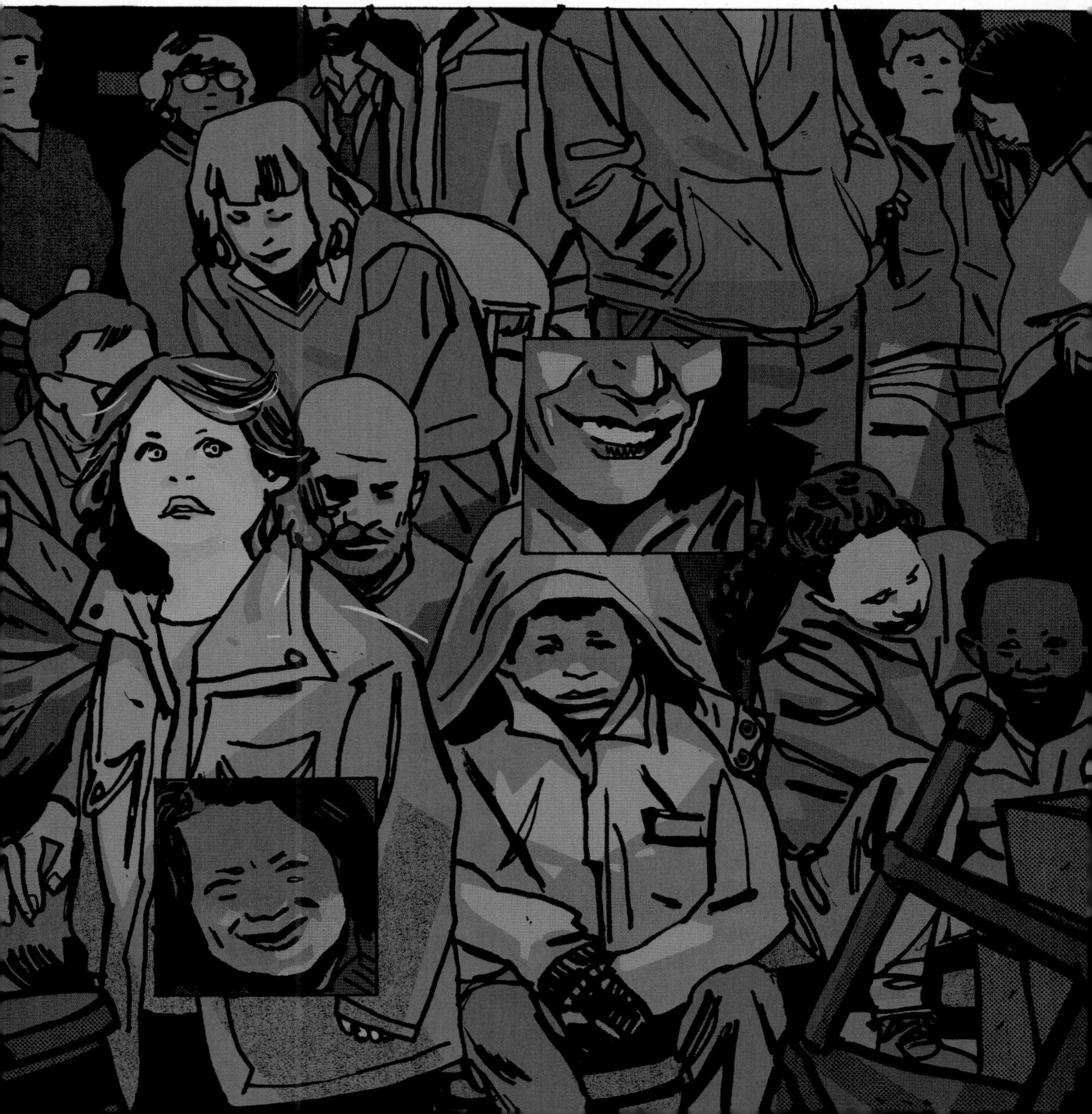

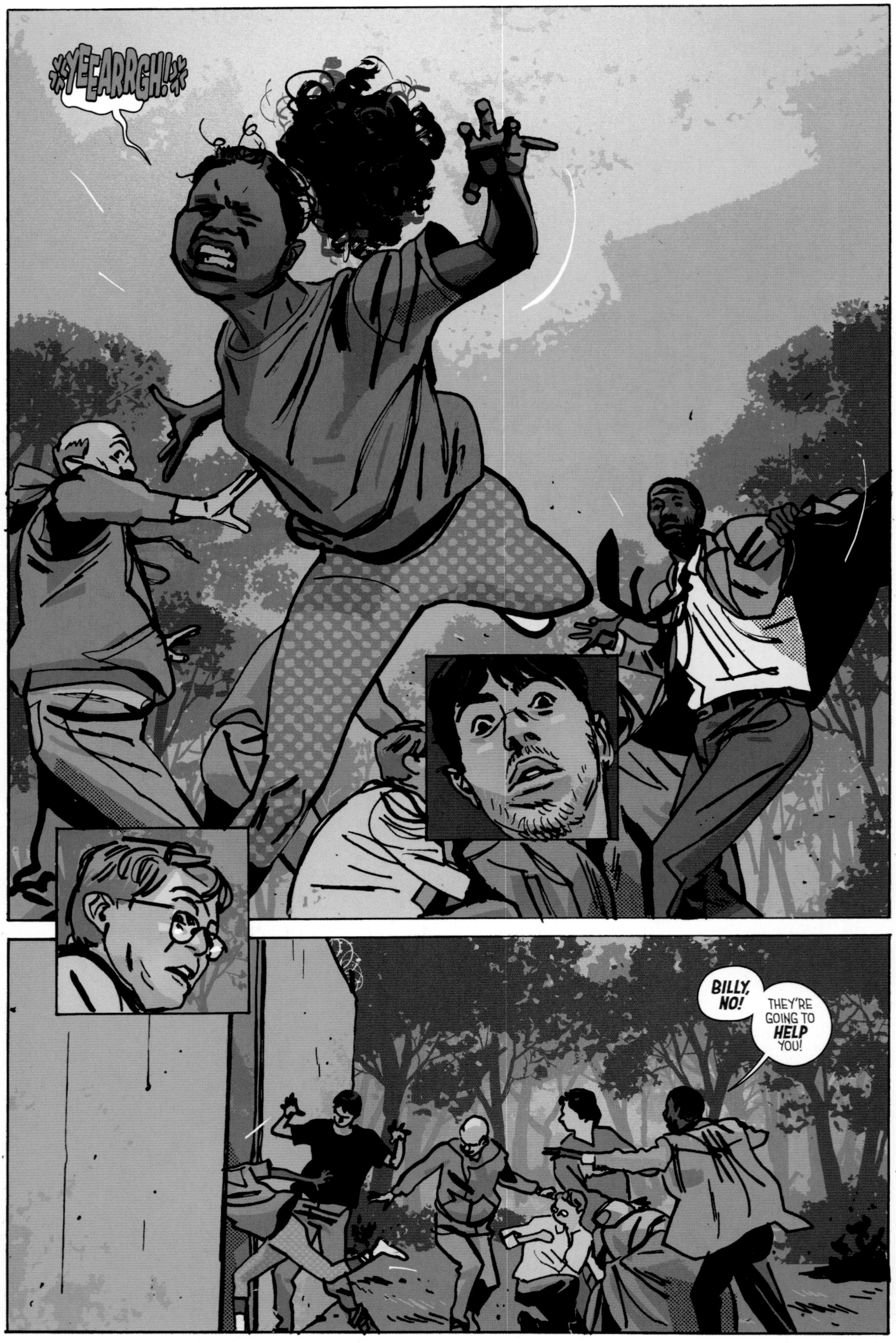
YEEARRGH!
BILLY, NO!
THEY'RE GOING TO HELP YOU!

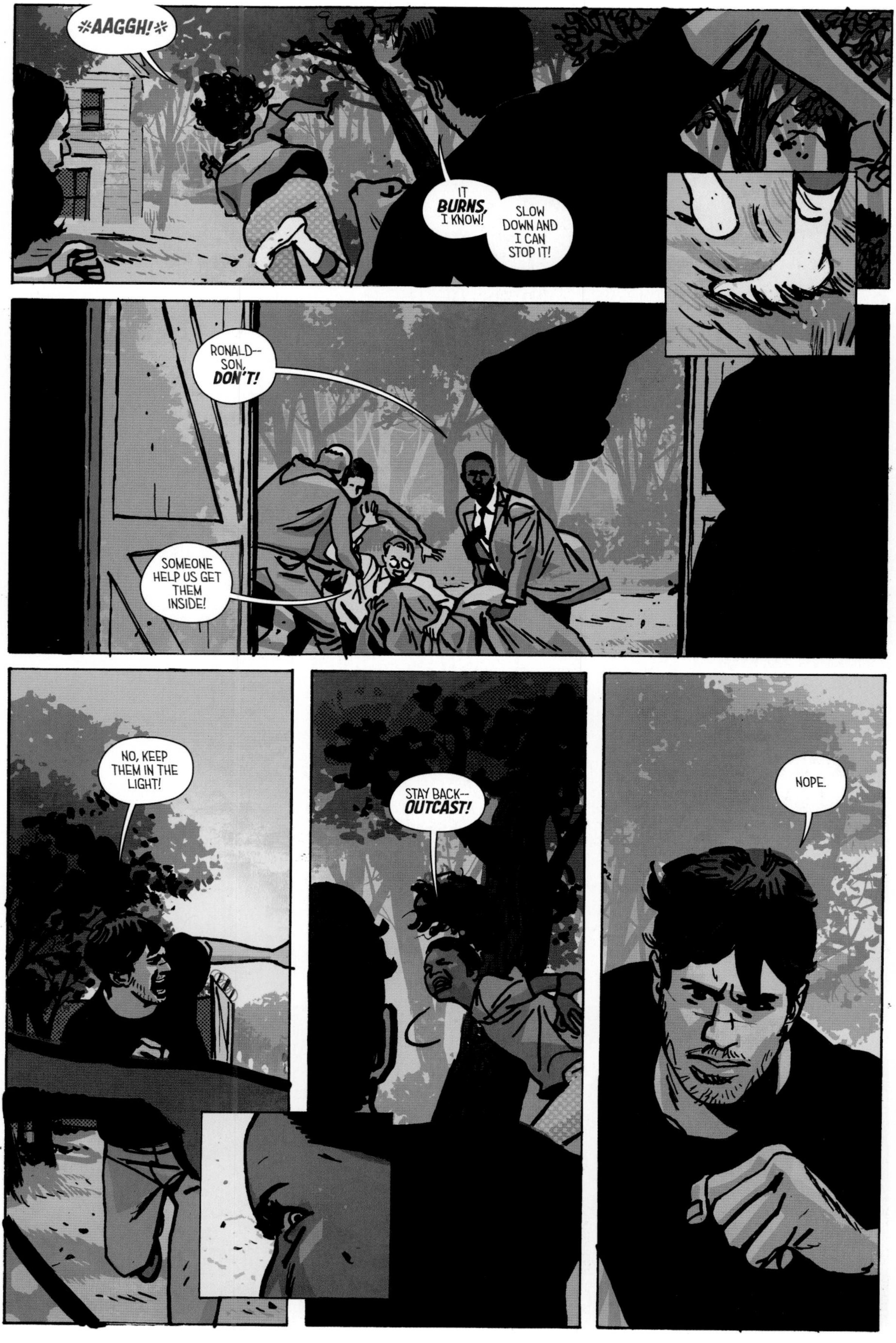

AAGGH!
IT BURNS, I KNOW!
SLOW DOWN AND I CAN STOP IT!
RONALD-- SON, DON'T!
SOMEONE HELP US GET THEM INSIDE!
NO, KEEP THEM IN THE LIGHT!
STAY BACK-- OUTCAST!
NOPE.

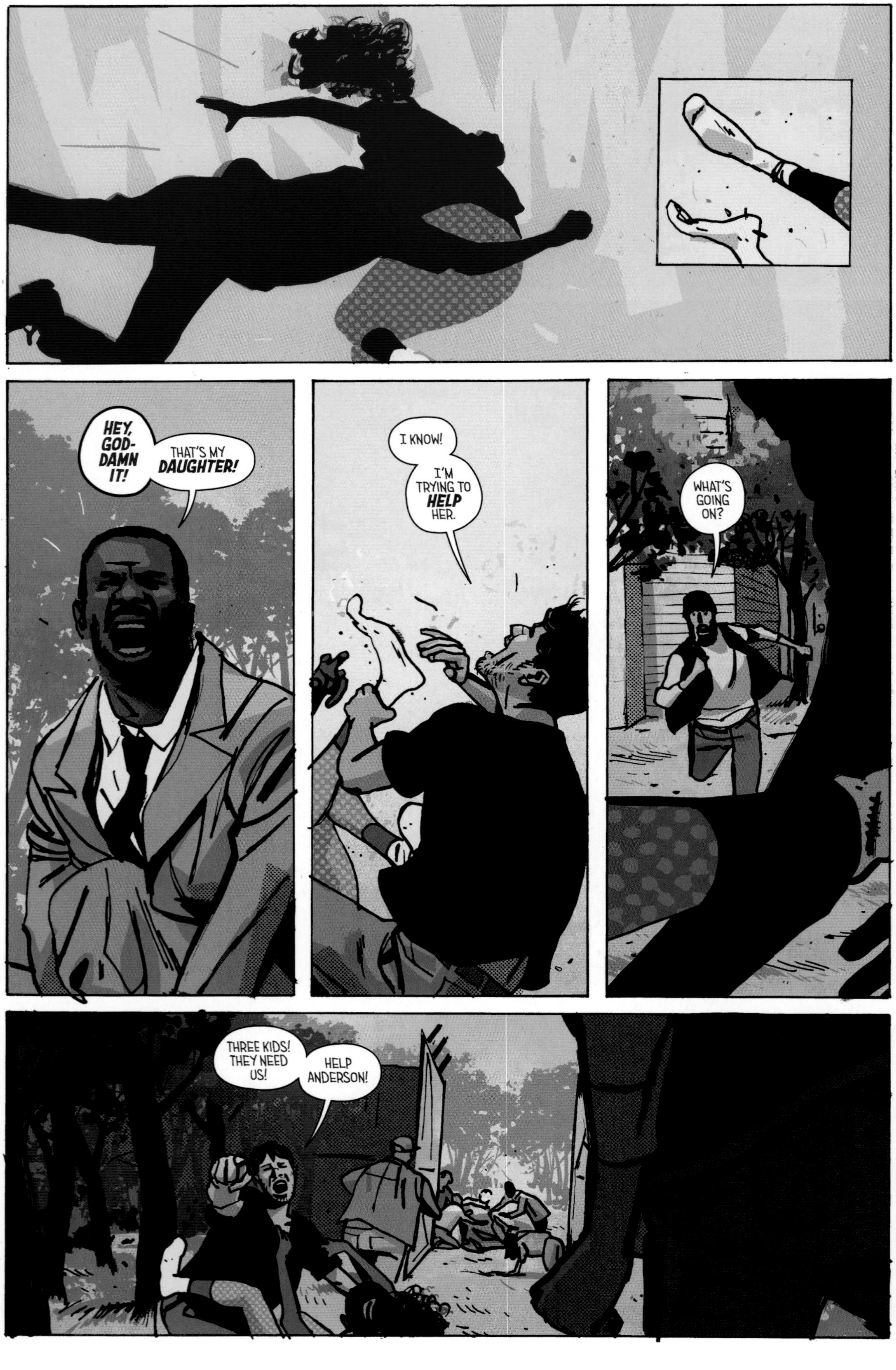
HEY, GOD-DAMN IT!
THAT'S MY DAUGHTER!
I KNOW!
I'M TRYING TO HELP HER.
WHAT'S GOING ON?
THREE KIDS! THEY NEED US!
HELP ANDERSON!

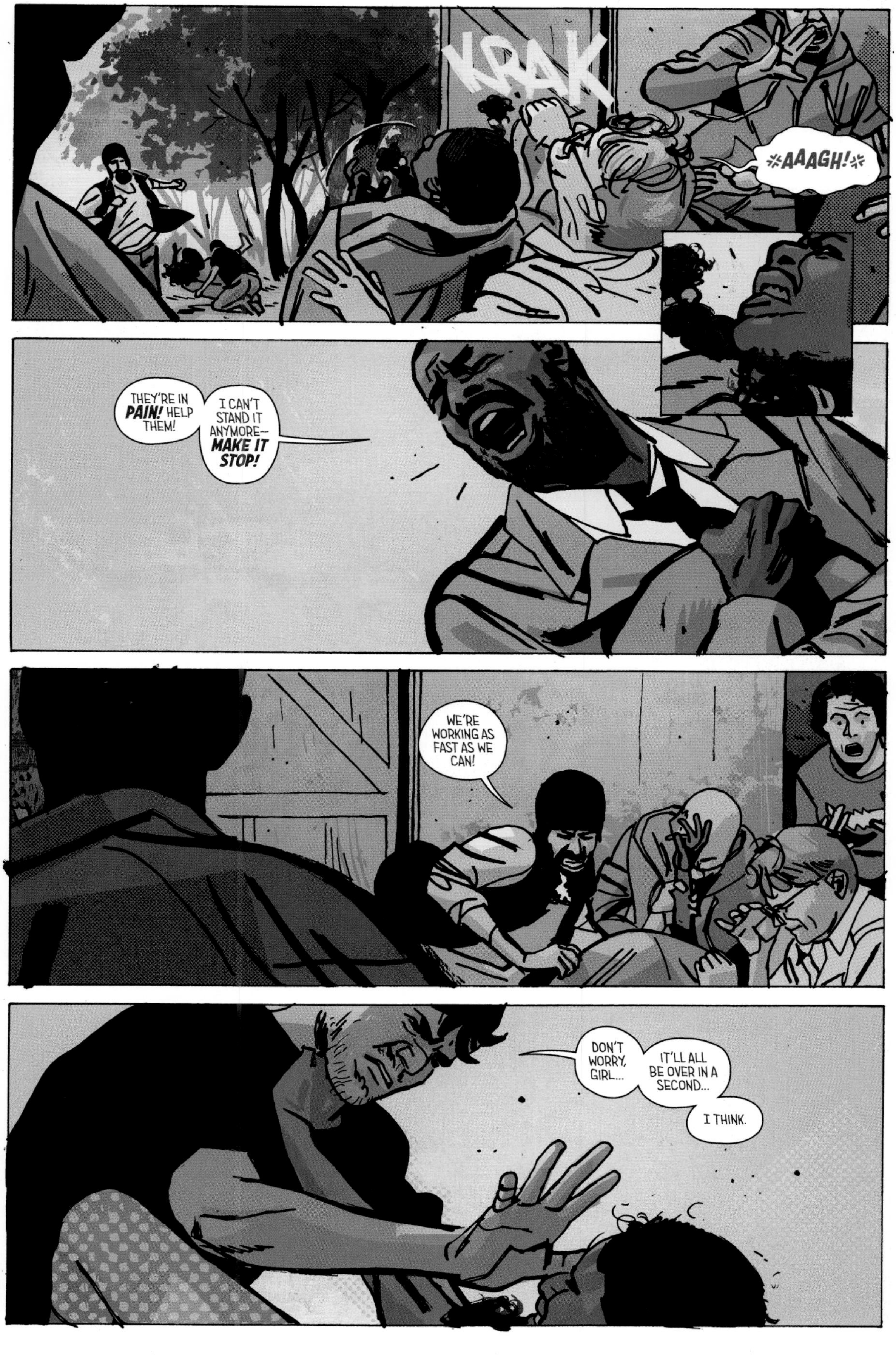
KRAK
#AAAGH!#
THEY'RE IN PAIN! HELP THEM!
I CAN'T STAND IT ANYMORE-- MAKE IT STOP!
WE'RE WORKING AS FAST AS WE CAN!
DON'T WORRY, GIRL...
IT'LL ALL BE OVER IN A SECOND...
I THINK.

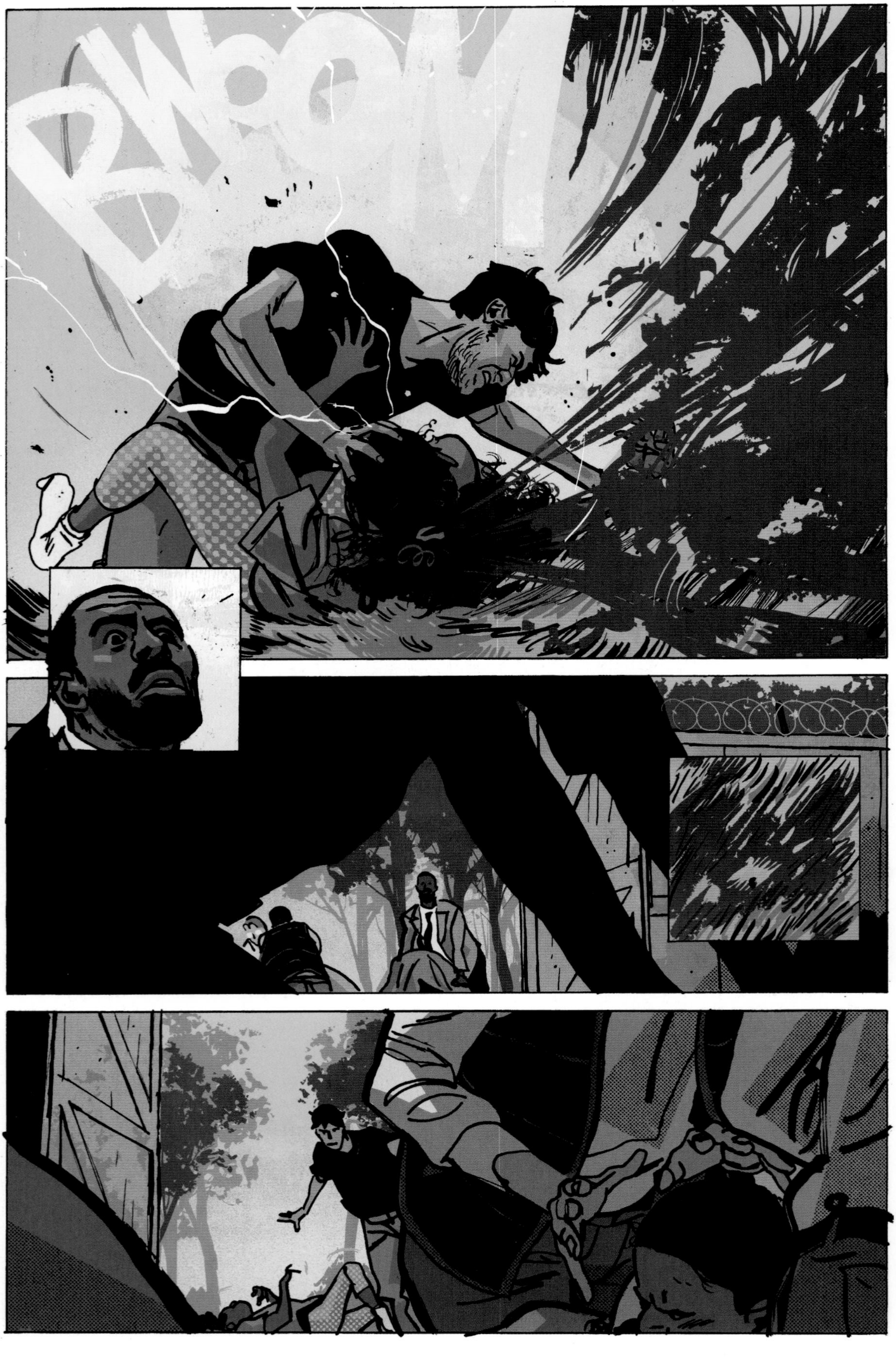
BWOOM

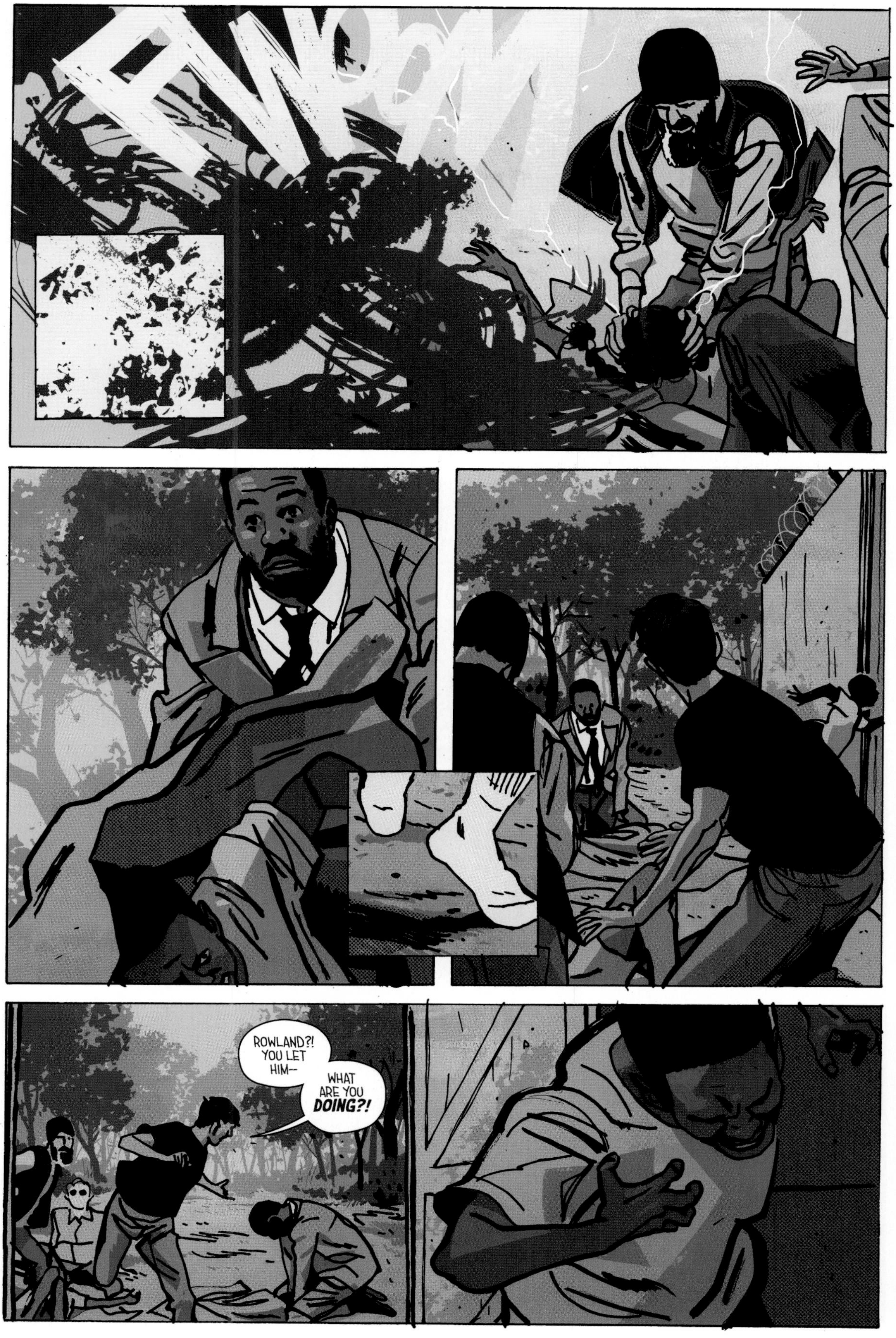
FWOOM
ROWLAND?! YOU LET HIM--
WHAT ARE YOU **DOING?!**

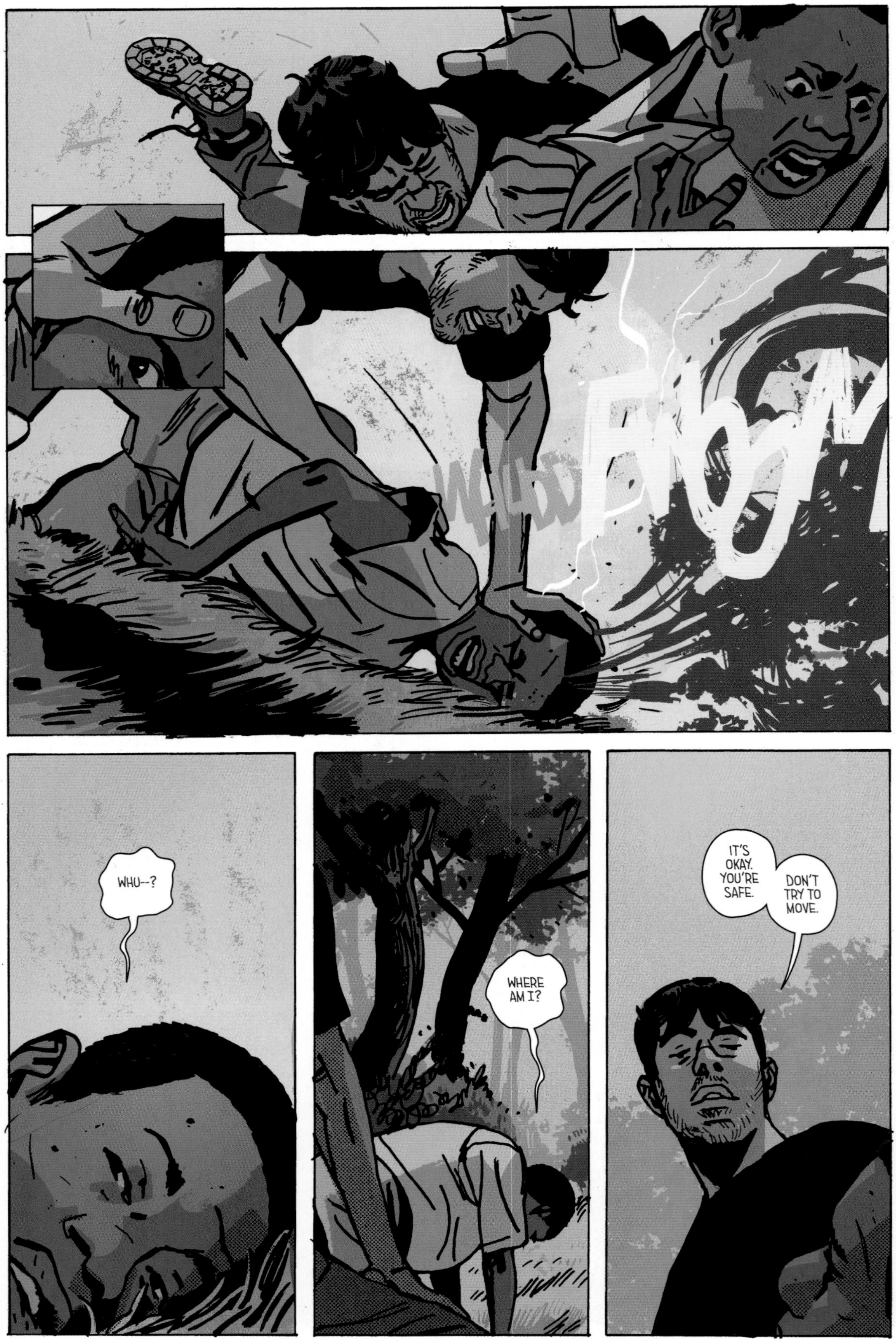
WHU--?
WHERE AM I?
IT'S OKAY. YOU'RE SAFE.
DON'T TRY TO MOVE.

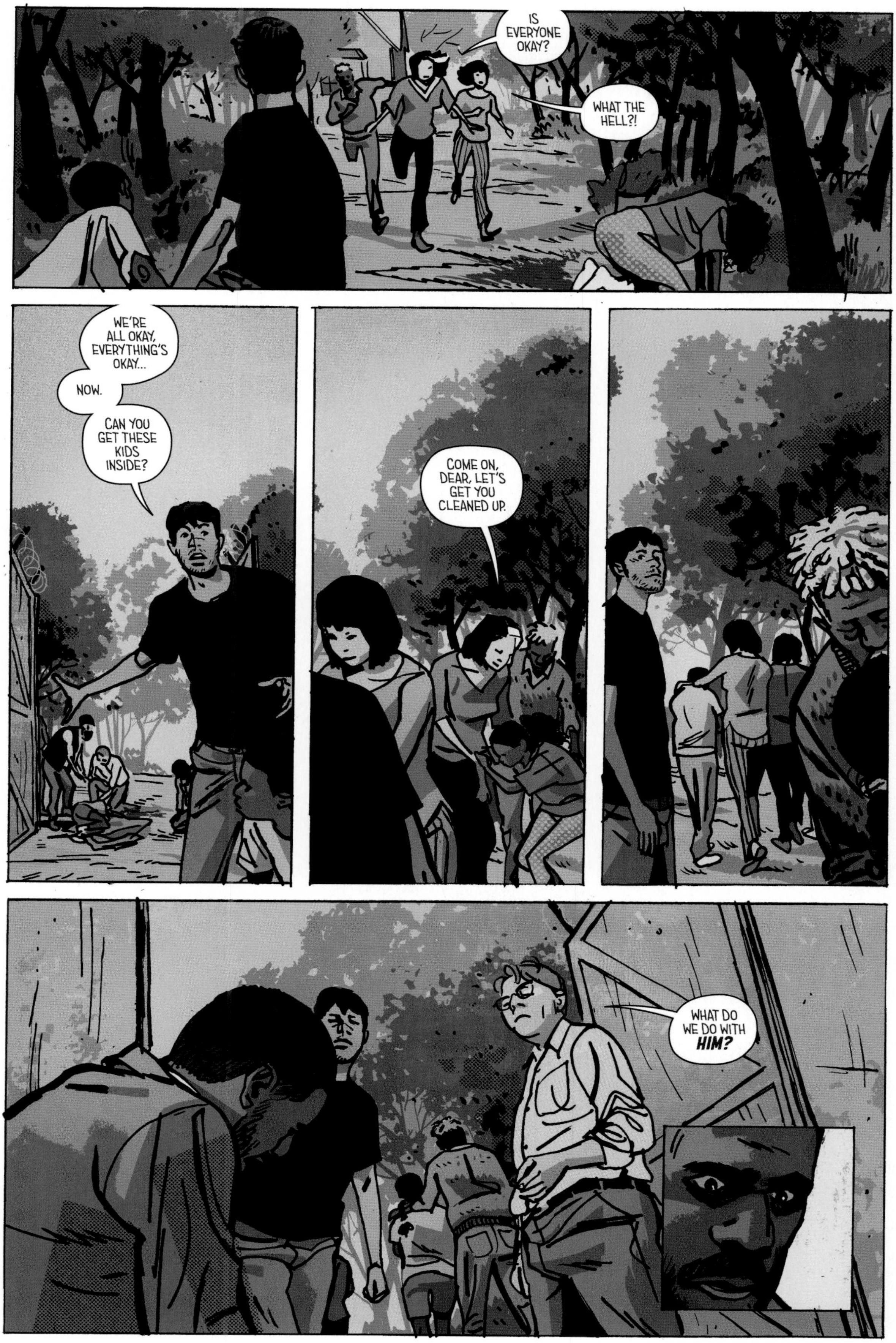
IS EVERYONE OKAY?
WHAT THE HELL?!
WE'RE ALL OKAY, EVERYTHING'S OKAY...
NOW.
CAN YOU GET THESE KIDS INSIDE?
COME ON, DEAR, LET'S GET YOU CLEANED UP.
WHAT DO WE DO WITH **HIM?**

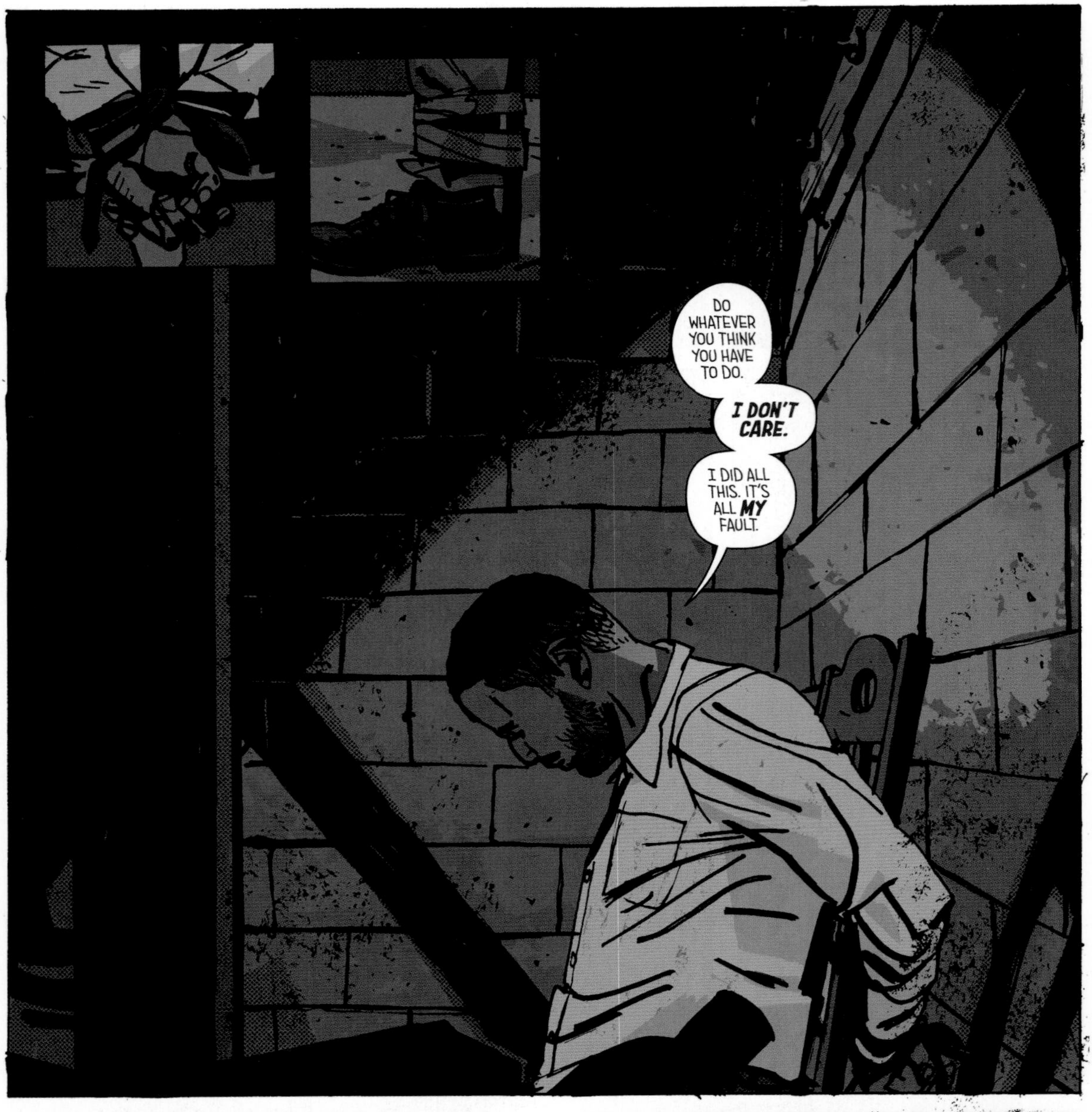
DO WHATEVER YOU THINK YOU HAVE TO DO.
I DON'T CARE.
I DID ALL THIS. IT'S ALL MY FAULT.

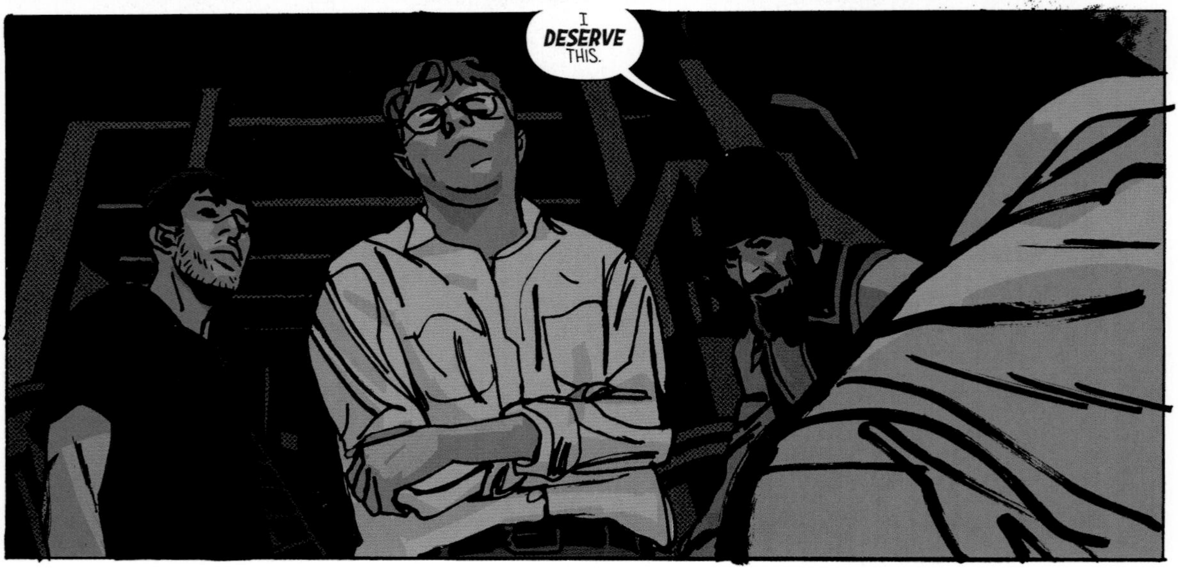
I DESERVE THIS.

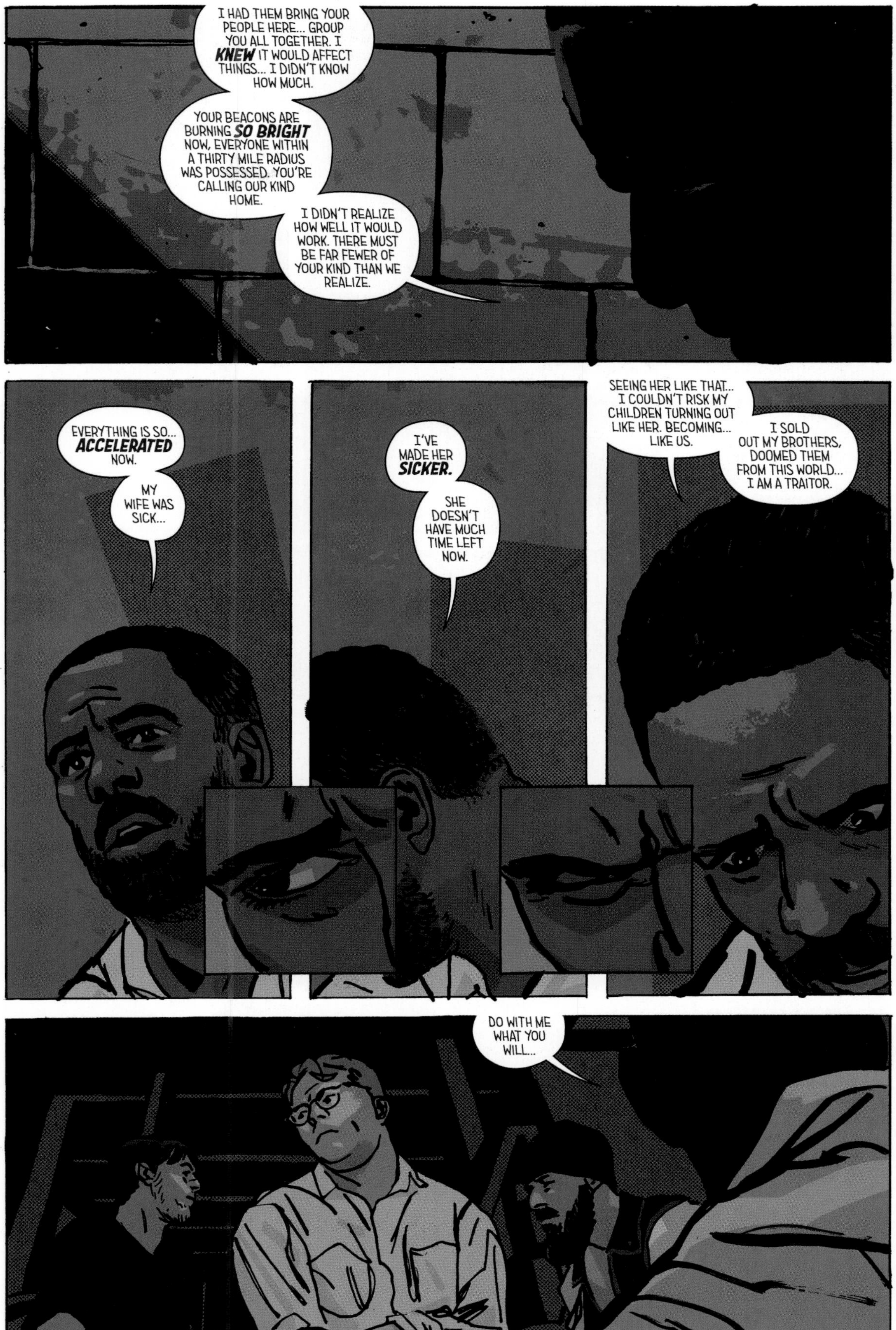
I HAD THEM BRING YOUR PEOPLE HERE... GROUP YOU ALL TOGETHER. I **KNEW** IT WOULD AFFECT THINGS... I DIDN'T KNOW HOW MUCH.
YOUR BEACONS ARE BURNING **SO BRIGHT** NOW, EVERYONE WITHIN A THIRTY MILE RADIUS WAS POSSESSED. YOU'RE CALLING OUR KIND HOME.
I DIDN'T REALIZE HOW WELL IT WOULD WORK. THERE MUST BE FAR FEWER OF YOUR KIND THAN WE REALIZE.
EVERYTHING IS SO... **ACCELERATED** NOW.
MY WIFE WAS SICK...
I'VE MADE HER **SICKER.**
SHE DOESN'T HAVE MUCH TIME LEFT NOW.
SEEING HER LIKE THAT... I COULDN'T RISK MY CHILDREN TURNING OUT LIKE HER. BECOMING... LIKE US.
I SOLD OUT MY BROTHERS, DOOMED THEM FROM THIS WORLD... I AM A TRAITOR.
DO WITH ME WHAT YOU WILL...

SHOW IT TO HIM. MAYBE HE KNOWS ABOUT IT.

WHAT IS *THIS?*

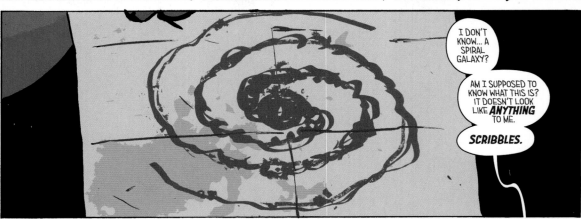

I DON'T KNOW... A SPIRAL GALAXY?

AM I SUPPOSED TO KNOW WHAT THIS IS? IT DOESN'T LOOK LIKE *ANYTHING* TO ME.

SCRIBBLES.

IT *SEEMS* LIKE HE'S TELLING THE TRUTH.

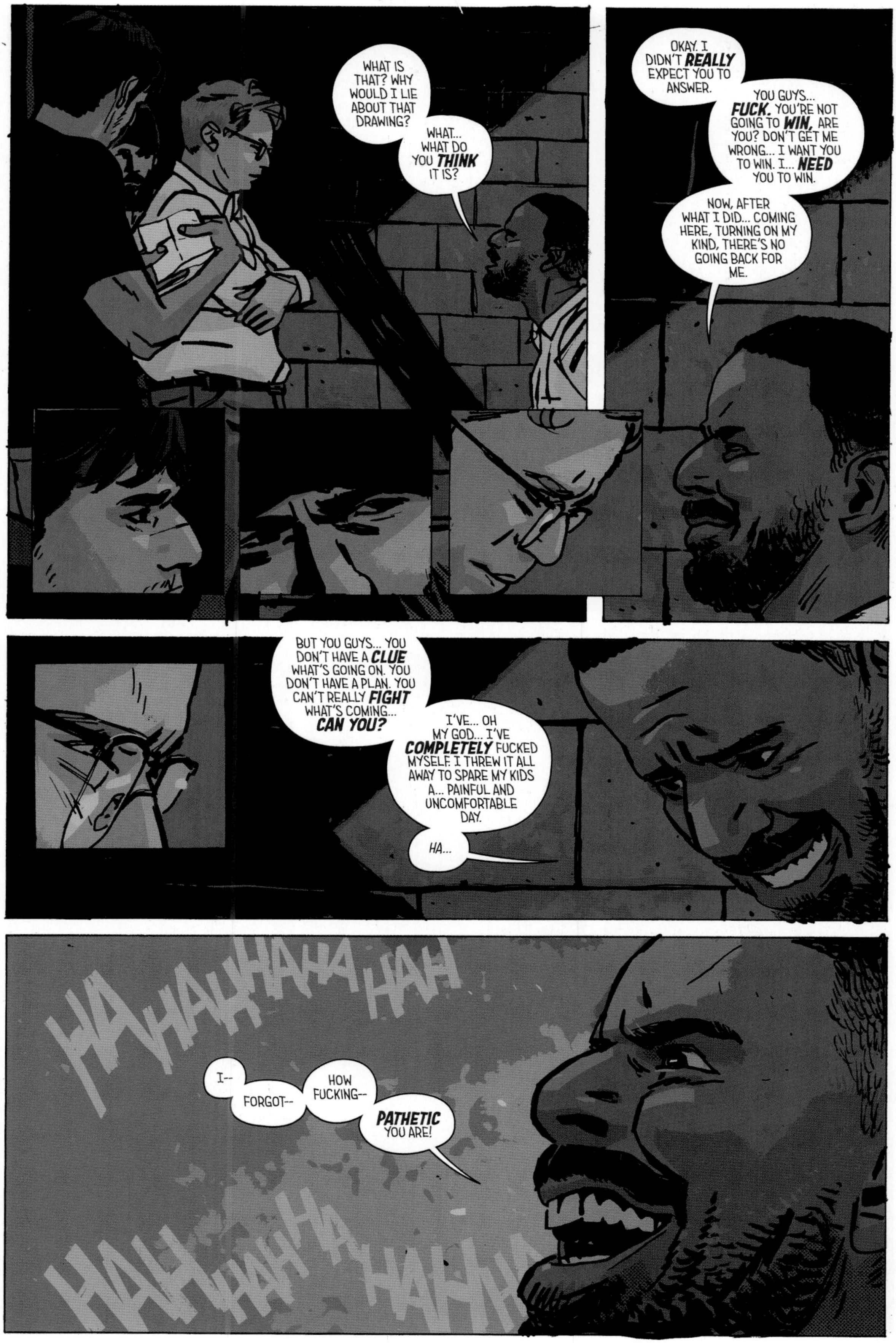

WHAT IS THAT? WHY WOULD I LIE ABOUT THAT DRAWING?
WHAT... WHAT DO YOU THINK IT IS?
OKAY. I DIDN'T REALLY EXPECT YOU TO ANSWER.
YOU GUYS... FUCK. YOU'RE NOT GOING TO WIN, ARE YOU? DON'T GET ME WRONG... I WANT YOU TO WIN. I... NEED YOU TO WIN.
NOW, AFTER WHAT I DID... COMING HERE, TURNING ON MY KIND, THERE'S NO GOING BACK FOR ME.
BUT YOU GUYS... YOU DON'T HAVE A CLUE WHAT'S GOING ON. YOU DON'T HAVE A PLAN. YOU CAN'T REALLY FIGHT WHAT'S COMING... CAN YOU?
I'VE... OH MY GOD... I'VE COMPLETELY FUCKED MYSELF. I THREW IT ALL AWAY TO SPARE MY KIDS A... PAINFUL AND UNCOMFORTABLE DAY.
HA...
HAHAHAHAHA HAH
I--
FORGOT--
HOW FUCKING--
PATHETIC YOU ARE!
HAHAHAHA HAHA

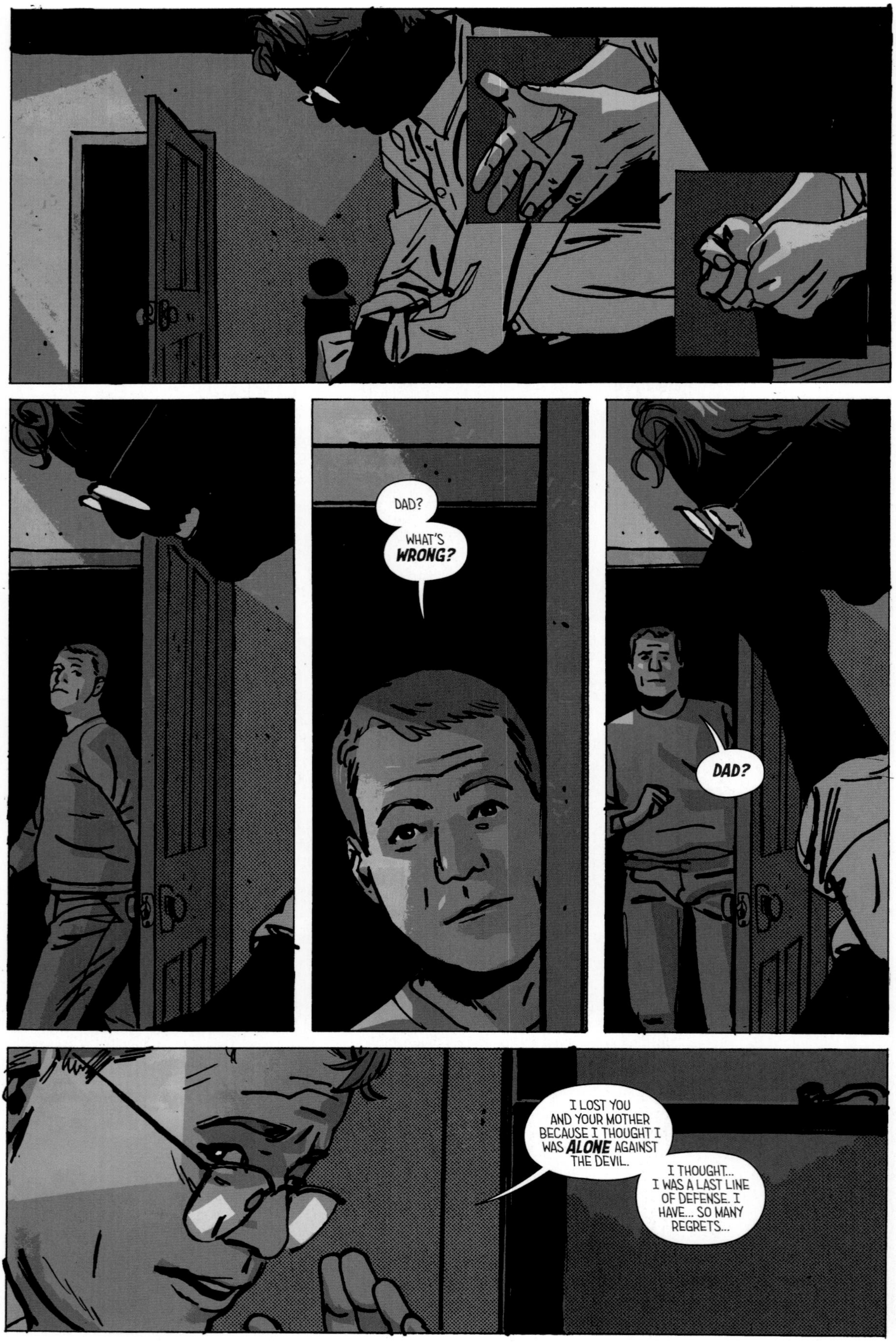
DAD?
WHAT'S **WRONG?**
DAD?
I LOST YOU AND YOUR MOTHER BECAUSE I THOUGHT I WAS **ALONE** AGAINST THE DEVIL.
I THOUGHT... I WAS A LAST LINE OF DEFENSE. I HAVE... SO MANY REGRETS...

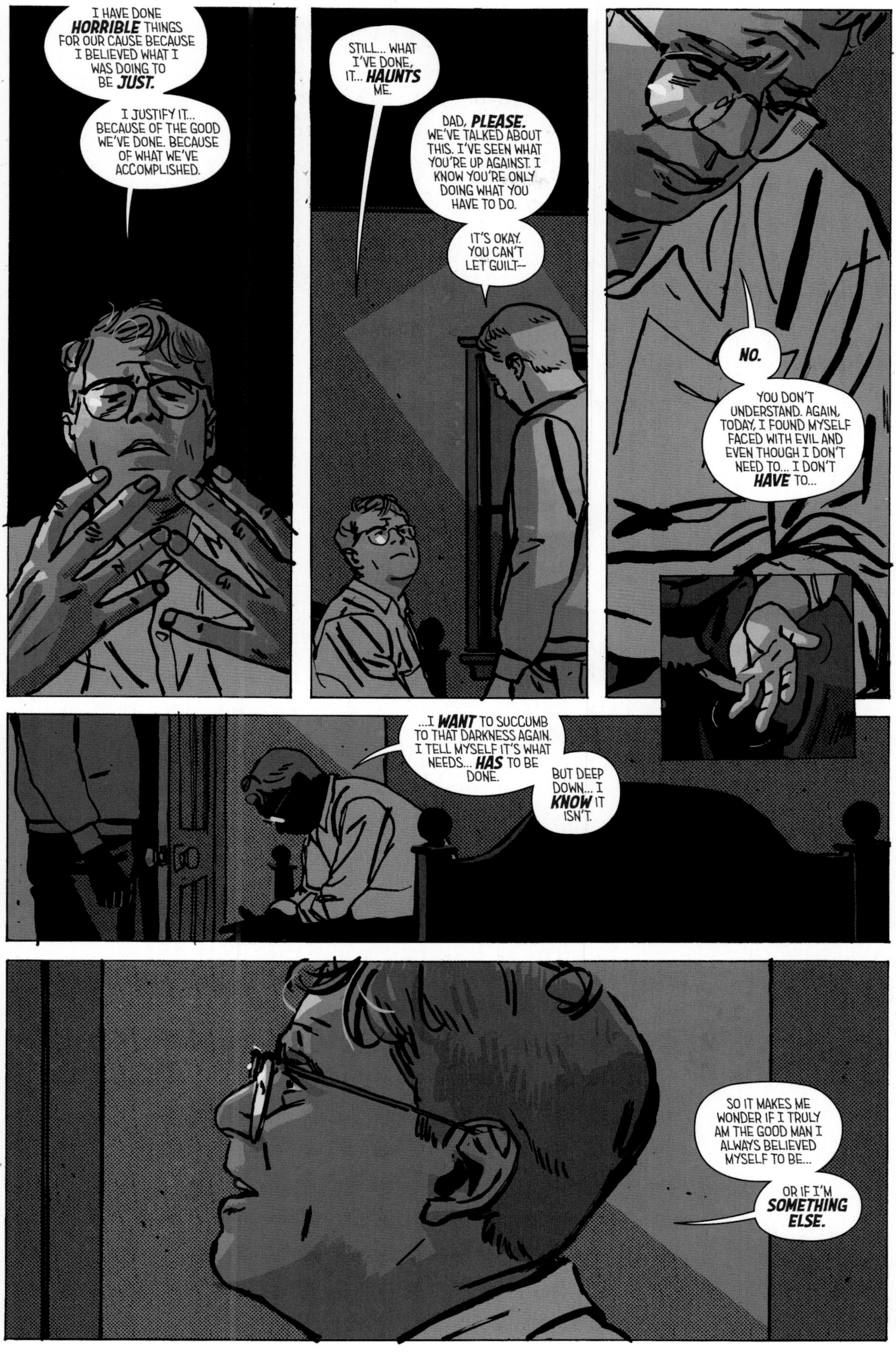
I HAVE DONE HORRIBLE THINGS FOR OUR CAUSE BECAUSE I BELIEVED WHAT I WAS DOING TO BE JUST.
I JUSTIFY IT... BECAUSE OF THE GOOD WE'VE DONE. BECAUSE OF WHAT WE'VE ACCOMPLISHED.
STILL... WHAT I'VE DONE, IT... HAUNTS ME.
DAD, PLEASE. WE'VE TALKED ABOUT THIS. I'VE SEEN WHAT YOU'RE UP AGAINST. I KNOW YOU'RE ONLY DOING WHAT YOU HAVE TO DO.
IT'S OKAY. YOU CAN'T LET GUILT--
NO.
YOU DON'T UNDERSTAND. AGAIN, TODAY, I FOUND MYSELF FACED WITH EVIL AND EVEN THOUGH I DON'T NEED TO... I DON'T HAVE TO...
...I WANT TO SUCCUMB TO THAT DARKNESS AGAIN. I TELL MYSELF IT'S WHAT NEEDS... HAS TO BE DONE.
BUT DEEP DOWN... I KNOW IT ISN'T.
SO IT MAKES ME WONDER IF I TRULY AM THE GOOD MAN I ALWAYS BELIEVED MYSELF TO BE...
OR IF I'M SOMETHING ELSE.

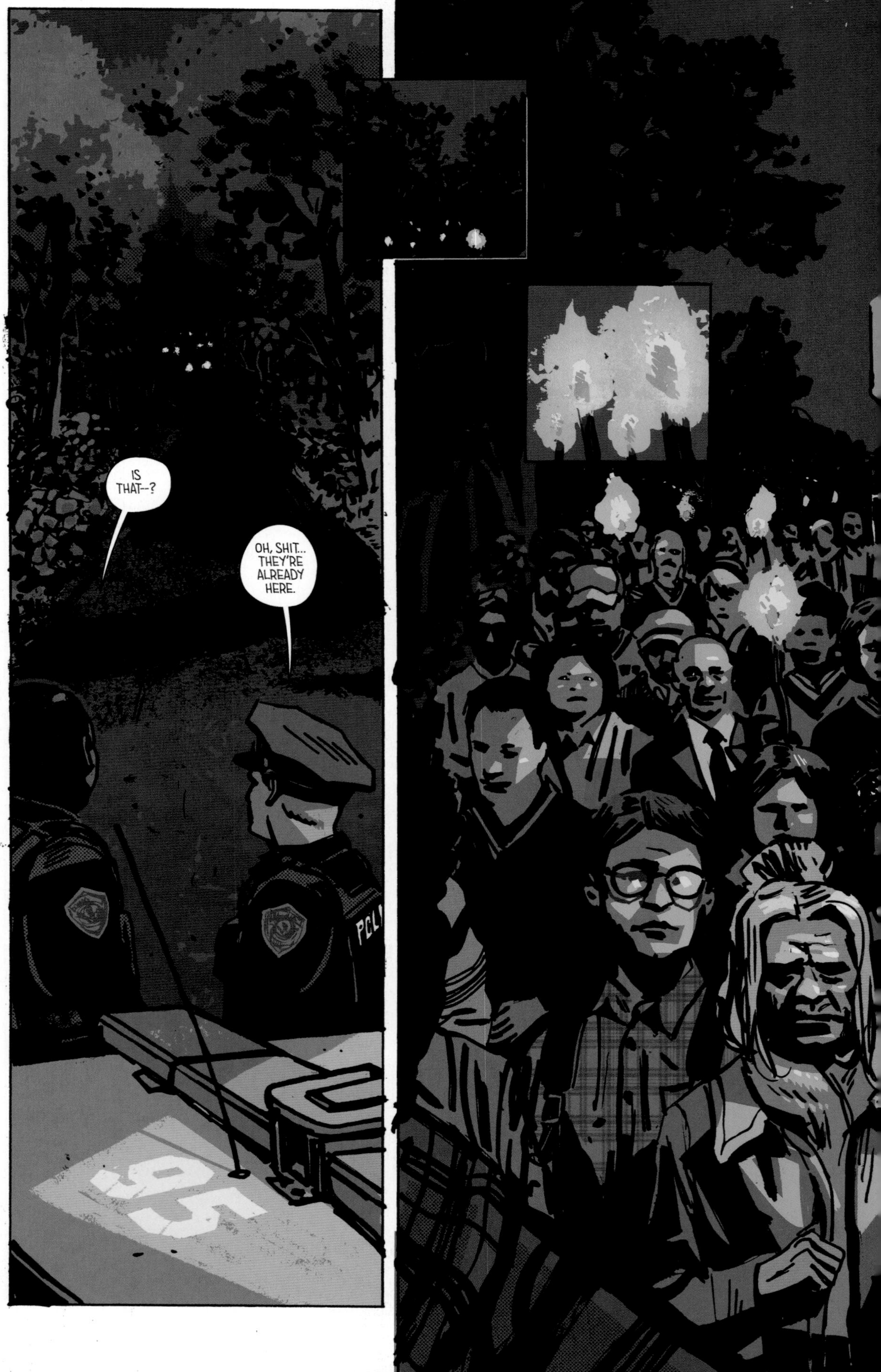
IS THAT--?
OH, SHIT... THEY'RE ALREADY HERE.

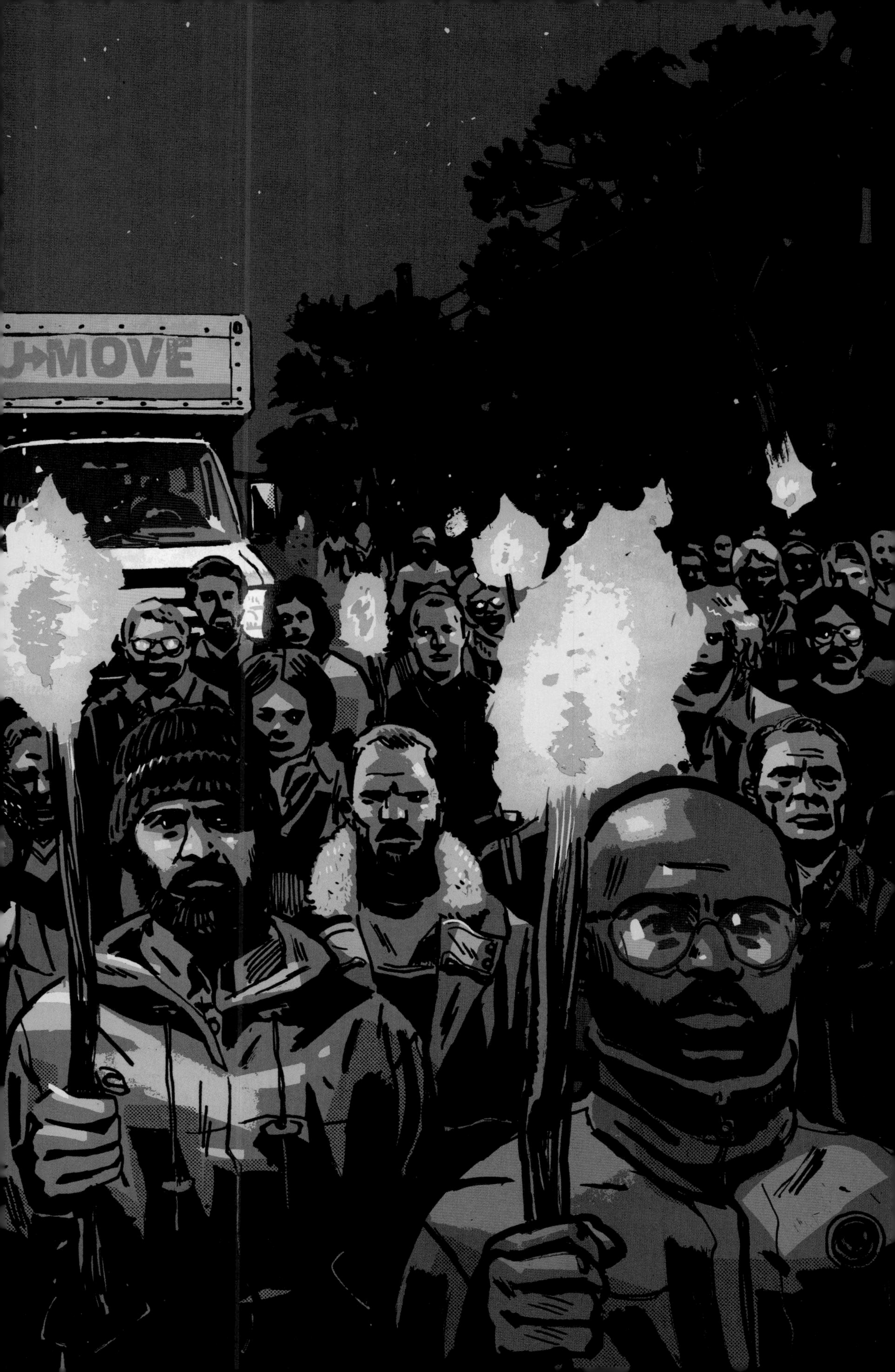
U→MOVE

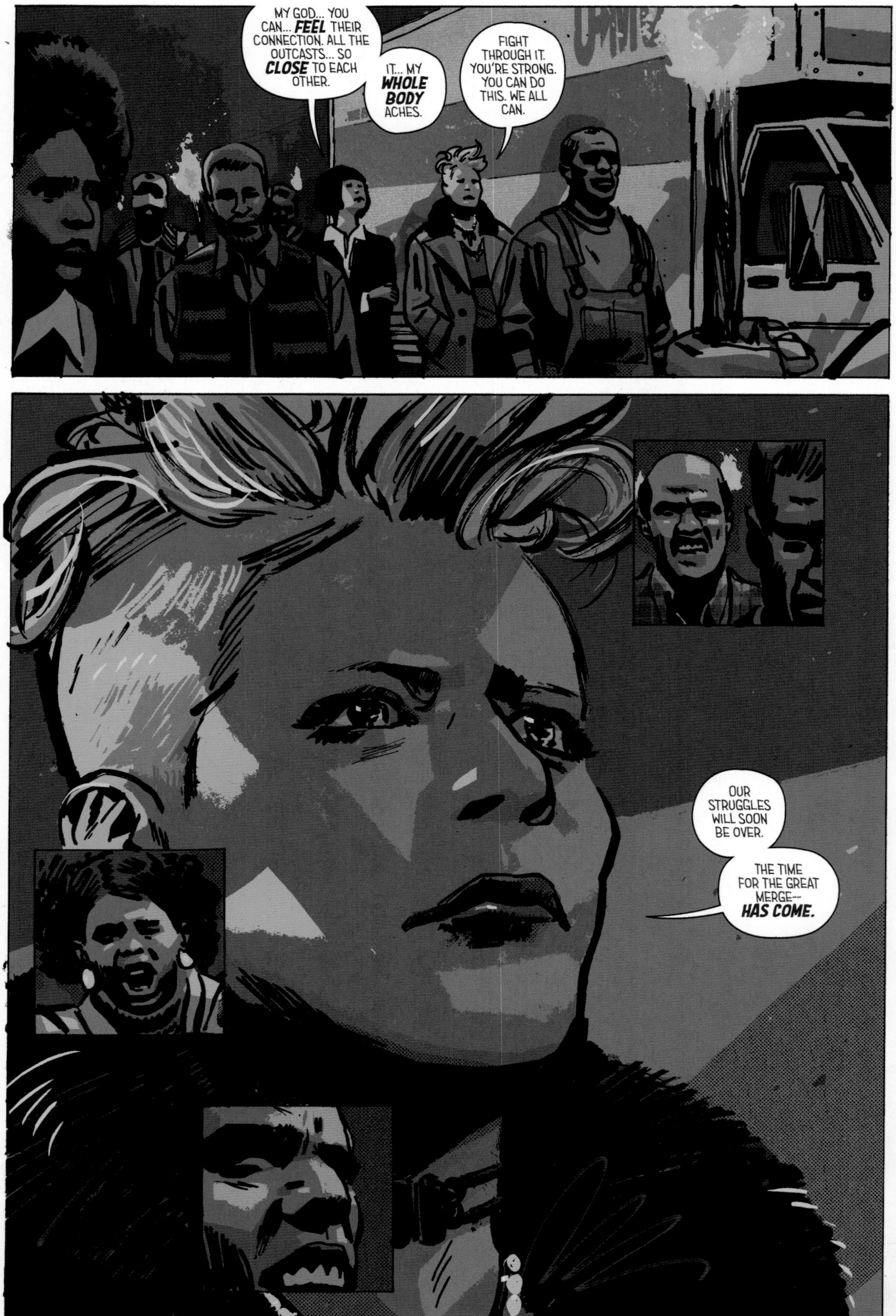
MY GOD... YOU CAN... FEEL THEIR CONNECTION. ALL THE OUTCASTS... SO CLOSE TO EACH OTHER.
IT... MY WHOLE BODY ACHES.
FIGHT THROUGH IT. YOU'RE STRONG. YOU CAN DO THIS. WE ALL CAN.
OUR STRUGGLES WILL SOON BE OVER.
THE TIME FOR THE GREAT MERGE-- HAS COME.

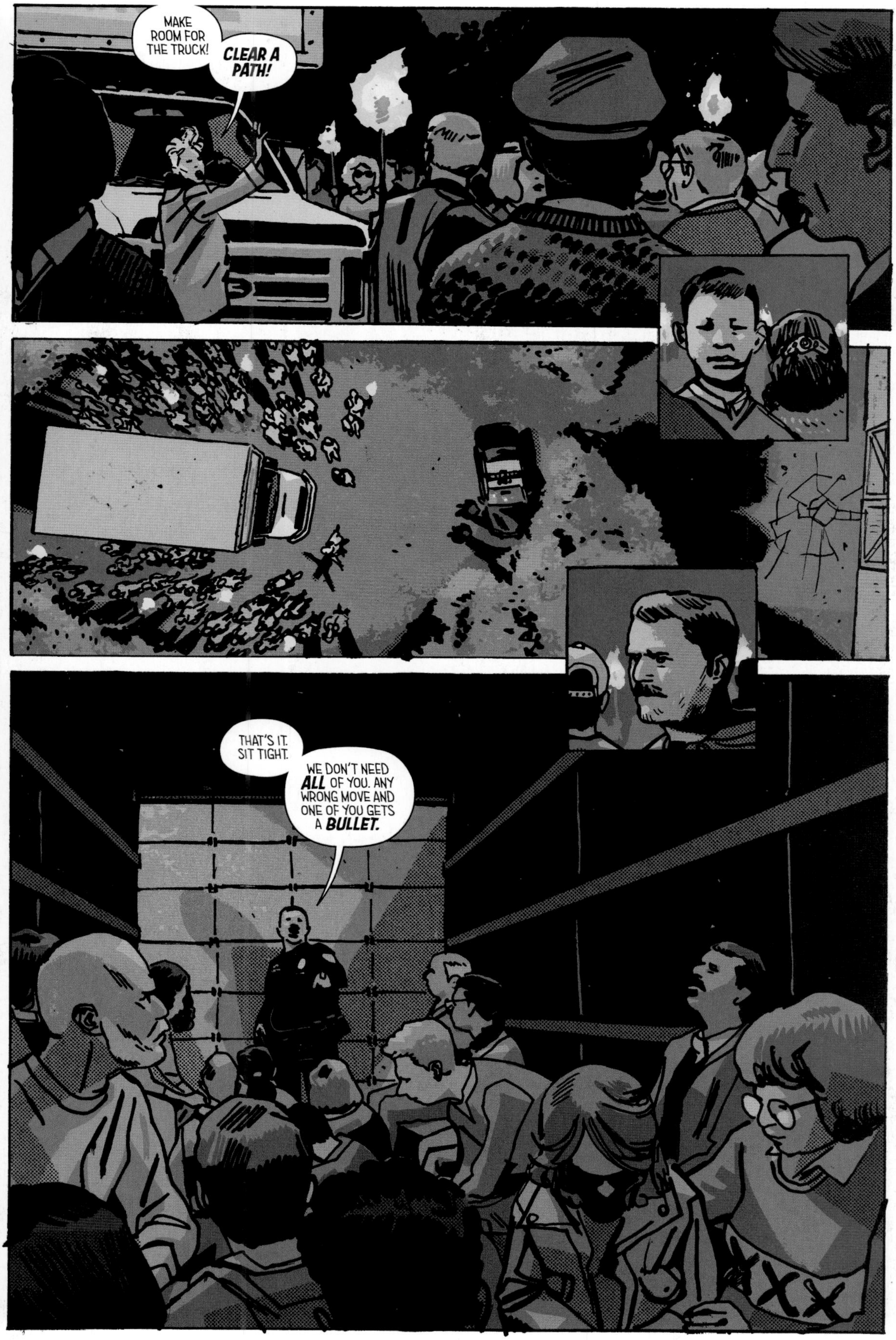
MAKE ROOM FOR THE TRUCK!
CLEAR A PATH!
THAT'S IT. SIT TIGHT.
WE DON'T NEED ALL OF YOU. ANY WRONG MOVE AND ONE OF YOU GETS A BULLET.

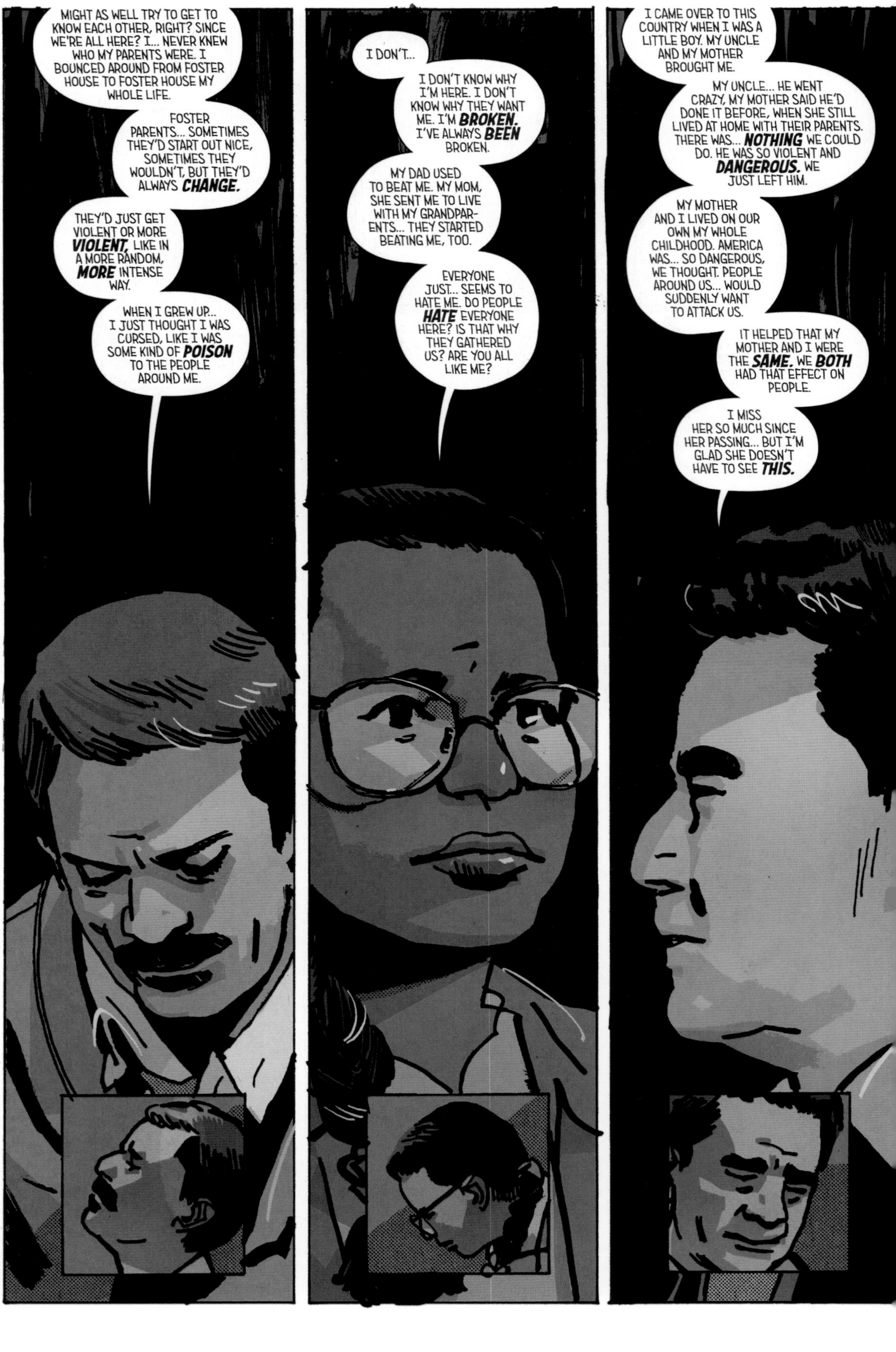
MIGHT AS WELL TRY TO GET TO KNOW EACH OTHER, RIGHT? SINCE WE'RE ALL HERE? I... NEVER KNEW WHO MY PARENTS WERE. I BOUNCED AROUND FROM FOSTER HOUSE TO FOSTER HOUSE MY WHOLE LIFE.
FOSTER PARENTS... SOMETIMES THEY'D START OUT NICE, SOMETIMES THEY WOULDN'T, BUT THEY'D ALWAYS CHANGE.
THEY'D JUST GET VIOLENT OR MORE VIOLENT, LIKE IN A MORE RANDOM, MORE INTENSE WAY.
WHEN I GREW UP... I JUST THOUGHT I WAS CURSED, LIKE I WAS SOME KIND OF POISON TO THE PEOPLE AROUND ME.
I DON'T...
I DON'T KNOW WHY I'M HERE. I DON'T KNOW WHY THEY WANT ME. I'M BROKEN. I'VE ALWAYS BEEN BROKEN.
MY DAD USED TO BEAT ME. MY MOM, SHE SENT ME TO LIVE WITH MY GRANDPAR-ENTS... THEY STARTED BEATING ME, TOO.
EVERYONE JUST... SEEMS TO HATE ME. DO PEOPLE HATE EVERYONE HERE? IS THAT WHY THEY GATHERED US? ARE YOU ALL LIKE ME?
I CAME OVER TO THIS COUNTRY WHEN I WAS A LITTLE BOY. MY UNCLE AND MY MOTHER BROUGHT ME.
MY UNCLE... HE WENT CRAZY, MY MOTHER SAID HE'D DONE IT BEFORE, WHEN SHE STILL LIVED AT HOME WITH THEIR PARENTS. THERE WAS... NOTHING WE COULD DO. HE WAS SO VIOLENT AND DANGEROUS. WE JUST LEFT HIM.
MY MOTHER AND I LIVED ON OUR OWN MY WHOLE CHILDHOOD. AMERICA WAS... SO DANGEROUS, WE THOUGHT. PEOPLE AROUND US... WOULD SUDDENLY WANT TO ATTACK US.
IT HELPED THAT MY MOTHER AND I WERE THE SAME. WE BOTH HAD THAT EFFECT ON PEOPLE.
I MISS HER SO MUCH SINCE HER PASSING... BUT I'M GLAD SHE DOESN'T HAVE TO SEE THIS.

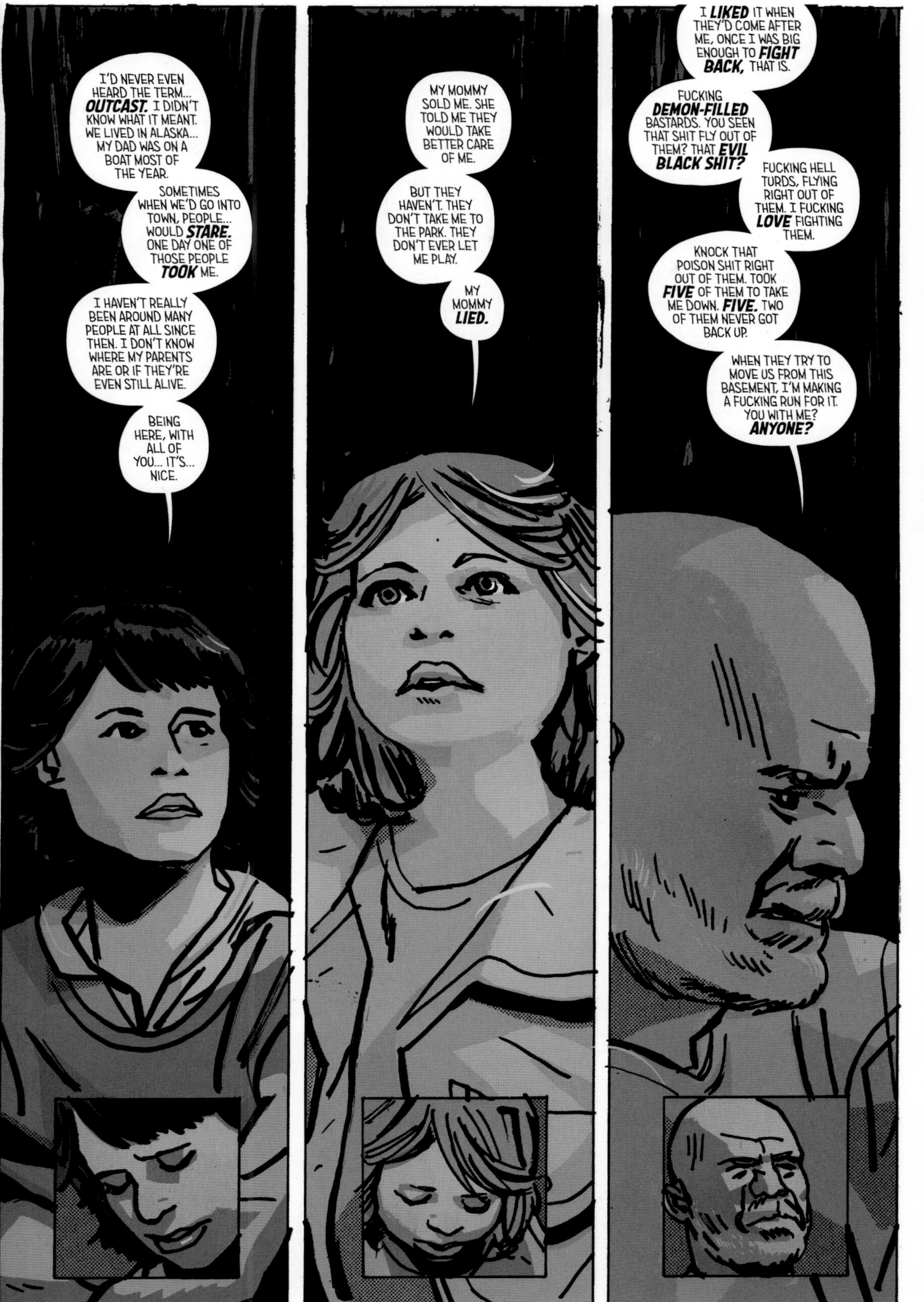
I'D NEVER EVEN HEARD THE TERM... OUTCAST. I DIDN'T KNOW WHAT IT MEANT. WE LIVED IN ALASKA... MY DAD WAS ON A BOAT MOST OF THE YEAR.
SOMETIMES WHEN WE'D GO INTO TOWN, PEOPLE... WOULD STARE. ONE DAY ONE OF THOSE PEOPLE TOOK ME.
I HAVEN'T REALLY BEEN AROUND MANY PEOPLE AT ALL SINCE THEN. I DON'T KNOW WHERE MY PARENTS ARE OR IF THEY'RE EVEN STILL ALIVE.
BEING HERE, WITH ALL OF YOU... IT'S... NICE.
MY MOMMY SOLD ME. SHE TOLD ME THEY WOULD TAKE BETTER CARE OF ME.
BUT THEY HAVEN'T. THEY DON'T TAKE ME TO THE PARK. THEY DON'T EVER LET ME PLAY.
MY MOMMY LIED.
I LIKED IT WHEN THEY'D COME AFTER ME, ONCE I WAS BIG ENOUGH TO FIGHT BACK, THAT IS.
FUCKING DEMON-FILLED BASTARDS. YOU SEEN THAT SHIT FLY OUT OF THEM? THAT EVIL BLACK SHIT?
FUCKING HELL TURDS, FLYING RIGHT OUT OF THEM. I FUCKING LOVE FIGHTING THEM.
KNOCK THAT POISON SHIT RIGHT OUT OF THEM. TOOK FIVE OF THEM TO TAKE ME DOWN. FIVE. TWO OF THEM NEVER GOT BACK UP.
WHEN THEY TRY TO MOVE US FROM THIS BASEMENT, I'M MAKING A FUCKING RUN FOR IT. YOU WITH ME? ANYONE?

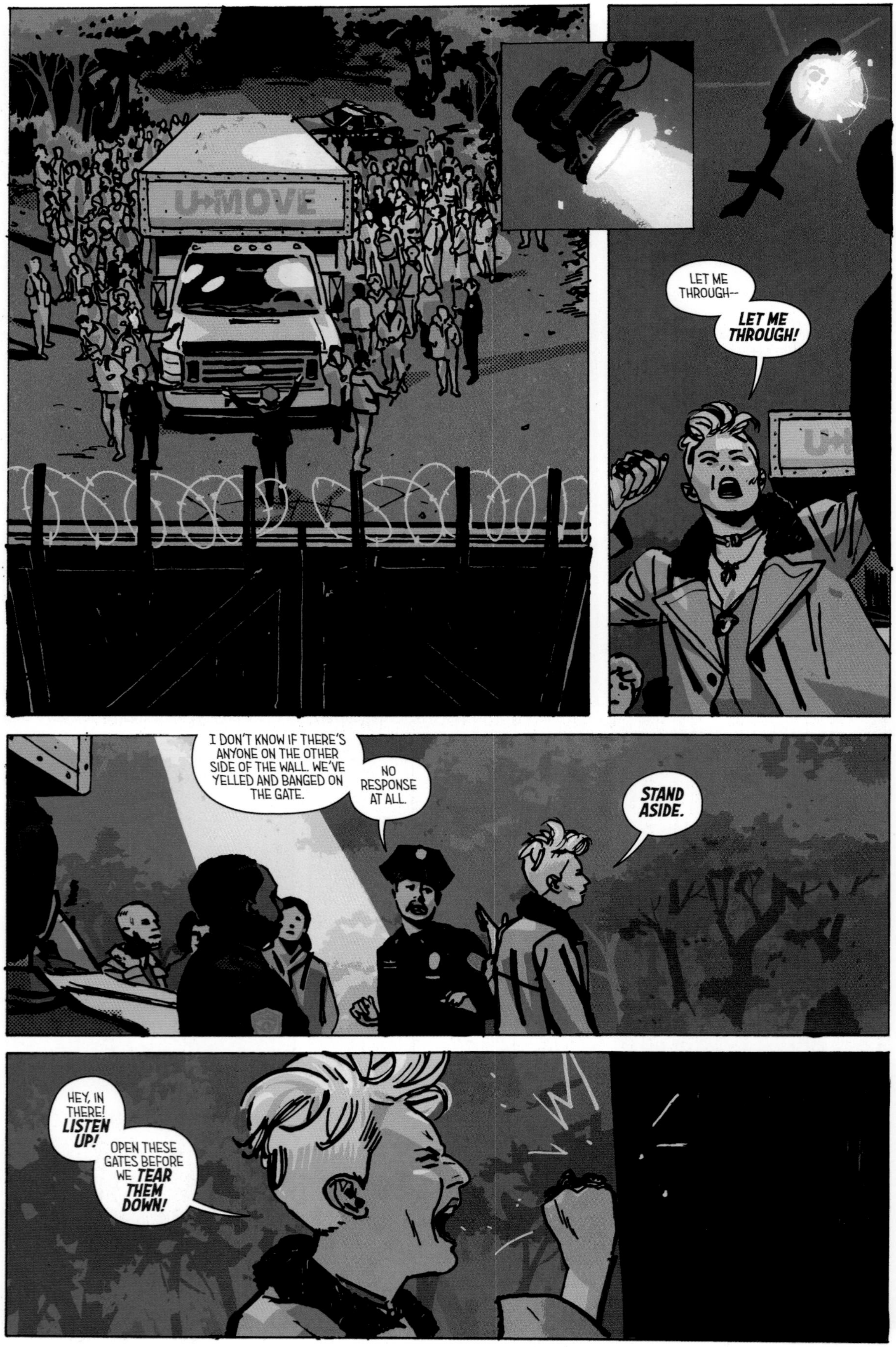
U-MOVE
LET ME THROUGH-- **LET ME THROUGH!**
I DON'T KNOW IF THERE'S ANYONE ON THE OTHER SIDE OF THE WALL. WE'VE YELLED AND BANGED ON THE GATE.
NO RESPONSE AT ALL.
STAND ASIDE.
HEY, IN THERE! **LISTEN UP!**
OPEN THESE GATES BEFORE WE **TEAR THEM DOWN!**

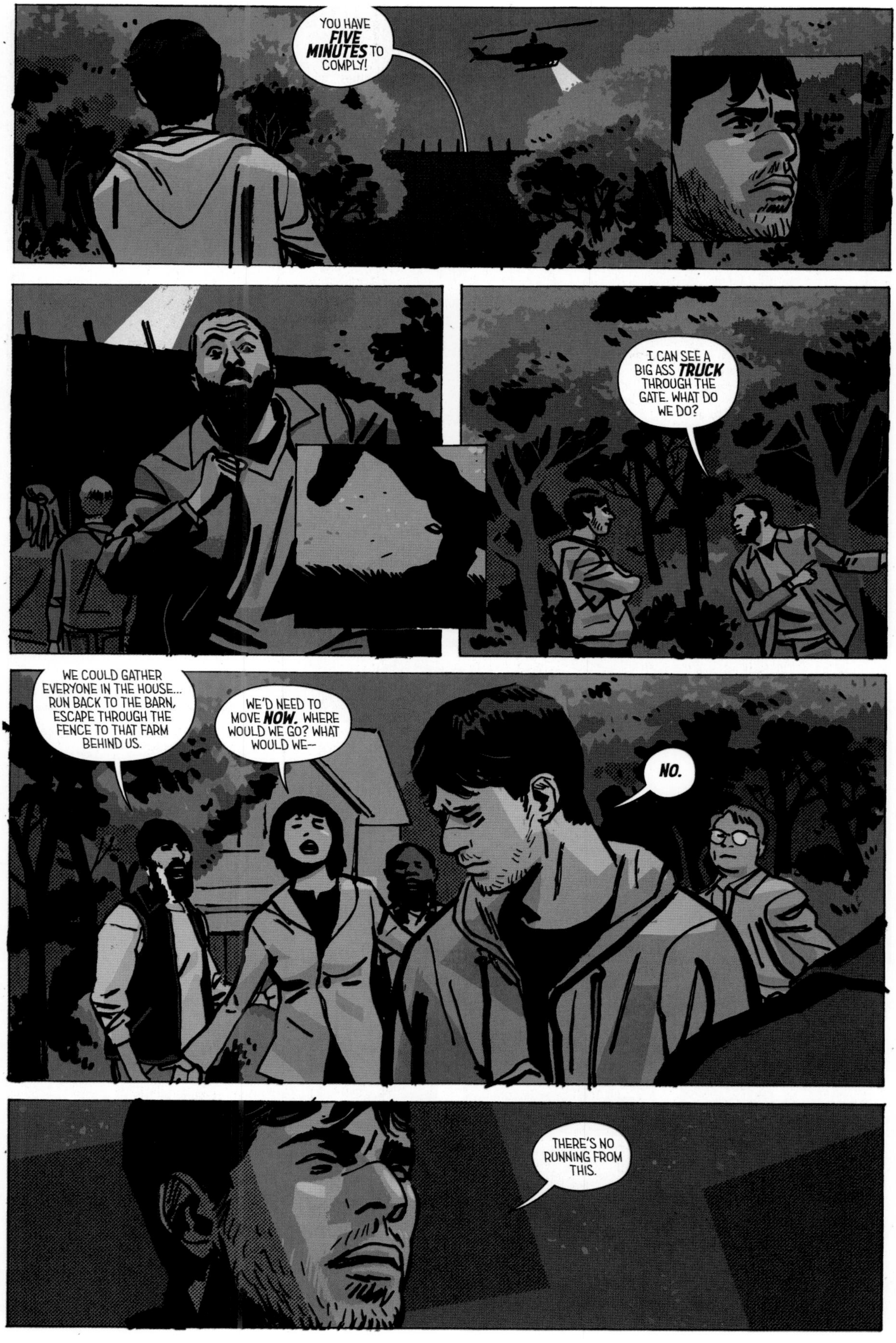
YOU HAVE FIVE MINUTES TO COMPLY!
I CAN SEE A BIG ASS TRUCK THROUGH THE GATE. WHAT DO WE DO?
WE COULD GATHER EVERYONE IN THE HOUSE... RUN BACK TO THE BARN, ESCAPE THROUGH THE FENCE TO THAT FARM BEHIND US.
WE'D NEED TO MOVE NOW. WHERE WOULD WE GO? WHAT WOULD WE--
NO.
THERE'S NO RUNNING FROM THIS.

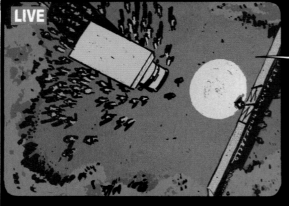

THIS IS THE SCENE TONIGHT IN **ROME, WEST VIRGINA.**

THERE'S NEW ACTIVITY IN THE LONG STANDOFF HAPPENING THERE.

STANDOFF IN ROME

3RD LIVE NEW ACTIVITY SURROUNDING WEST VIRGINIA CULT

WE HAVEN'T REPORTED ON THE KYLE BARNES CULT AND THEIR STANDOFF IN A SMALL FARM JUST OUTSIDE OF ROME IN SOME WEEKS, BUT THERE'S NEW DEVELOPMENTS TONIGHT.

IT SEEMS THE PEOPLE OF THE TOWN HAVE GATHERED OUTSIDE THE WALLS EN MASSE, TO FINALLY PUT AN END TO THIS CONFLICT.

FOR MONTHS NOW, KYLE BARNES AND HIS FOLLOWERS HAVE BEEN LIVING ON THE FARM. THEY ERECTED A WALL AROUND THE PERIMETER AND CLOSED OFF ALL CONTACT WITH THE OUTSIDE WORLD.

THE FEDERAL GOVERNMENT HAVE YET TO STEP IN AS THERE ISN'T COMPELLING EVIDENCE OF VIOLENCE OR MISTREATMENT ON THE FARM. THE TWO SIDES HAVE BEEN LOCKED IN STALEMATE UNTIL NOW.

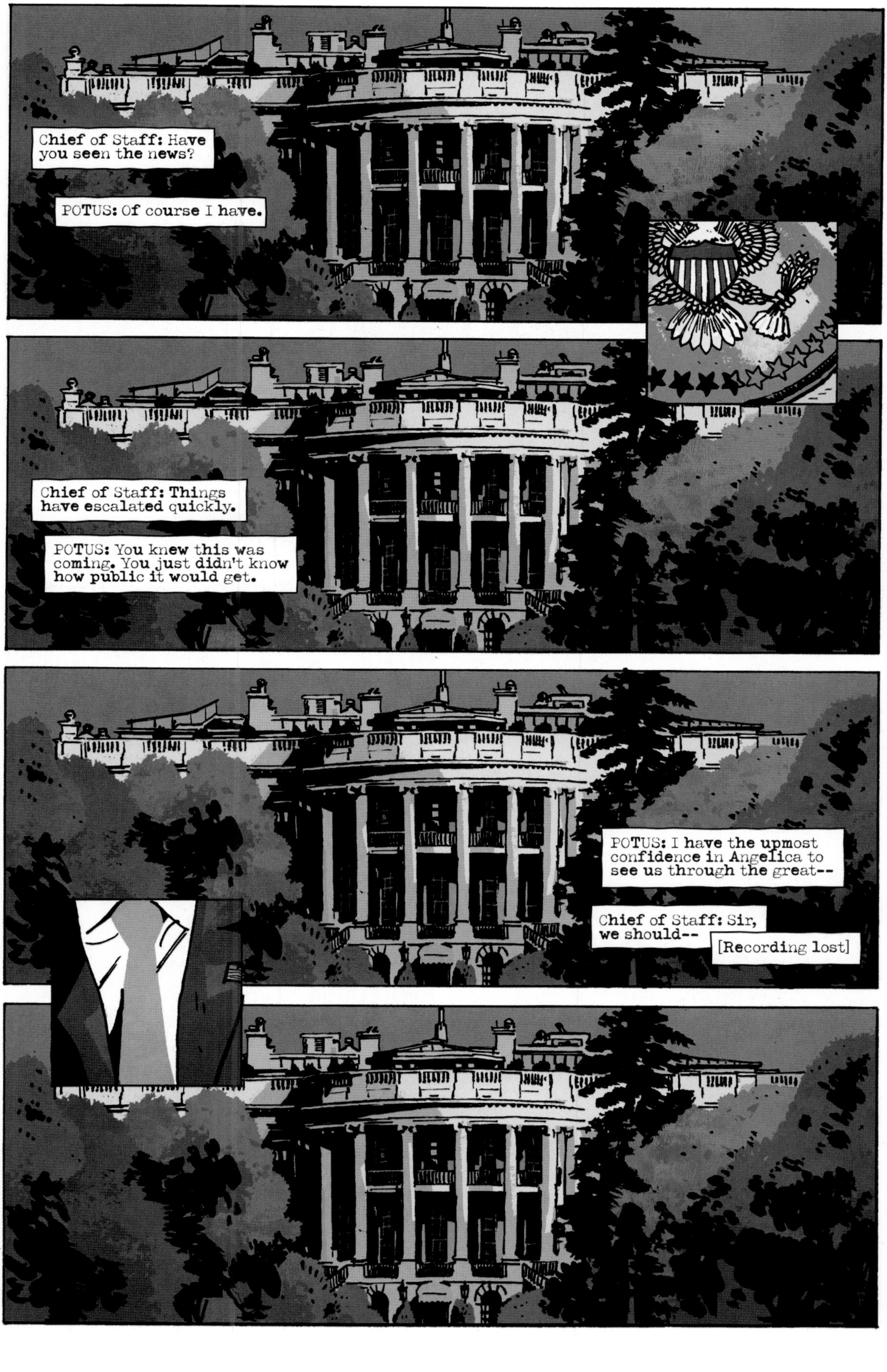
Chief of Staff: Have you seen the news?
POTUS: Of course I have.
Chief of Staff: Things have escalated quickly.
POTUS: You knew this was coming. You just didn't know how public it would get.
POTUS: I have the upmost confidence in Angelica to see us through the great--
Chief of Staff: Sir, we should--
[Recording lost]

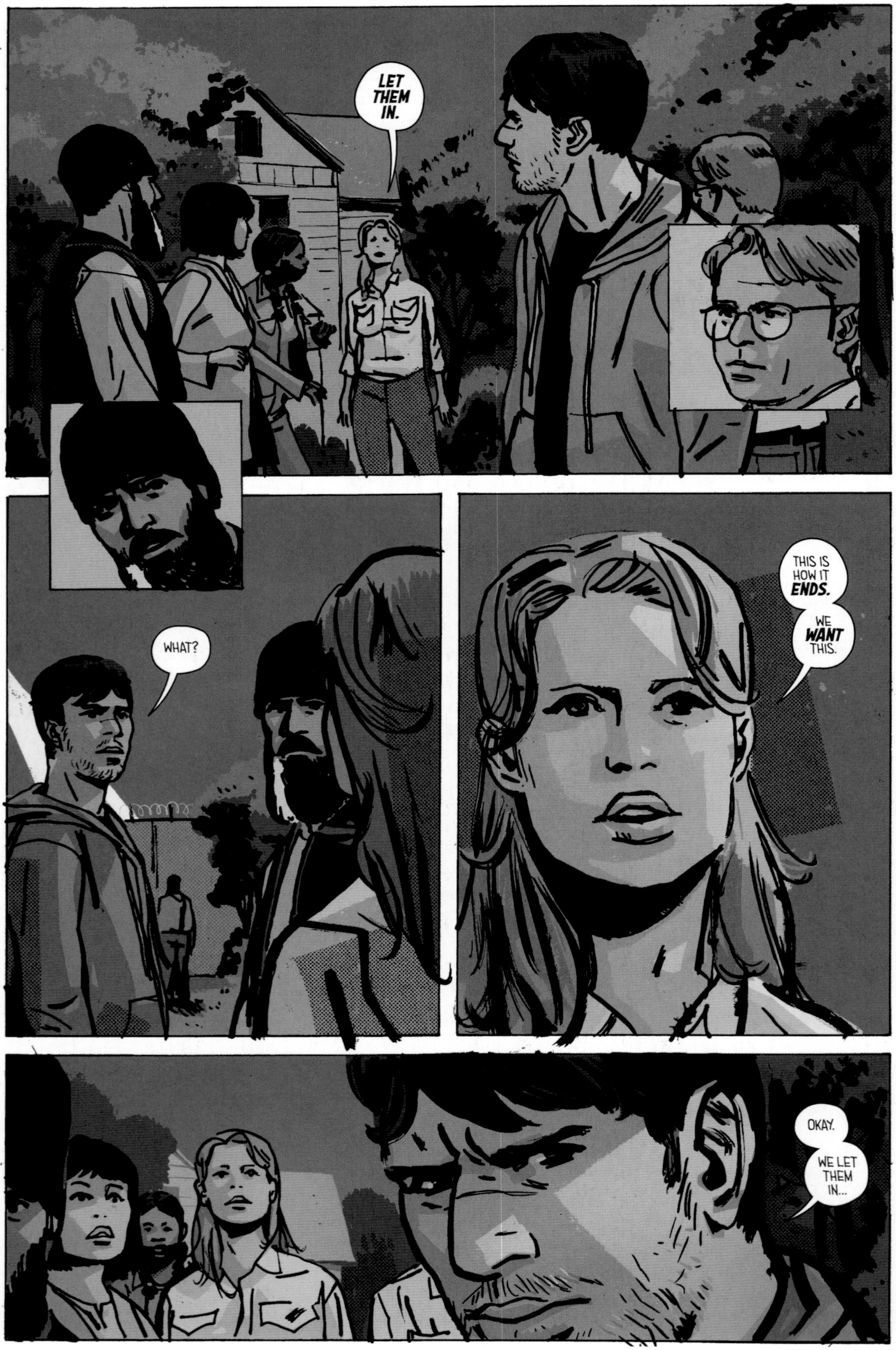
LET THEM IN.
WHAT?
THIS IS HOW IT ENDS.
WE WANT THIS.
OKAY.
WE LET THEM IN...

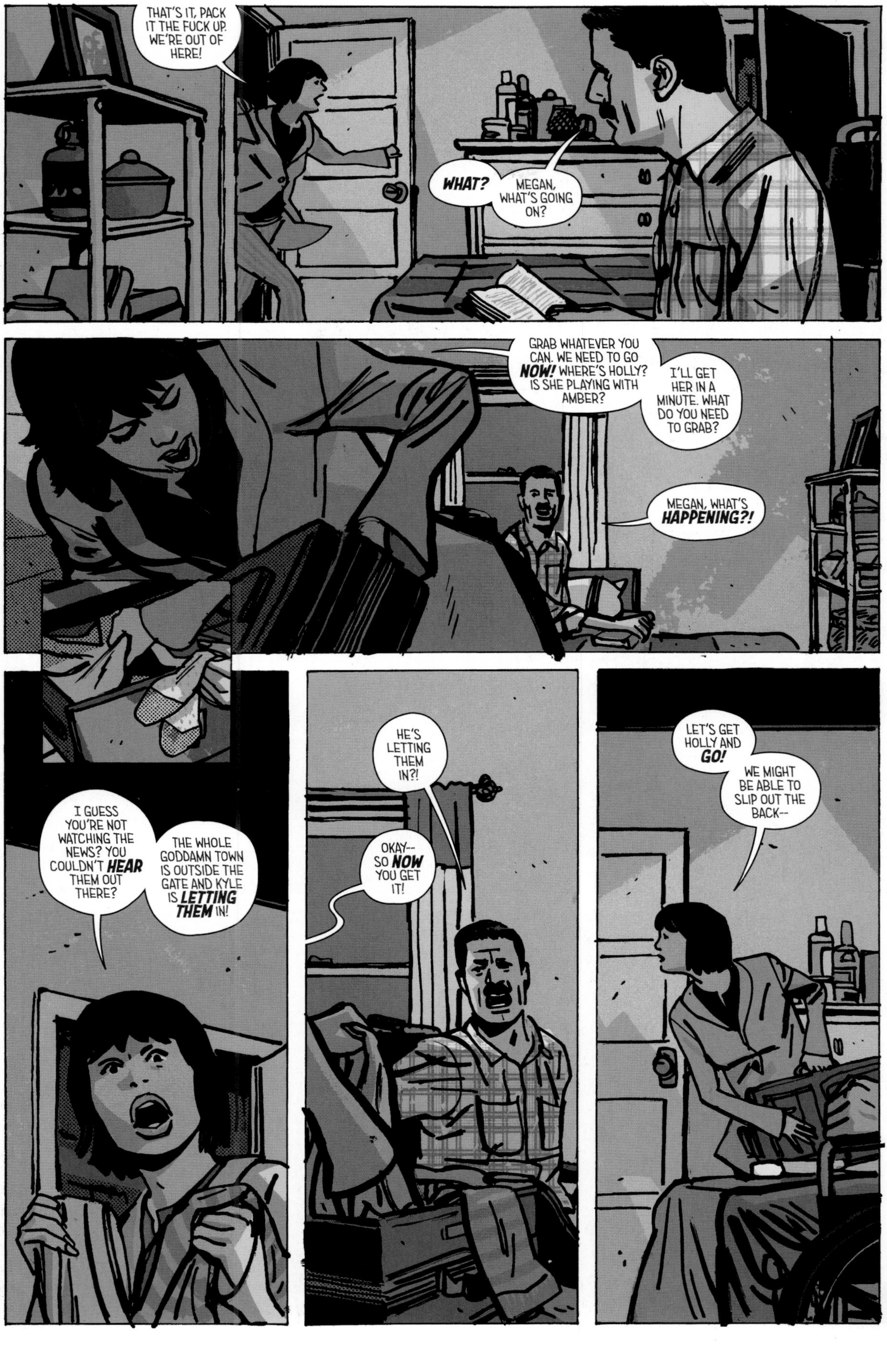
THAT'S IT, PACK IT THE FUCK UP. WE'RE OUT OF HERE!
WHAT?
MEGAN, WHAT'S GOING ON?
GRAB WHATEVER YOU CAN. WE NEED TO GO NOW! WHERE'S HOLLY? IS SHE PLAYING WITH AMBER?
I'LL GET HER IN A MINUTE. WHAT DO YOU NEED TO GRAB?
MEGAN, WHAT'S HAPPENING?!
I GUESS YOU'RE NOT WATCHING THE NEWS? YOU COULDN'T HEAR THEM OUT THERE?
THE WHOLE GODDAMN TOWN IS OUTSIDE THE GATE AND KYLE IS LETTING THEM IN!
HE'S LETTING THEM IN?!
OKAY-- SO NOW YOU GET IT!
LET'S GET HOLLY AND GO!
WE MIGHT BE ABLE TO SLIP OUT THE BACK--

MEGAN-- STOP. JUST STOP.

WHAT?!

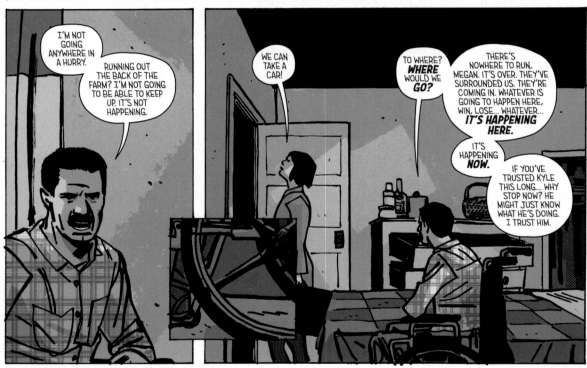

I'M NOT GOING ANYWHERE IN A HURRY.

RUNNING OUT THE BACK OF THE FARM? I'M NOT GOING TO BE ABLE TO KEEP UP. IT'S NOT HAPPENING.

WE CAN TAKE A CAR!

TO WHERE? WHERE WOULD WE GO?

THERE'S NOWHERE TO RUN, MEGAN. IT'S OVER. THEY'VE SURROUNDED US. THEY'RE COMING IN. WHATEVER IS GOING TO HAPPEN HERE, WIN, LOSE... WHATEVER... IT'S HAPPENING HERE.

IT'S HAPPENING NOW.

IF YOU'VE TRUSTED KYLE THIS LONG... WHY STOP NOW? HE MIGHT JUST KNOW WHAT HE'S DOING. I TRUST HIM.

SO THAT'S IT? YOU'RE JUST GIVING UP?!

WHAT? FUCK YOU. NO.

I HAVEN'T GIVEN UP YET, AND I'M NOT ABOUT TO NOW! I JUST KNOW WE'RE OUT OF OPTIONS.

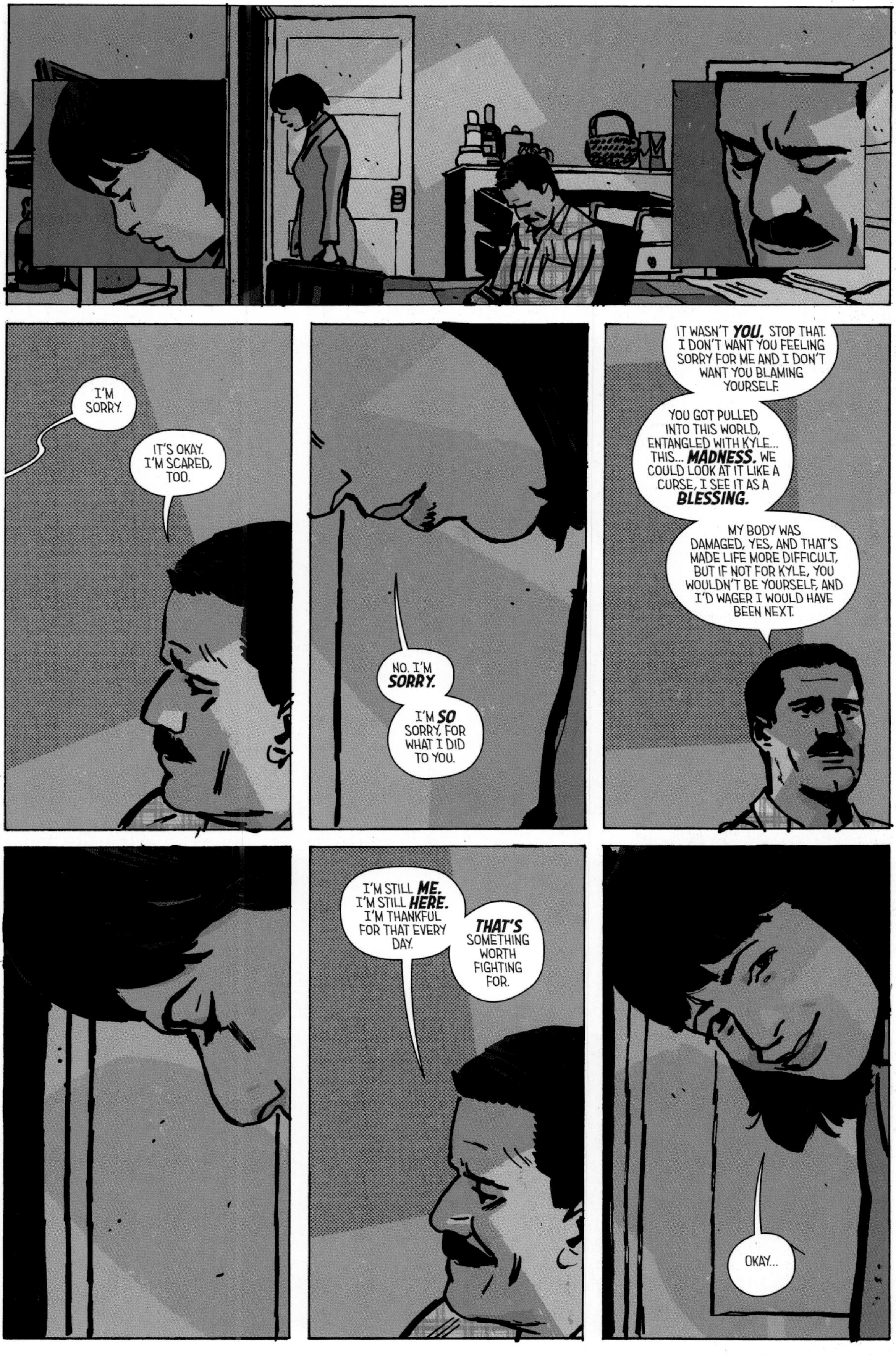
I'M SORRY.
IT'S OKAY. I'M SCARED, TOO.
NO. I'M SORRY.
I'M SO SORRY, FOR WHAT I DID TO YOU.
IT WASN'T YOU. STOP THAT. I DON'T WANT YOU FEELING SORRY FOR ME AND I DON'T WANT YOU BLAMING YOURSELF.
YOU GOT PULLED INTO THIS WORLD, ENTANGLED WITH KYLE... THIS... MADNESS. WE COULD LOOK AT IT LIKE A CURSE, I SEE IT AS A BLESSING.
MY BODY WAS DAMAGED, YES, AND THAT'S MADE LIFE MORE DIFFICULT, BUT IF NOT FOR KYLE, YOU WOULDN'T BE YOURSELF, AND I'D WAGER I WOULD HAVE BEEN NEXT.
I'M STILL ME. I'M STILL HERE. I'M THANKFUL FOR THAT EVERY DAY.
THAT'S SOMETHING WORTH FIGHTING FOR.
OKAY...

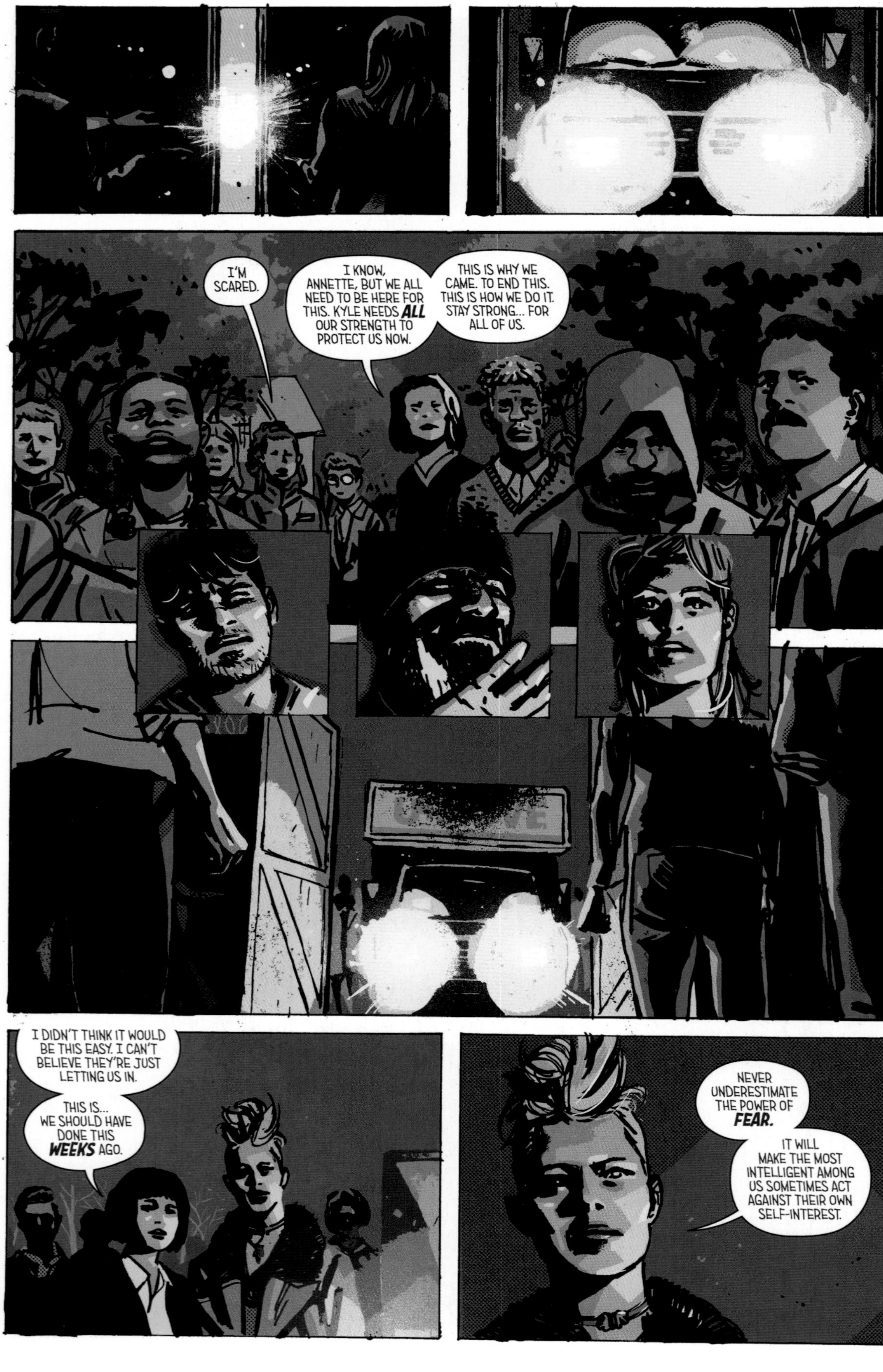
I'M SCARED.
I KNOW, ANNETTE, BUT WE ALL NEED TO BE HERE FOR THIS. KYLE NEEDS ALL OUR STRENGTH TO PROTECT US NOW.
THIS IS WHY WE CAME. TO END THIS. THIS IS HOW WE DO IT. STAY STRONG... FOR ALL OF US.
I DIDN'T THINK IT WOULD BE THIS EASY. I CAN'T BELIEVE THEY'RE JUST LETTING US IN.
THIS IS... WE SHOULD HAVE DONE THIS WEEKS AGO.
NEVER UNDERESTIMATE THE POWER OF FEAR.
IT WILL MAKE THE MOST INTELLIGENT AMONG US SOMETIMES ACT AGAINST THEIR OWN SELF-INTEREST.

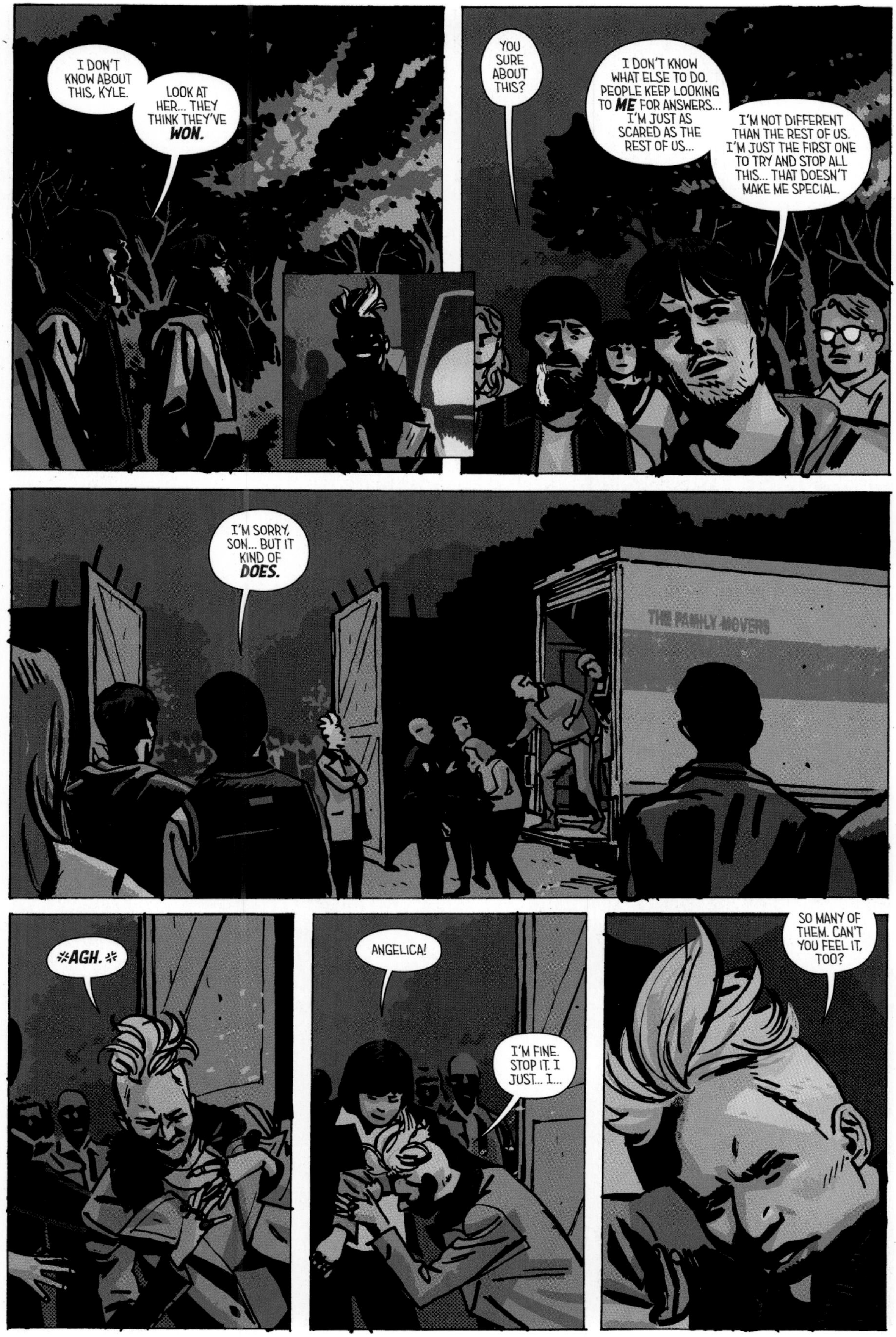

I DON'T KNOW ABOUT THIS, KYLE.
LOOK AT HER... THEY THINK THEY'VE **WON.**
YOU SURE ABOUT THIS?
I DON'T KNOW WHAT ELSE TO DO. PEOPLE KEEP LOOKING TO **ME** FOR ANSWERS... I'M JUST AS SCARED AS THE REST OF US...
I'M NOT DIFFERENT THAN THE REST OF US. I'M JUST THE FIRST ONE TO TRY AND STOP ALL THIS... THAT DOESN'T MAKE ME SPECIAL.
I'M SORRY, SON... BUT IT KIND OF **DOES.**
THE FAMILY MOVERS
AGH.
ANGELICA!
I'M FINE. STOP IT. I JUST... I...
SO MANY OF THEM. CAN'T YOU FEEL IT, TOO?

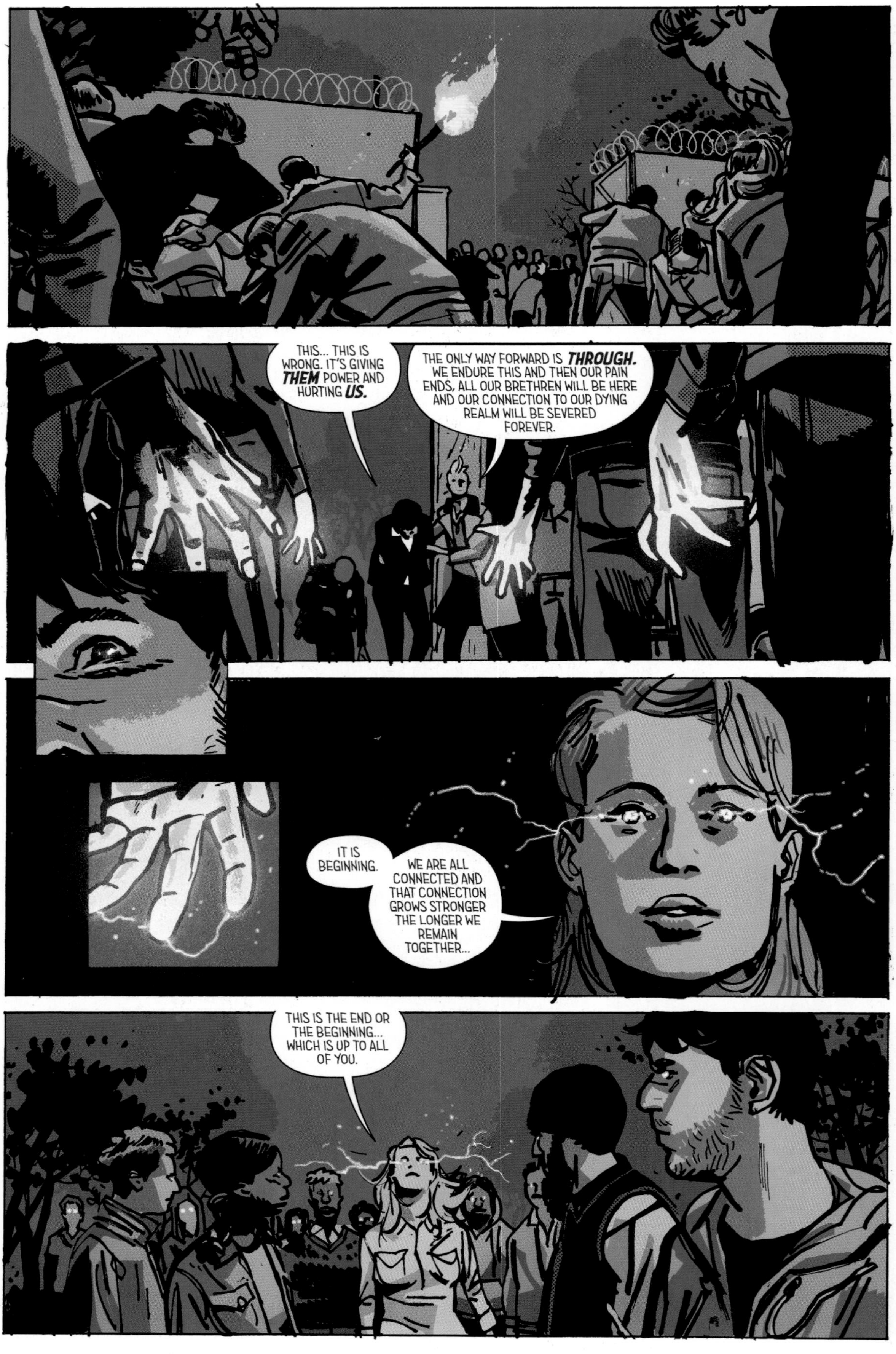
THIS... THIS IS WRONG. IT'S GIVING *THEM* POWER AND HURTING *US.*
THE ONLY WAY FORWARD IS *THROUGH.* WE ENDURE THIS AND THEN OUR PAIN ENDS, ALL OUR BRETHREN WILL BE HERE AND OUR CONNECTION TO OUR DYING REALM WILL BE SEVERED FOREVER.
IT IS BEGINNING.
WE ARE ALL CONNECTED AND THAT CONNECTION GROWS STRONGER THE LONGER WE REMAIN TOGETHER...
THIS IS THE END OR THE BEGINNING... WHICH IS UP TO ALL OF YOU.

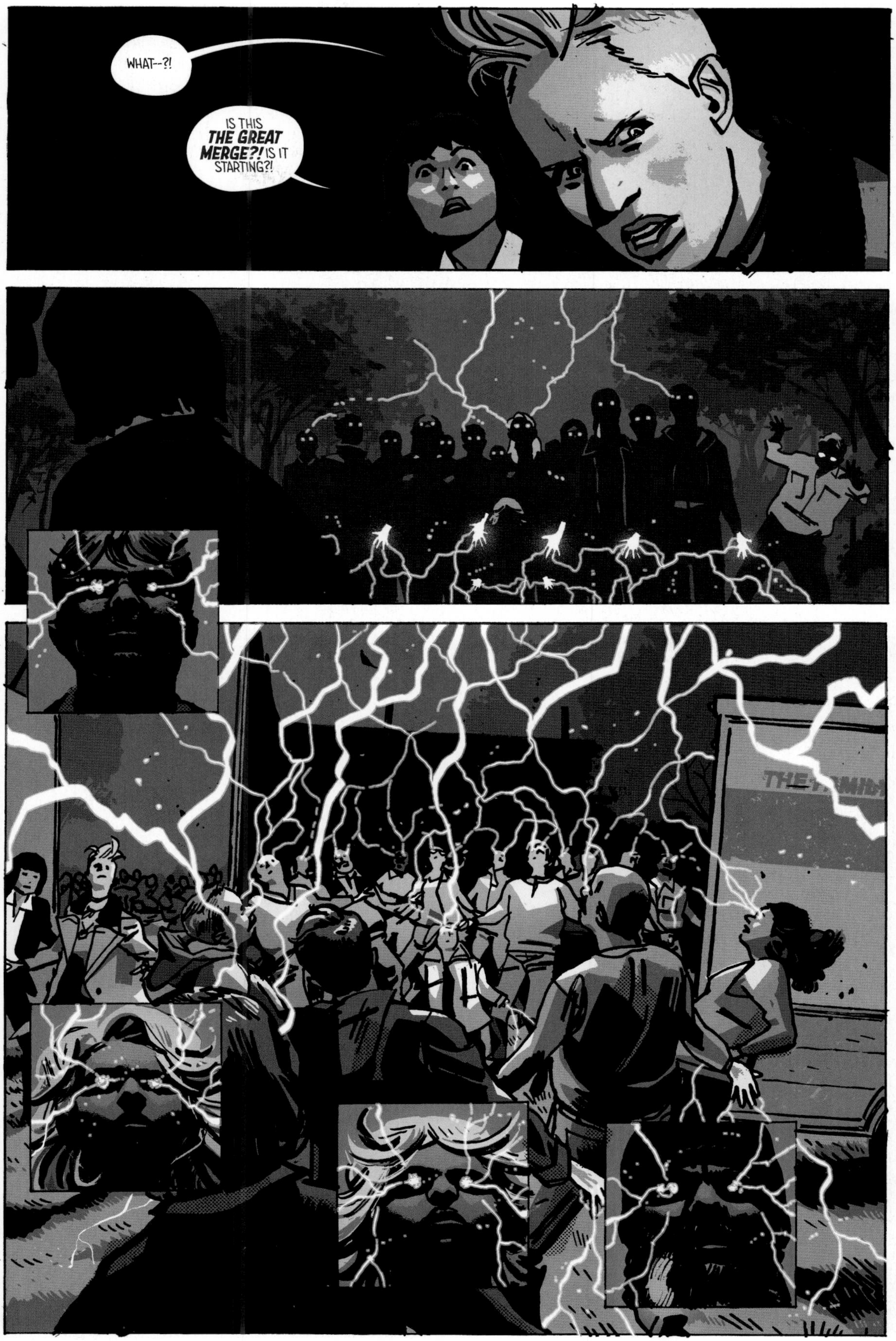
WHAT--?!
IS THIS THE GREAT MERGE?! IS IT STARTING?!

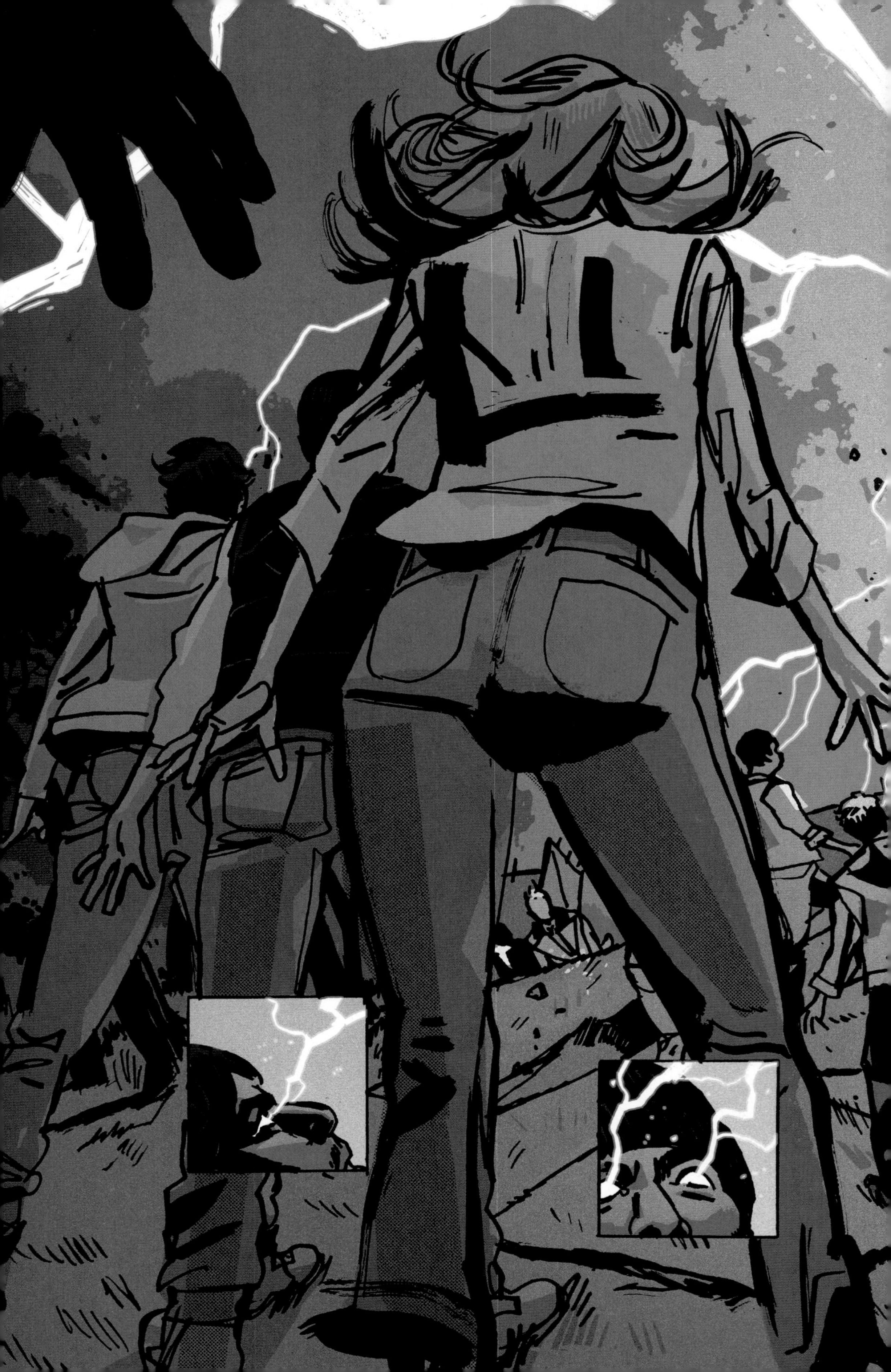

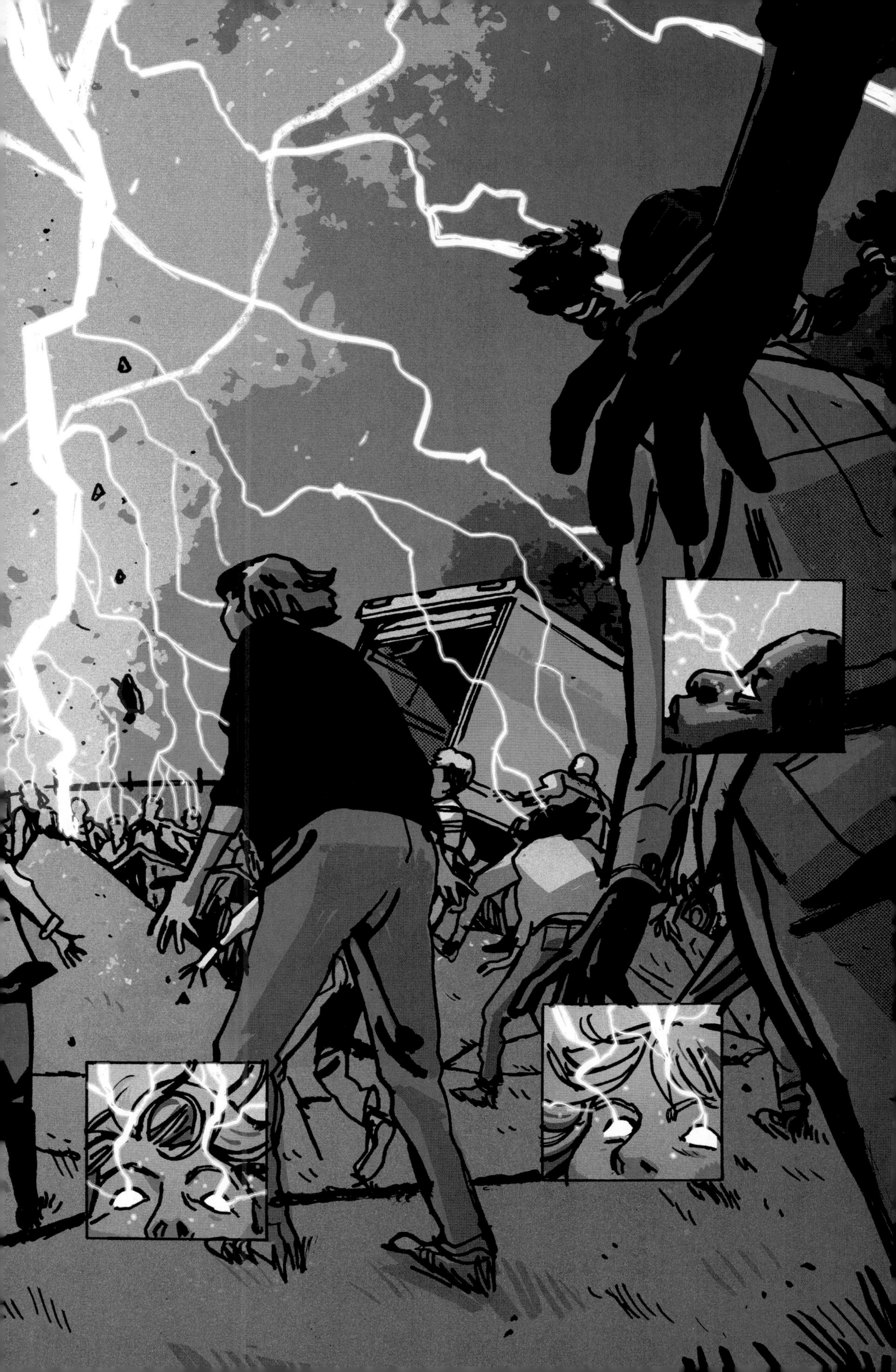

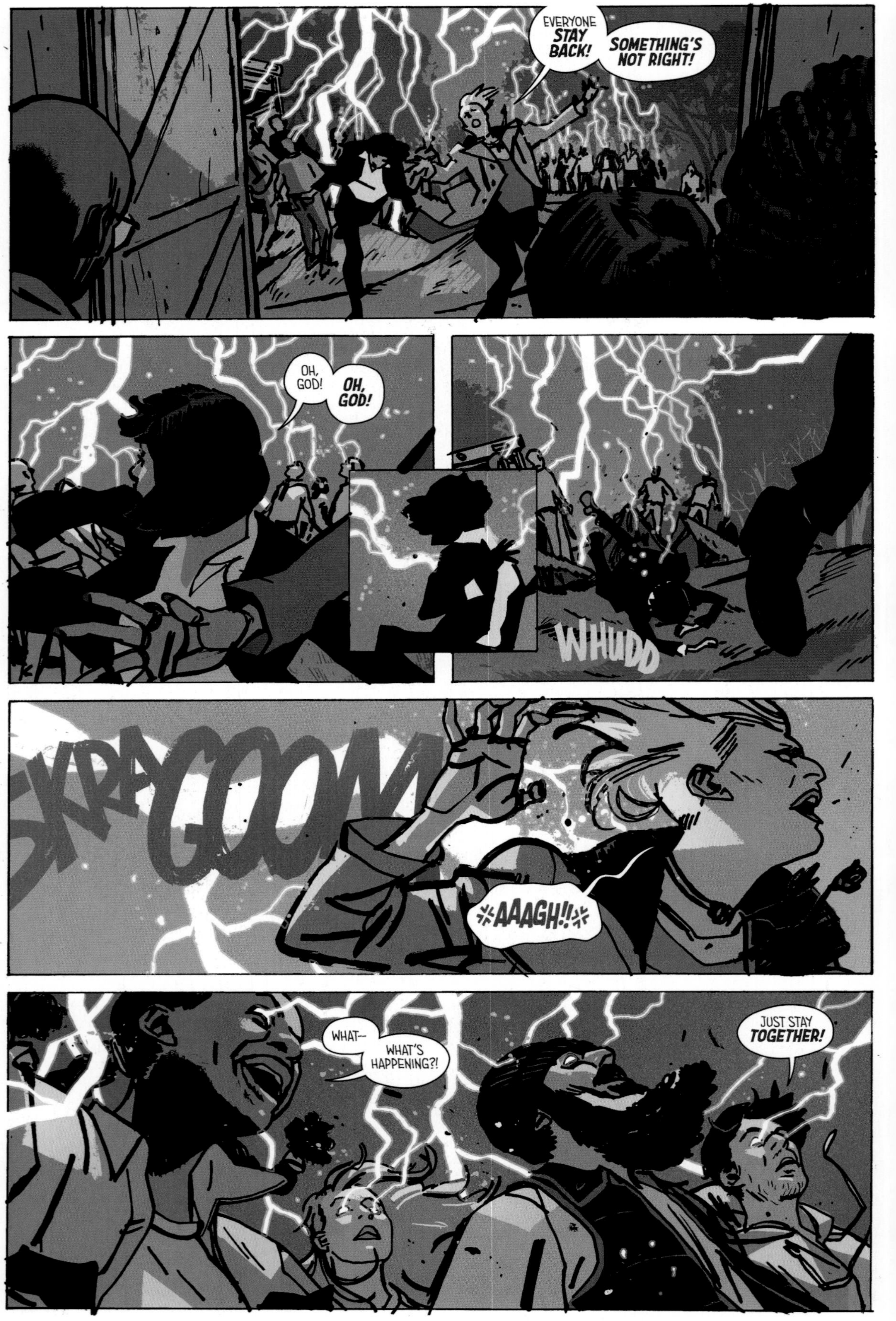
EVERYONE STAY BACK!
SOMETHING'S NOT RIGHT!
OH, GOD!
OH, GOD!
WHUDD
SKRAGOOM
AAAGH!!
WHAT--
WHAT'S HAPPENING?!
JUST STAY TOGETHER!

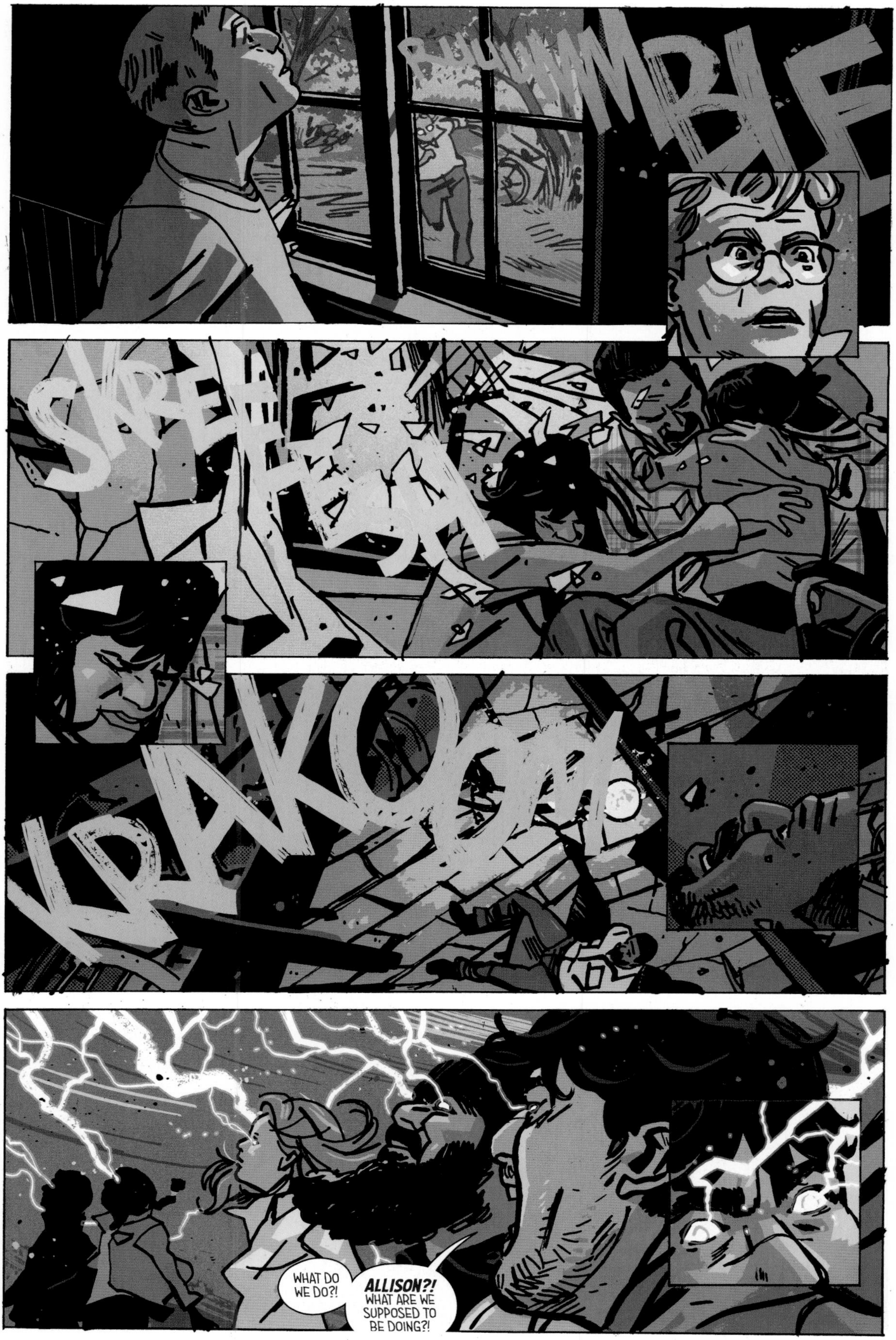
KRAKOOM
WHAT DO WE DO?!
ALLISON?! WHAT ARE WE SUPPOSED TO BE DOING?!

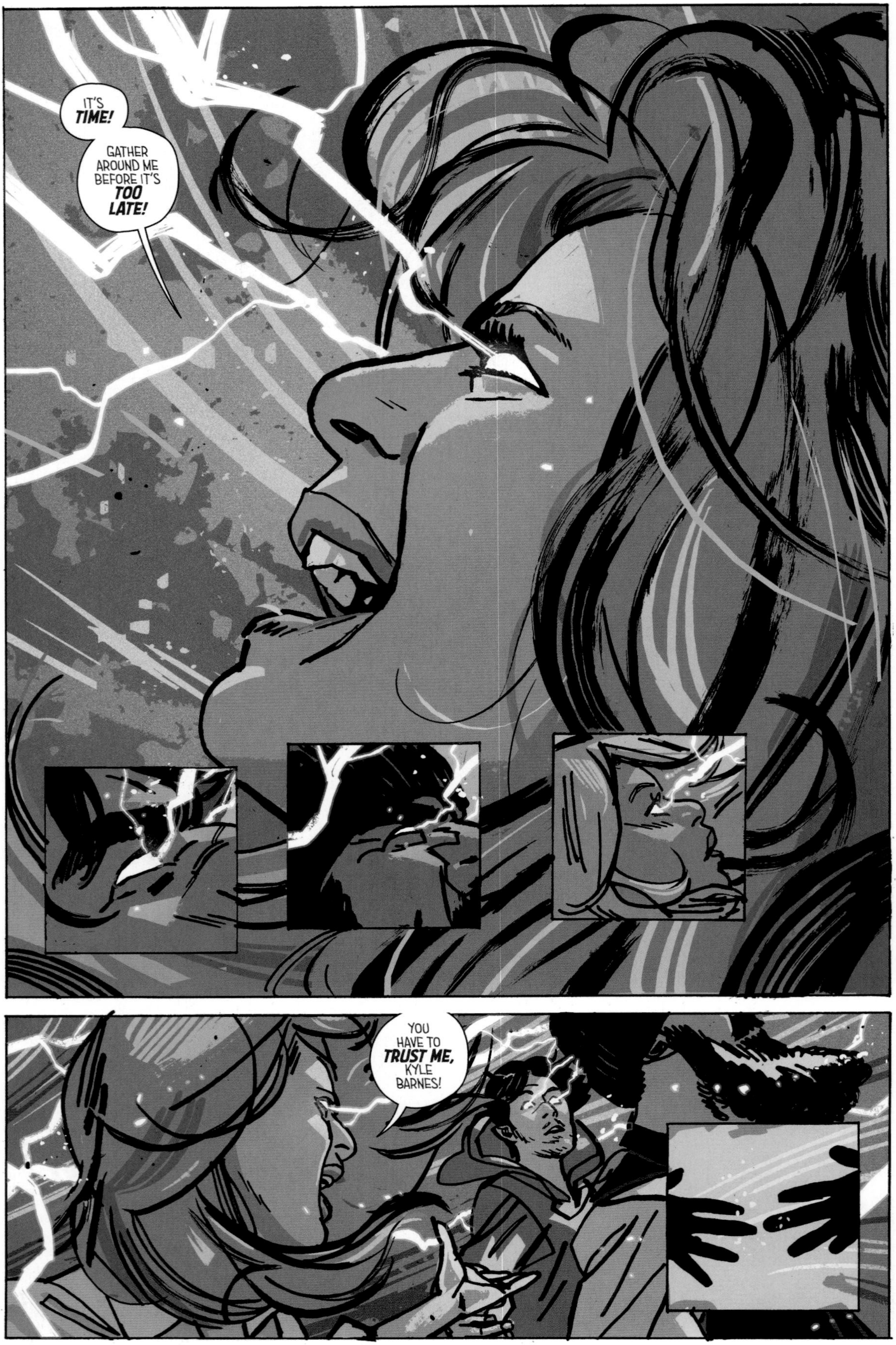
IT'S TIME!
GATHER AROUND ME BEFORE IT'S TOO LATE!
YOU HAVE TO TRUST ME, KYLE BARNES!

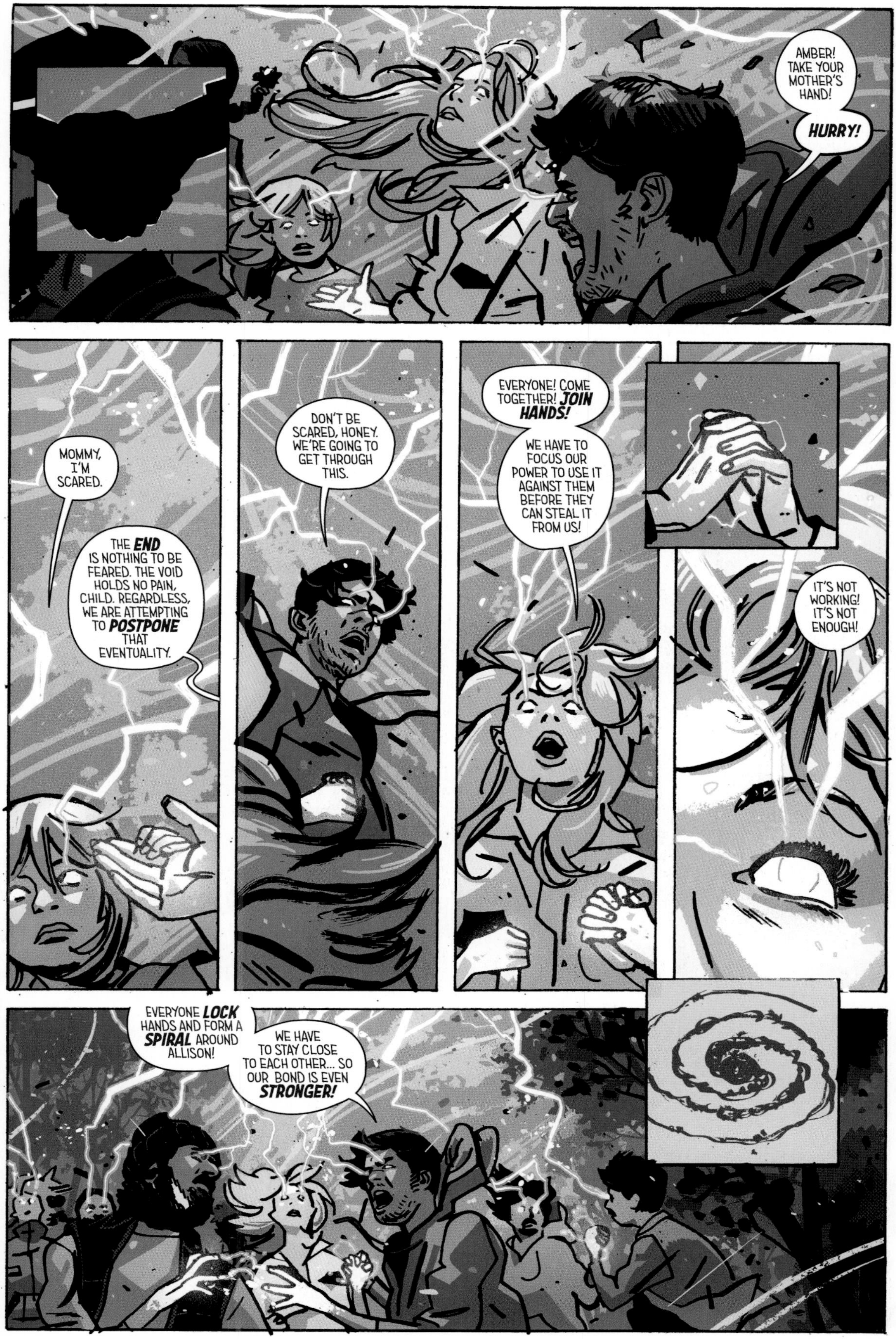
AMBER! TAKE YOUR MOTHER'S HAND!
HURRY!
MOMMY, I'M SCARED.
THE END IS NOTHING TO BE FEARED. THE VOID HOLDS NO PAIN, CHILD. REGARDLESS, WE ARE ATTEMPTING TO POSTPONE THAT EVENTUALITY.
DON'T BE SCARED, HONEY. WE'RE GOING TO GET THROUGH THIS.
EVERYONE! COME TOGETHER! JOIN HANDS!
WE HAVE TO FOCUS OUR POWER TO USE IT AGAINST THEM BEFORE THEY CAN STEAL IT FROM US!
IT'S NOT WORKING! IT'S NOT ENOUGH!
EVERYONE LOCK HANDS AND FORM A SPIRAL AROUND ALLISON!
WE HAVE TO STAY CLOSE TO EACH OTHER... SO OUR BOND IS EVEN STRONGER!

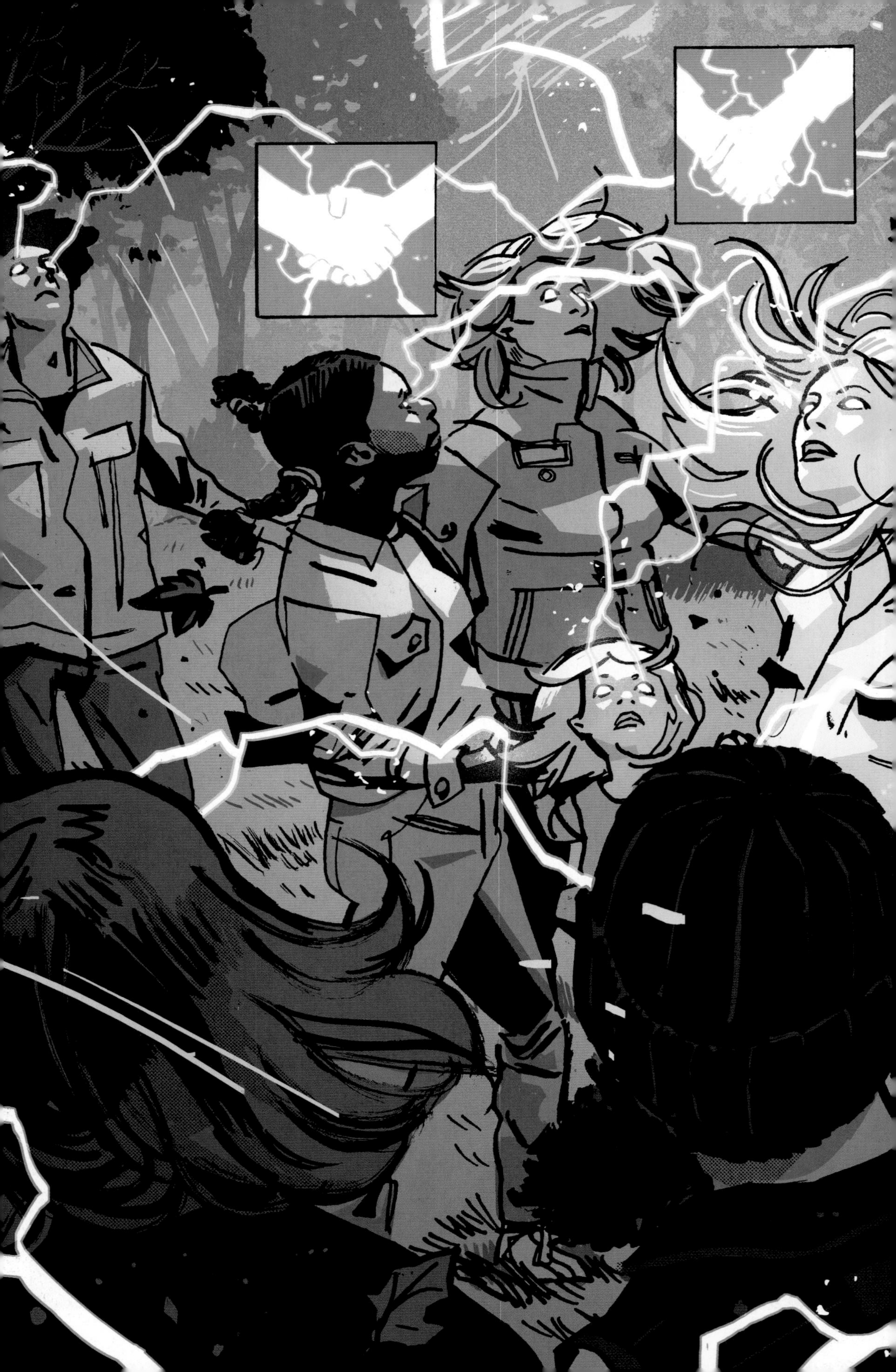

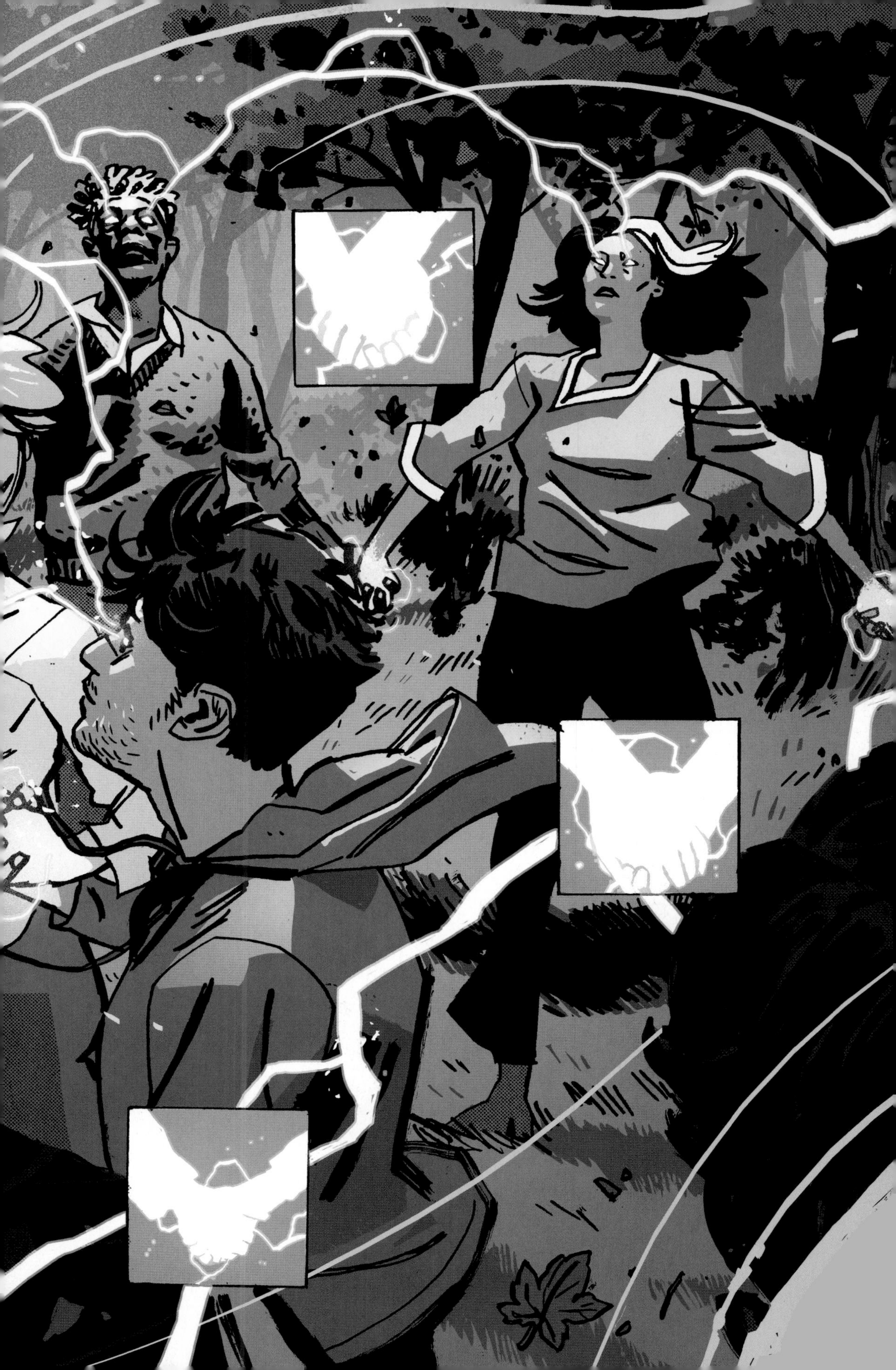

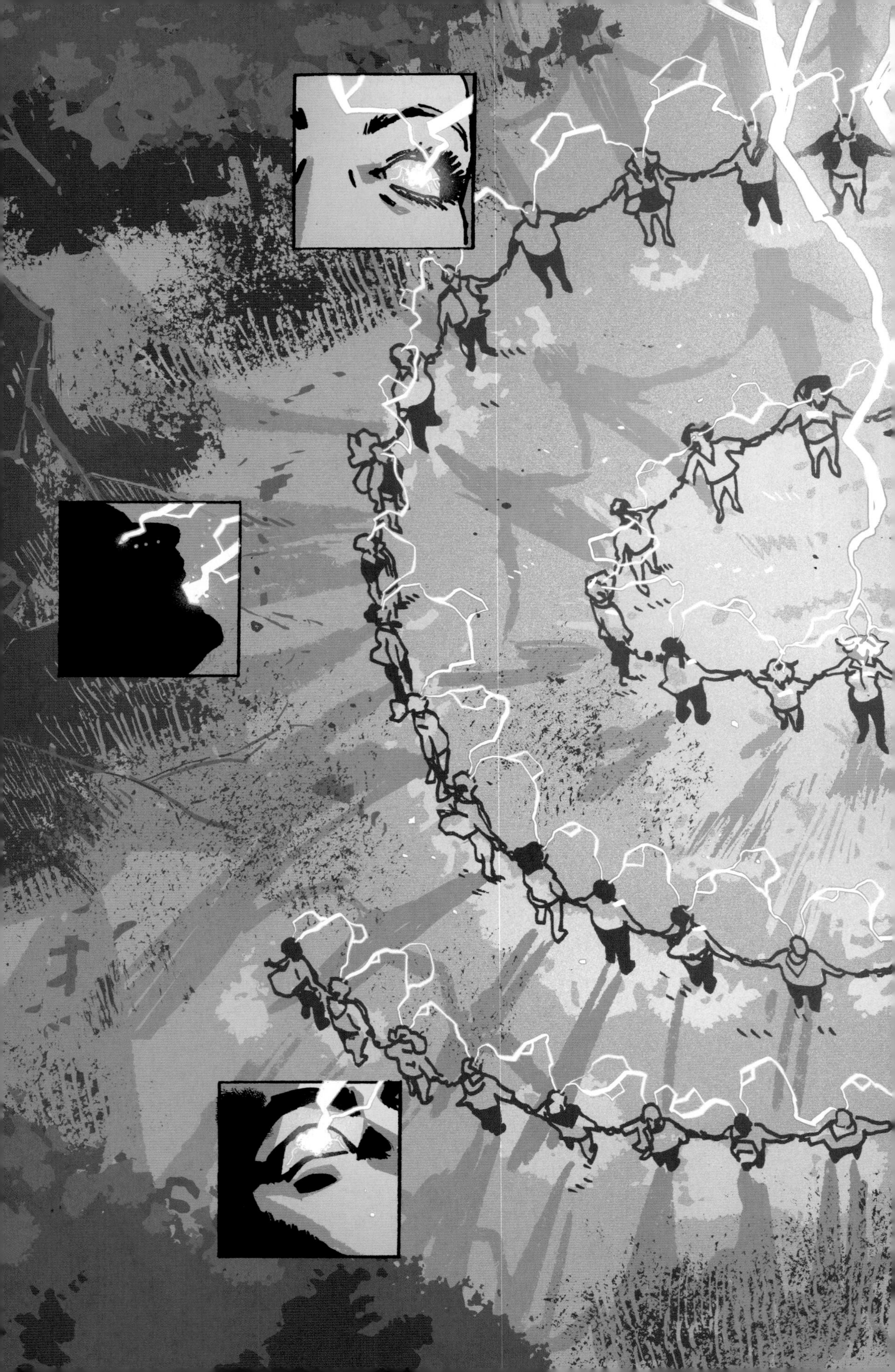

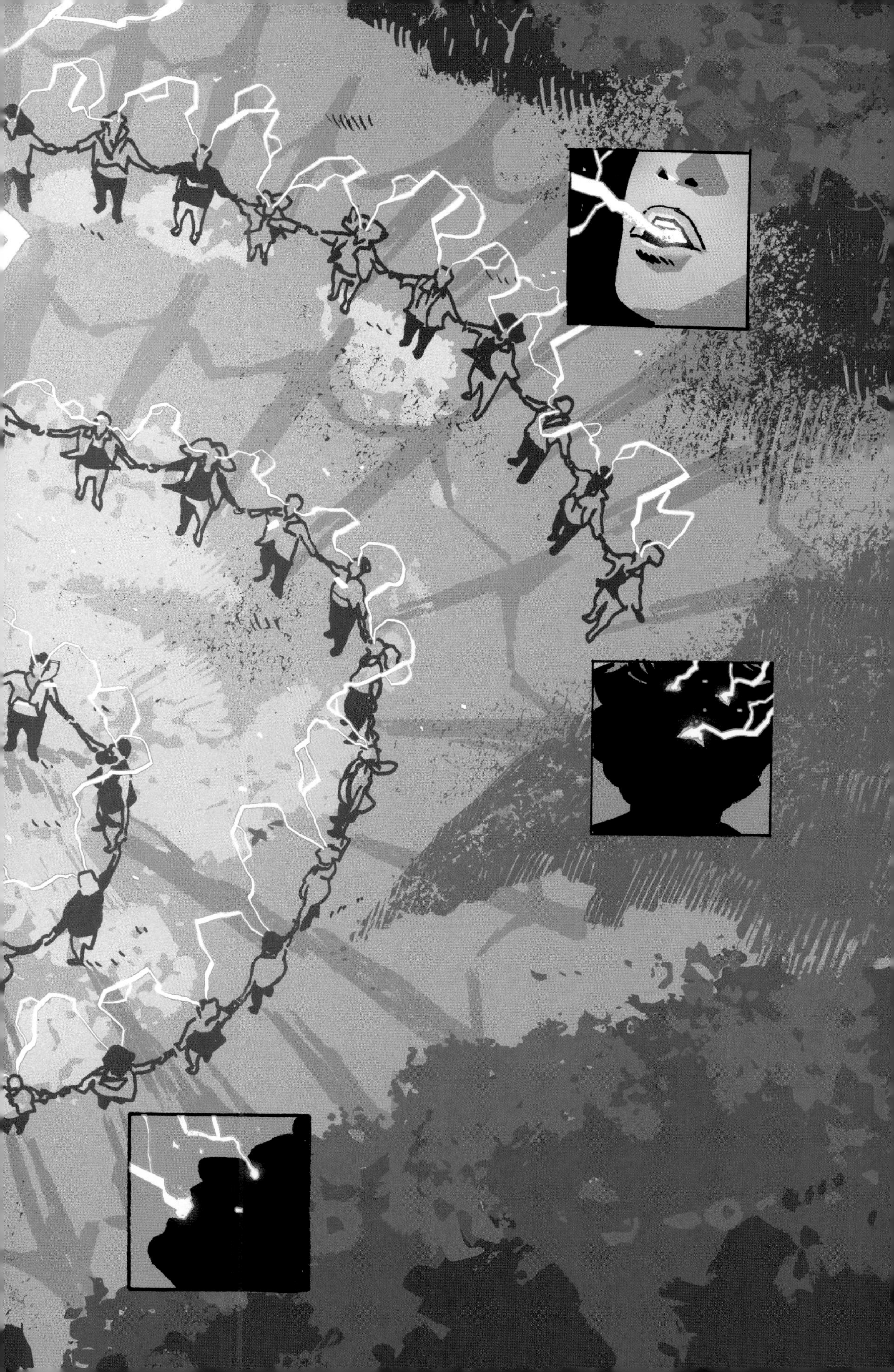

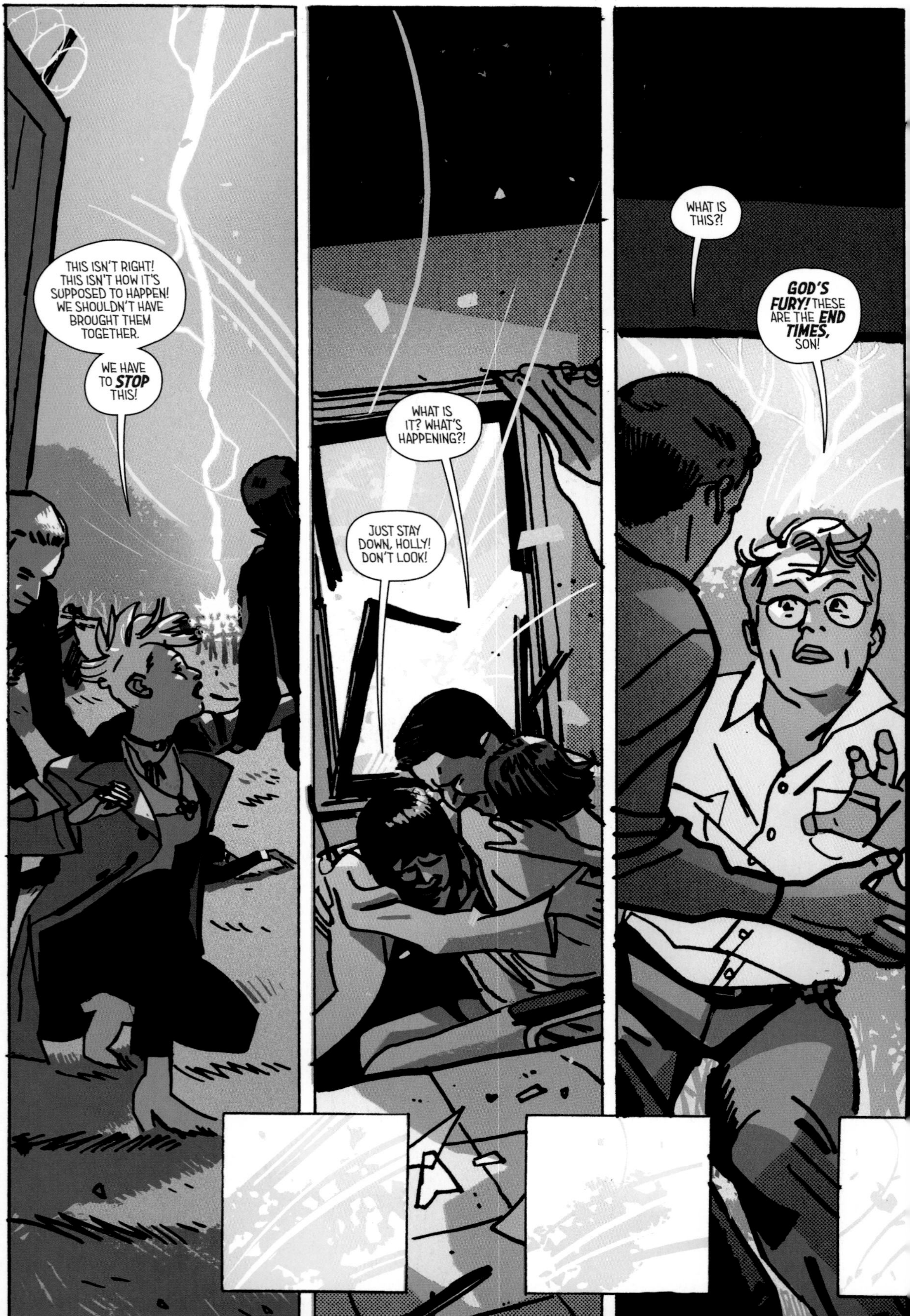
THIS ISN'T RIGHT! THIS ISN'T HOW IT'S SUPPOSED TO HAPPEN! WE SHOULDN'T HAVE BROUGHT THEM TOGETHER.
WE HAVE TO **STOP** THIS!
WHAT IS IT? WHAT'S HAPPENING?!
JUST STAY DOWN, HOLLY! DON'T LOOK!
WHAT IS THIS?!
GOD'S FURY! THESE ARE THE **END TIMES,** SON!

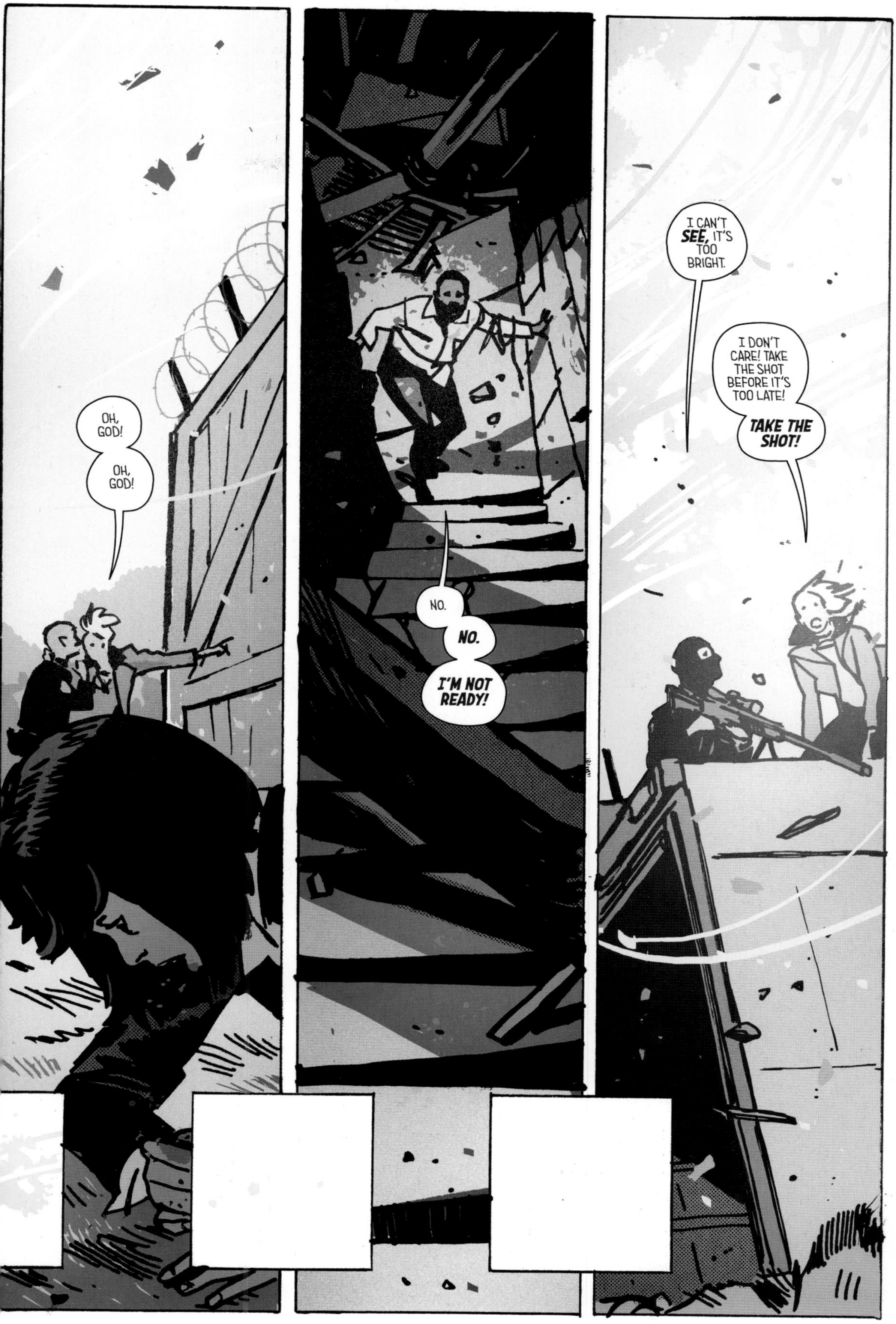
OH, GOD!
OH, GOD!
NO.
NO.
I'M NOT READY!
I CAN'T SEE, IT'S TOO BRIGHT.
I DON'T CARE! TAKE THE SHOT BEFORE IT'S TOO LATE!
TAKE THE SHOT!

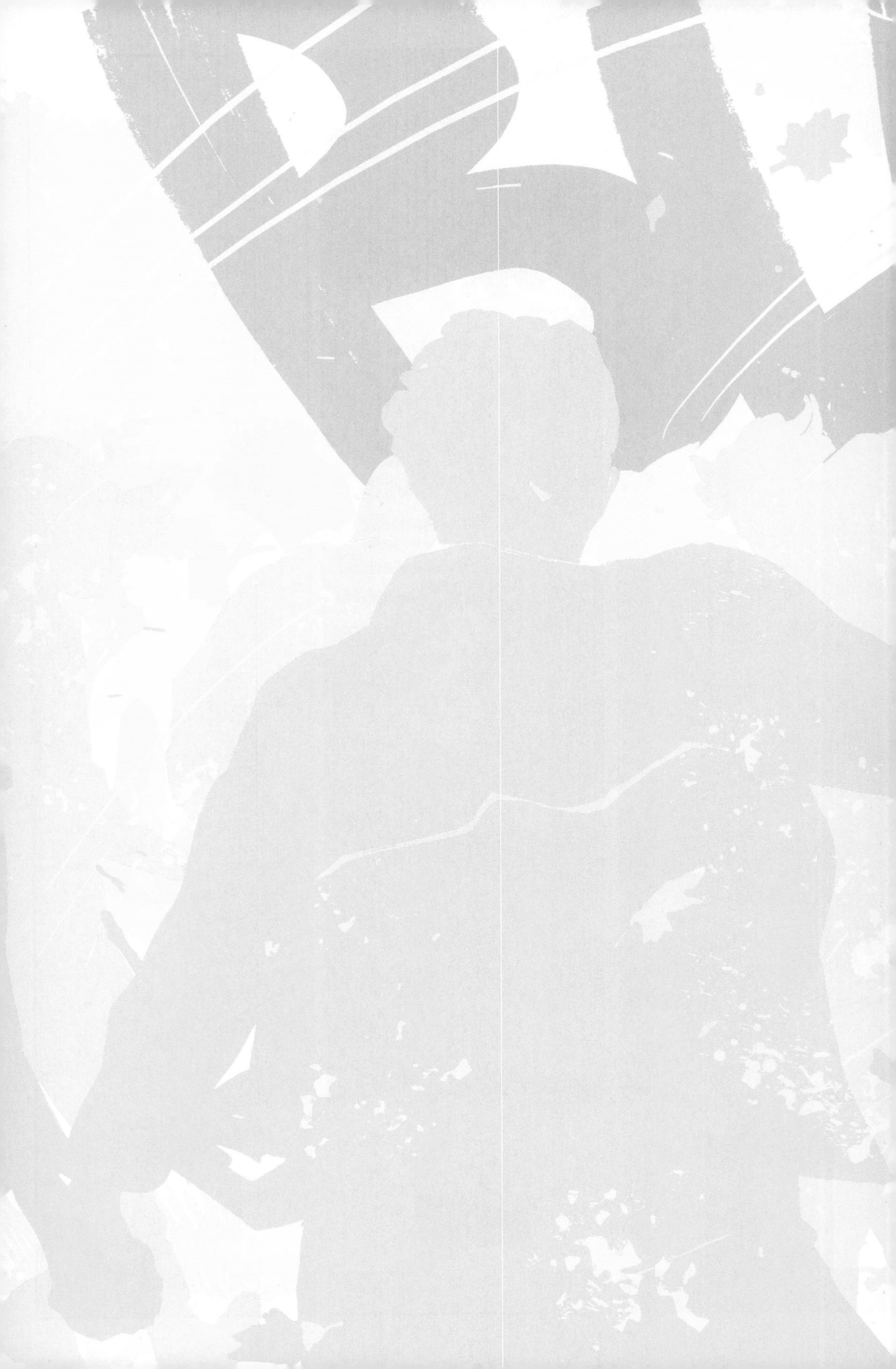

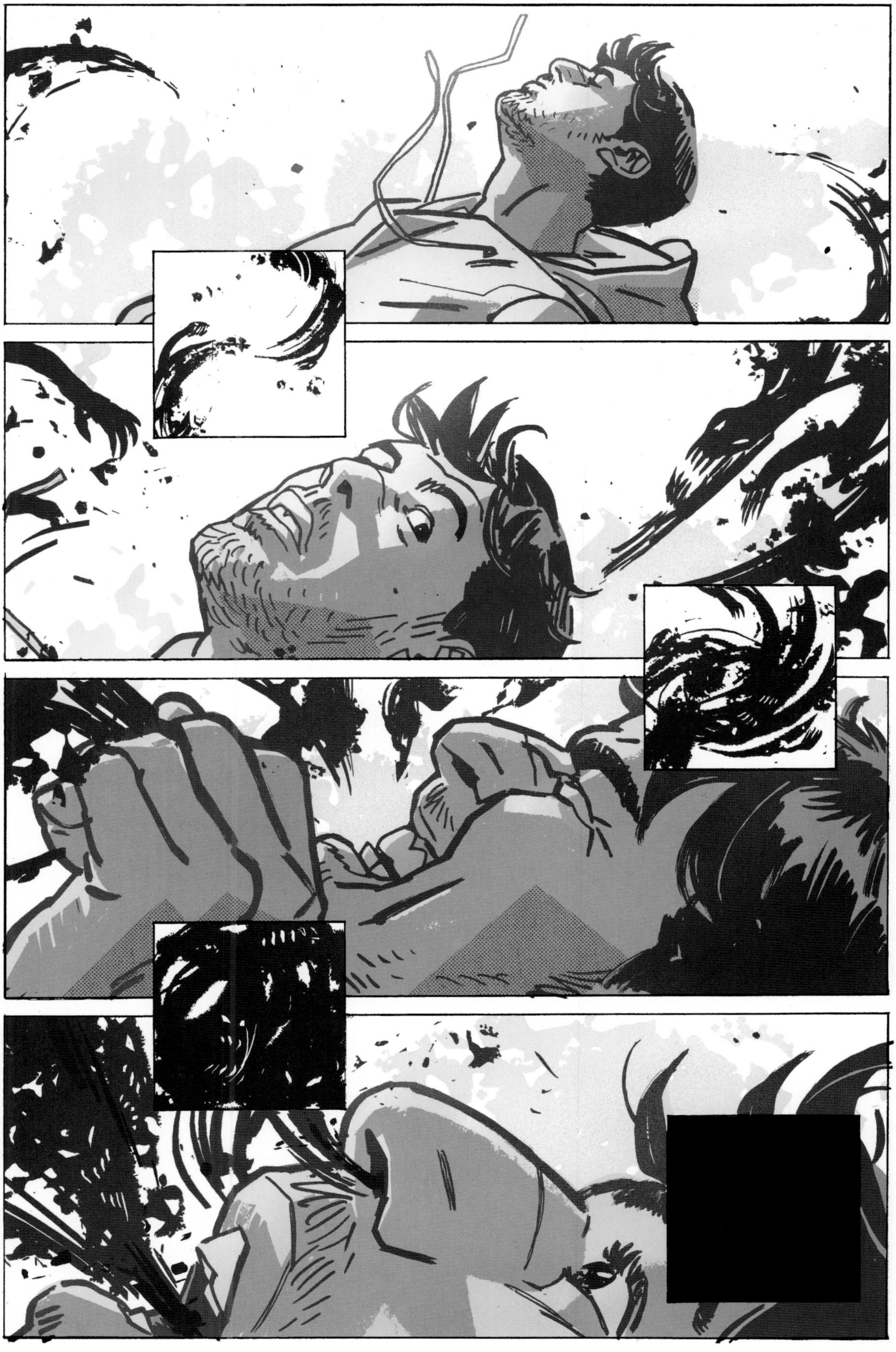
[redacted]

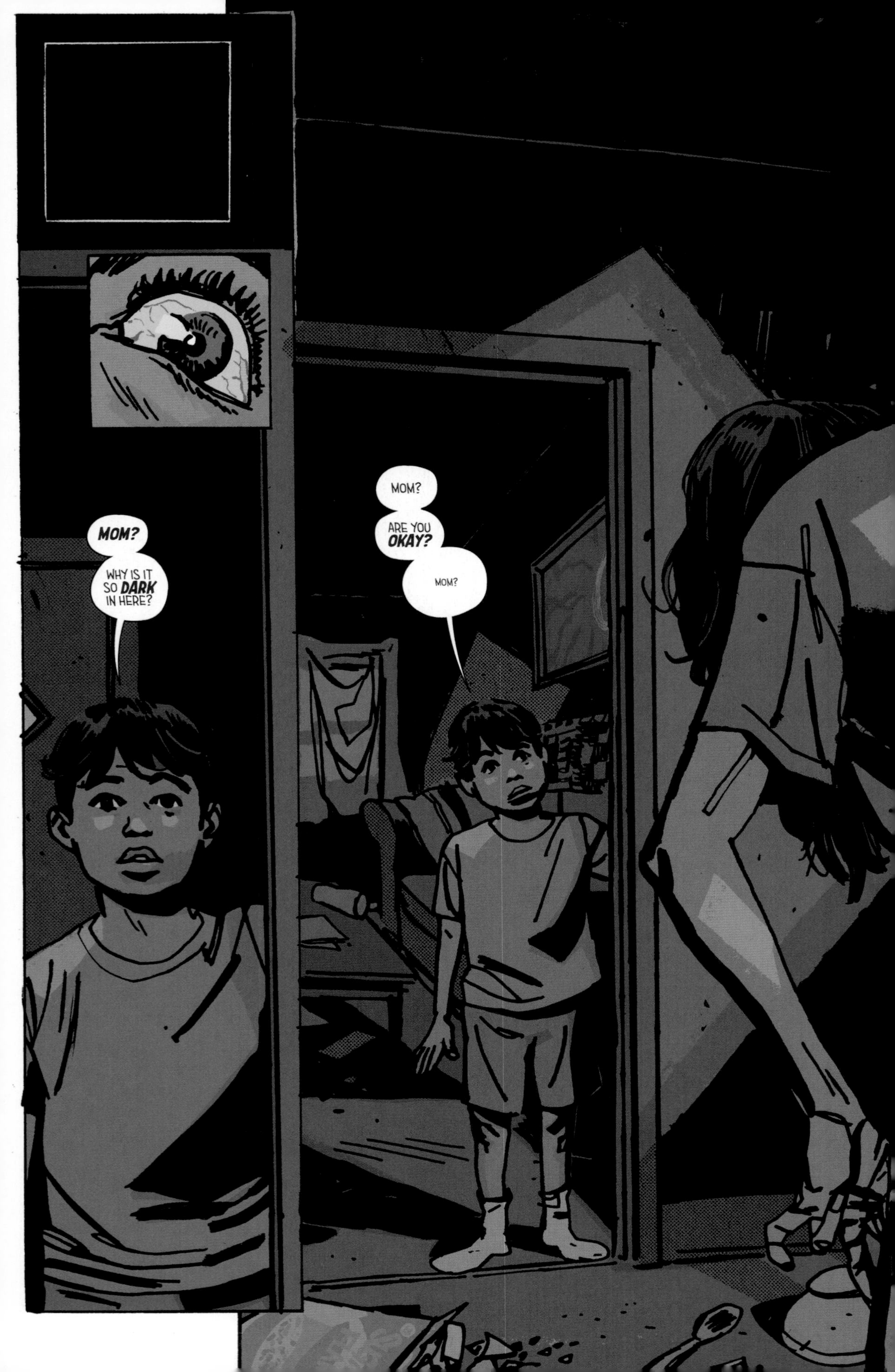
MOM?
WHY IS IT SO DARK IN HERE?
MOM?
ARE YOU OKAY?
MOM?

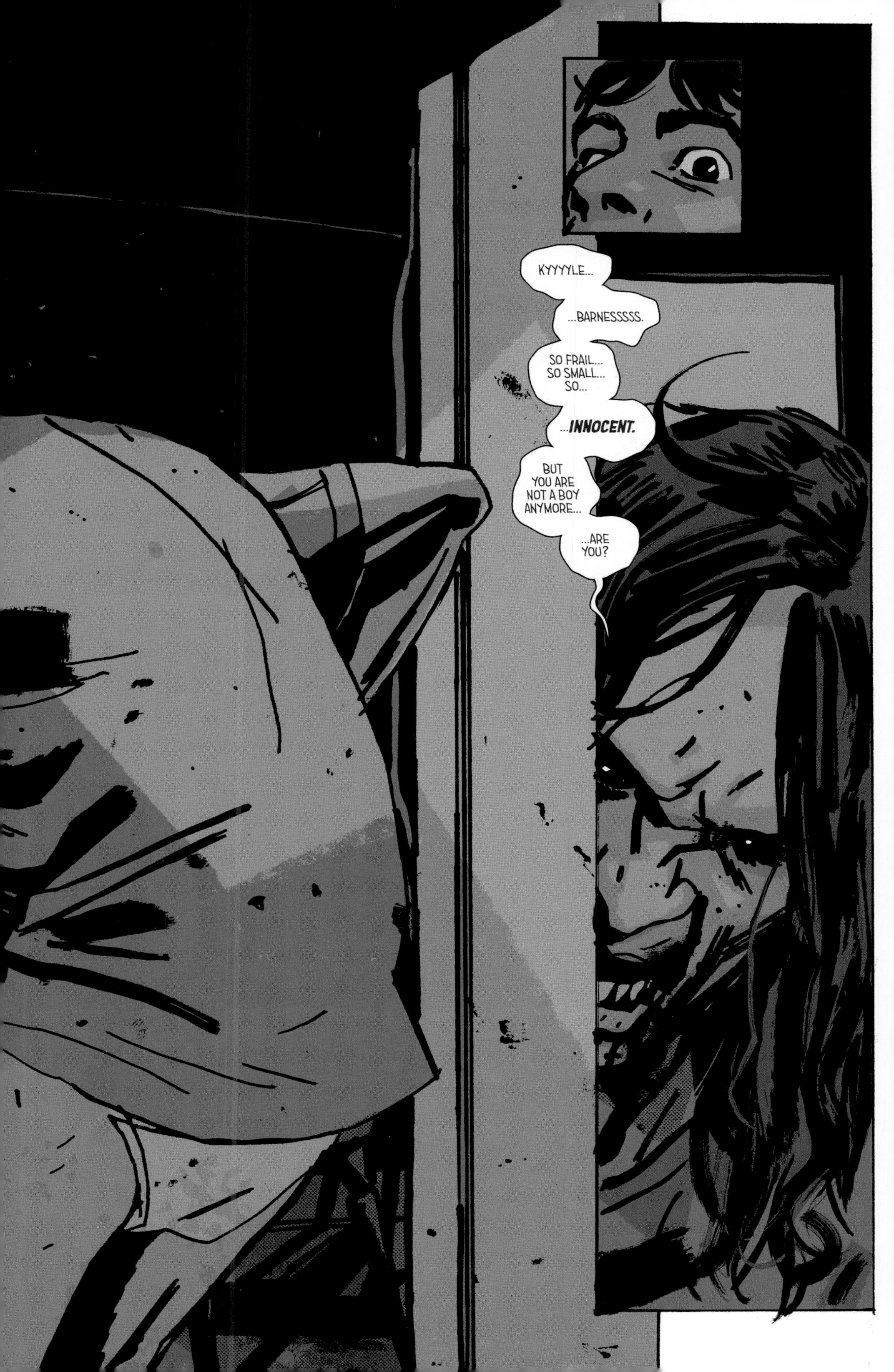
KYYYYLE...
...BARNESSSSS.
SO FRAIL... SO SMALL... SO...
...INNOCENT.
BUT YOU ARE NOT A BOY ANYMORE...
...ARE YOU?

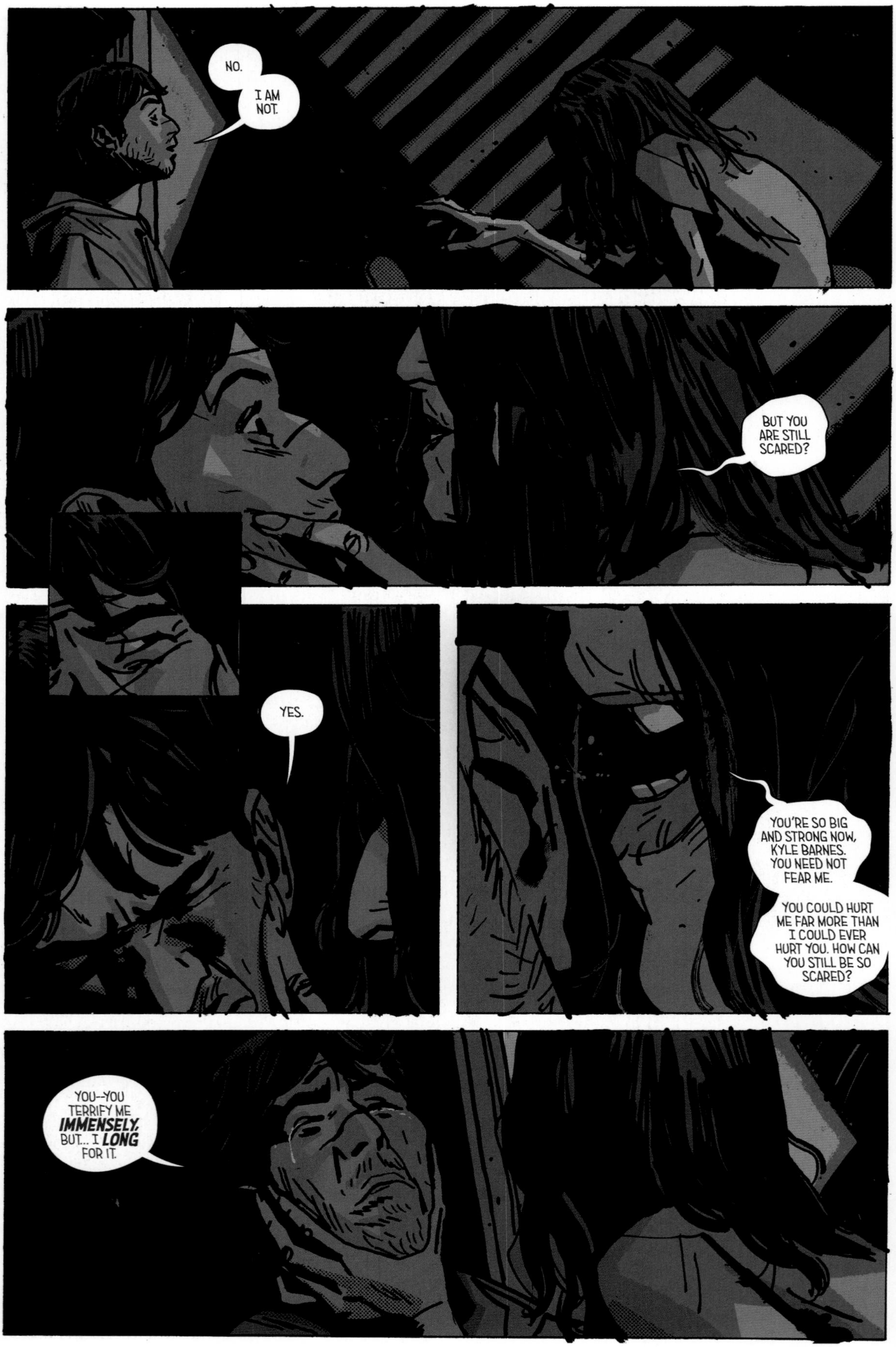
NO.
I AM NOT.
BUT YOU ARE STILL SCARED?
YES.
YOU'RE SO BIG AND STRONG NOW, KYLE BARNES. YOU NEED NOT FEAR ME.
YOU COULD HURT ME FAR MORE THAN I COULD EVER HURT YOU. HOW CAN YOU STILL BE SO SCARED?
YOU--YOU TERRIFY ME **IMMENSELY,** BUT... I **LONG** FOR IT.

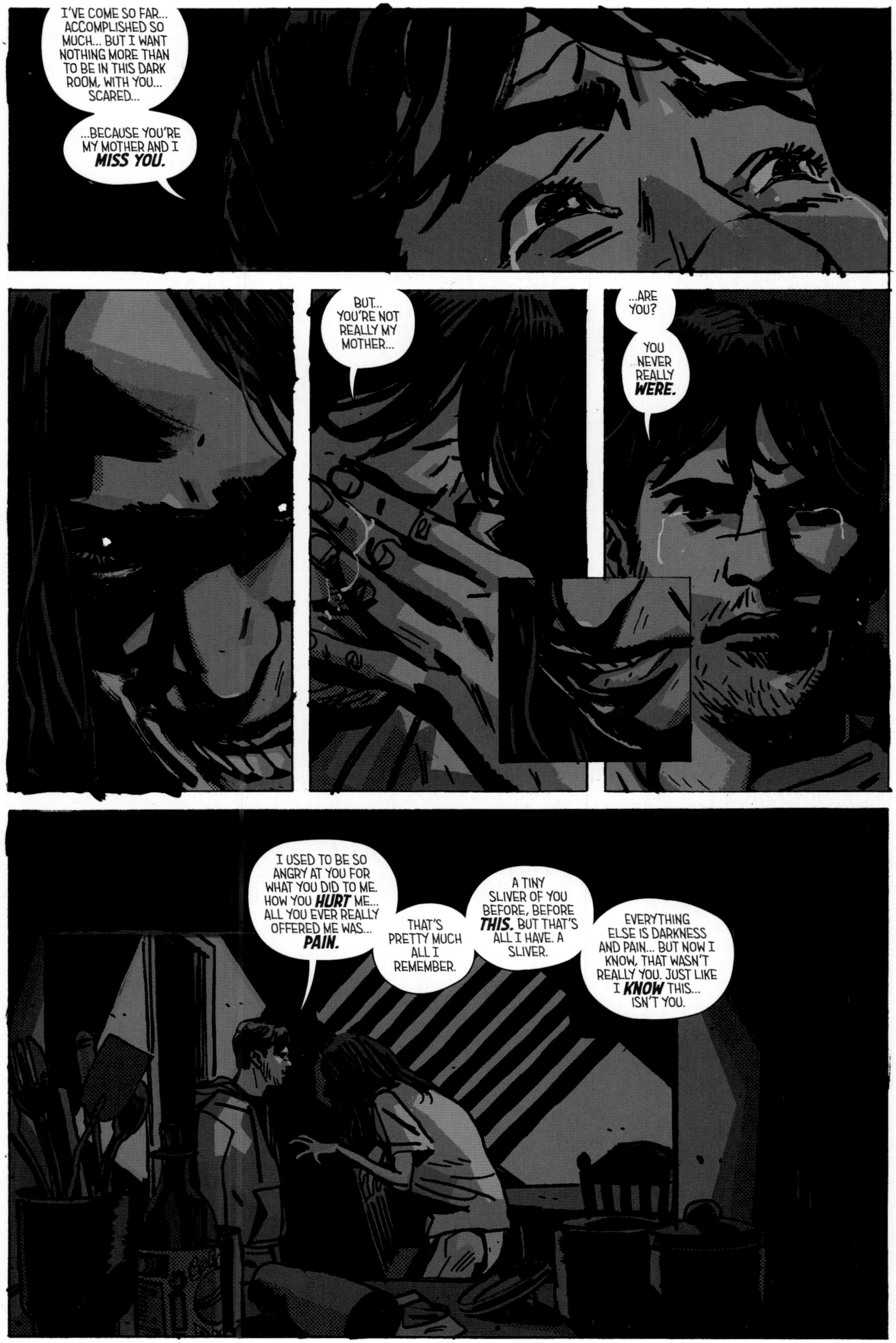

I'VE COME SO FAR... ACCOMPLISHED SO MUCH... BUT I WANT NOTHING MORE THAN TO BE IN THIS DARK ROOM, WITH YOU... SCARED...
...BECAUSE YOU'RE MY MOTHER AND I MISS YOU.
BUT... YOU'RE NOT REALLY MY MOTHER...
...ARE YOU?
YOU NEVER REALLY WERE.
I USED TO BE SO ANGRY AT YOU FOR WHAT YOU DID TO ME. HOW YOU HURT ME... ALL YOU EVER REALLY OFFERED ME WAS... PAIN.
THAT'S PRETTY MUCH ALL I REMEMBER.
A TINY SLIVER OF YOU BEFORE, BEFORE THIS. BUT THAT'S ALL I HAVE. A SLIVER.
EVERYTHING ELSE IS DARKNESS AND PAIN... BUT NOW I KNOW, THAT WASN'T REALLY YOU. JUST LIKE I KNOW THIS... ISN'T YOU.

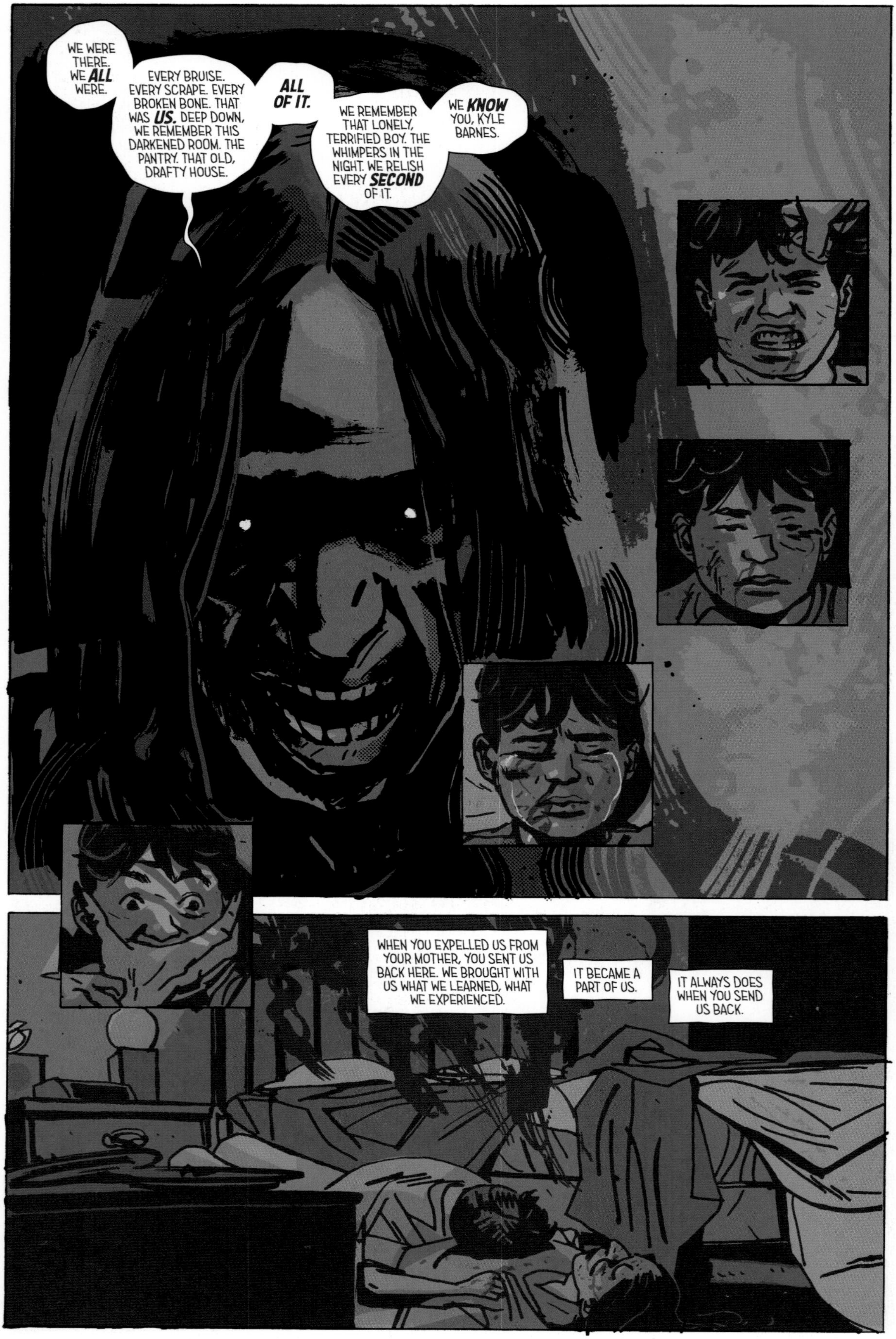
WE WERE THERE. WE ALL WERE.
EVERY BRUISE. EVERY SCRAPE. EVERY BROKEN BONE. THAT WAS US. DEEP DOWN, WE REMEMBER THIS DARKENED ROOM. THE PANTRY. THAT OLD, DRAFTY HOUSE.
ALL OF IT.
WE REMEMBER THAT LONELY, TERRIFIED BOY. THE WHIMPERS IN THE NIGHT. WE RELISH EVERY SECOND OF IT.
WE KNOW YOU, KYLE BARNES.
WHEN YOU EXPELLED US FROM YOUR MOTHER, YOU SENT US BACK HERE. WE BROUGHT WITH US WHAT WE LEARNED, WHAT WE EXPERIENCED.
IT BECAME A PART OF US.
IT ALWAYS DOES WHEN YOU SEND US BACK.

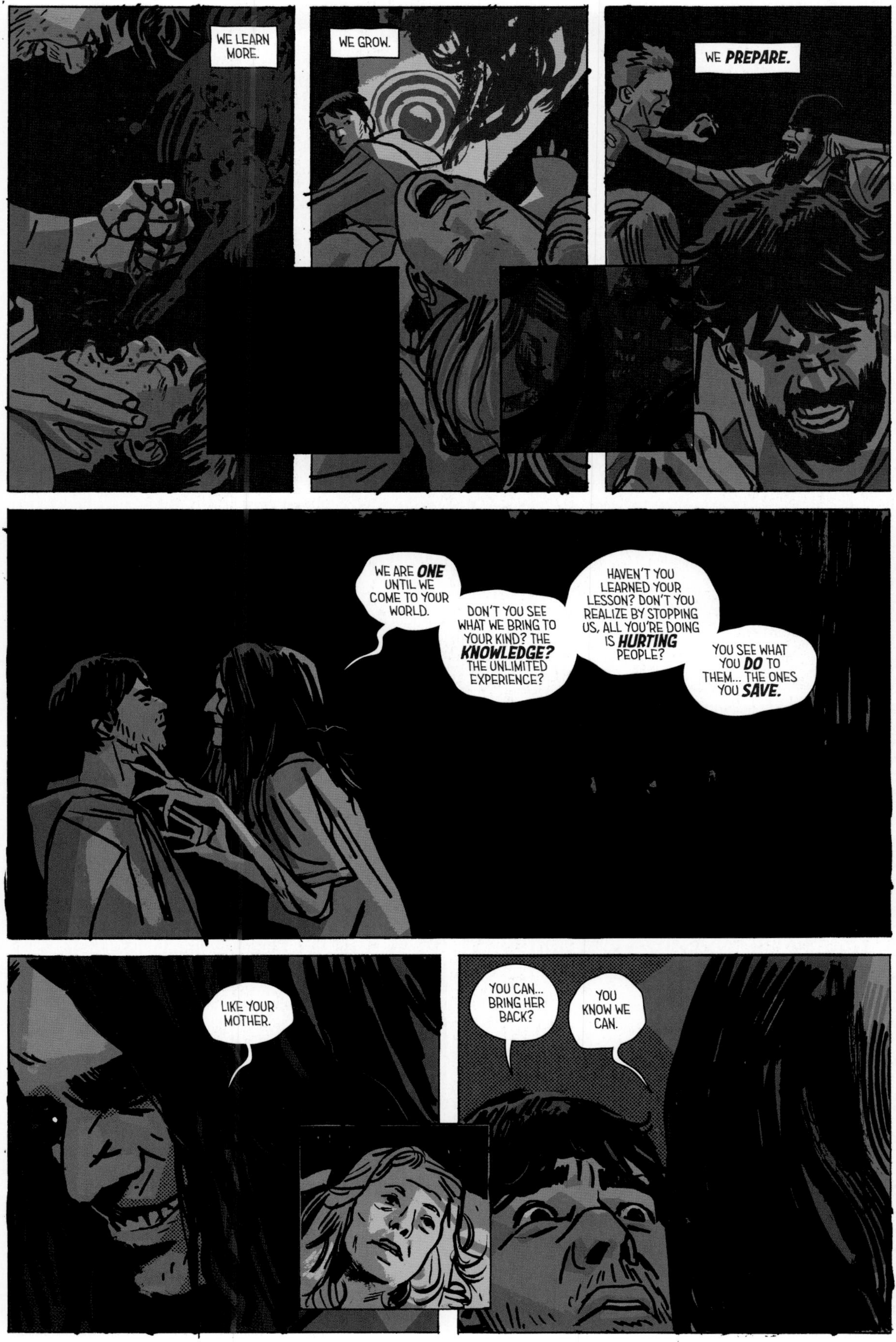
WE LEARN MORE.
WE GROW.
WE PREPARE.
WE ARE ONE UNTIL WE COME TO YOUR WORLD.
DON'T YOU SEE WHAT WE BRING TO YOUR KIND? THE KNOWLEDGE? THE UNLIMITED EXPERIENCE?
HAVEN'T YOU LEARNED YOUR LESSON? DON'T YOU REALIZE BY STOPPING US, ALL YOU'RE DOING IS HURTING PEOPLE?
YOU SEE WHAT YOU DO TO THEM... THE ONES YOU SAVE.
LIKE YOUR MOTHER.
YOU CAN... BRING HER BACK?
YOU KNOW WE CAN.

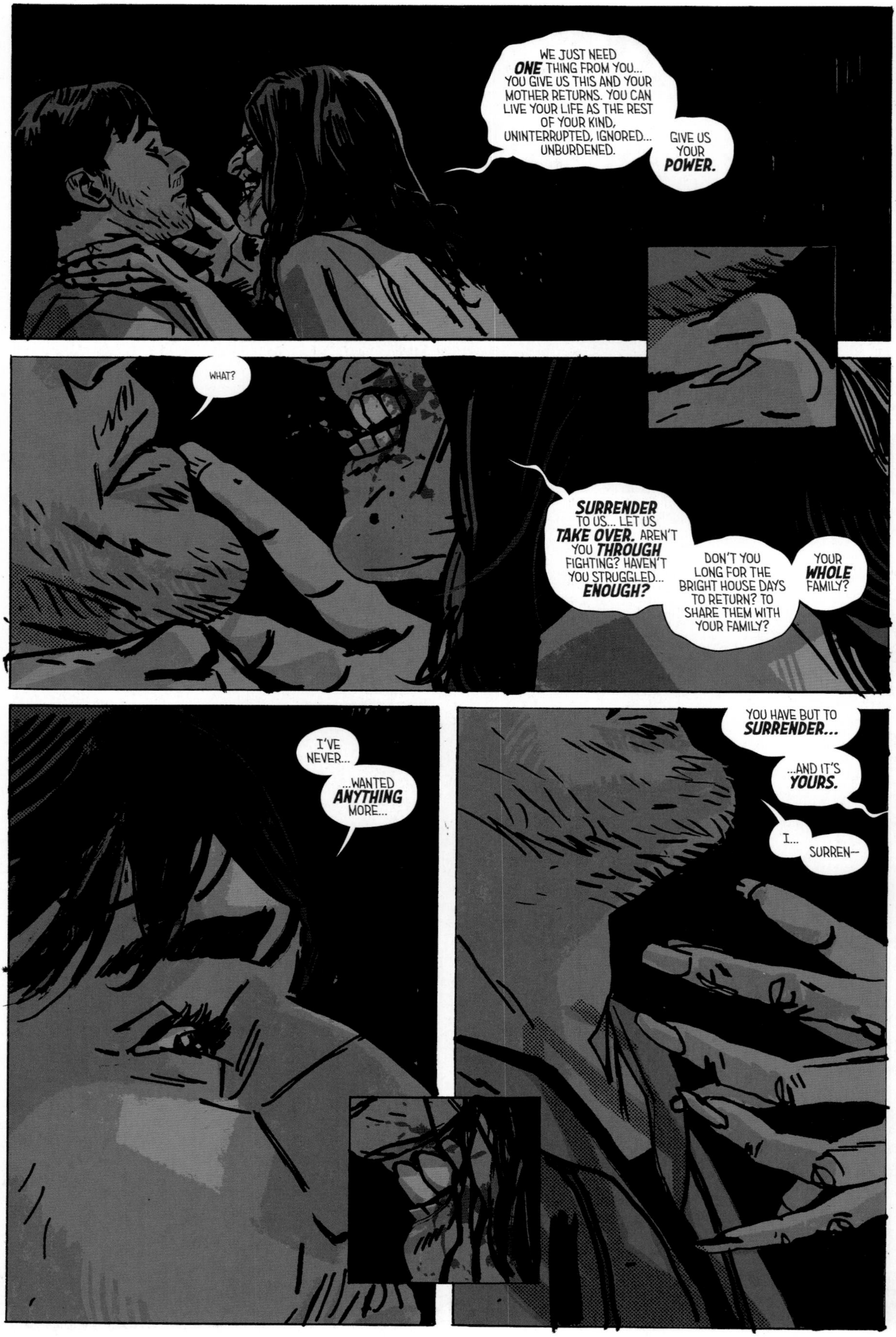

WE JUST NEED ONE THING FROM YOU... YOU GIVE US THIS AND YOUR MOTHER RETURNS. YOU CAN LIVE YOUR LIFE AS THE REST OF YOUR KIND, UNINTERRUPTED, IGNORED... UNBURDENED.
GIVE US YOUR POWER.
WHAT?
SURRENDER TO US... LET US TAKE OVER. AREN'T YOU THROUGH FIGHTING? HAVEN'T YOU STRUGGLED... ENOUGH?
DON'T YOU LONG FOR THE BRIGHT HOUSE DAYS TO RETURN? TO SHARE THEM WITH YOUR FAMILY?
YOUR WHOLE FAMILY?
I'VE NEVER...
...WANTED ANYTHING MORE...
YOU HAVE BUT TO SURRENDER...
...AND IT'S YOURS.
I...
SURREN--

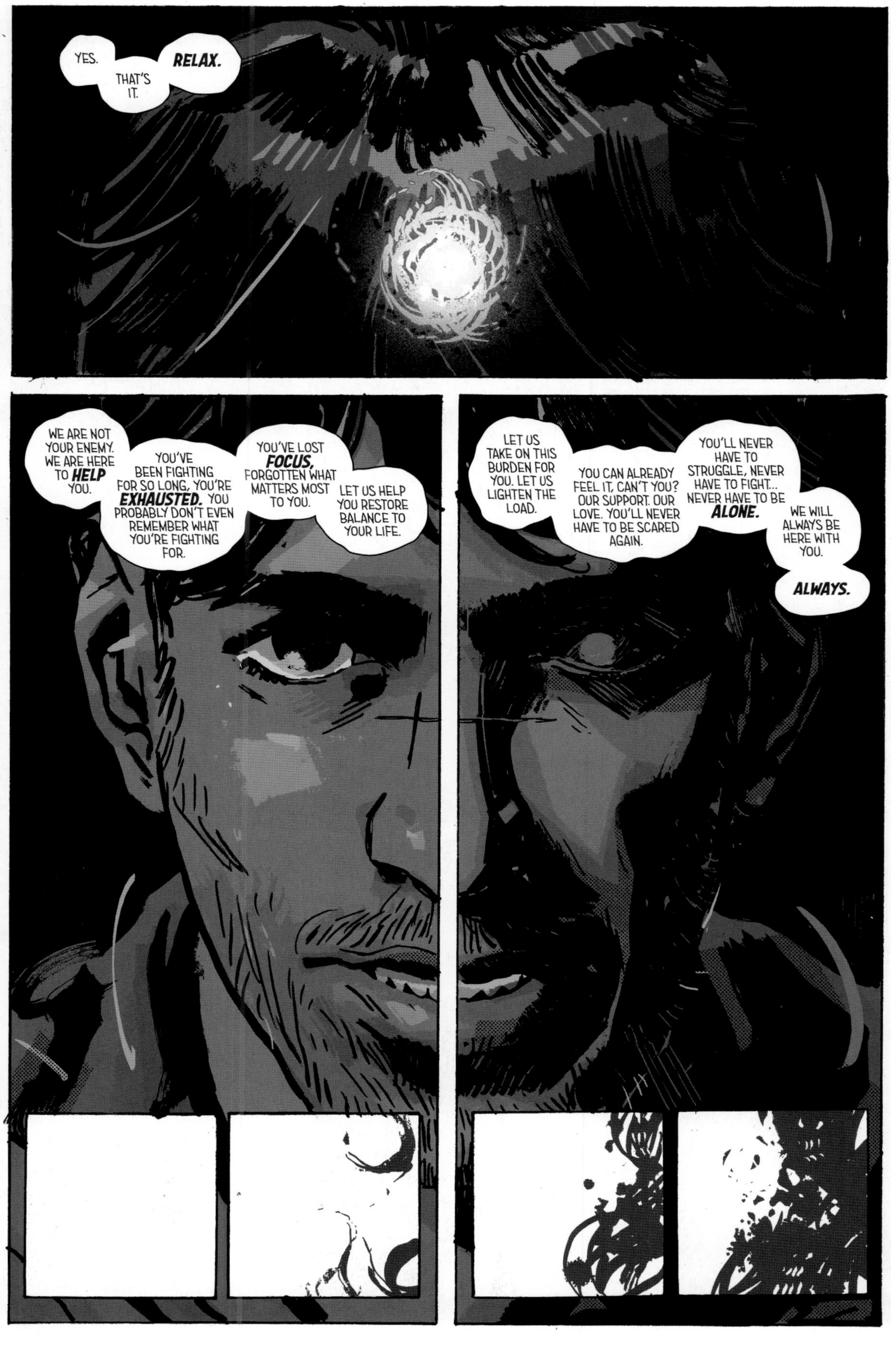
YES.
THAT'S IT.
RELAX.
WE ARE NOT YOUR ENEMY. WE ARE HERE TO HELP YOU.
YOU'VE BEEN FIGHTING FOR SO LONG, YOU'RE EXHAUSTED. YOU PROBABLY DON'T EVEN REMEMBER WHAT YOU'RE FIGHTING FOR.
YOU'VE LOST FOCUS, FORGOTTEN WHAT MATTERS MOST TO YOU.
LET US HELP YOU RESTORE BALANCE TO YOUR LIFE.
LET US TAKE ON THIS BURDEN FOR YOU. LET US LIGHTEN THE LOAD.
YOU CAN ALREADY FEEL IT, CAN'T YOU? OUR SUPPORT. OUR LOVE. YOU'LL NEVER HAVE TO BE SCARED AGAIN.
YOU'LL NEVER HAVE TO STRUGGLE, NEVER HAVE TO FIGHT... NEVER HAVE TO BE ALONE.
WE WILL ALWAYS BE HERE WITH YOU.
ALWAYS.

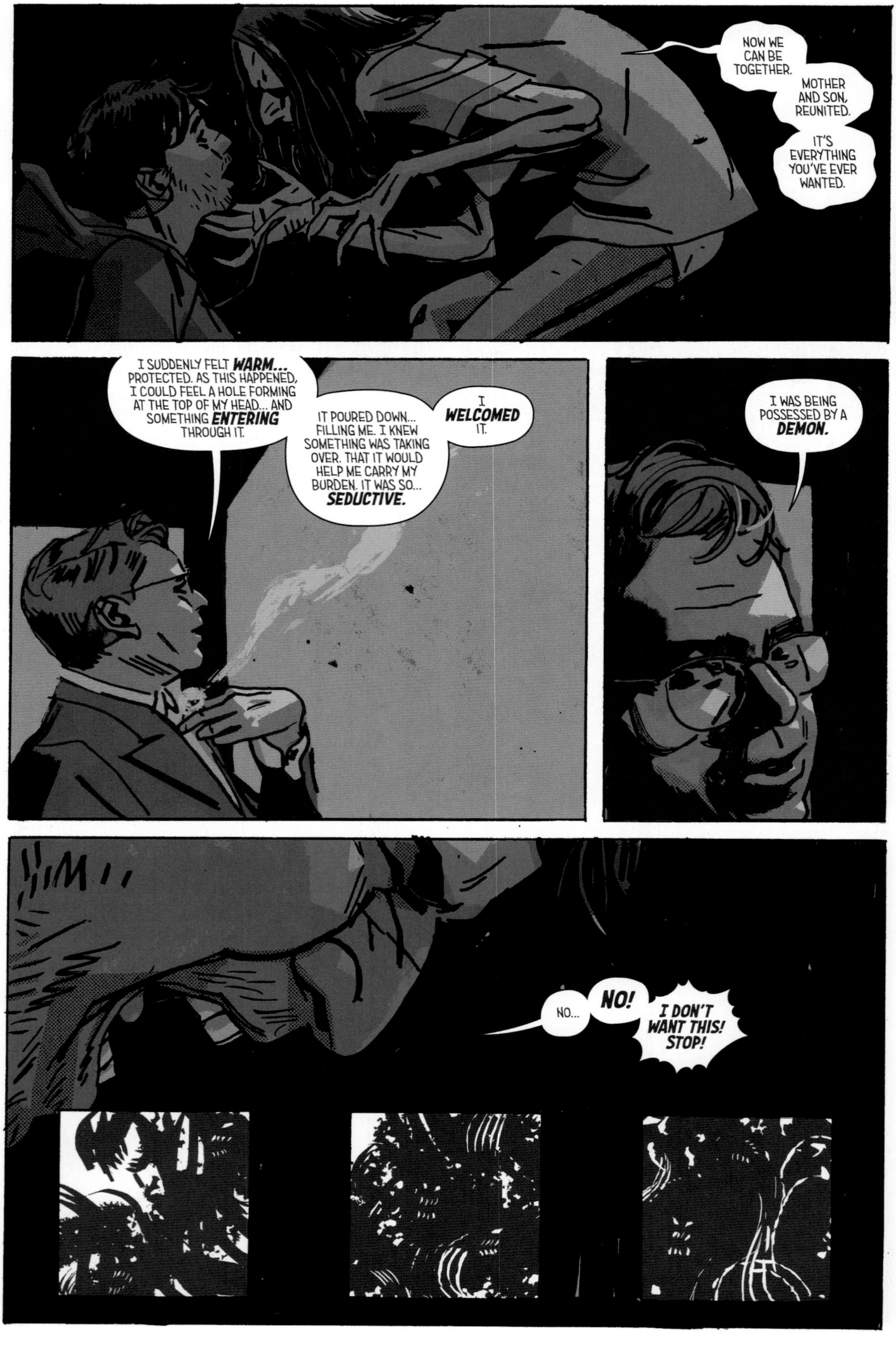
NOW WE CAN BE TOGETHER.
MOTHER AND SON, REUNITED.
IT'S EVERYTHING YOU'VE EVER WANTED.
I SUDDENLY FELT WARM... PROTECTED. AS THIS HAPPENED, I COULD FEEL A HOLE FORMING AT THE TOP OF MY HEAD... AND SOMETHING ENTERING THROUGH IT.
IT POURED DOWN... FILLING ME. I KNEW SOMETHING WAS TAKING OVER. THAT IT WOULD HELP ME CARRY MY BURDEN. IT WAS SO... SEDUCTIVE.
I WELCOMED IT.
I WAS BEING POSSESSED BY A DEMON.
NO...
NO!
I DON'T WANT THIS! STOP!

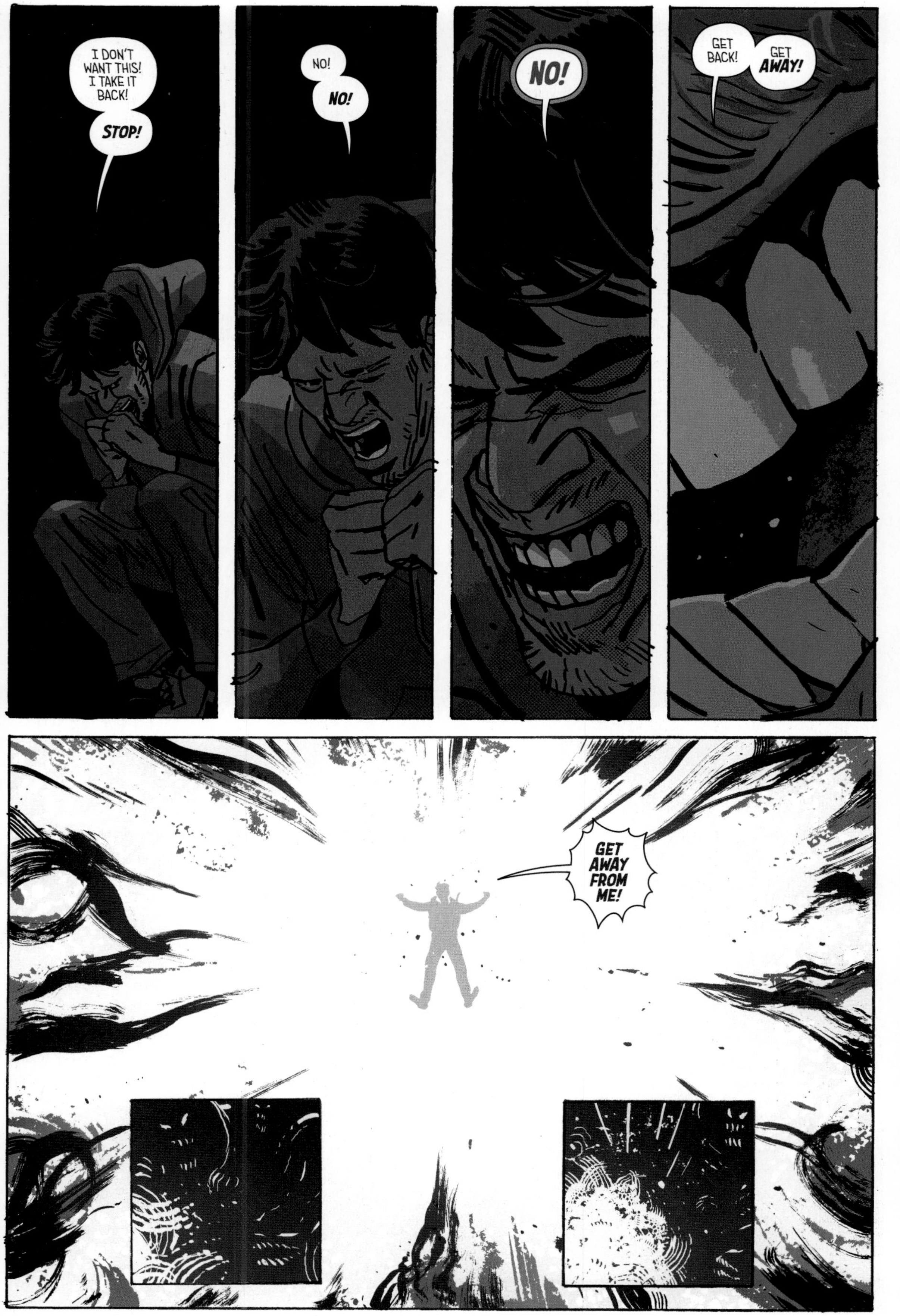
I DON'T WANT THIS! I TAKE IT BACK!
STOP!
NO!
NO!
NO!
GET BACK!
GET AWAY!
GET AWAY FROM ME!

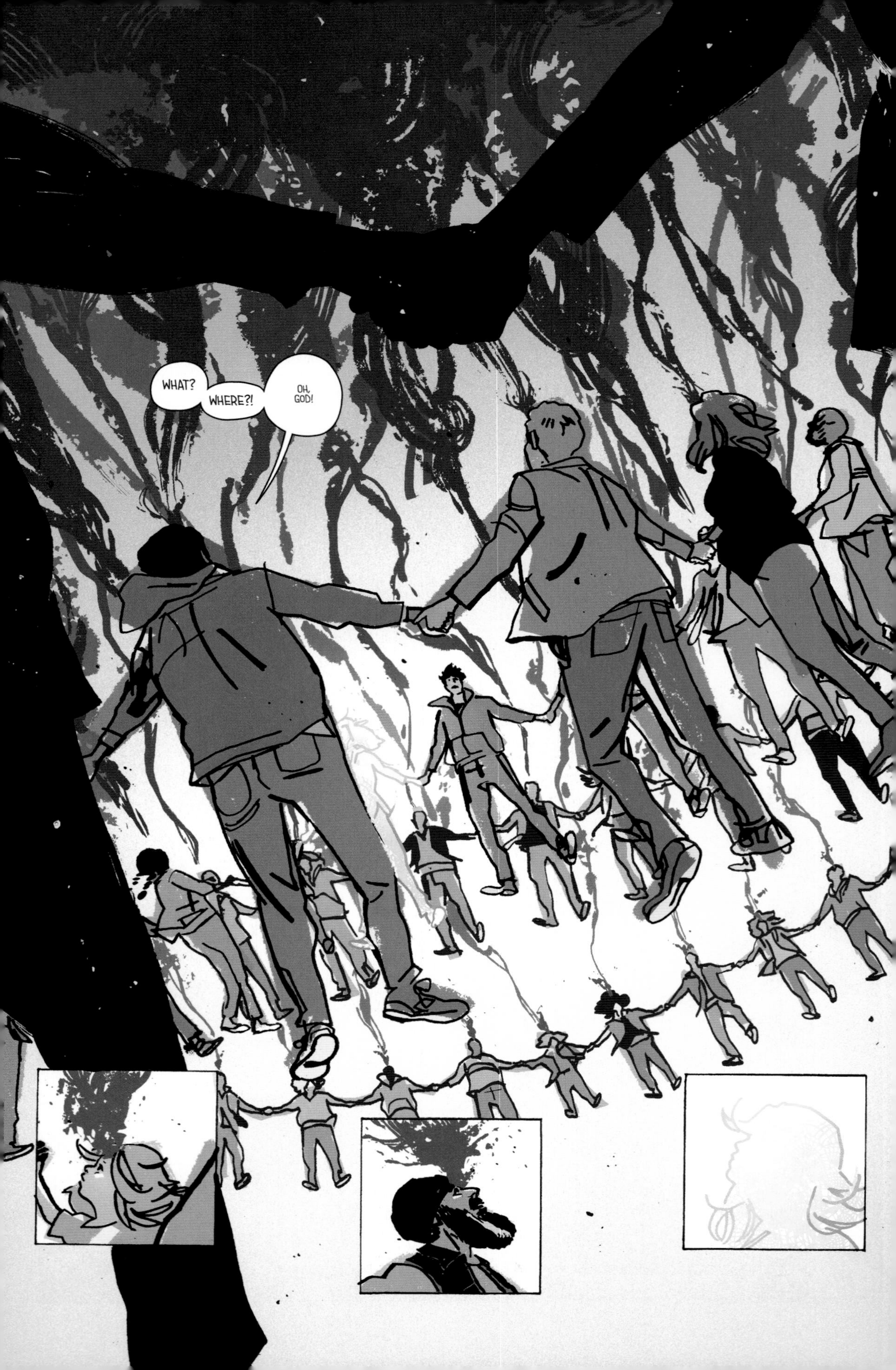
WHAT?
WHERE?!
OH, GOD!

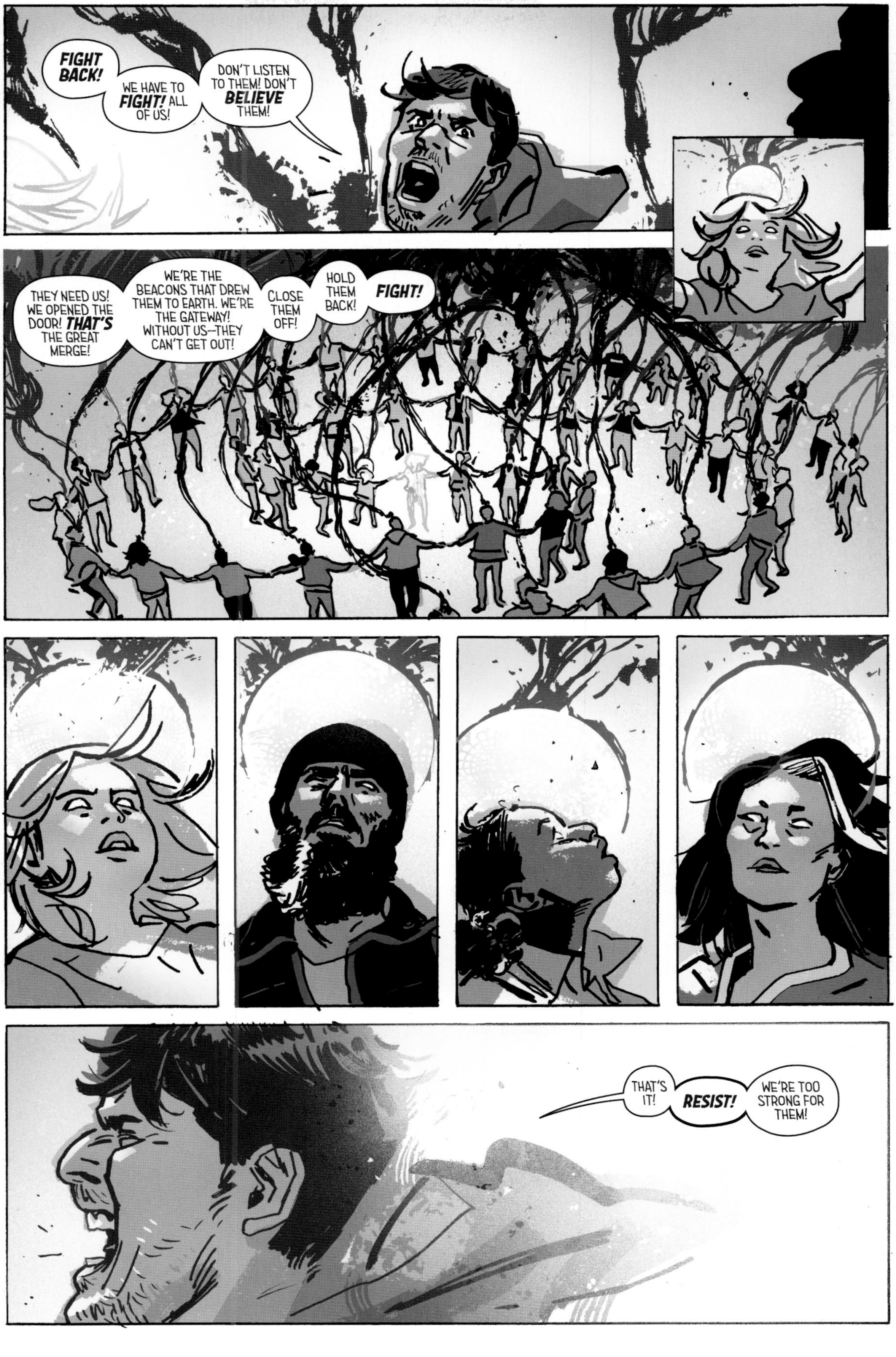
FIGHT BACK!
WE HAVE TO FIGHT! ALL OF US!
DON'T LISTEN TO THEM! DON'T BELIEVE THEM!
THEY NEED US! WE OPENED THE DOOR! THAT'S THE GREAT MERGE!
WE'RE THE BEACONS THAT DREW THEM TO EARTH. WE'RE THE GATEWAY! WITHOUT US--THEY CAN'T GET OUT!
CLOSE THEM OFF!
HOLD THEM BACK!
FIGHT!
THAT'S IT!
RESIST!
WE'RE TOO STRONG FOR THEM!

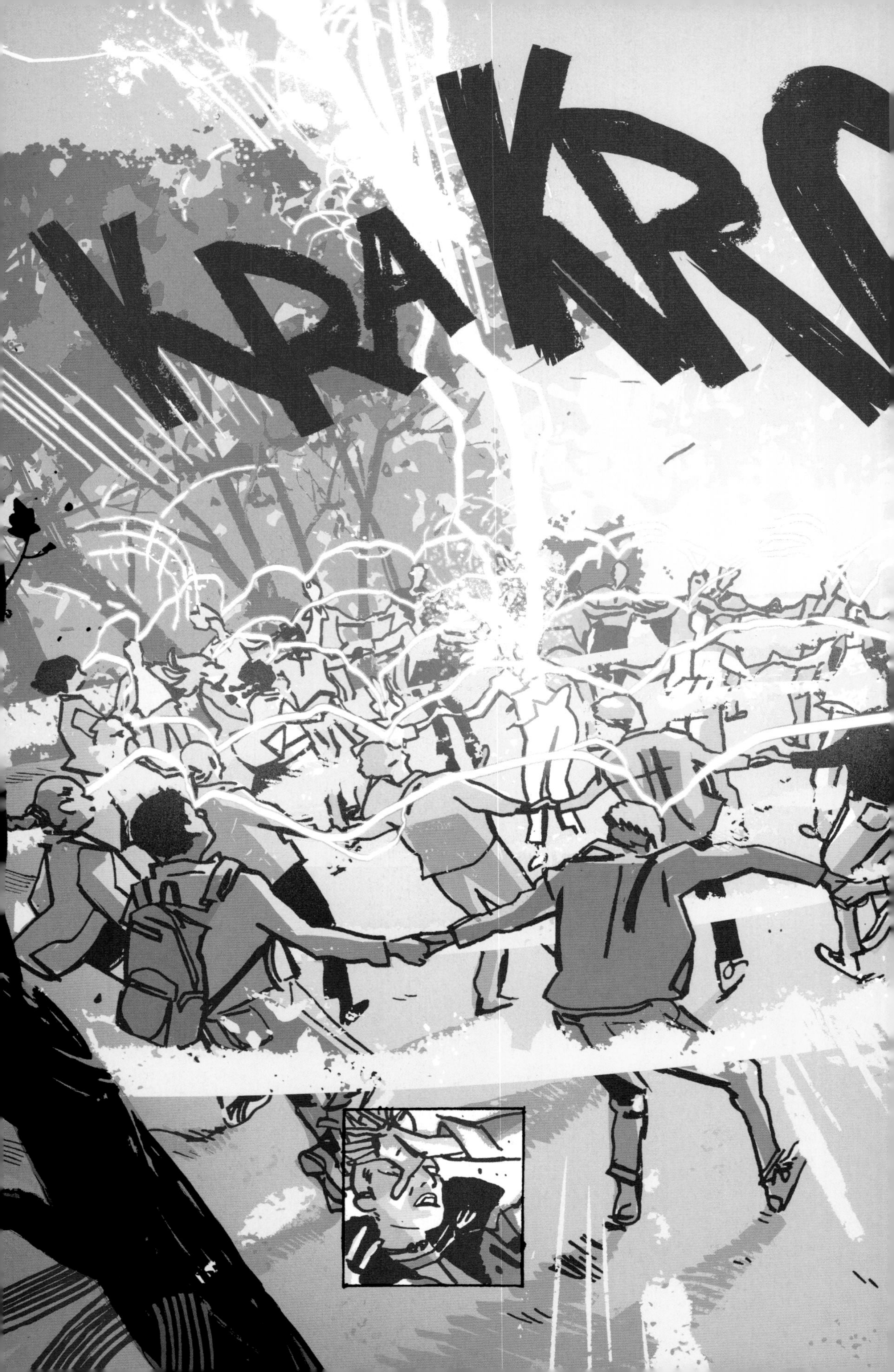
KRAKR

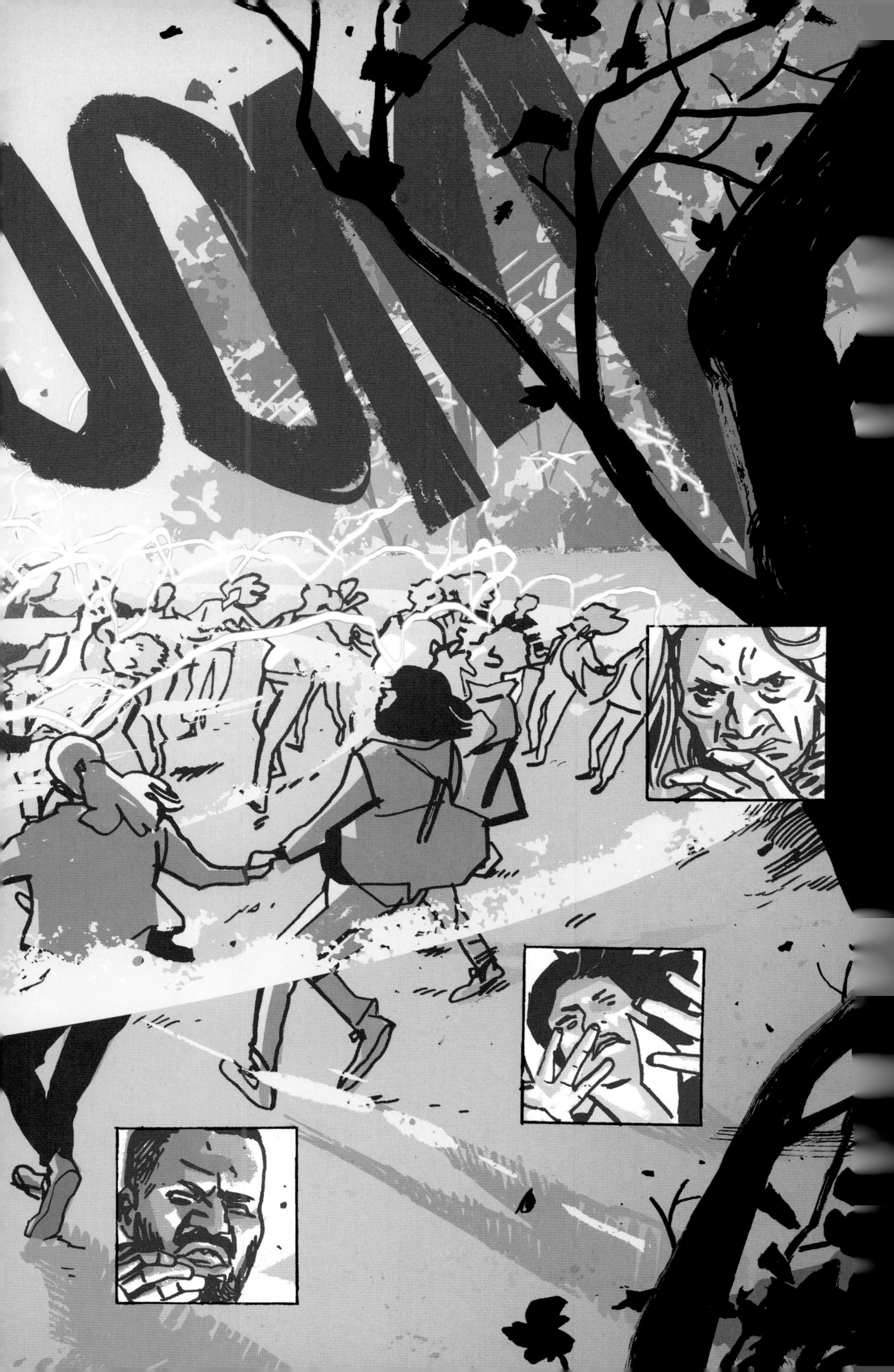

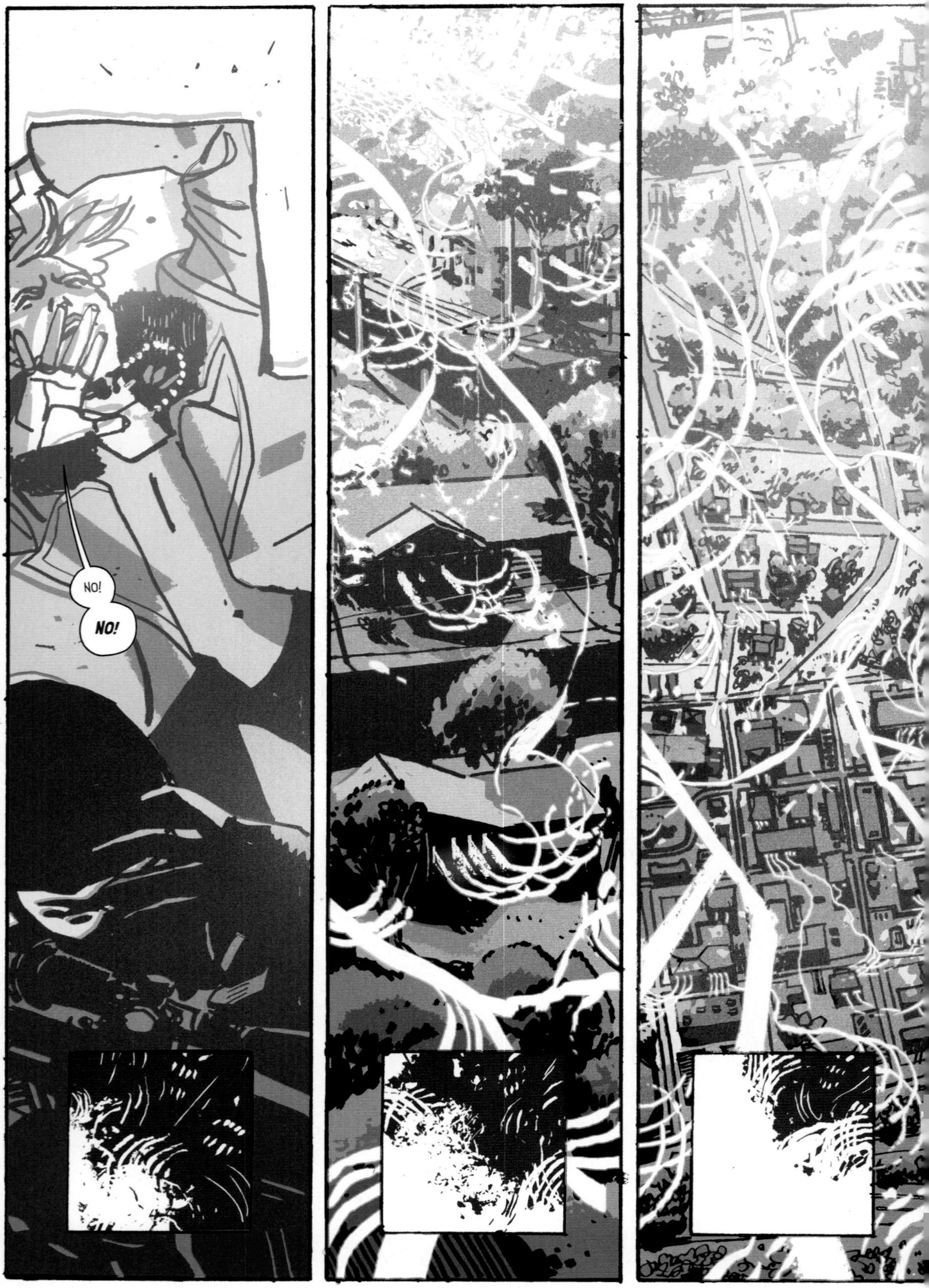
NO!
NO!

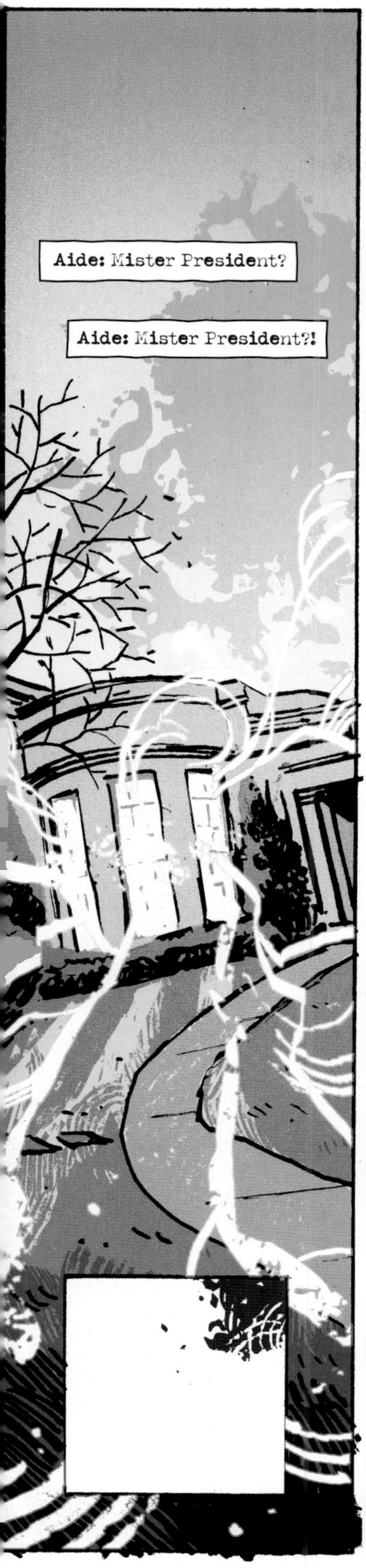
Aide: Mister President?
Aide: Mister President?!

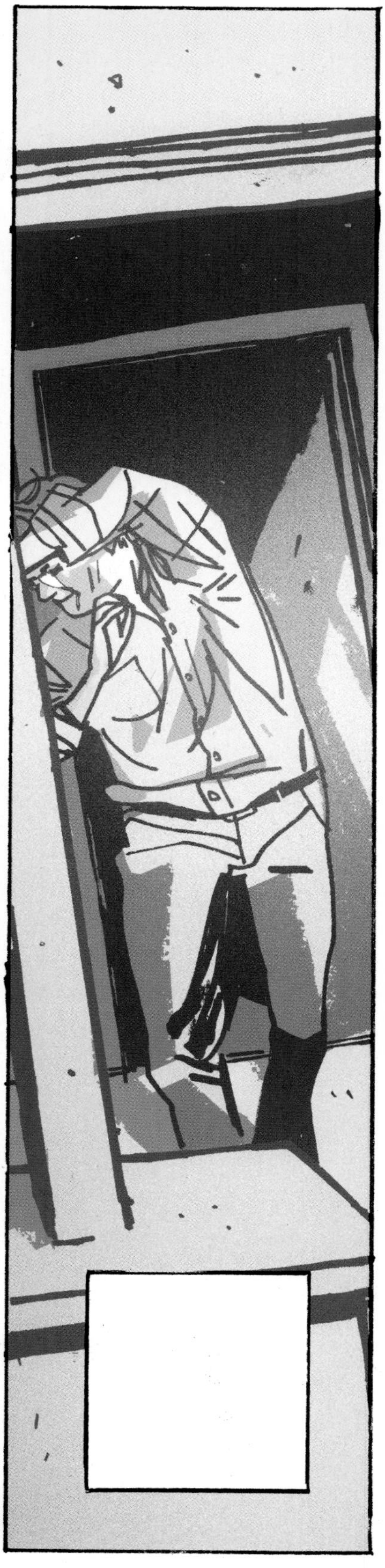

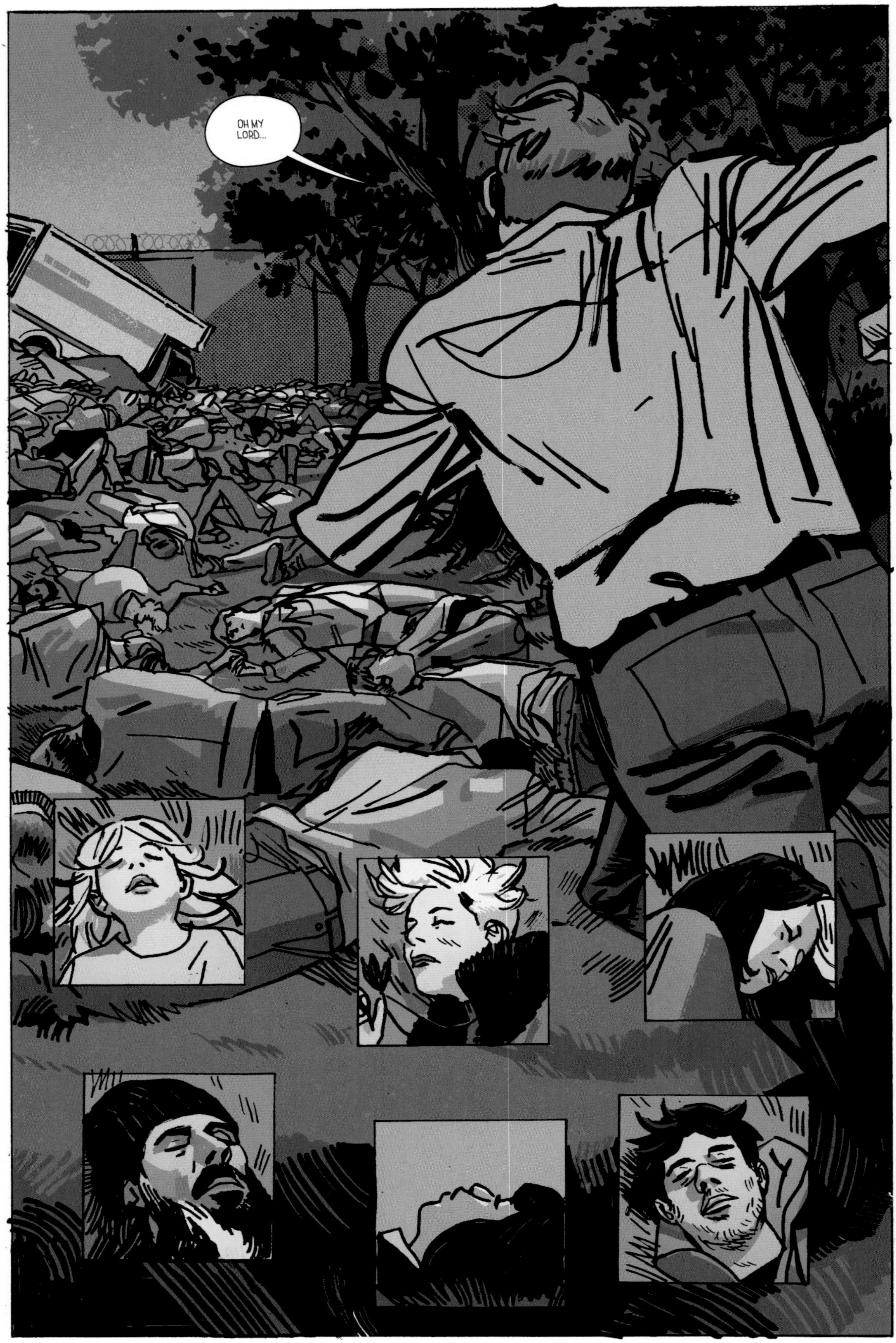
OH MY LORD...

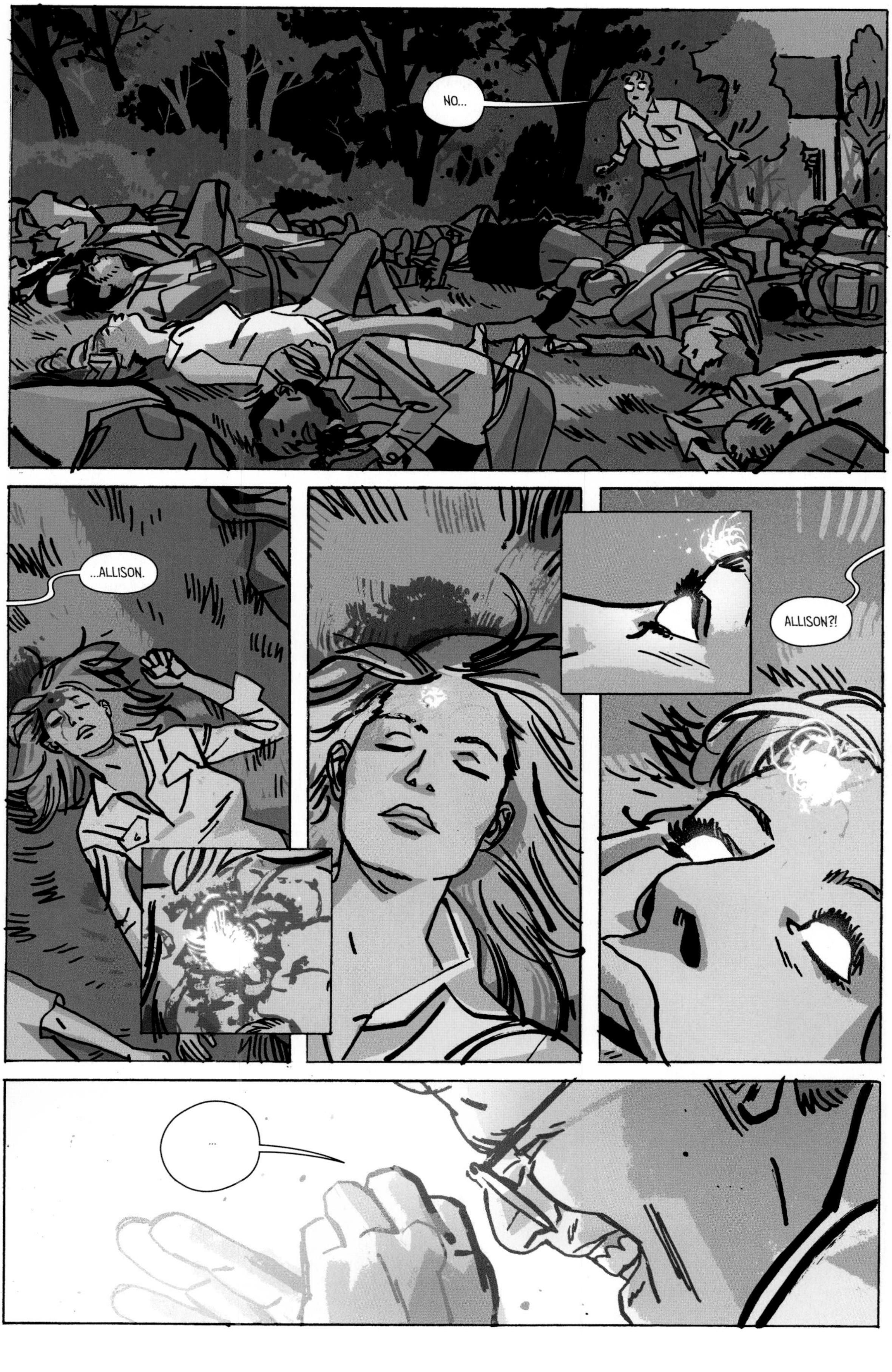
NO...
...ALLISON.
ALLISON?!
...

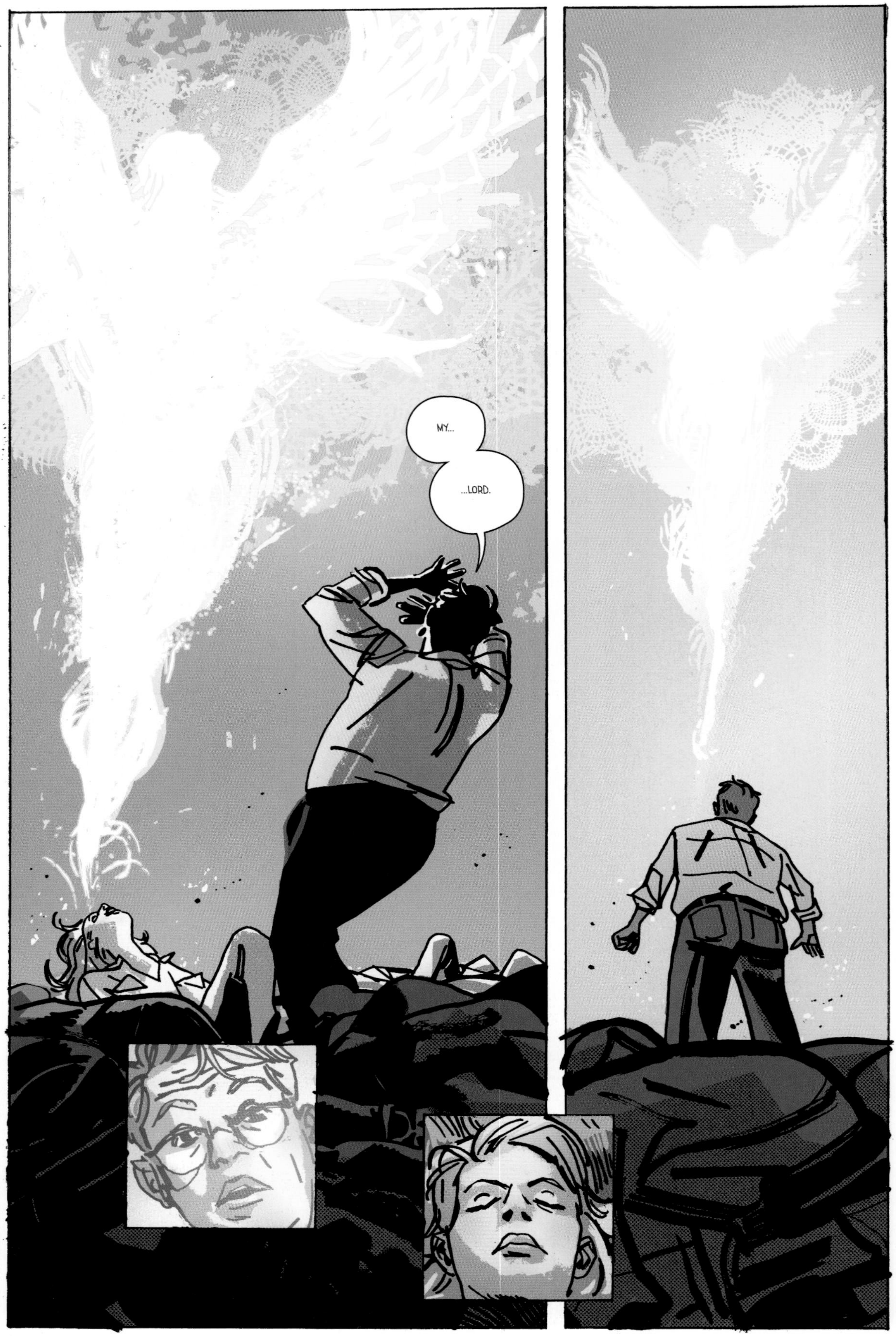
MY...
...LORD.

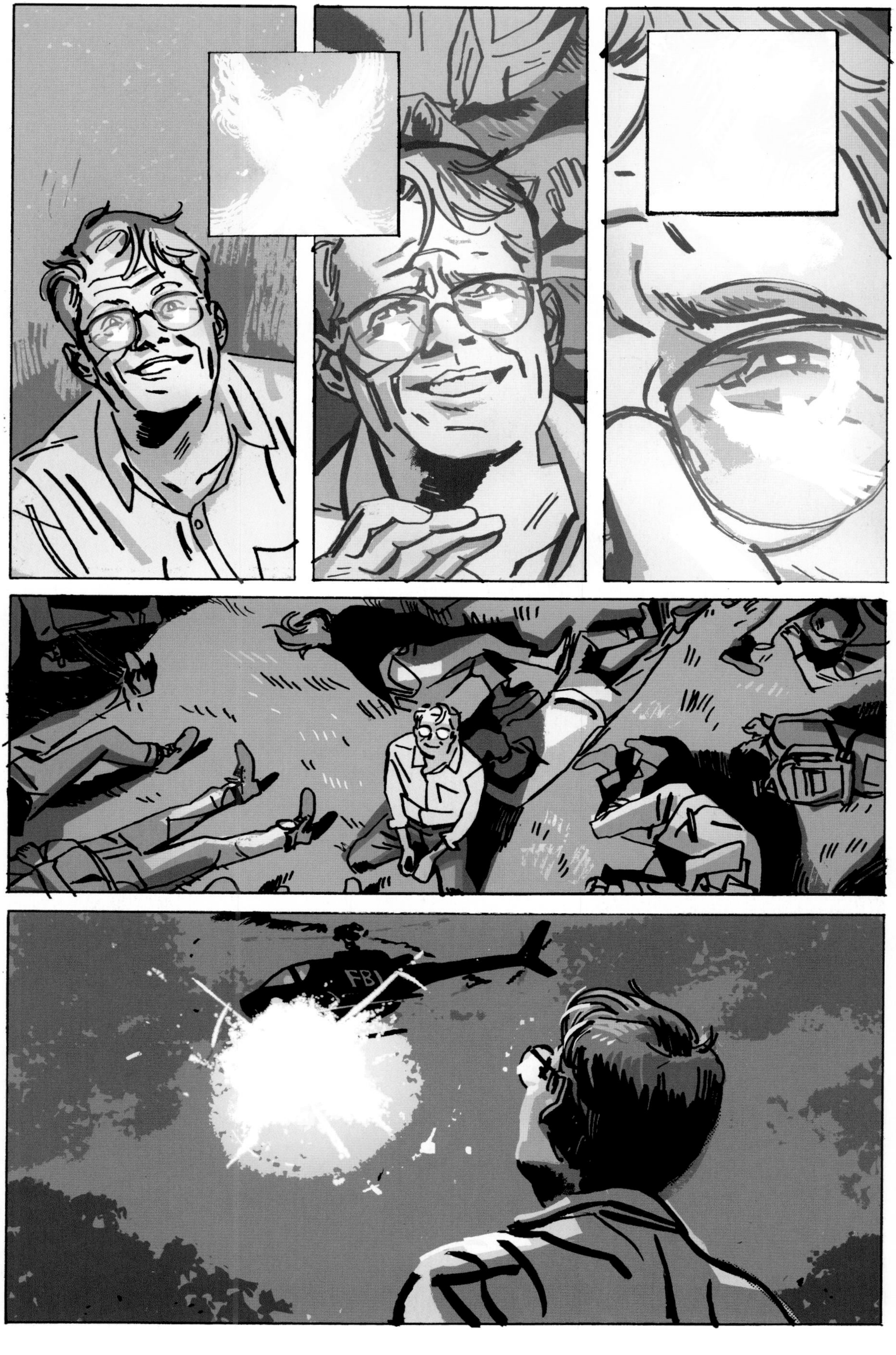
FBI

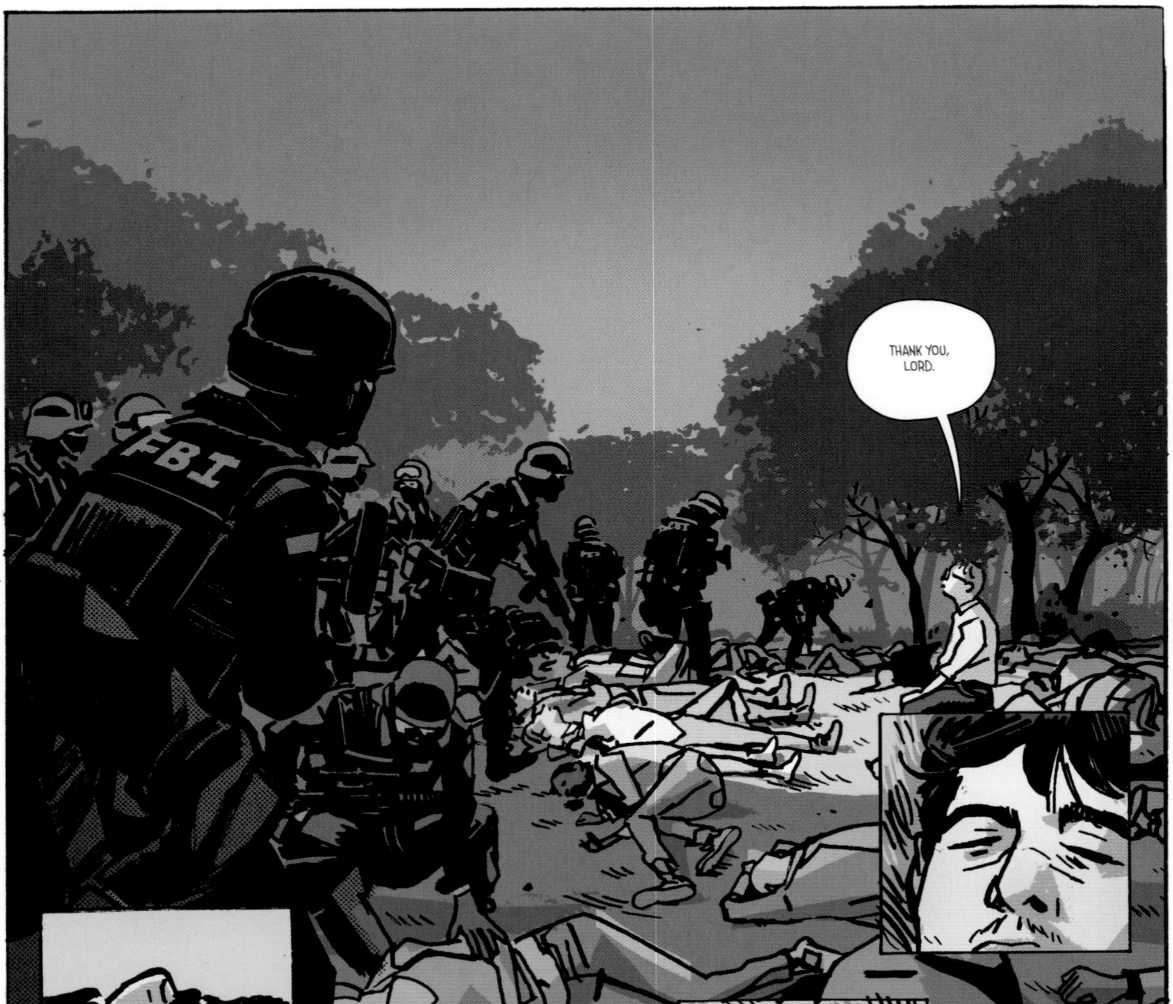
THANK YOU, LORD.

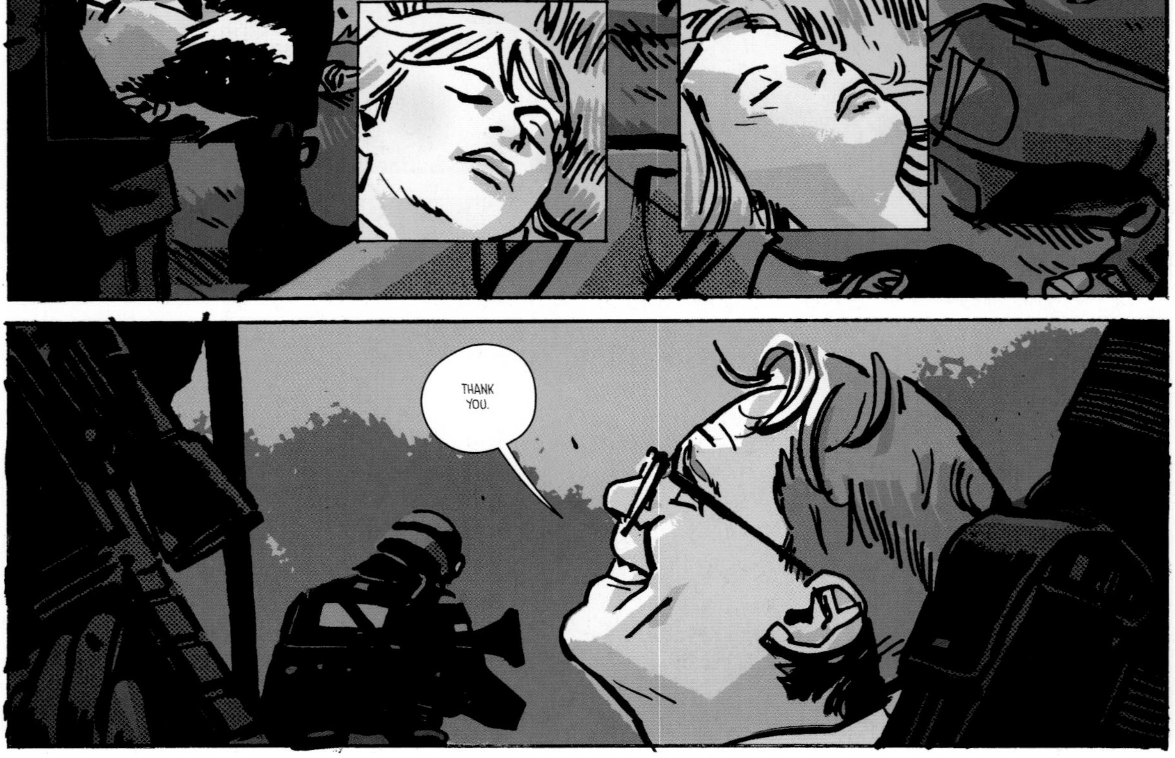
THANK YOU.

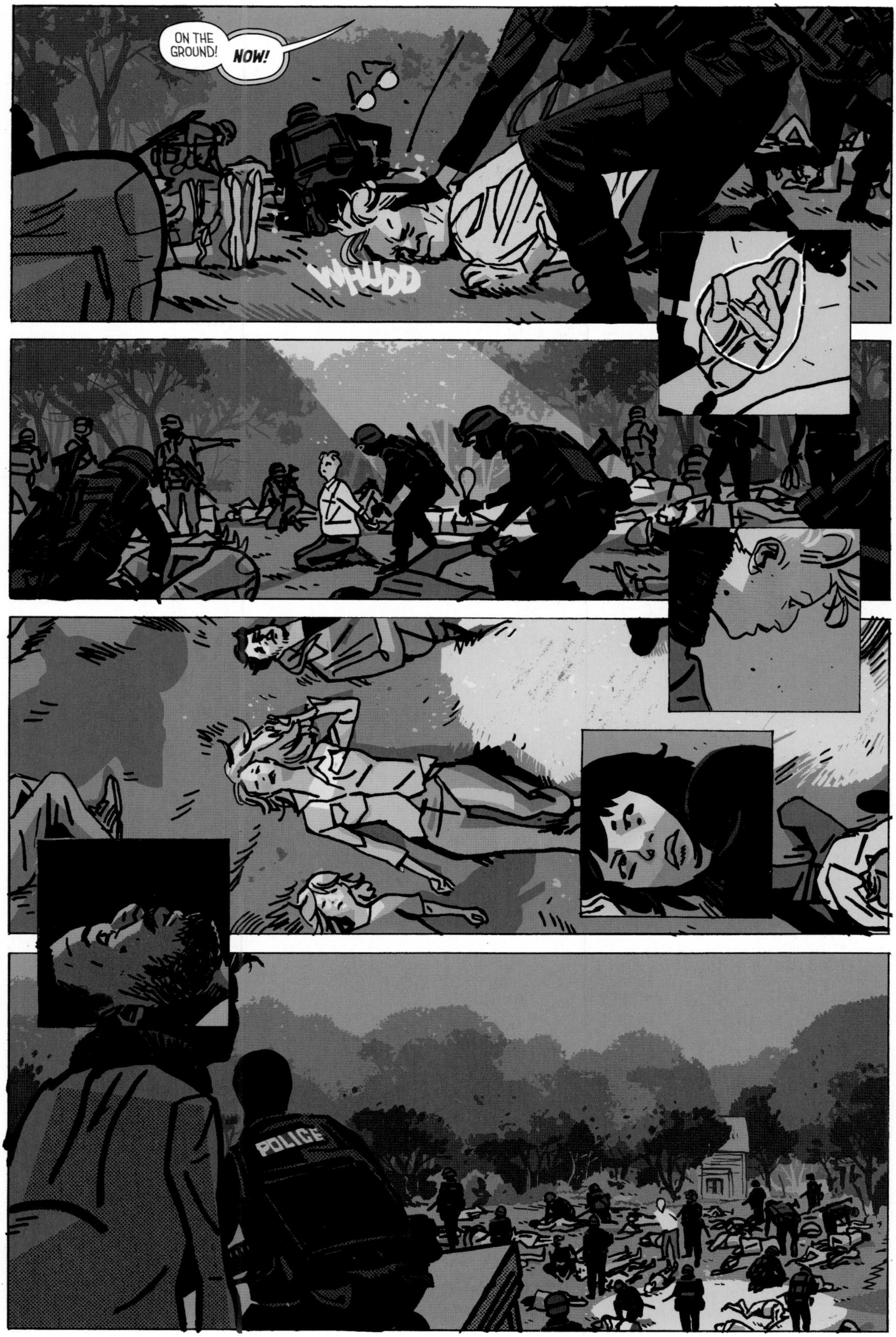
ON THE GROUND!
NOW!
WHUDD
POLICE

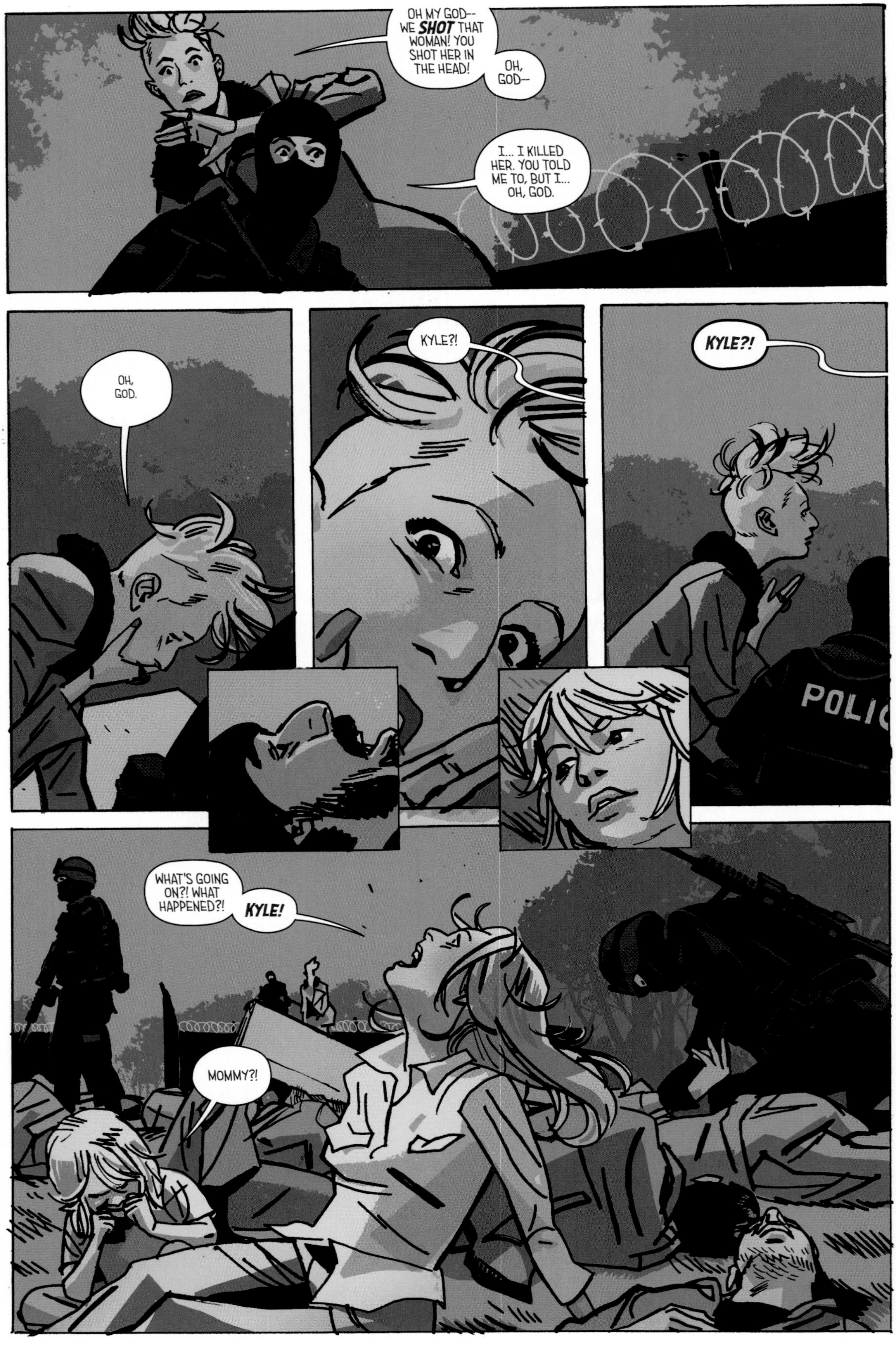
OH MY GOD-- WE SHOT THAT WOMAN! YOU SHOT HER IN THE HEAD!
OH, GOD--
I... I KILLED HER. YOU TOLD ME TO, BUT I... OH, GOD.
OH, GOD.
KYLE?!
KYLE?!
POLIC
WHAT'S GOING ON?! WHAT HAPPENED?!
KYLE!
MOMMY?!

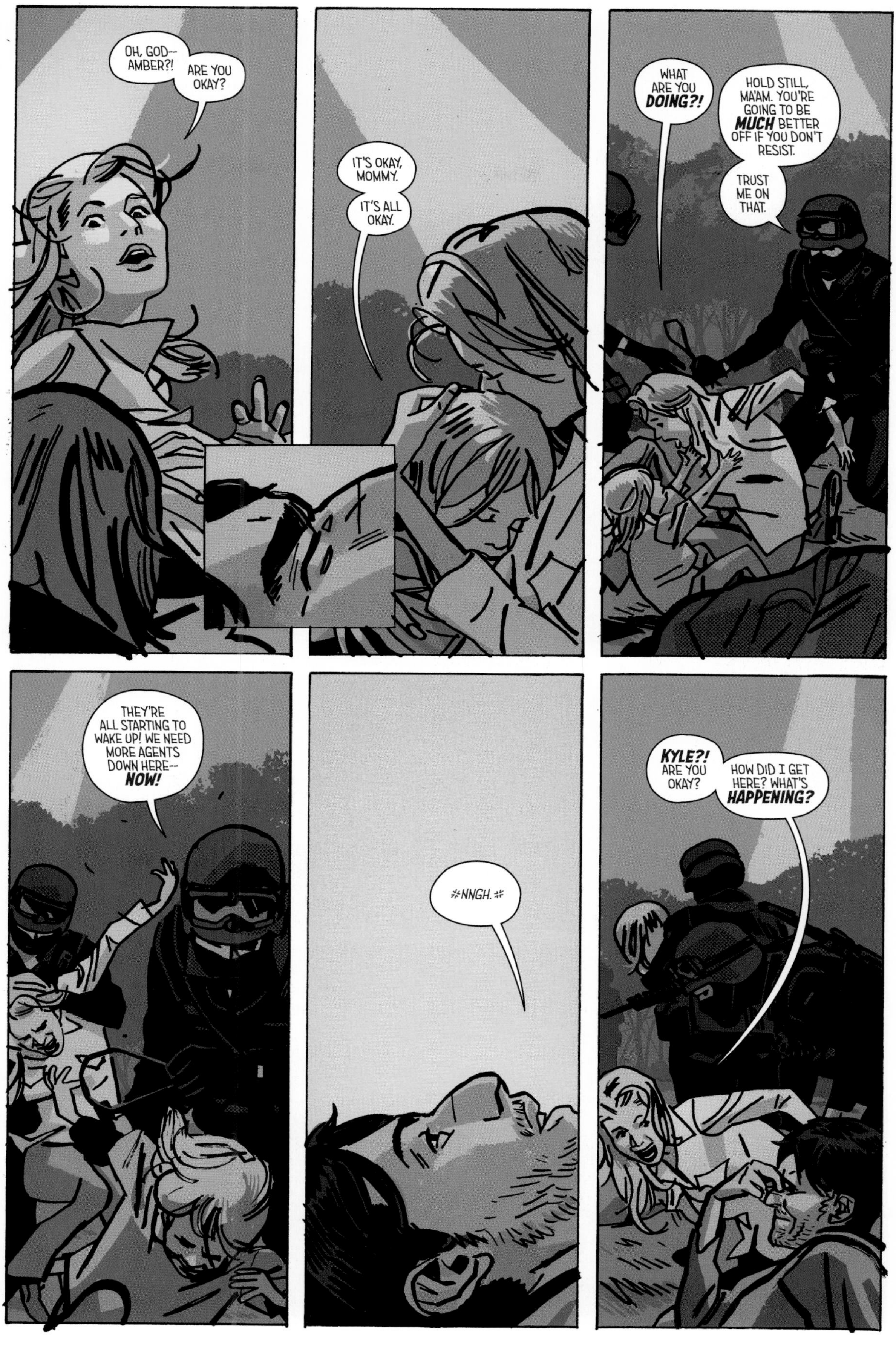
OH, GOD-- AMBER?!
ARE YOU OKAY?
IT'S OKAY, MOMMY.
IT'S ALL OKAY.
WHAT ARE YOU DOING?!
HOLD STILL, MA'AM. YOU'RE GOING TO BE MUCH BETTER OFF IF YOU DON'T RESIST.
TRUST ME ON THAT.
THEY'RE ALL STARTING TO WAKE UP! WE NEED MORE AGENTS DOWN HERE-- NOW!
#NNGH.#
KYLE?! ARE YOU OKAY?
HOW DID I GET HERE? WHAT'S HAPPENING?

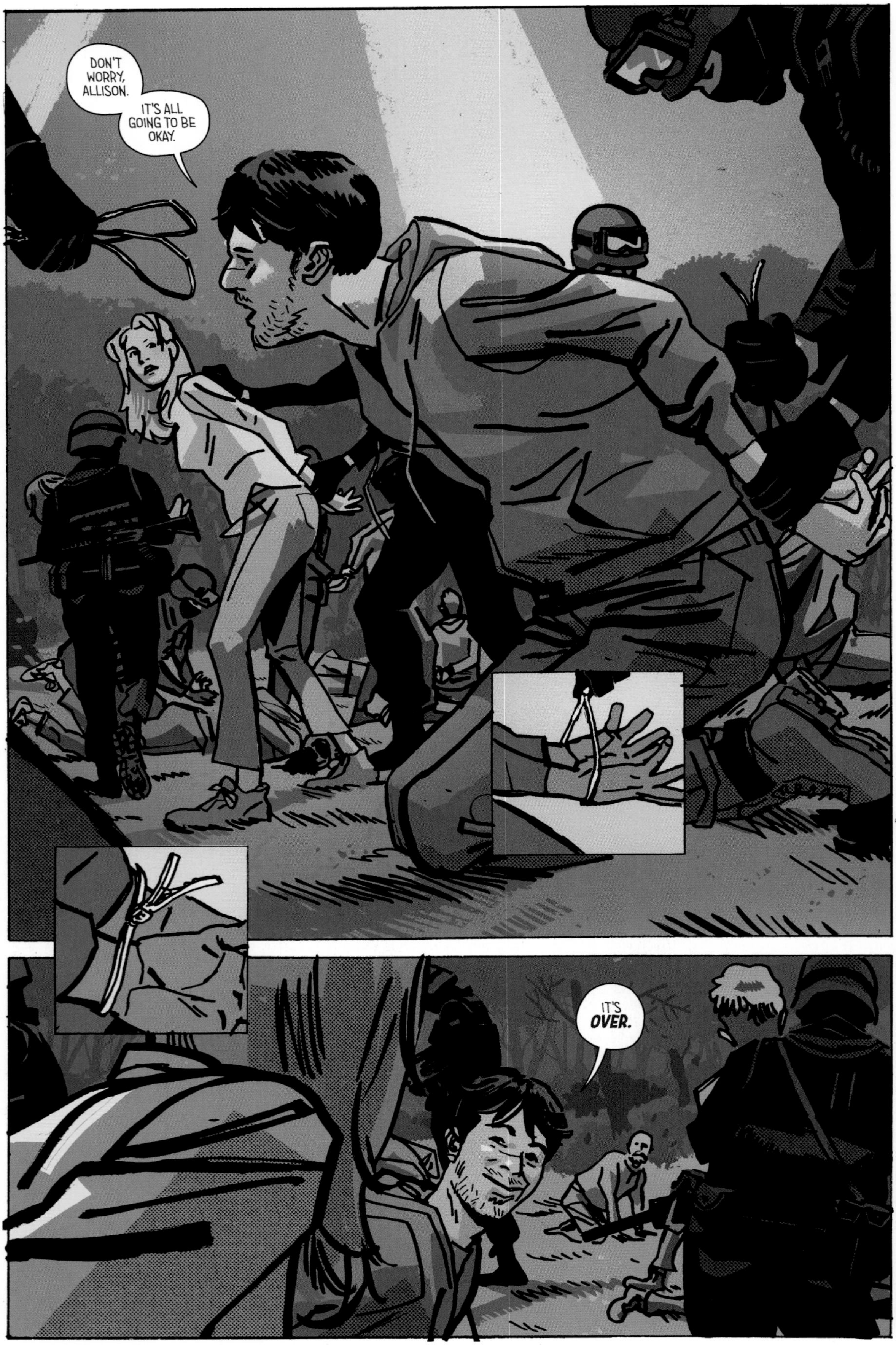
DON'T WORRY, ALLISON.
IT'S ALL GOING TO BE OKAY.
IT'S OVER.

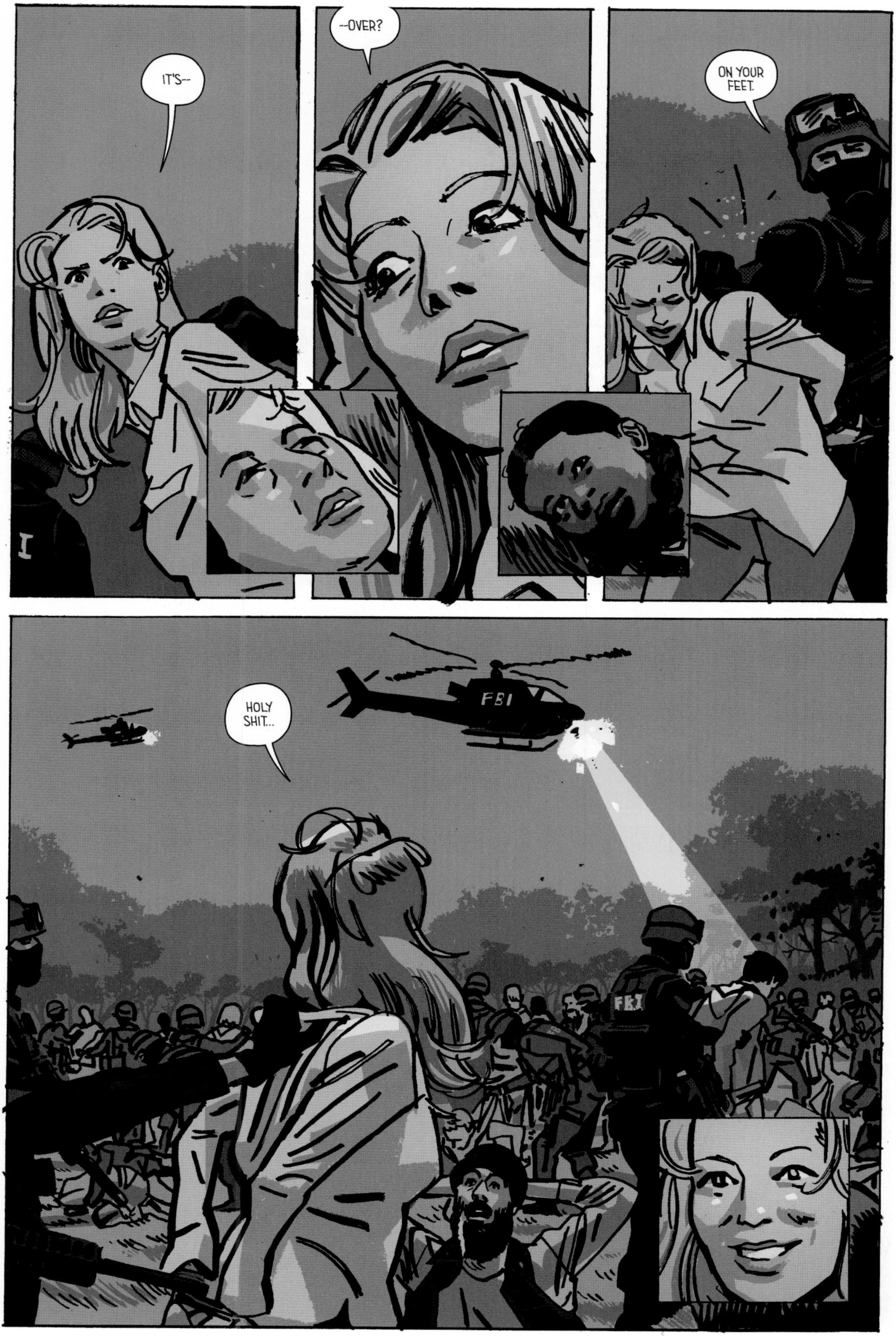
IT'S--
--OVER?
ON YOUR FEET.
HOLY SHIT...
FBI
FBI

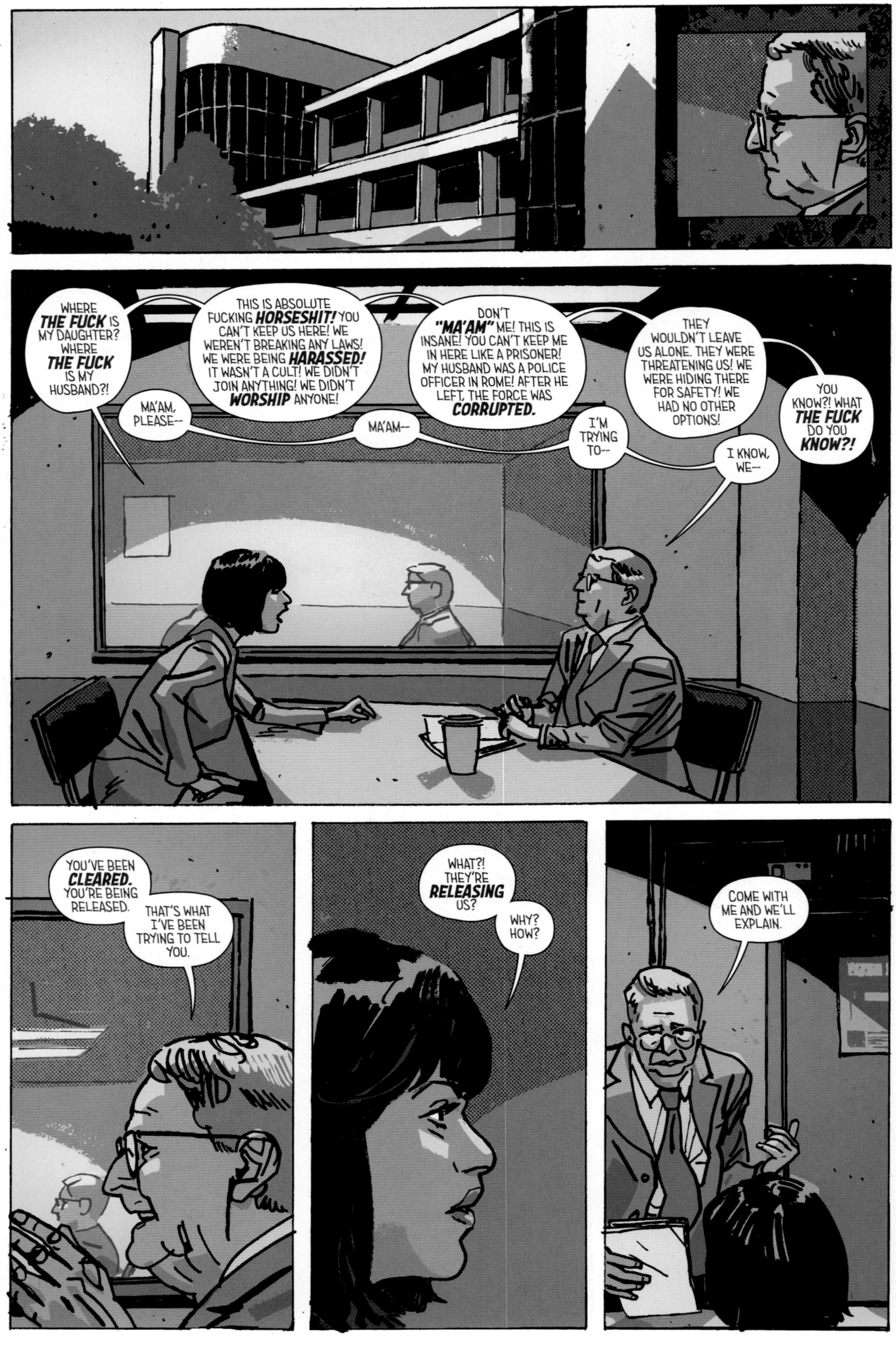
WHERE THE FUCK IS MY DAUGHTER? WHERE THE FUCK IS MY HUSBAND?!
MA'AM, PLEASE--
THIS IS ABSOLUTE FUCKING HORSESHIT! YOU CAN'T KEEP US HERE! WE WEREN'T BREAKING ANY LAWS! WE WERE BEING HARASSED! IT WASN'T A CULT! WE DIDN'T JOIN ANYTHING! WE DIDN'T WORSHIP ANYONE!
MA'AM--
DON'T "MA'AM" ME! THIS IS INSANE! YOU CAN'T KEEP ME IN HERE LIKE A PRISONER! MY HUSBAND WAS A POLICE OFFICER IN ROME! AFTER HE LEFT, THE FORCE WAS CORRUPTED.
I'M TRYING TO--
THEY WOULDN'T LEAVE US ALONE. THEY WERE THREATENING US! WE WERE HIDING THERE FOR SAFETY! WE HAD NO OTHER OPTIONS!
I KNOW, WE--
YOU KNOW?! WHAT THE FUCK DO YOU KNOW?!
YOU'VE BEEN CLEARED. YOU'RE BEING RELEASED.
THAT'S WHAT I'VE BEEN TRYING TO TELL YOU.
WHAT?! THEY'RE RELEASING US?
WHY? HOW?
COME WITH ME AND WE'LL EXPLAIN.

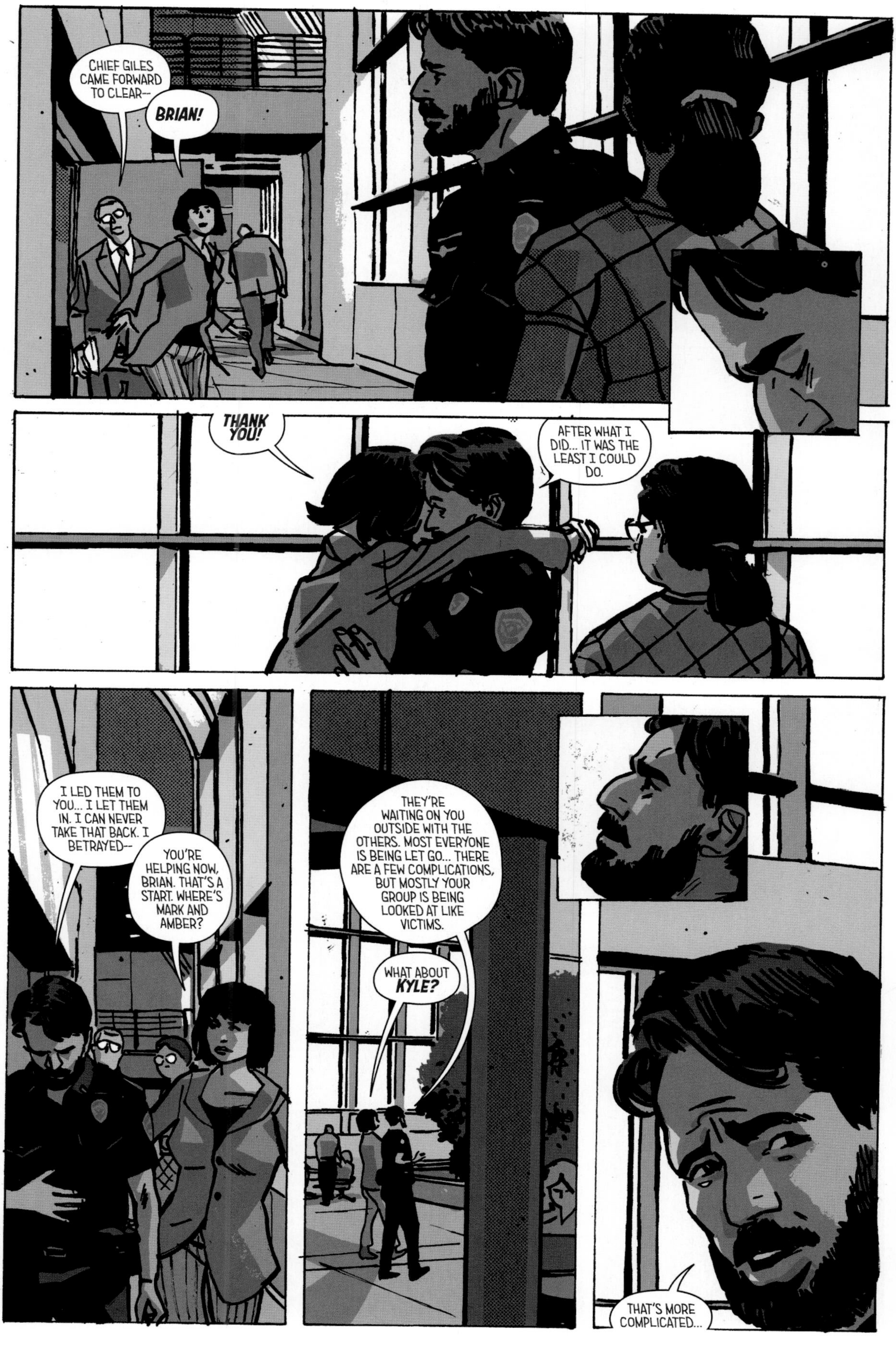
CHIEF GILES CAME FORWARD TO CLEAR--
BRIAN!
THANK YOU!
AFTER WHAT I DID... IT WAS THE LEAST I COULD DO.
I LED THEM TO YOU... I LET THEM IN. I CAN NEVER TAKE THAT BACK. I BETRAYED--
YOU'RE HELPING NOW, BRIAN. THAT'S A START. WHERE'S MARK AND AMBER?
THEY'RE WAITING ON YOU OUTSIDE WITH THE OTHERS. MOST EVERYONE IS BEING LET GO... THERE ARE A FEW COMPLICATIONS, BUT MOSTLY YOUR GROUP IS BEING LOOKED AT LIKE VICTIMS.
WHAT ABOUT KYLE?
THAT'S MORE COMPLICATED...

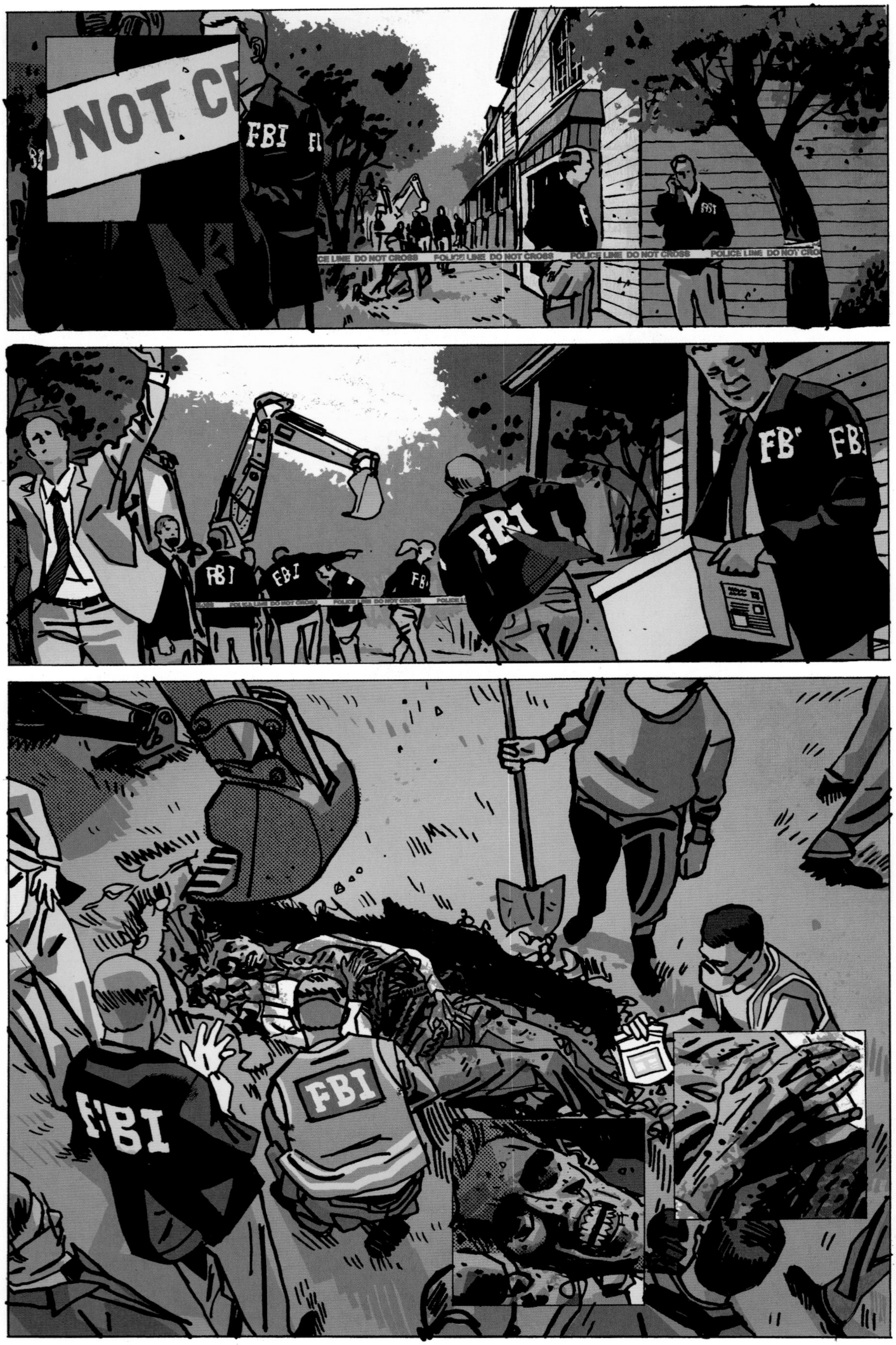

FBI
POLICE LINE DO NOT CROSS
FBI
POLICE LINE DO NOT CROSS
FBI

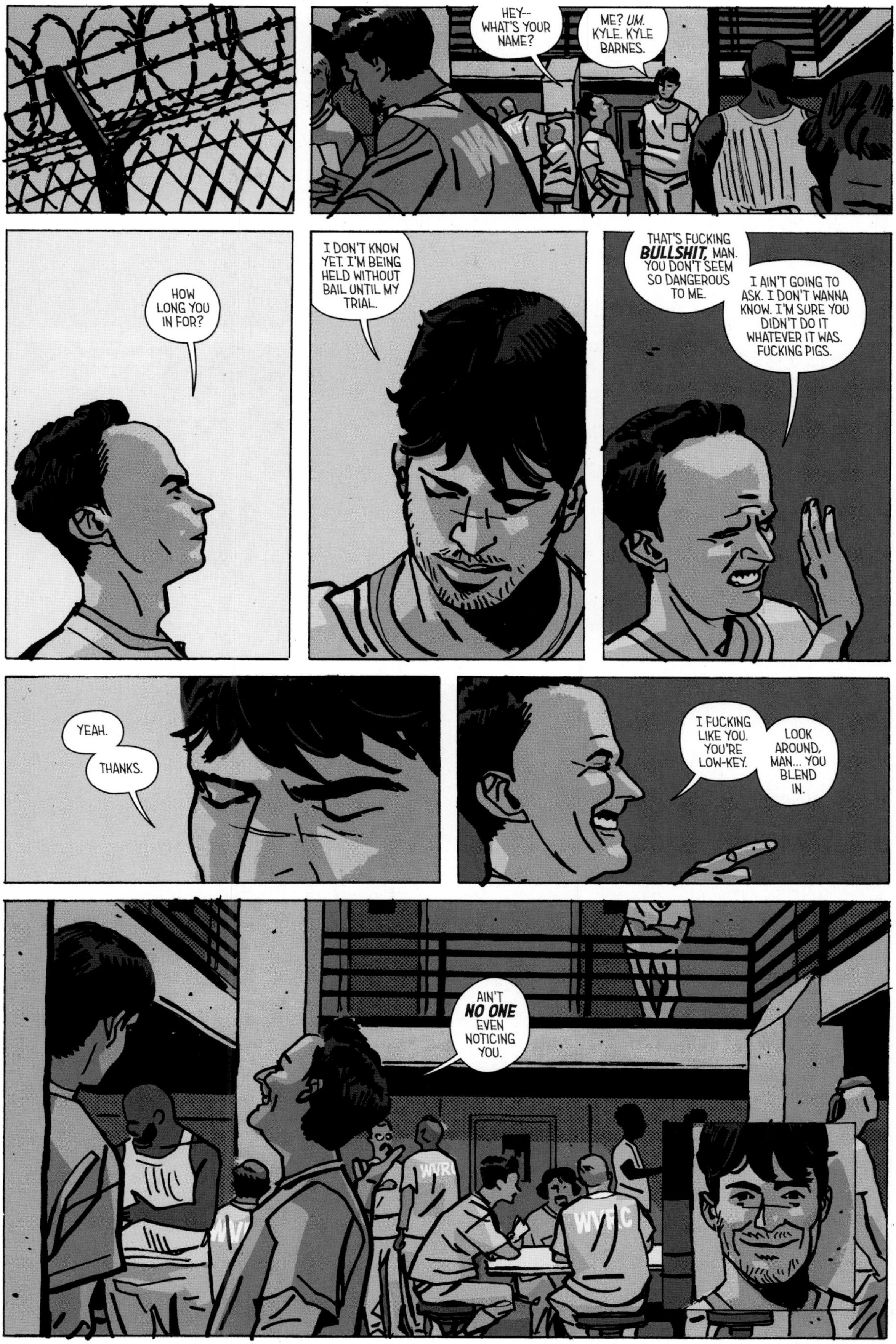
HEY-- WHAT'S YOUR NAME?
ME? *UM.* KYLE. KYLE BARNES.
HOW LONG YOU IN FOR?
I DON'T KNOW YET. I'M BEING HELD WITHOUT BAIL UNTIL MY TRIAL.
THAT'S FUCKING ***BULLSHIT,*** MAN. YOU DON'T SEEM SO DANGEROUS TO ME.
I AIN'T GOING TO ASK. I DON'T WANNA KNOW. I'M SURE YOU DIDN'T DO IT WHATEVER IT WAS. FUCKING PIGS.
YEAH.
THANKS.
I FUCKING LIKE YOU. YOU'RE LOW-KEY.
LOOK AROUND, MAN... YOU BLEND IN.
AIN'T ***NO ONE*** EVEN NOTICING YOU.

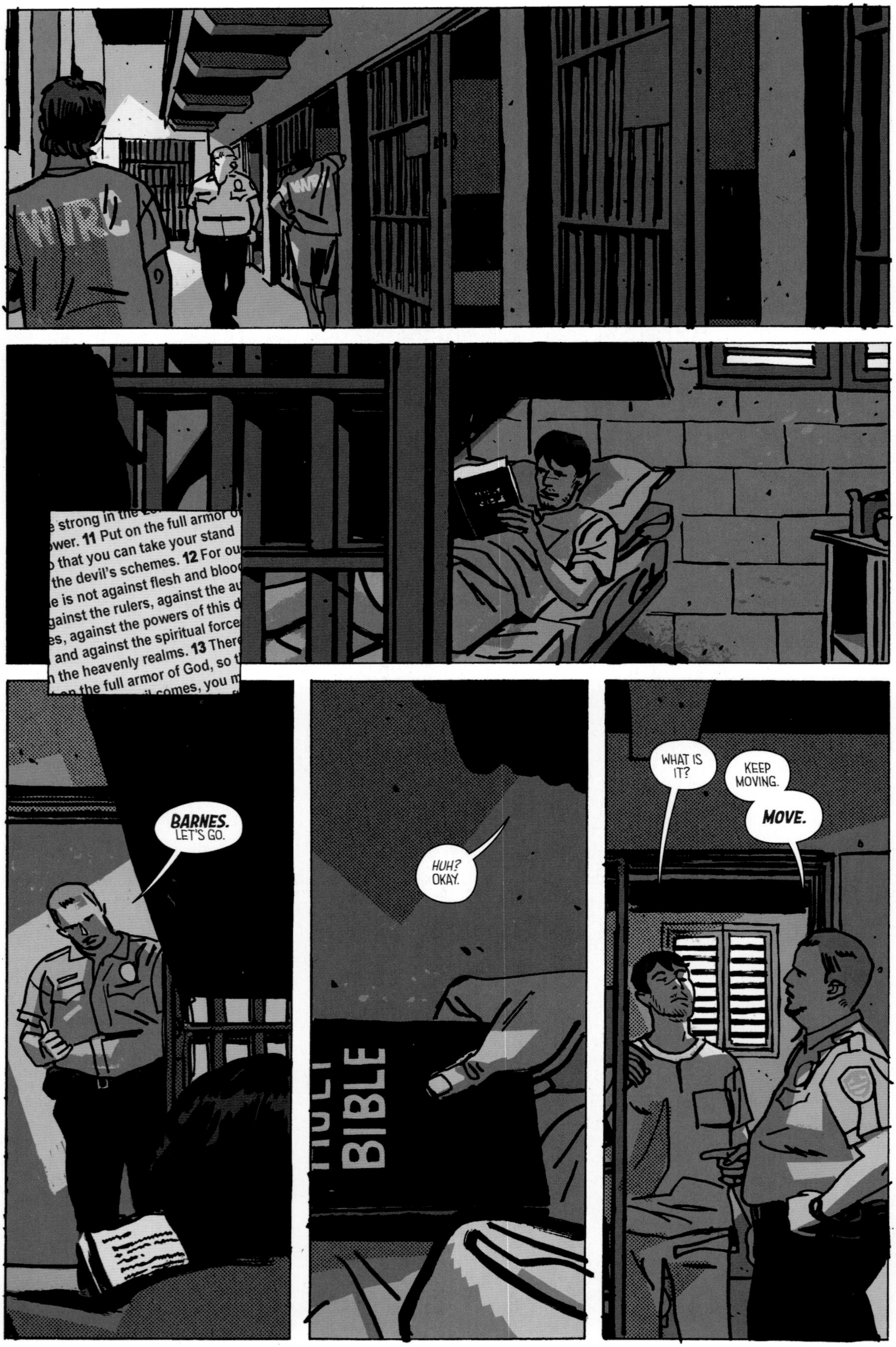
e strong in the
ower. 11 Put on the full armor o
o that you can take your stand
the devil's schemes. 12 For ou
e is not against flesh and bloo
gainst the rulers, against the au
es, against the powers of this d
and against the spiritual force
n the heavenly realms. 13 There
n the full armor of God, so th
comes, you m
BARNES. LET'S GO.
HUH? OKAY.
BIBLE
WHAT IS IT?
KEEP MOVING.
MOVE.

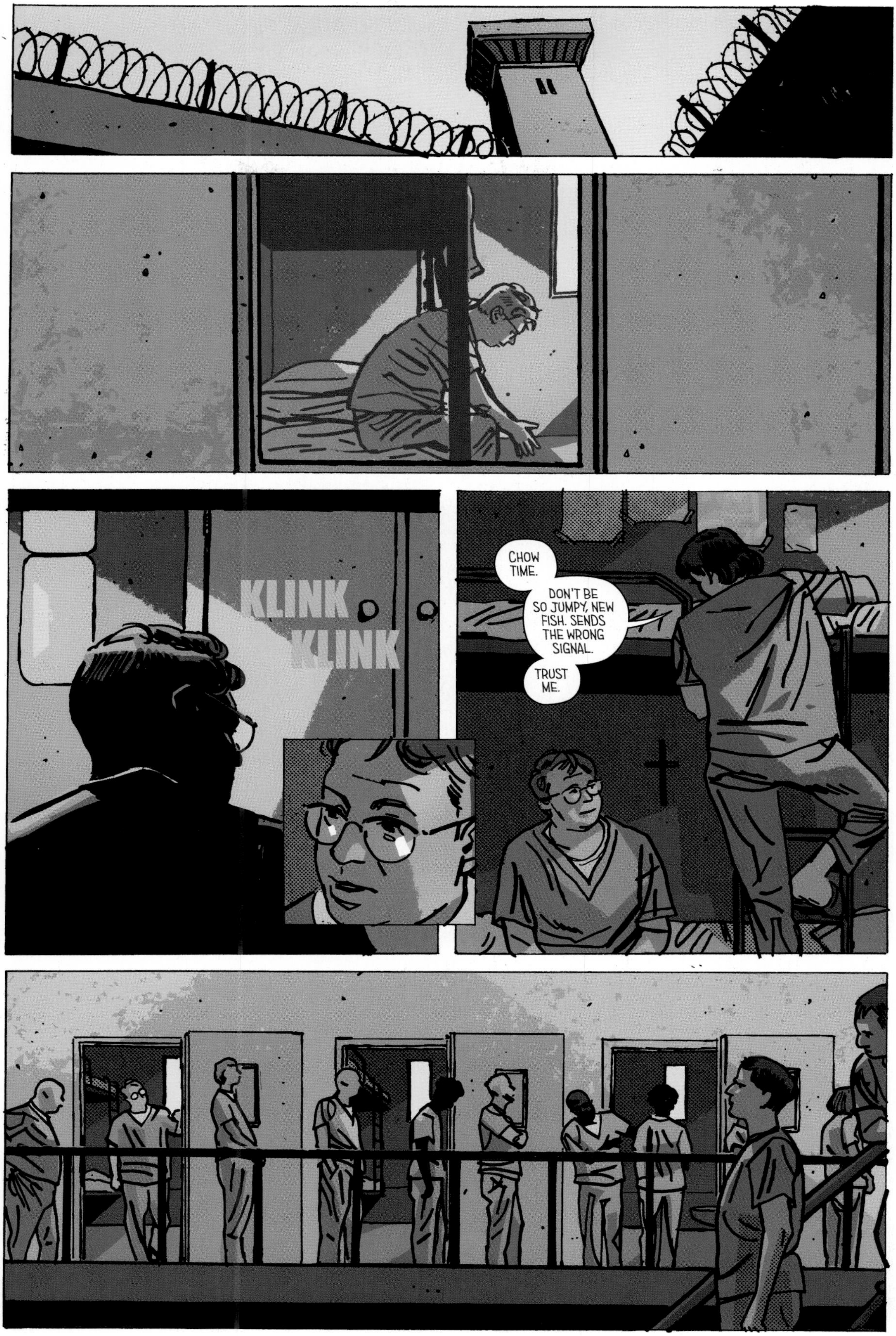
KLINK
KLINK
CHOW TIME.
DON'T BE SO JUMPY, NEW FISH. SENDS THE WRONG SIGNAL.
TRUST ME.

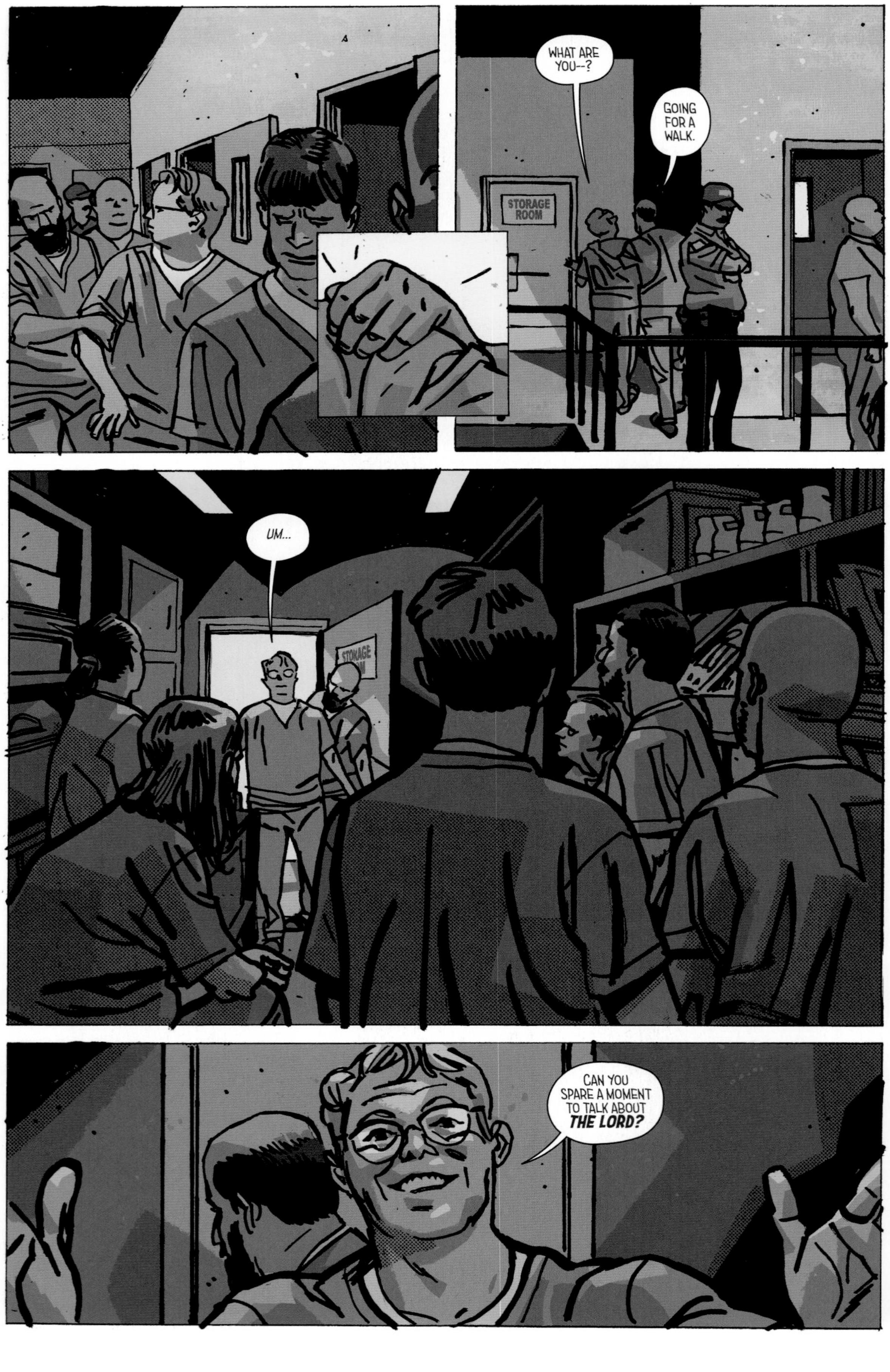
WHAT ARE YOU--?
GOING FOR A WALK.
STORAGE ROOM
UM...
CAN YOU SPARE A MOMENT TO TALK ABOUT ***THE LORD?***

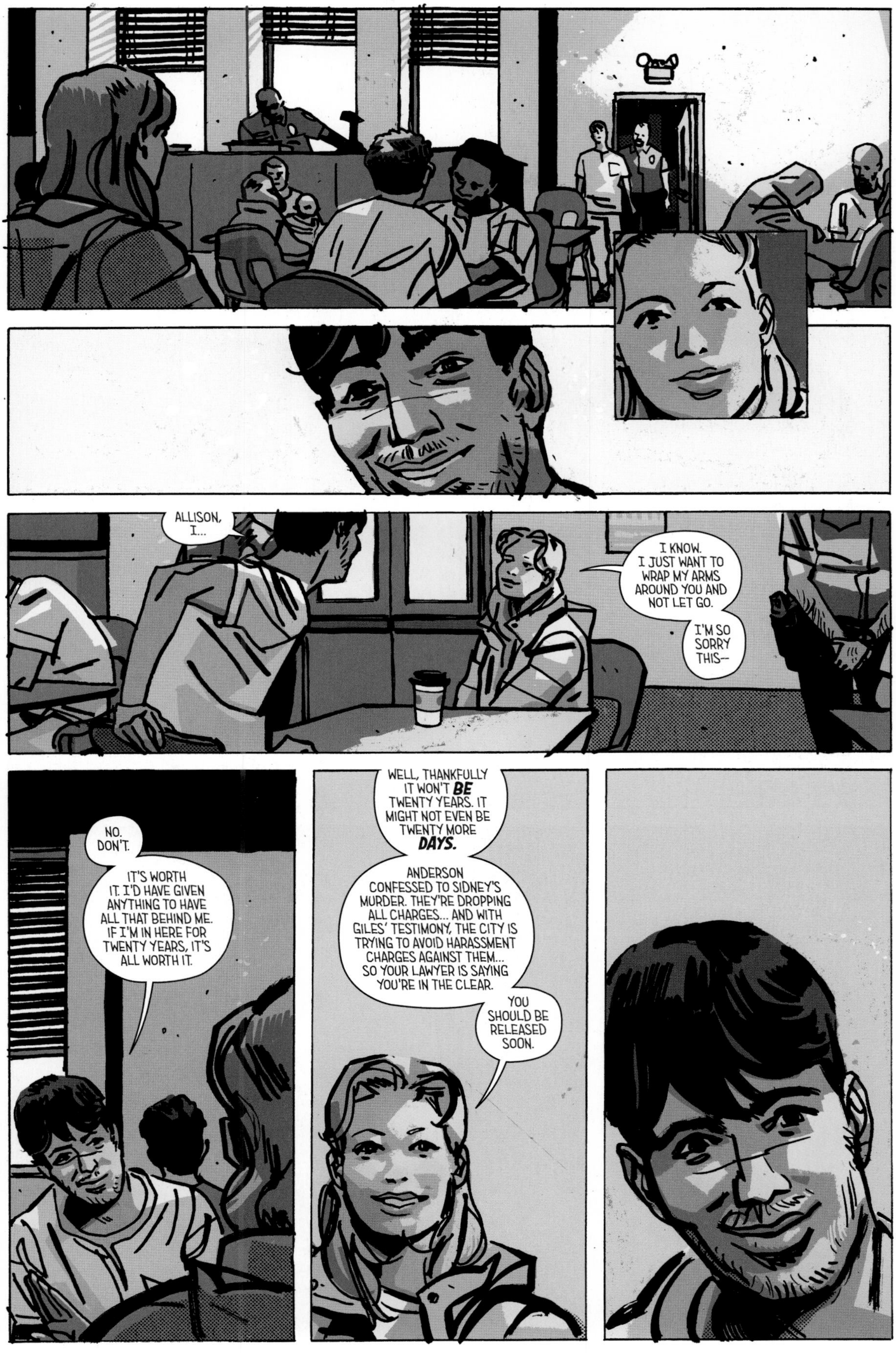
ALLISON, I...
I KNOW. I JUST WANT TO WRAP MY ARMS AROUND YOU AND NOT LET GO.
I'M SO SORRY THIS--
NO. DON'T.
IT'S WORTH IT. I'D HAVE GIVEN ANYTHING TO HAVE ALL THAT BEHIND ME. IF I'M IN HERE FOR TWENTY YEARS, IT'S ALL WORTH IT.
WELL, THANKFULLY IT WON'T **BE** TWENTY YEARS. IT MIGHT NOT EVEN BE TWENTY MORE ***DAYS.***
ANDERSON CONFESSED TO SIDNEY'S MURDER. THEY'RE DROPPING ALL CHARGES... AND WITH GILES' TESTIMONY, THE CITY IS TRYING TO AVOID HARASSMENT CHARGES AGAINST THEM... SO YOUR LAWYER IS SAYING YOU'RE IN THE CLEAR.
YOU SHOULD BE RELEASED SOON.

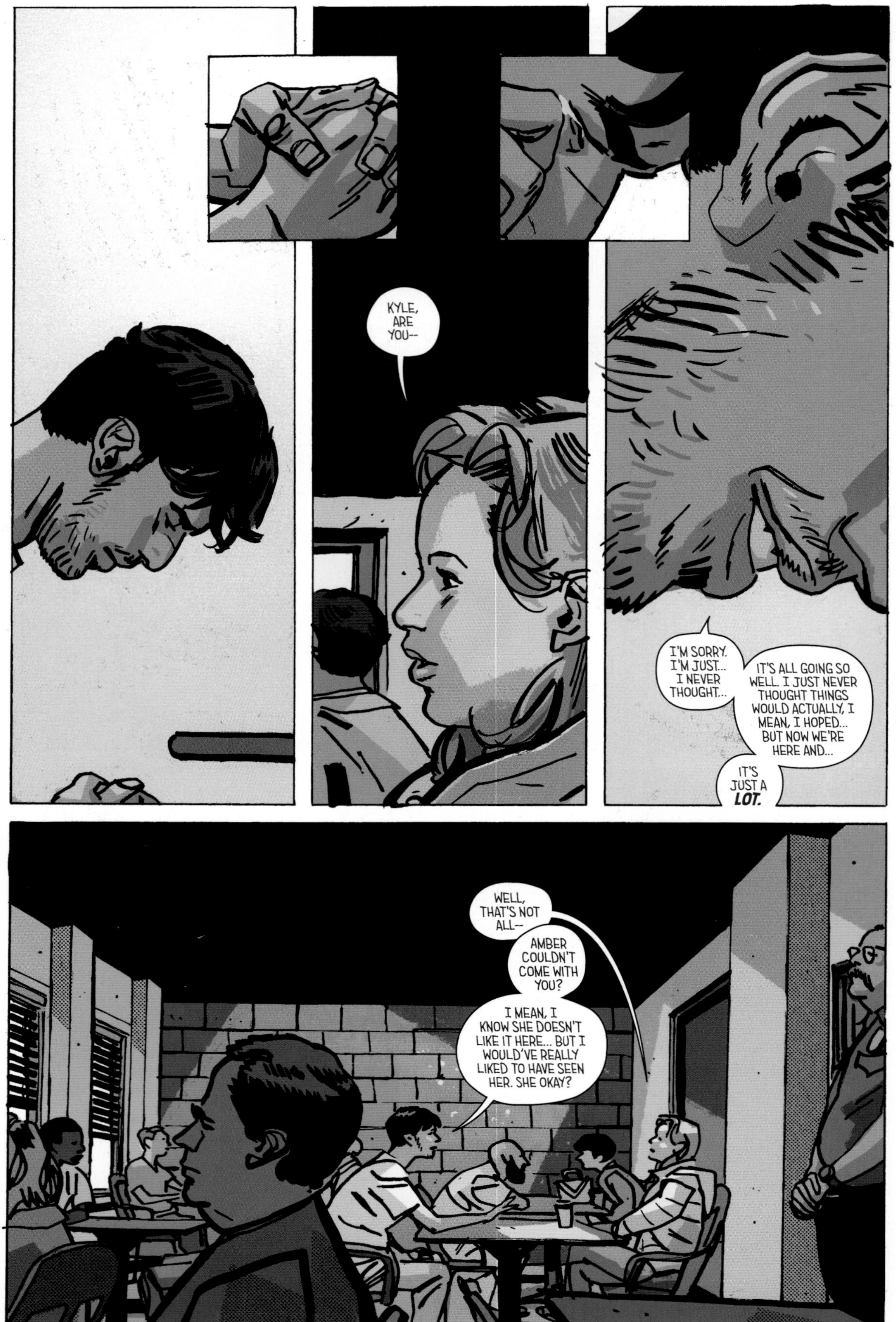
KYLE, ARE YOU--
I'M SORRY. I'M JUST... I NEVER THOUGHT...
IT'S ALL GOING SO WELL. I JUST NEVER THOUGHT THINGS WOULD ACTUALLY, I MEAN, I HOPED... BUT NOW WE'RE HERE AND...
IT'S JUST A **LOT.**
WELL, THAT'S NOT ALL--
AMBER COULDN'T COME WITH YOU?
I MEAN, I KNOW SHE DOESN'T LIKE IT HERE... BUT I WOULD'VE REALLY LIKED TO HAVE SEEN HER. SHE OKAY?

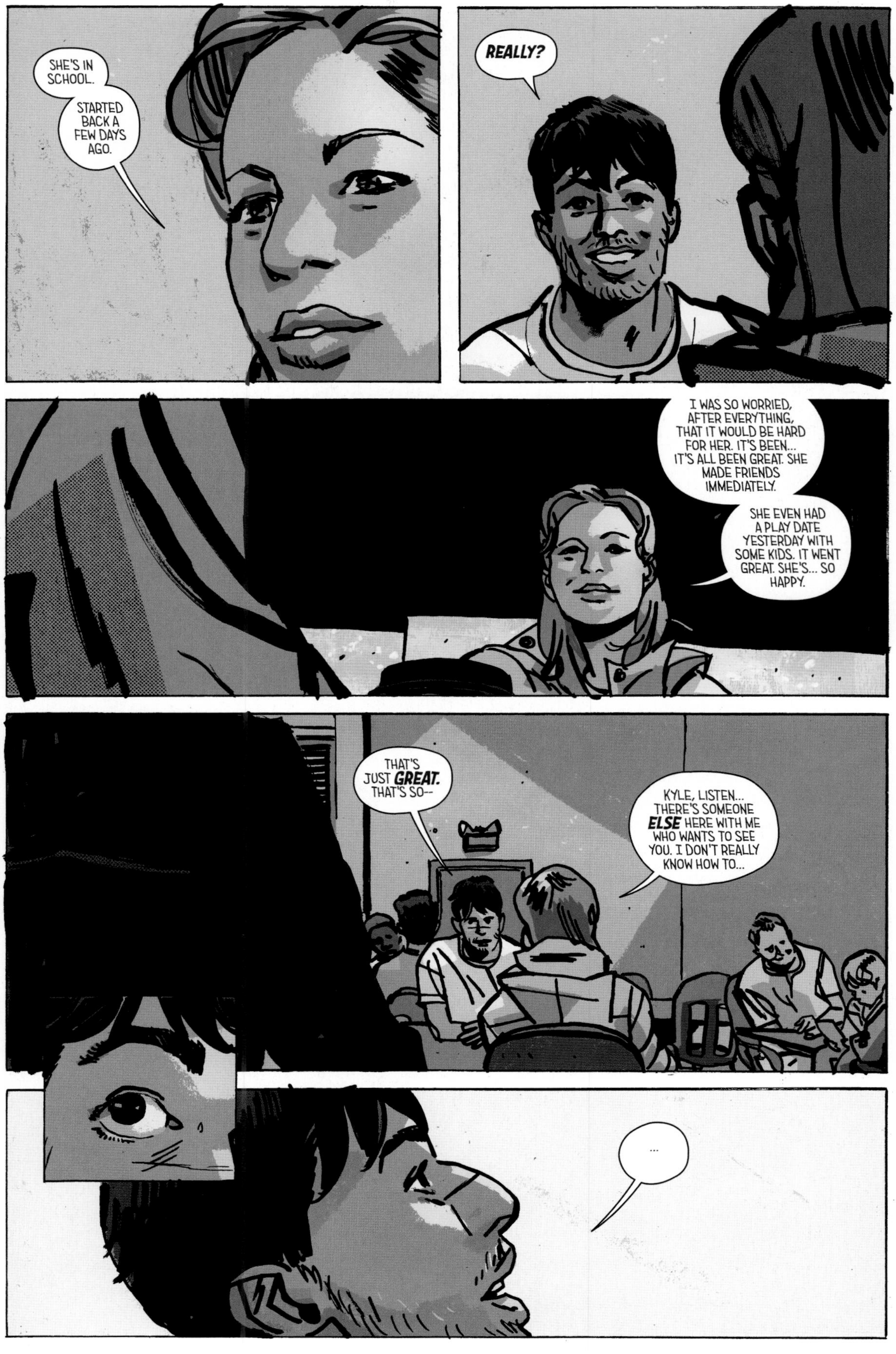
SHE'S IN SCHOOL.
STARTED BACK A FEW DAYS AGO.
REALLY?
I WAS SO WORRIED, AFTER EVERYTHING, THAT IT WOULD BE HARD FOR HER. IT'S BEEN... IT'S ALL BEEN GREAT. SHE MADE FRIENDS IMMEDIATELY.
SHE EVEN HAD A PLAY DATE YESTERDAY WITH SOME KIDS. IT WENT GREAT. SHE'S... SO HAPPY.
THAT'S JUST GREAT. THAT'S SO--
KYLE, LISTEN... THERE'S SOMEONE ELSE HERE WITH ME WHO WANTS TO SEE YOU. I DON'T REALLY KNOW HOW TO...
...

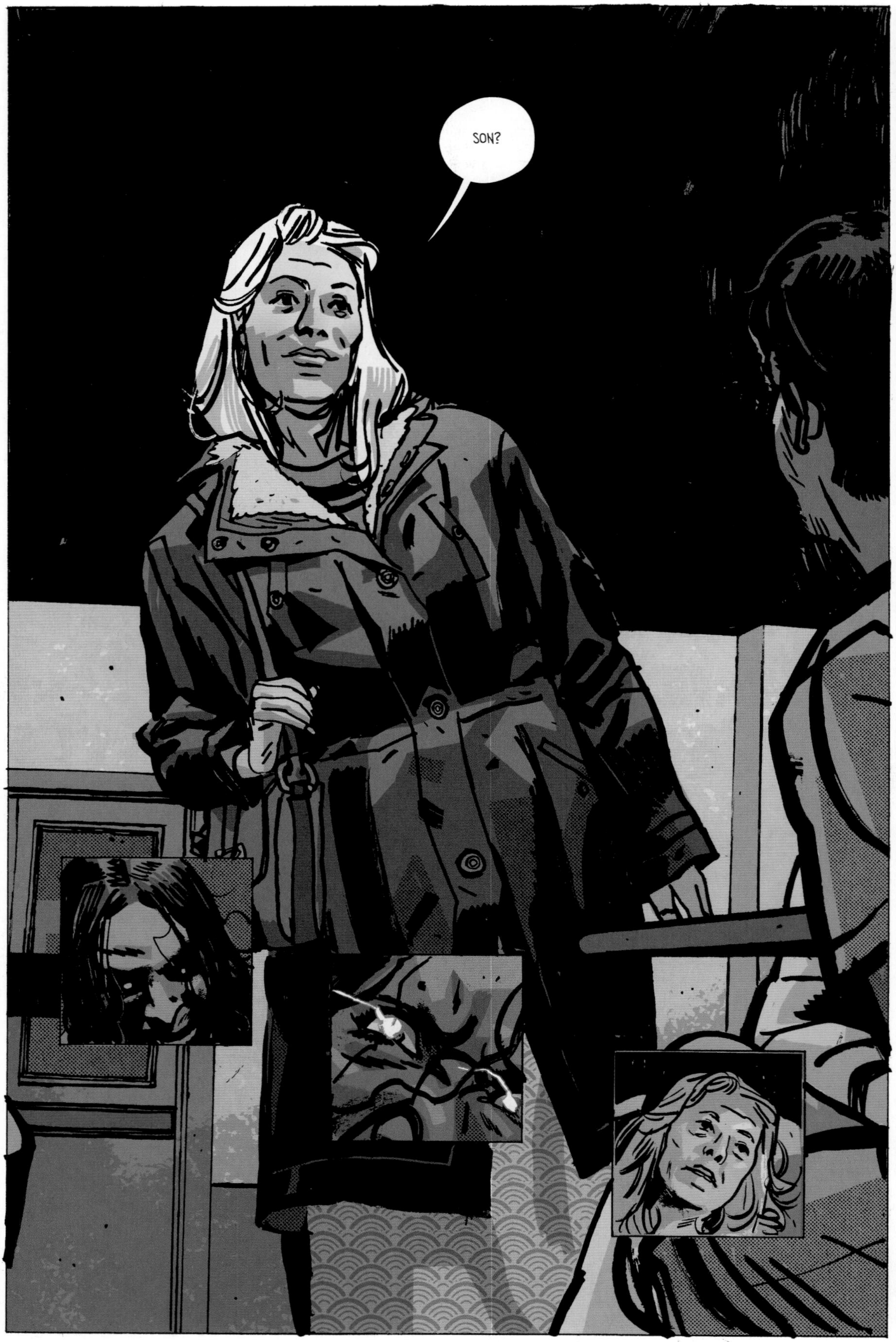
SON?

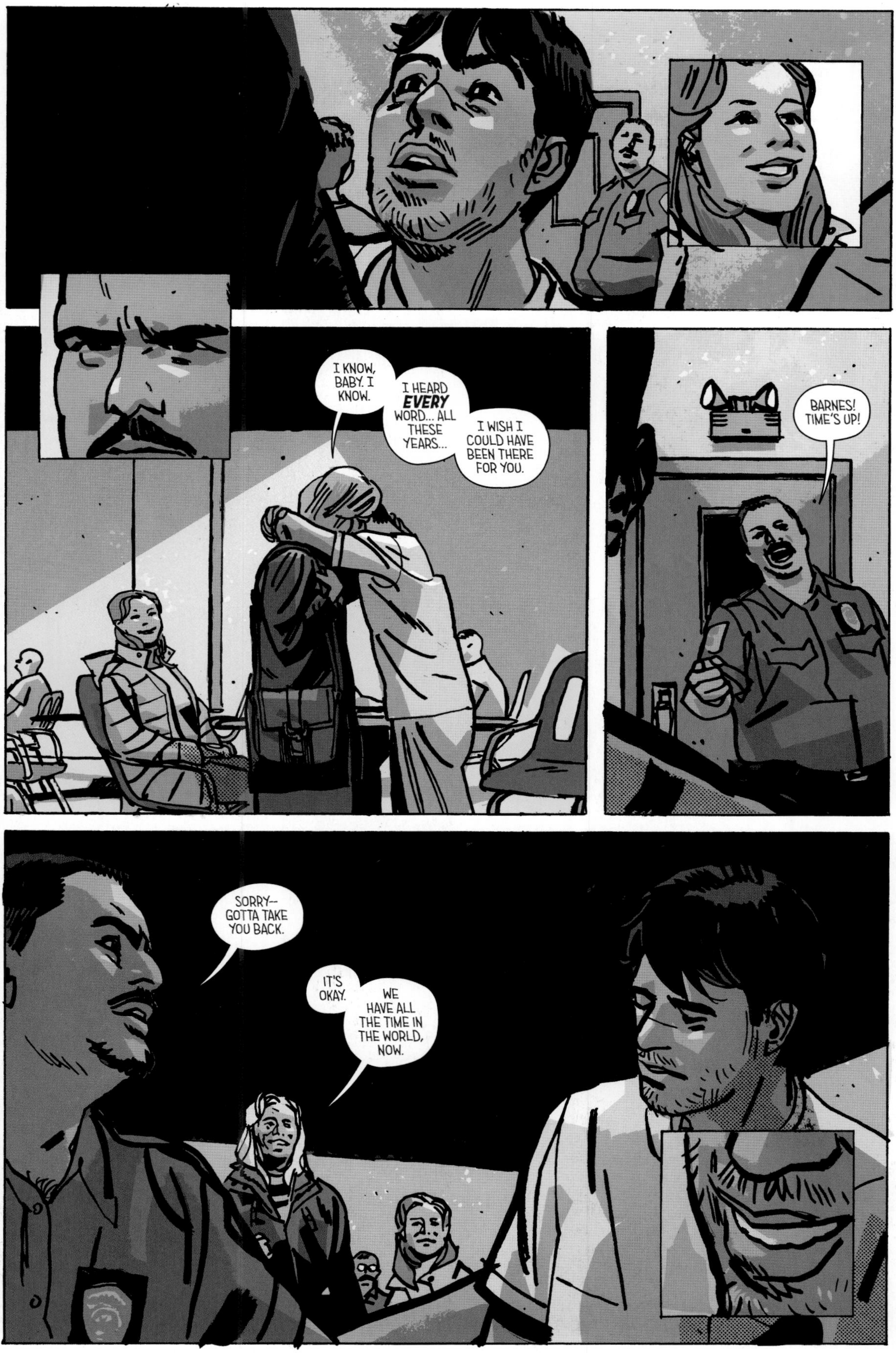
I KNOW, BABY. I KNOW.
I HEARD EVERY WORD... ALL THESE YEARS...
I WISH I COULD HAVE BEEN THERE FOR YOU.
BARNES! TIME'S UP!
SORRY-- GOTTA TAKE YOU BACK.
IT'S OKAY.
WE HAVE ALL THE TIME IN THE WORLD, NOW.

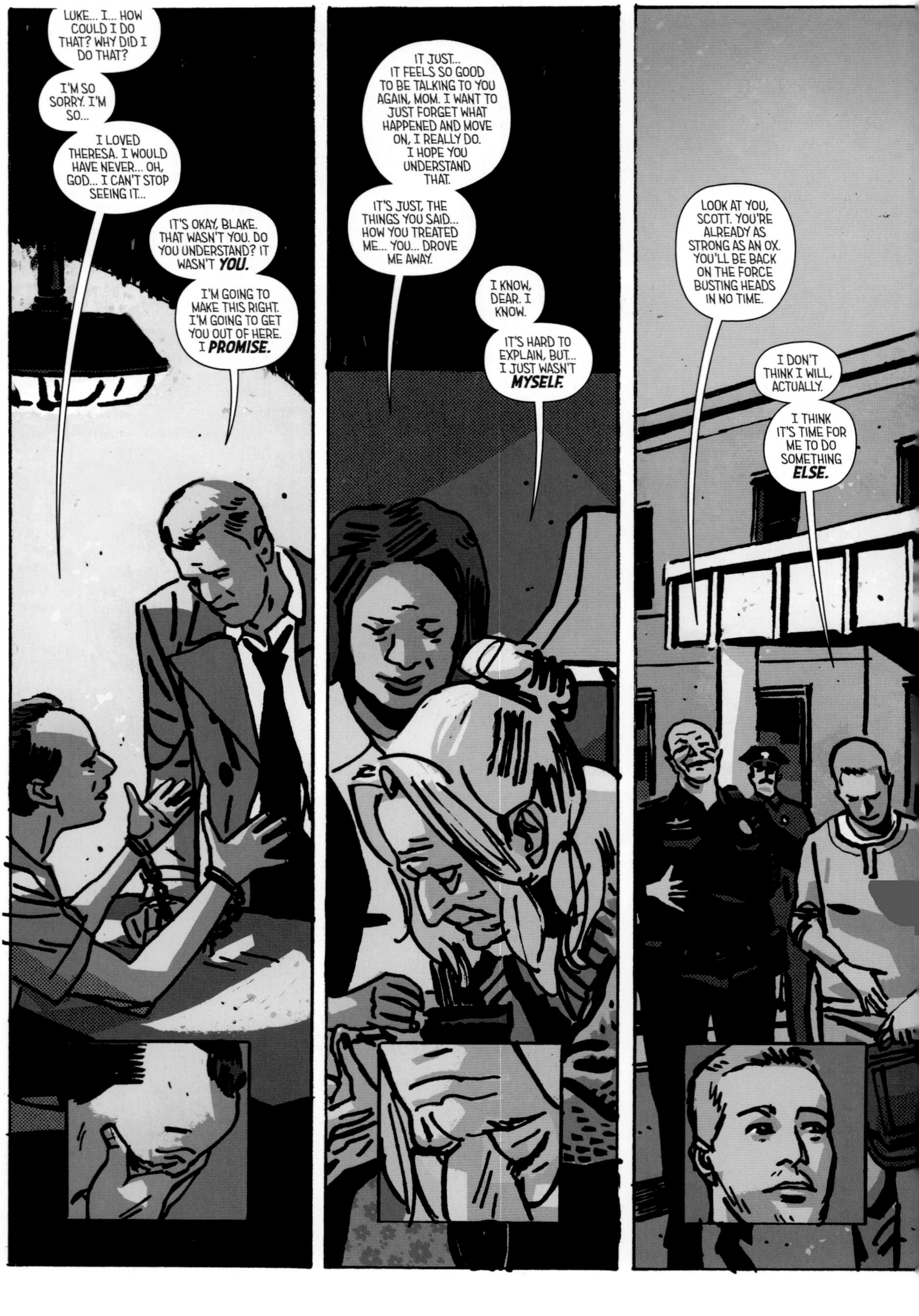

LUKE... I... HOW COULD I DO THAT? WHY DID I DO THAT?
I'M SO SORRY. I'M SO...
I LOVED THERESA. I WOULD HAVE NEVER... OH, GOD... I CAN'T STOP SEEING IT...
IT'S OKAY, BLAKE. THAT WASN'T YOU. DO YOU UNDERSTAND? IT WASN'T *YOU.*
I'M GOING TO MAKE THIS RIGHT. I'M GOING TO GET YOU OUT OF HERE. I *PROMISE.*
IT JUST... IT FEELS SO GOOD TO BE TALKING TO YOU AGAIN, MOM. I WANT TO JUST FORGET WHAT HAPPENED AND MOVE ON, I REALLY DO. I HOPE YOU UNDERSTAND THAT.
IT'S JUST, THE THINGS YOU SAID... HOW YOU TREATED ME... YOU... DROVE ME AWAY.
I KNOW, DEAR. I KNOW.
IT'S HARD TO EXPLAIN, BUT... I JUST WASN'T *MYSELF.*
LOOK AT YOU, SCOTT. YOU'RE ALREADY AS STRONG AS AN OX. YOU'LL BE BACK ON THE FORCE BUSTING HEADS IN NO TIME.
I DON'T THINK I WILL, ACTUALLY.
I THINK IT'S TIME FOR ME TO DO SOMETHING *ELSE.*

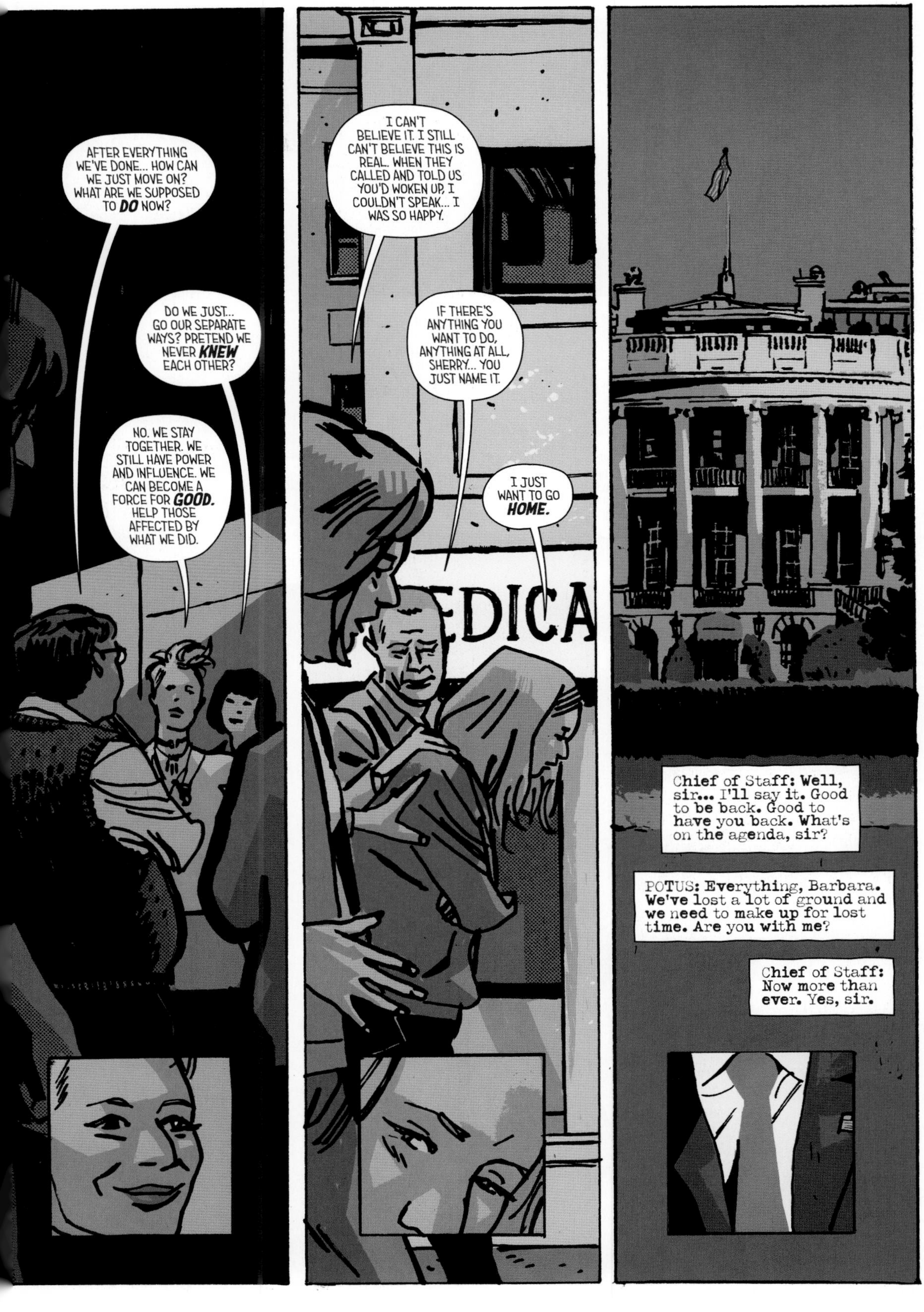
AFTER EVERYTHING WE'VE DONE... HOW CAN WE JUST MOVE ON? WHAT ARE WE SUPPOSED TO **DO** NOW?
DO WE JUST... GO OUR SEPARATE WAYS? PRETEND WE NEVER **KNEW** EACH OTHER?
NO. WE STAY TOGETHER. WE STILL HAVE POWER AND INFLUENCE. WE CAN BECOME A FORCE FOR **GOOD.** HELP THOSE AFFECTED BY WHAT WE DID.
I CAN'T BELIEVE IT. I STILL CAN'T BELIEVE THIS IS REAL. WHEN THEY CALLED AND TOLD US YOU'D WOKEN UP, I COULDN'T SPEAK... I WAS SO HAPPY.
IF THERE'S ANYTHING YOU WANT TO DO, ANYTHING AT ALL, SHERRY... YOU JUST NAME IT.
I JUST WANT TO GO **HOME.**
EDICA
Chief of Staff: Well, sir... I'll say it. Good to be back. Good to have you back. What's on the agenda, sir?
POTUS: Everything, Barbara. We've lost a lot of ground and we need to make up for lost time. Are you with me?
Chief of Staff: Now more than ever. Yes, sir.

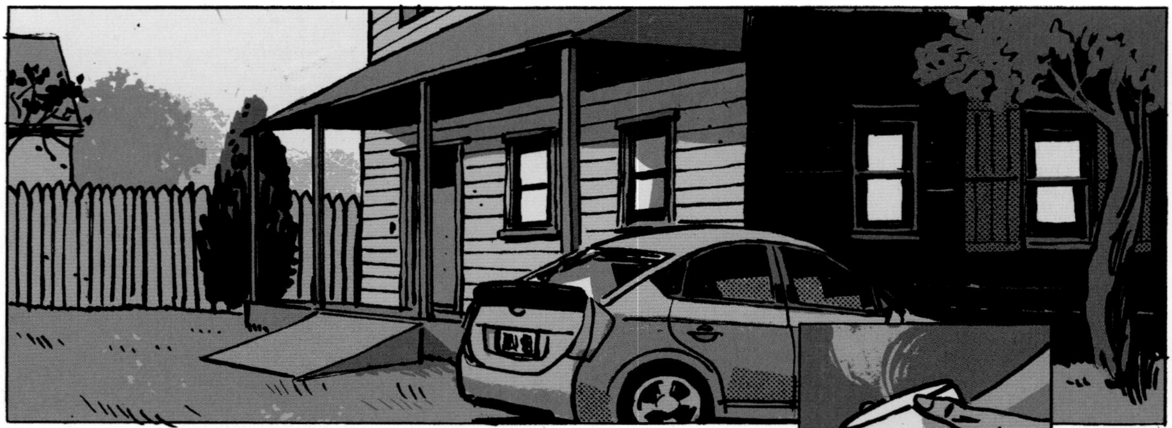
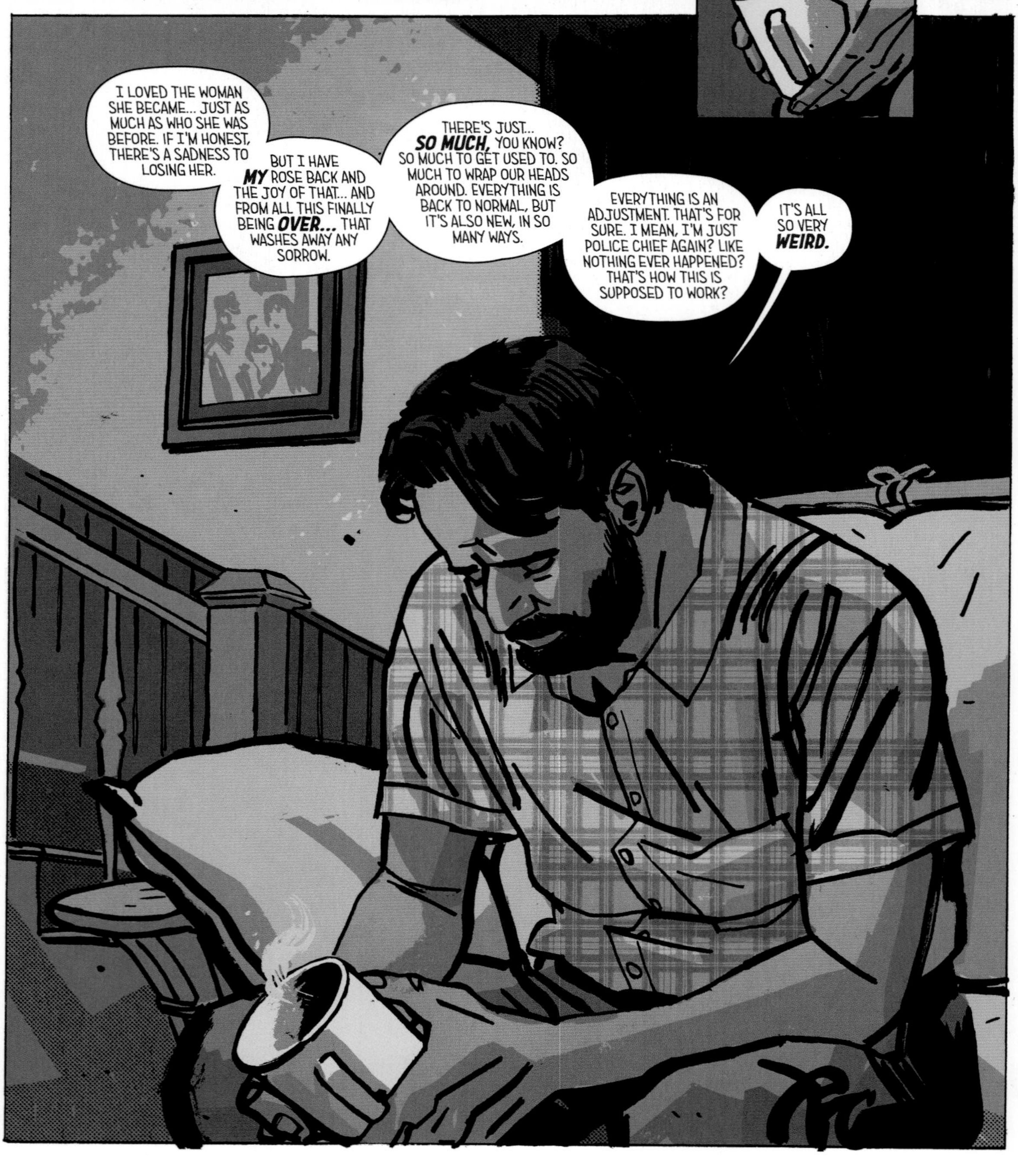
I LOVED THE WOMAN SHE BECAME... JUST AS MUCH AS WHO SHE WAS BEFORE. IF I'M HONEST, THERE'S A SADNESS TO LOSING HER.
BUT I HAVE **MY** ROSE BACK AND THE JOY OF THAT... AND FROM ALL THIS FINALLY BEING **OVER...** THAT WASHES AWAY ANY SORROW.
THERE'S JUST... **SO MUCH,** YOU KNOW? SO MUCH TO GET USED TO. SO MUCH TO WRAP OUR HEADS AROUND. EVERYTHING IS BACK TO NORMAL, BUT IT'S ALSO NEW, IN SO MANY WAYS.
EVERYTHING IS AN ADJUSTMENT. THAT'S FOR SURE. I MEAN, I'M JUST POLICE CHIEF AGAIN? LIKE NOTHING EVER HAPPENED? THAT'S HOW THIS IS SUPPOSED TO WORK?
IT'S ALL SO VERY **WEIRD.**

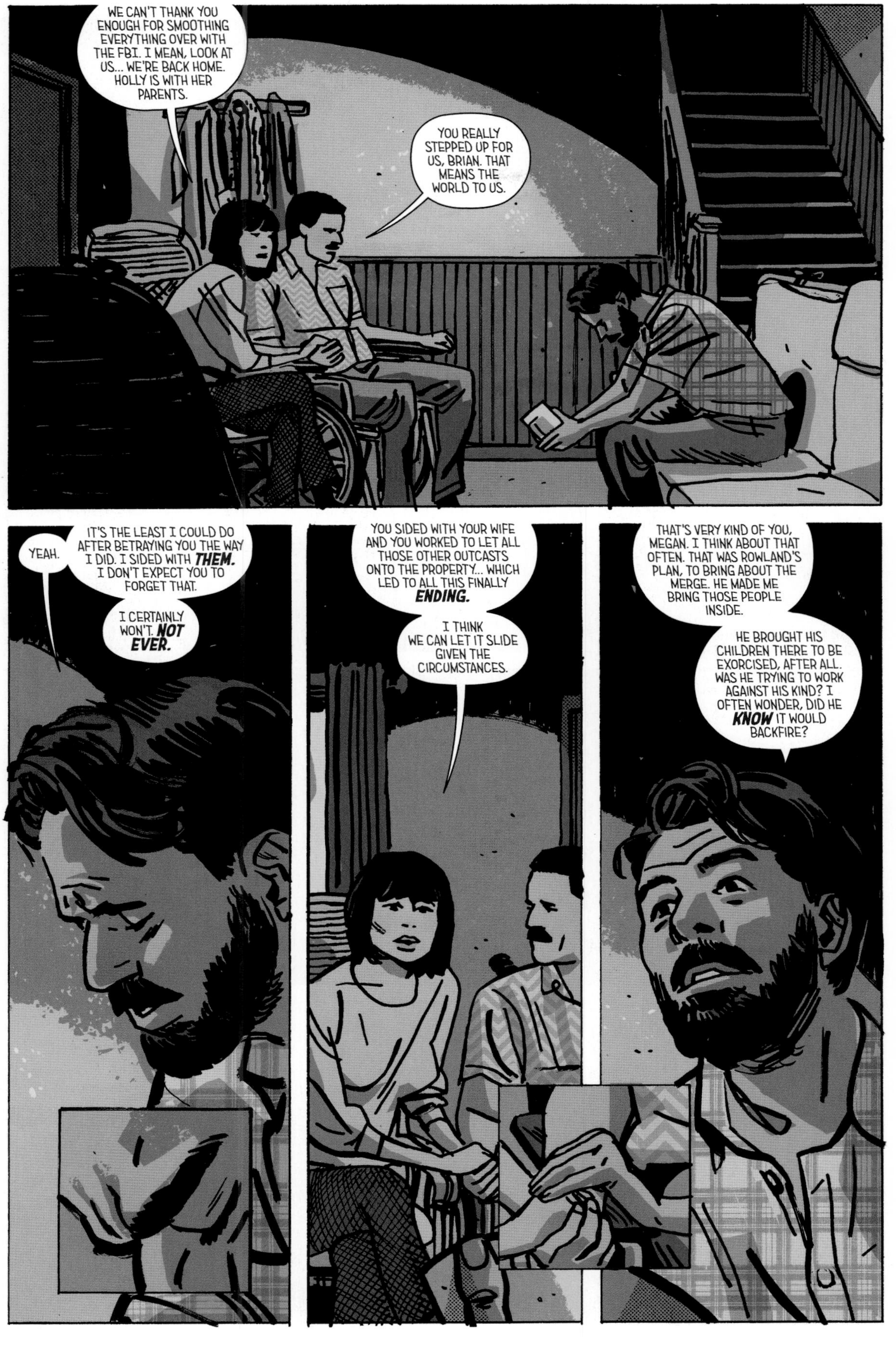
WE CAN'T THANK YOU ENOUGH FOR SMOOTHING EVERYTHING OVER WITH THE FBI. I MEAN, LOOK AT US... WE'RE BACK HOME. HOLLY IS WITH HER PARENTS.
YOU REALLY STEPPED UP FOR US, BRIAN. THAT MEANS THE WORLD TO US.
YEAH.
IT'S THE LEAST I COULD DO AFTER BETRAYING YOU THE WAY I DID. I SIDED WITH **THEM.** I DON'T EXPECT YOU TO FORGET THAT.
I CERTAINLY WON'T. **NOT EVER.**
YOU SIDED WITH YOUR WIFE AND YOU WORKED TO LET ALL THOSE OTHER OUTCASTS ONTO THE PROPERTY... WHICH LED TO ALL THIS FINALLY **ENDING.**
I THINK WE CAN LET IT SLIDE GIVEN THE CIRCUMSTANCES.
THAT'S VERY KIND OF YOU, MEGAN. I THINK ABOUT THAT OFTEN. THAT WAS ROWLAND'S PLAN, TO BRING ABOUT THE MERGE. HE MADE ME BRING THOSE PEOPLE INSIDE.
HE BROUGHT HIS CHILDREN THERE TO BE EXORCISED, AFTER ALL. WAS HE TRYING TO WORK AGAINST HIS KIND? I OFTEN WONDER, DID HE **KNOW** IT WOULD BACKFIRE?

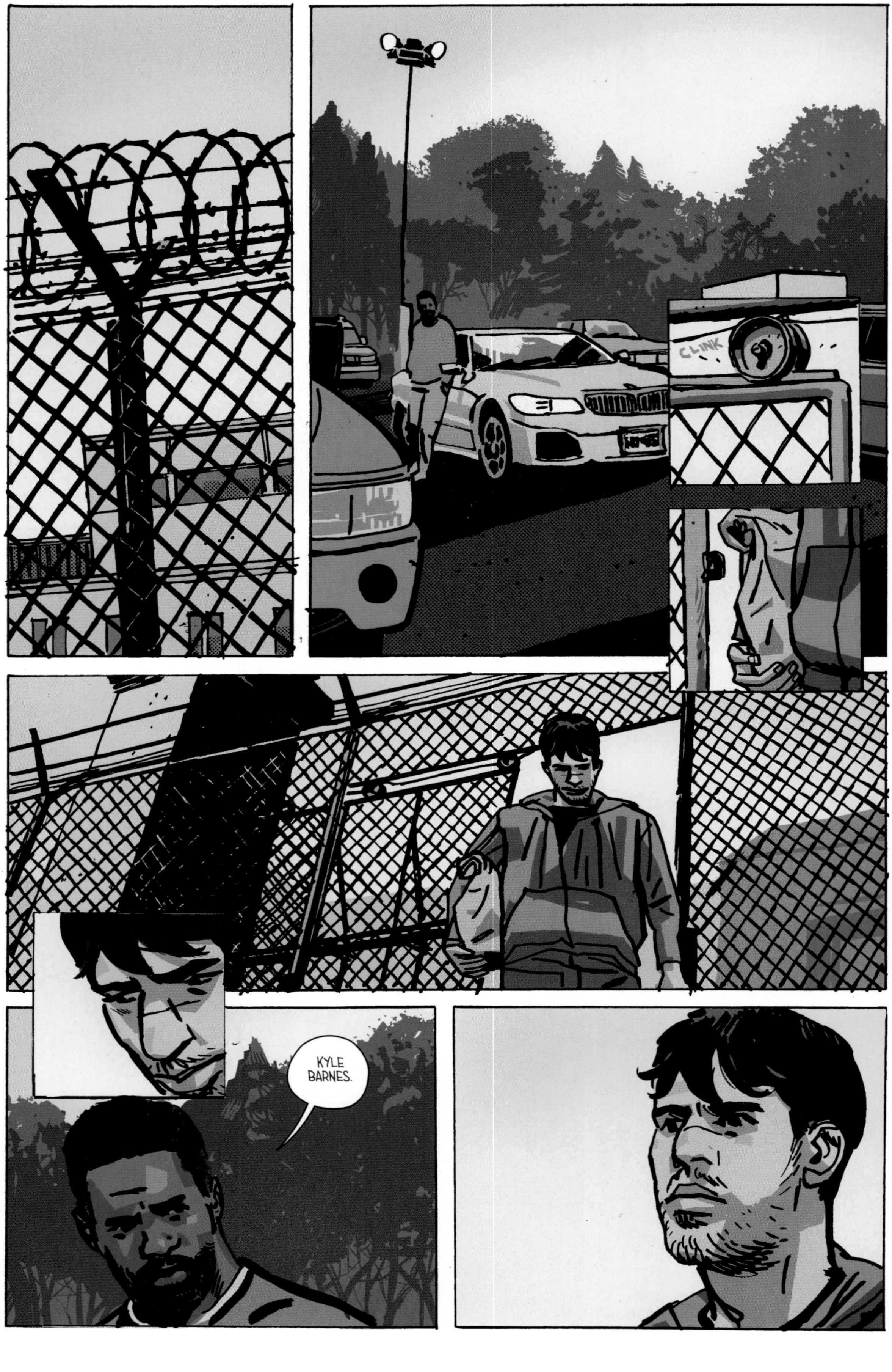

CLINK
KYLE BARNES.

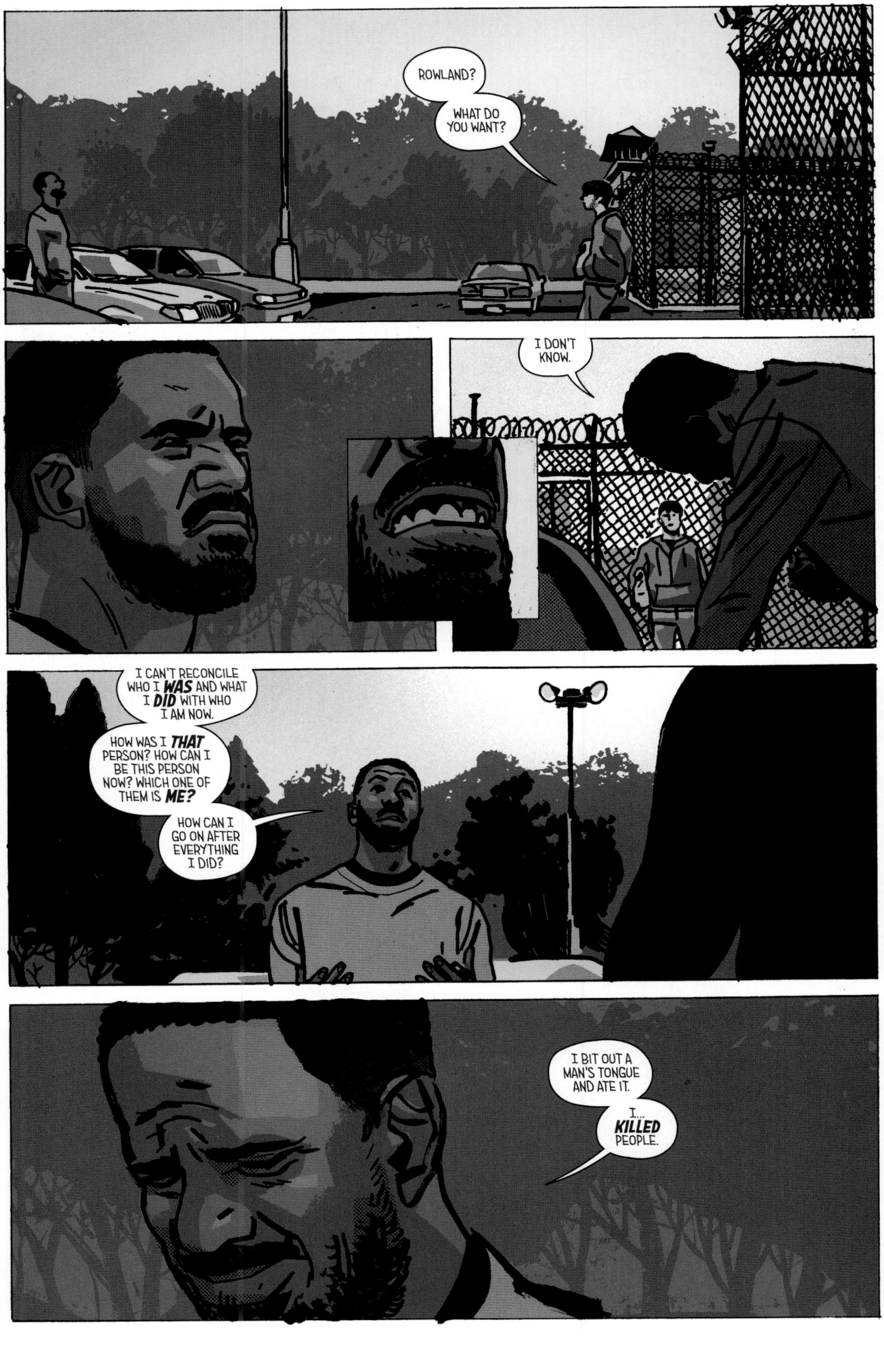
ROWLAND?
WHAT DO YOU WANT?
I DON'T KNOW.
I CAN'T RECONCILE WHO I **WAS** AND WHAT I **DID** WITH WHO I AM NOW.
HOW WAS I **THAT** PERSON? HOW CAN I BE THIS PERSON NOW? WHICH ONE OF THEM IS **ME?**
HOW CAN I GO ON AFTER EVERYTHING I DID?
I BIT OUT A MAN'S TONGUE AND ATE IT.
I... **KILLED** PEOPLE.

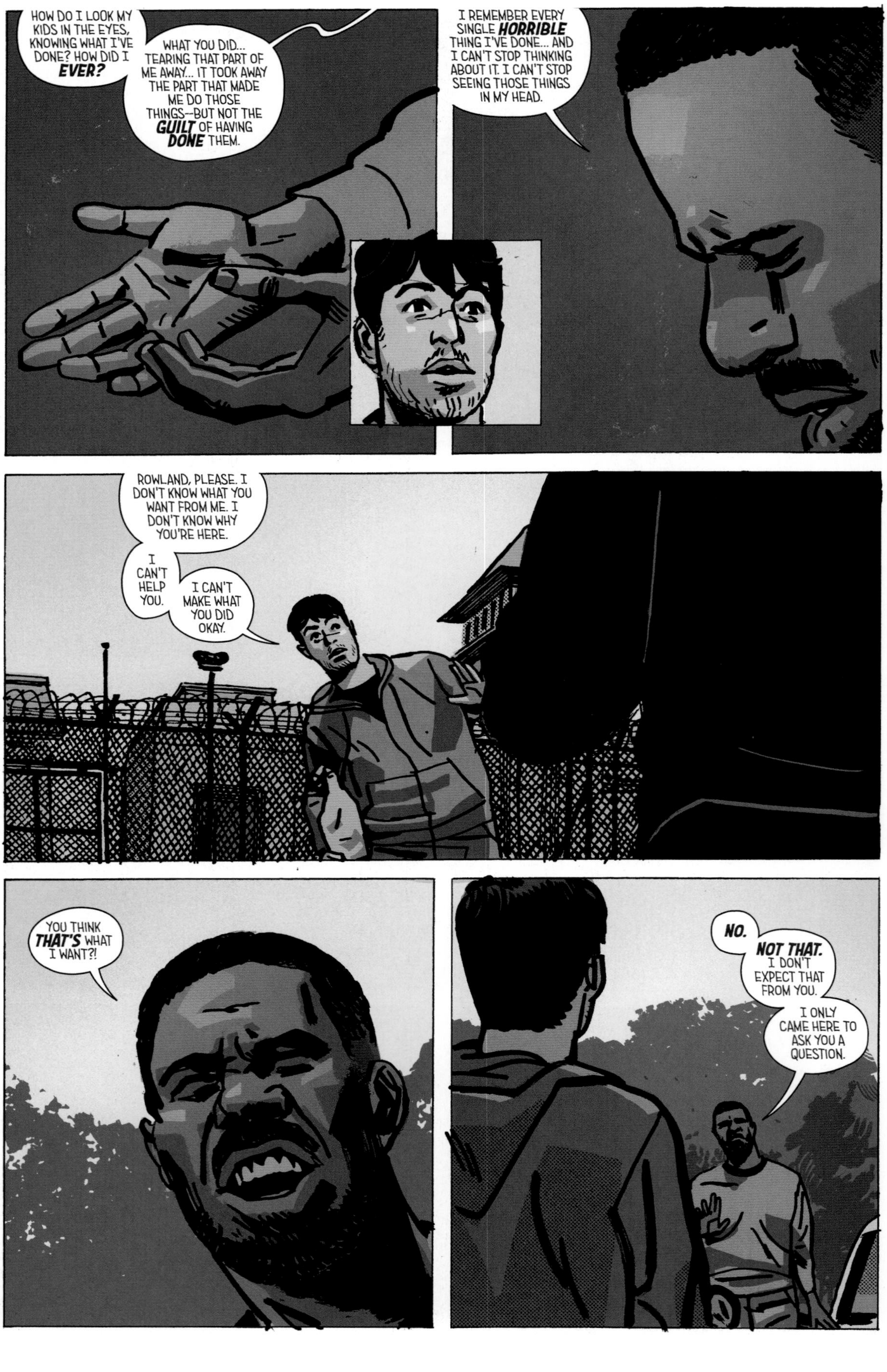
HOW DO I LOOK MY KIDS IN THE EYES, KNOWING WHAT I'VE DONE? HOW DID I **EVER?**
WHAT YOU DID... TEARING THAT PART OF ME AWAY... IT TOOK AWAY THE PART THAT MADE ME DO THOSE THINGS--BUT NOT THE **GUILT** OF HAVING **DONE** THEM.
I REMEMBER EVERY SINGLE **HORRIBLE** THING I'VE DONE... AND I CAN'T STOP THINKING ABOUT IT. I CAN'T STOP SEEING THOSE THINGS IN MY HEAD.
ROWLAND, PLEASE. I DON'T KNOW WHAT YOU WANT FROM ME. I DON'T KNOW WHY YOU'RE HERE.
I CAN'T HELP YOU.
I CAN'T MAKE WHAT YOU DID OKAY.
YOU THINK **THAT'S** WHAT I WANT?!
NO.
NOT THAT. I DON'T EXPECT THAT FROM YOU.
I ONLY CAME HERE TO ASK YOU A QUESTION.

THE WORST THING IS... I HAD YOU EXORCISE MY DAUGHTERS BECAUSE I COULDN'T BEAR THE THOUGHT OF THEM CEASING TO BE WHO THEY WERE.

I ALSO BROUGHT ALL THE OUTCASTS TOGETHER... I GAVE YOU POWER... ENOUGH TO PLAN AND REVERSE THE MERGE.

I *BETRAYED* MY SIDE.

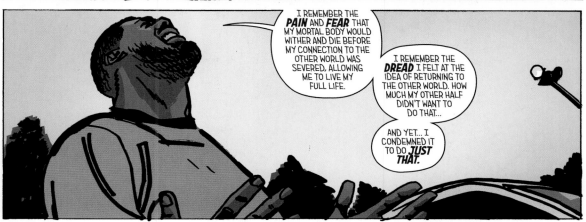

I REMEMBER THE *PAIN* AND *FEAR* THAT MY MORTAL BODY WOULD WITHER AND DIE BEFORE MY CONNECTION TO THE OTHER WORLD WAS SEVERED, ALLOWING ME TO LIVE MY FULL LIFE.

I REMEMBER THE *DREAD* I FELT AT THE IDEA OF RETURNING TO THE OTHER WORLD. HOW MUCH MY OTHER HALF DIDN'T WANT TO DO THAT...

AND YET... I CONDEMNED IT TO DO *JUST THAT.*

THEY WERE *ESCAPING* THEIR WORLD BECAUSE IT WAS *DYING.* IT WAS GOING TO TAKE THEM WITH IT. COMING HERE WAS THEIR ONLY HOPE.

WHEN YOU CLOSED THE DOOR AND CUT THEM OFF, I HAVE TO KNOW... DID THEIR WORLD COLLAPSE? ARE THEY GONE FOREVER? OR DID THEIR RETURN RESTORE STABILITY TO THEIR WORLD?

PLEASE TELL ME I DIDN'T *KILL* THEM ALL.

I... I *DON'T KNOW.*

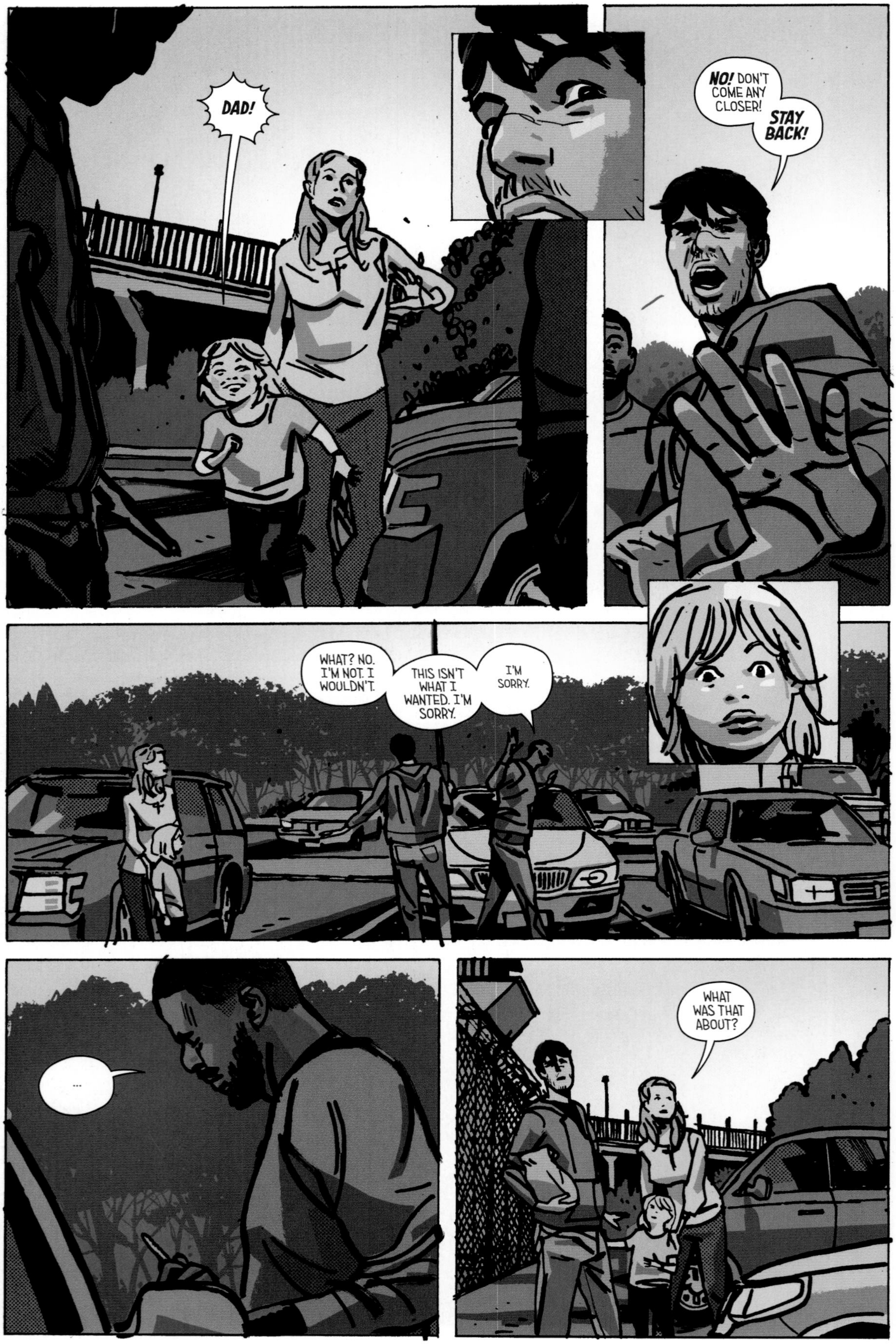
DAD!
NO! DON'T COME ANY CLOSER! STAY BACK!
WHAT? NO. I'M NOT. I WOULDN'T.
THIS ISN'T WHAT I WANTED. I'M SORRY.
I'M SORRY.
...
WHAT WAS THAT ABOUT?

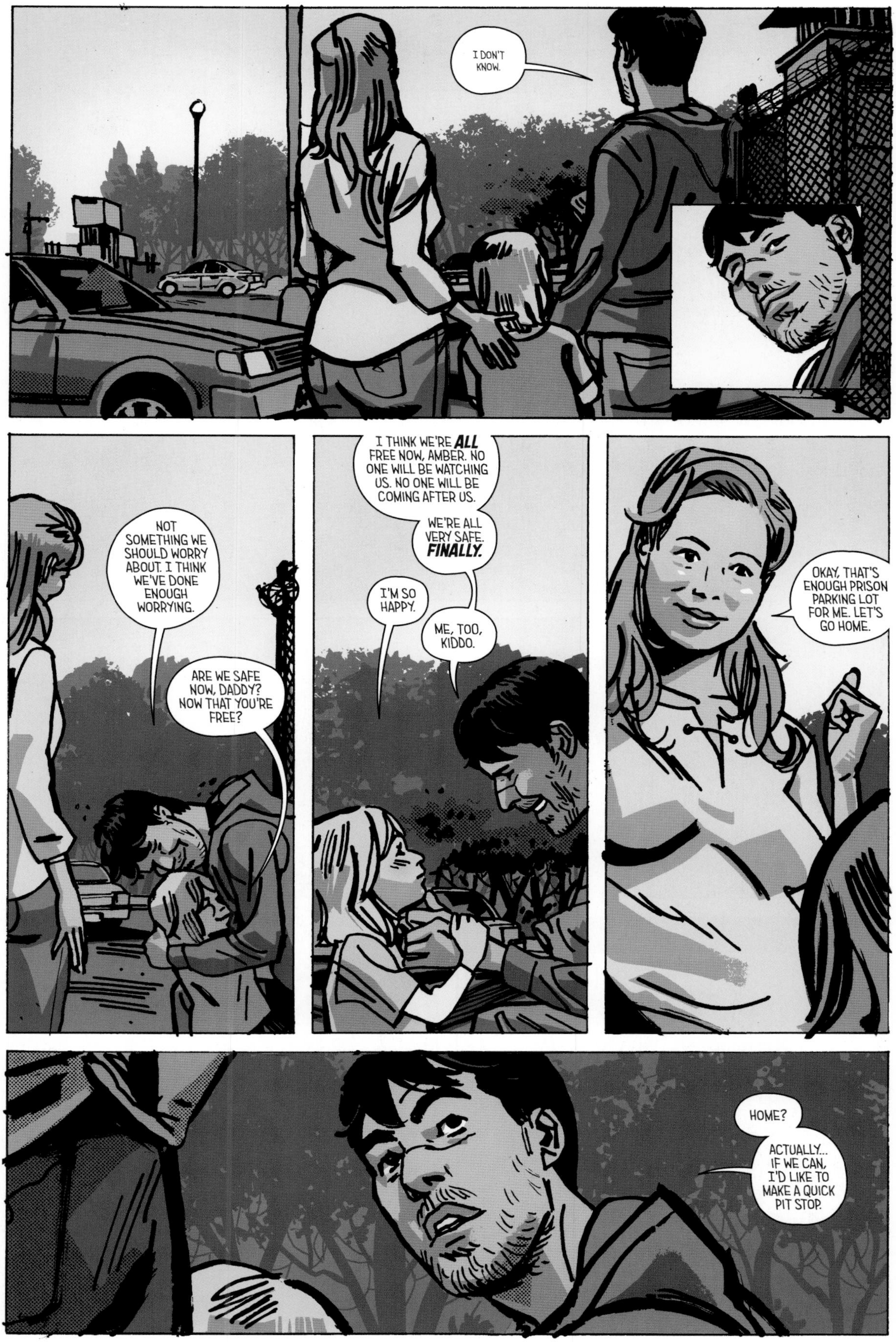

I DON'T KNOW.
NOT SOMETHING WE SHOULD WORRY ABOUT. I THINK WE'VE DONE ENOUGH WORRYING.
ARE WE SAFE NOW, DADDY? NOW THAT YOU'RE FREE?
I THINK WE'RE ALL FREE NOW, AMBER. NO ONE WILL BE WATCHING US. NO ONE WILL BE COMING AFTER US.
WE'RE ALL VERY SAFE. FINALLY.
I'M SO HAPPY.
ME, TOO, KIDDO.
OKAY, THAT'S ENOUGH PRISON PARKING LOT FOR ME. LET'S GO HOME.
HOME?
ACTUALLY... IF WE CAN, I'D LIKE TO MAKE A QUICK PIT STOP.

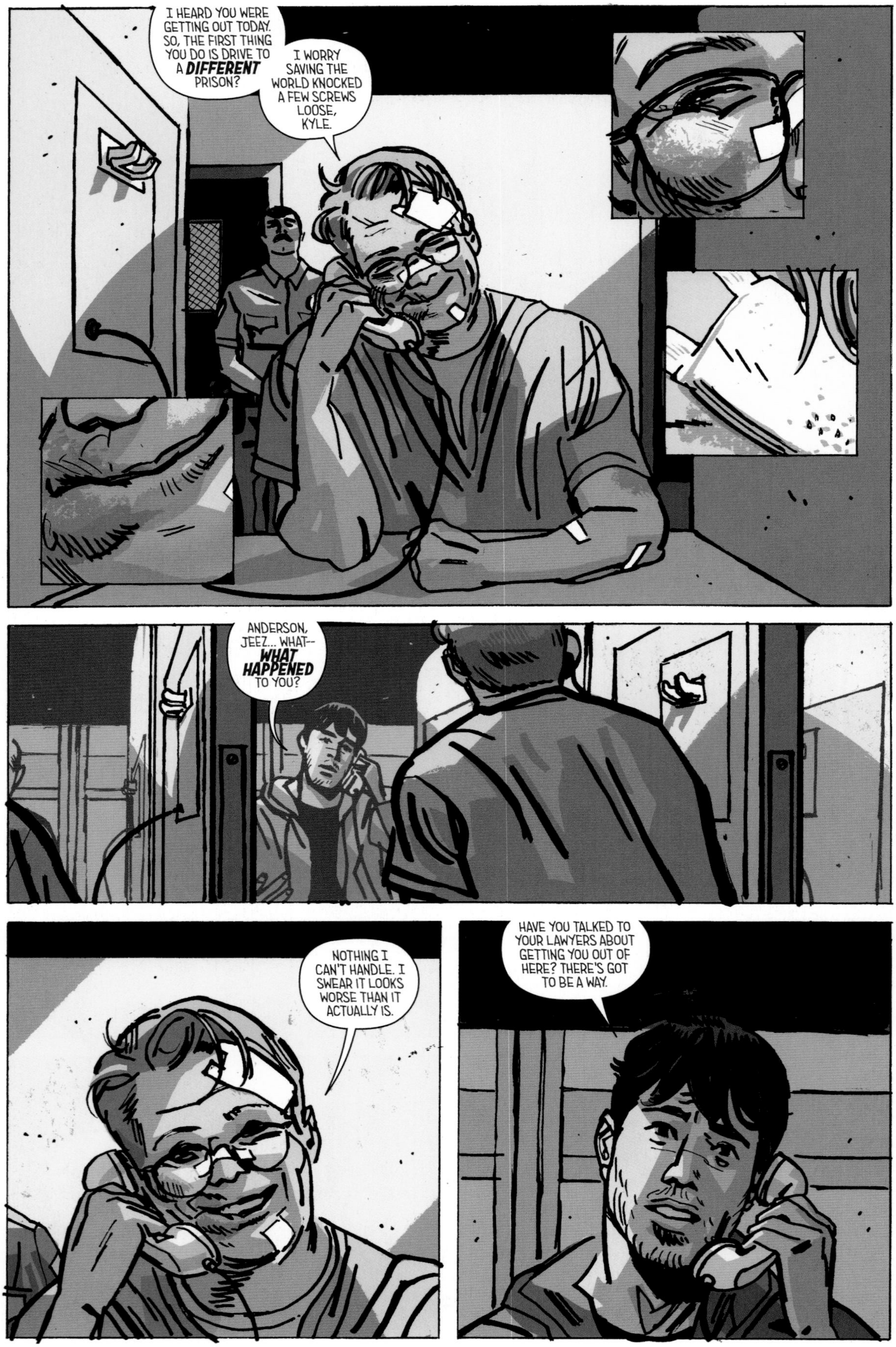
I HEARD YOU WERE GETTING OUT TODAY. SO, THE FIRST THING YOU DO IS DRIVE TO A ***DIFFERENT*** PRISON?
I WORRY SAVING THE WORLD KNOCKED A FEW SCREWS LOOSE, KYLE.
ANDERSON, JEEZ... WHAT-- ***WHAT HAPPENED*** TO YOU?
NOTHING I CAN'T HANDLE. I SWEAR IT LOOKS WORSE THAN IT ACTUALLY IS.
HAVE YOU TALKED TO YOUR LAWYERS ABOUT GETTING YOU OUT OF HERE? THERE'S GOT TO BE A WAY.

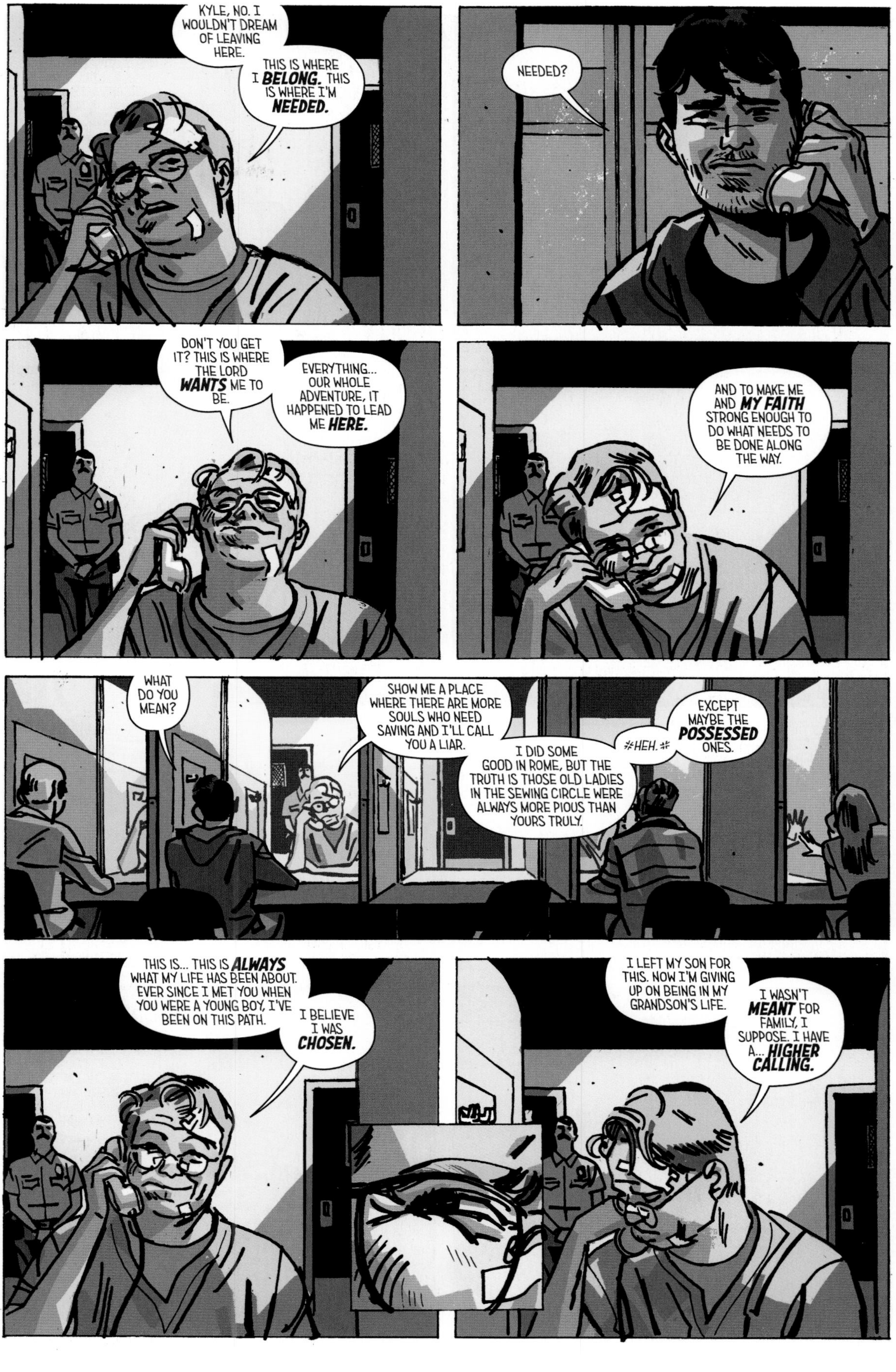

KYLE, NO. I WOULDN'T DREAM OF LEAVING HERE.
THIS IS WHERE I BELONG. THIS IS WHERE I'M NEEDED.
NEEDED?
DON'T YOU GET IT? THIS IS WHERE THE LORD WANTS ME TO BE.
EVERYTHING... OUR WHOLE ADVENTURE, IT HAPPENED TO LEAD ME HERE.
AND TO MAKE ME AND MY FAITH STRONG ENOUGH TO DO WHAT NEEDS TO BE DONE ALONG THE WAY.
WHAT DO YOU MEAN?
SHOW ME A PLACE WHERE THERE ARE MORE SOULS WHO NEED SAVING AND I'LL CALL YOU A LIAR.
I DID SOME GOOD IN ROME, BUT THE TRUTH IS THOSE OLD LADIES IN THE SEWING CIRCLE WERE ALWAYS MORE PIOUS THAN YOURS TRULY.
#HEH.#
EXCEPT MAYBE THE POSSESSED ONES.
THIS IS... THIS IS ALWAYS WHAT MY LIFE HAS BEEN ABOUT. EVER SINCE I MET YOU WHEN YOU WERE A YOUNG BOY, I'VE BEEN ON THIS PATH.
I BELIEVE I WAS CHOSEN.
I LEFT MY SON FOR THIS. NOW I'M GIVING UP ON BEING IN MY GRANDSON'S LIFE.
I WASN'T MEANT FOR FAMILY, I SUPPOSE. I HAVE A... HIGHER CALLING.

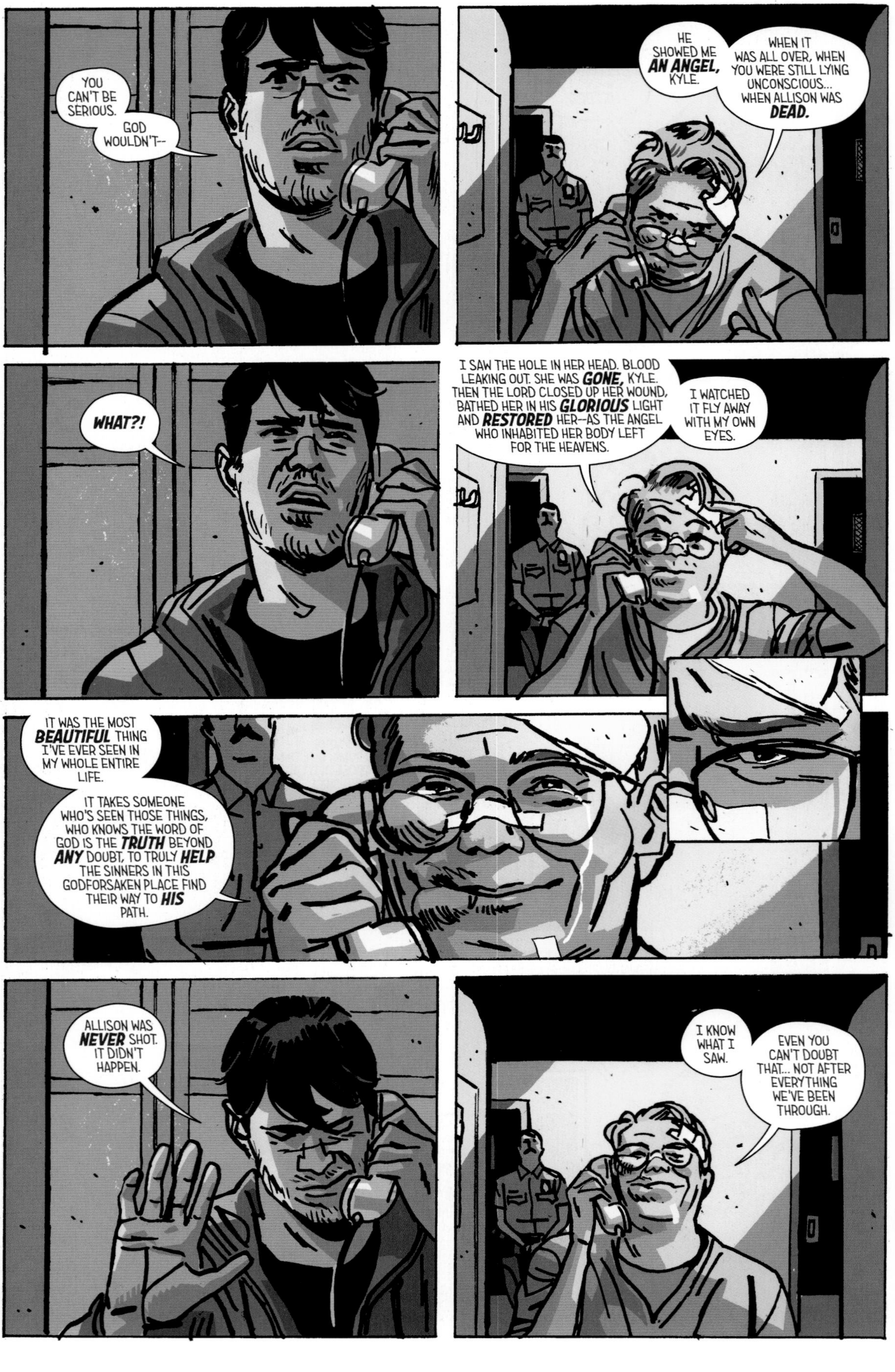

YOU CAN'T BE SERIOUS.
GOD WOULDN'T--
HE SHOWED ME AN ANGEL, KYLE.
WHEN IT WAS ALL OVER, WHEN YOU WERE STILL LYING UNCONSCIOUS... WHEN ALLISON WAS DEAD.
WHAT?!
I SAW THE HOLE IN HER HEAD. BLOOD LEAKING OUT. SHE WAS GONE, KYLE. THEN THE LORD CLOSED UP HER WOUND, BATHED HER IN HIS GLORIOUS LIGHT AND RESTORED HER--AS THE ANGEL WHO INHABITED HER BODY LEFT FOR THE HEAVENS.
I WATCHED IT FLY AWAY WITH MY OWN EYES.
IT WAS THE MOST BEAUTIFUL THING I'VE EVER SEEN IN MY WHOLE ENTIRE LIFE.
IT TAKES SOMEONE WHO'S SEEN THOSE THINGS, WHO KNOWS THE WORD OF GOD IS THE TRUTH BEYOND ANY DOUBT, TO TRULY HELP THE SINNERS IN THIS GODFORSAKEN PLACE FIND THEIR WAY TO HIS PATH.
ALLISON WAS NEVER SHOT. IT DIDN'T HAPPEN.
I KNOW WHAT I SAW.
EVEN YOU CAN'T DOUBT THAT... NOT AFTER EVERYTHING WE'VE BEEN THROUGH.

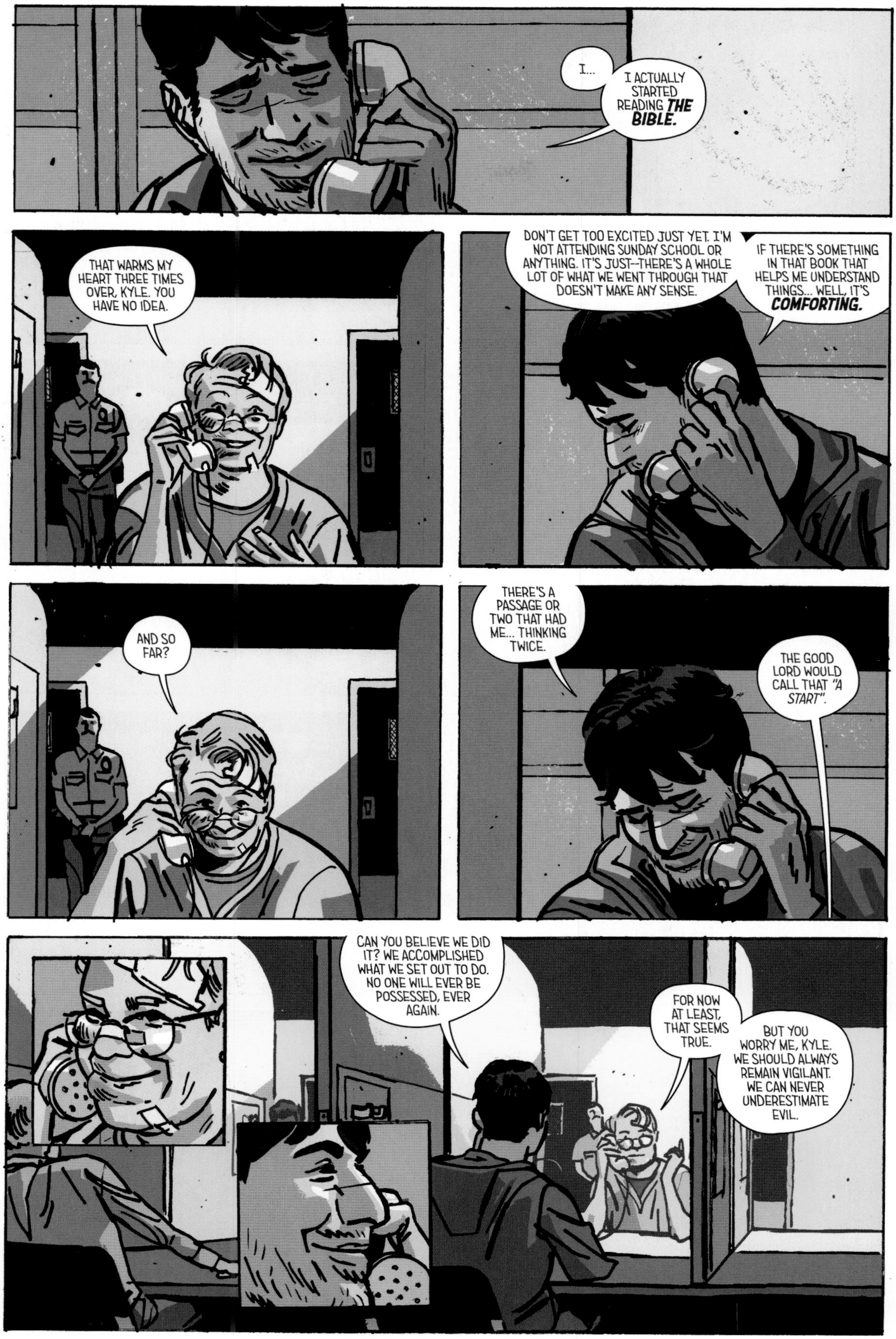
I...
I ACTUALLY STARTED READING ***THE BIBLE.***
THAT WARMS MY HEART THREE TIMES OVER, KYLE. YOU HAVE NO IDEA.
DON'T GET TOO EXCITED JUST YET. I'M NOT ATTENDING SUNDAY SCHOOL OR ANYTHING. IT'S JUST--THERE'S A WHOLE LOT OF WHAT WE WENT THROUGH THAT DOESN'T MAKE ANY SENSE.
IF THERE'S SOMETHING IN THAT BOOK THAT HELPS ME UNDERSTAND THINGS... WELL, IT'S ***COMFORTING.***
AND SO FAR?
THERE'S A PASSAGE OR TWO THAT HAD ME... THINKING TWICE.
THE GOOD LORD WOULD CALL THAT *"A START"*.
CAN YOU BELIEVE WE DID IT? WE ACCOMPLISHED WHAT WE SET OUT TO DO. NO ONE WILL EVER BE POSSESSED, EVER AGAIN.
FOR NOW AT LEAST, THAT SEEMS TRUE.
BUT YOU WORRY ME, KYLE. WE SHOULD ALWAYS REMAIN VIGILANT. WE CAN NEVER UNDERESTIMATE EVIL.

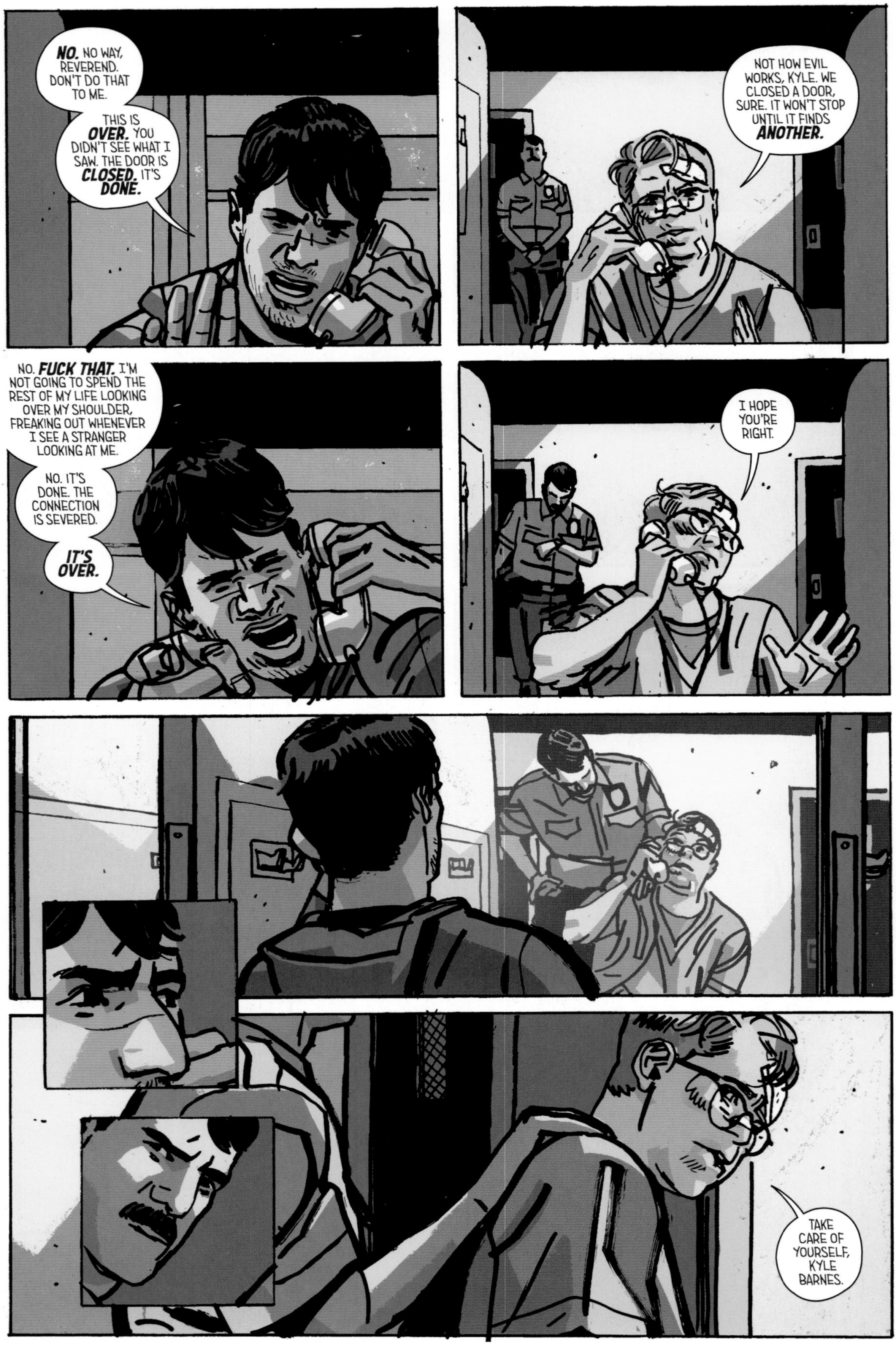
NO. NO WAY, REVEREND. DON'T DO THAT TO ME.
THIS IS OVER. YOU DIDN'T SEE WHAT I SAW. THE DOOR IS CLOSED. IT'S DONE.
NOT HOW EVIL WORKS, KYLE. WE CLOSED A DOOR, SURE. IT WON'T STOP UNTIL IT FINDS ANOTHER.
NO. FUCK THAT. I'M NOT GOING TO SPEND THE REST OF MY LIFE LOOKING OVER MY SHOULDER, FREAKING OUT WHENEVER I SEE A STRANGER LOOKING AT ME.
NO. IT'S DONE. THE CONNECTION IS SEVERED.
IT'S OVER.
I HOPE YOU'RE RIGHT.
TAKE CARE OF YOURSELF, KYLE BARNES.

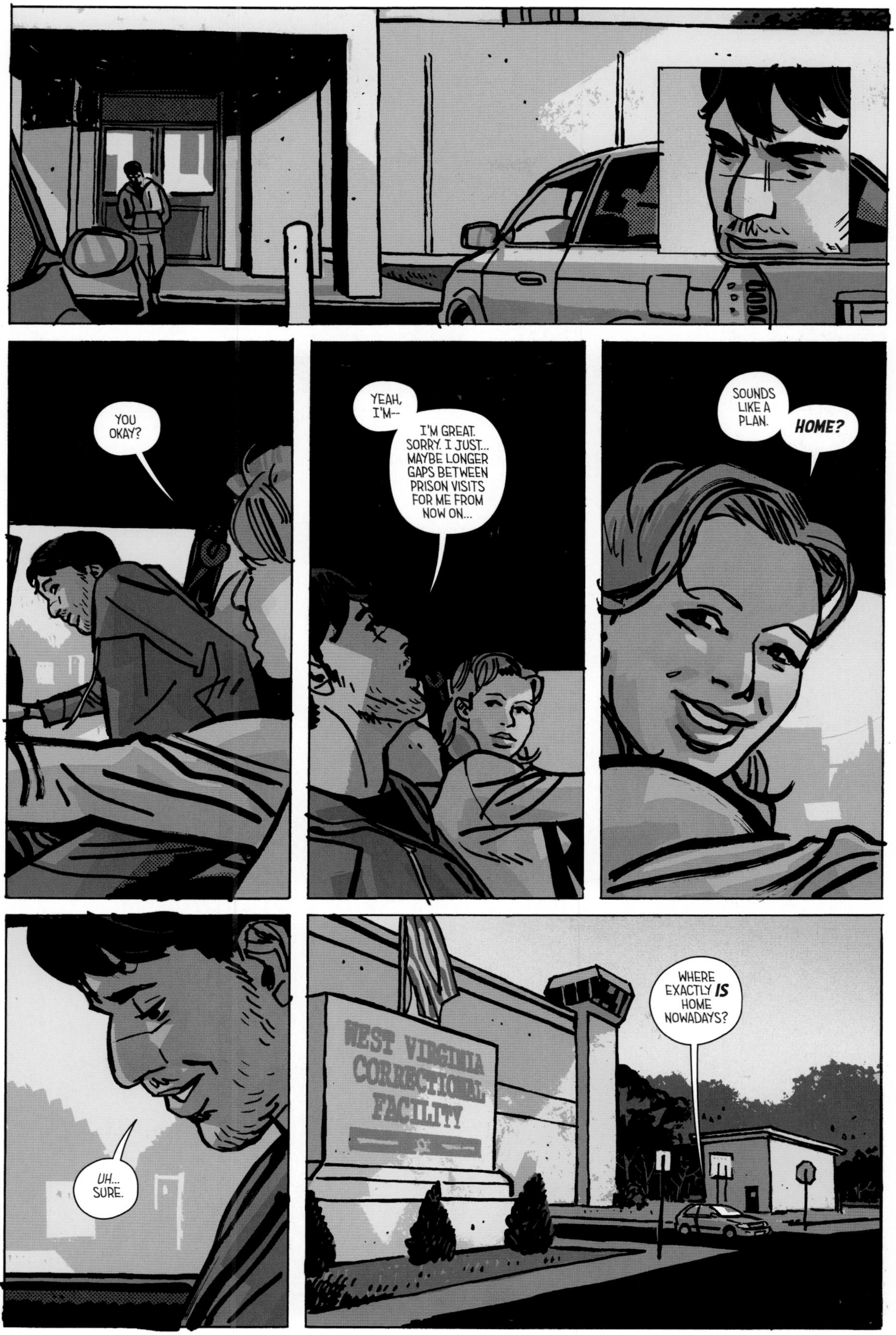

YOU OKAY?
YEAH, I'M--
I'M GREAT. SORRY. I JUST... MAYBE LONGER GAPS BETWEEN PRISON VISITS FOR ME FROM NOW ON...
SOUNDS LIKE A PLAN.
HOME?
UH... SURE.
WEST VIRGINIA CORRECTIONAL FACILITY
WHERE EXACTLY IS HOME NOWADAYS?

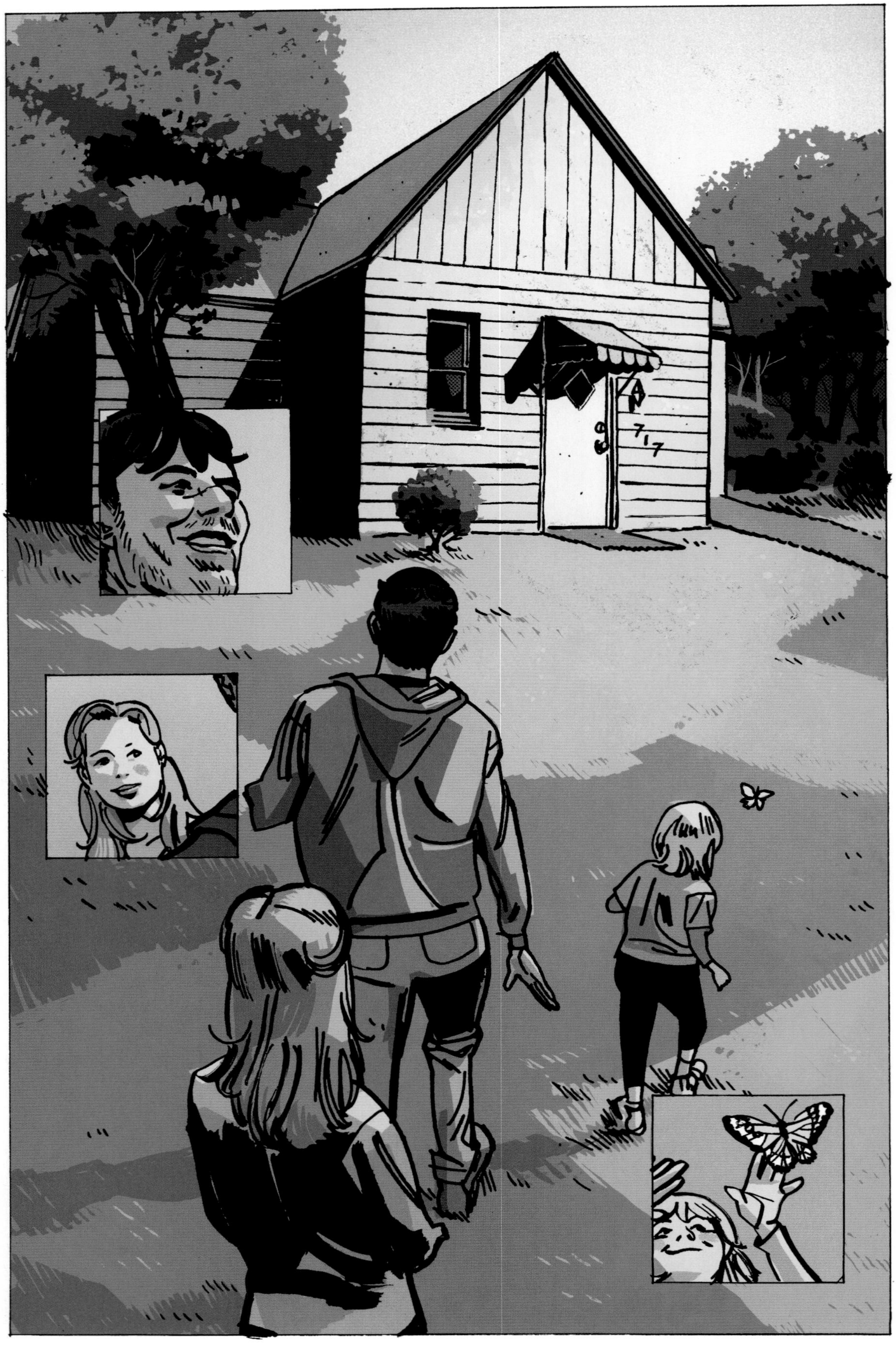

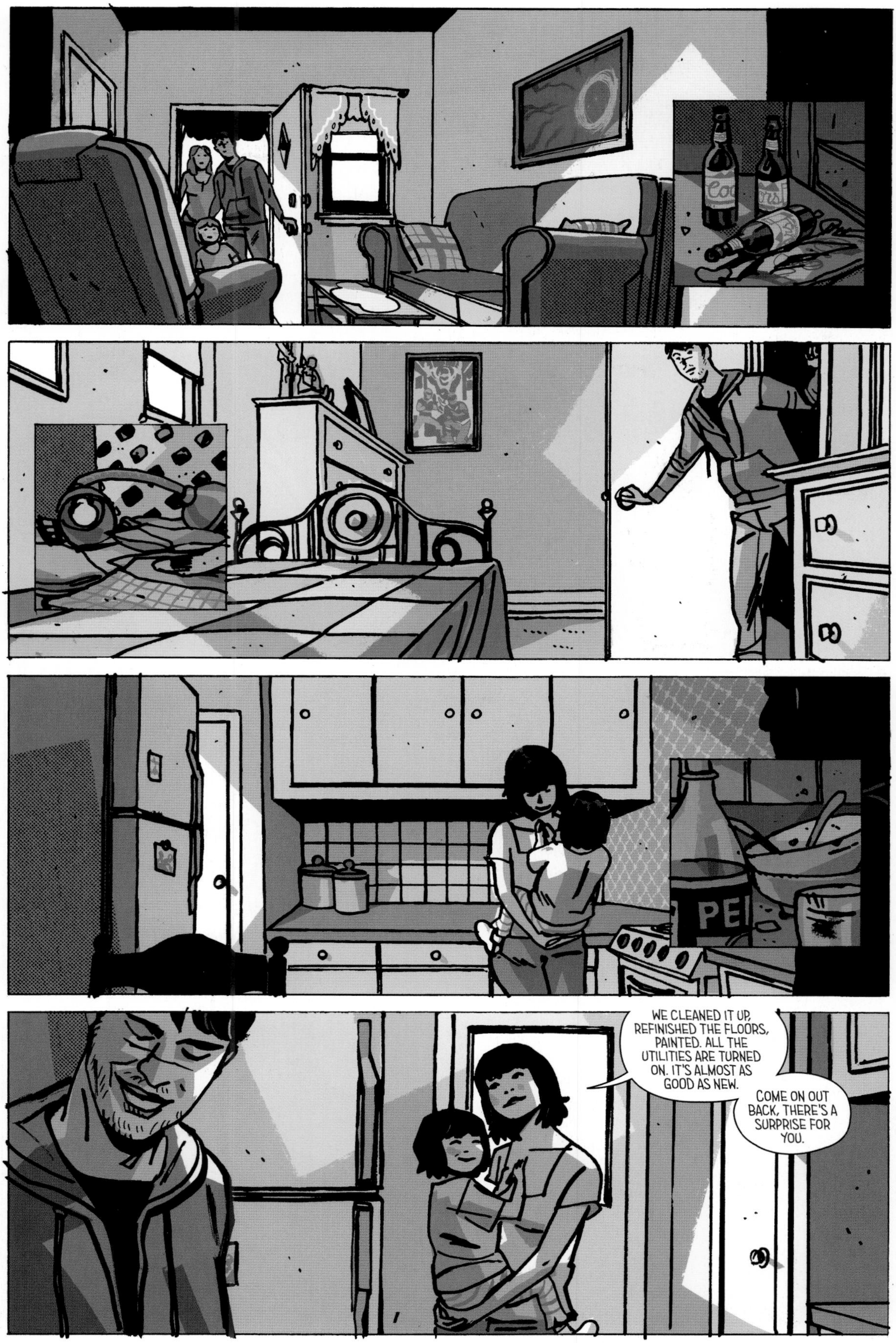
Coors
PE
WE CLEANED IT UP, REFINISHED THE FLOORS, PAINTED. ALL THE UTILITIES ARE TURNED ON. IT'S ALMOST AS GOOD AS NEW.
COME ON OUT BACK, THERE'S A SURPRISE FOR YOU.

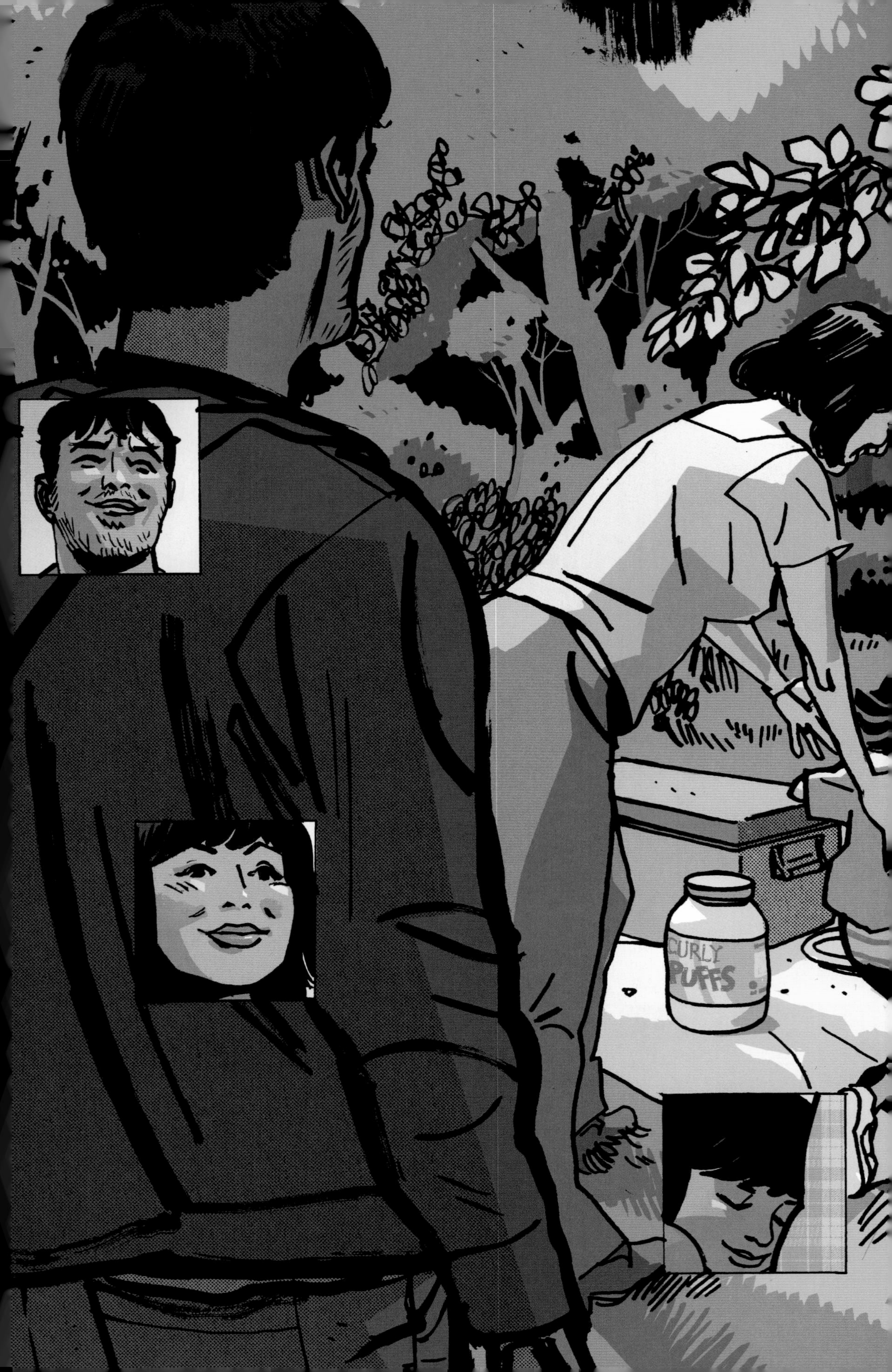
CURLY PUFFS

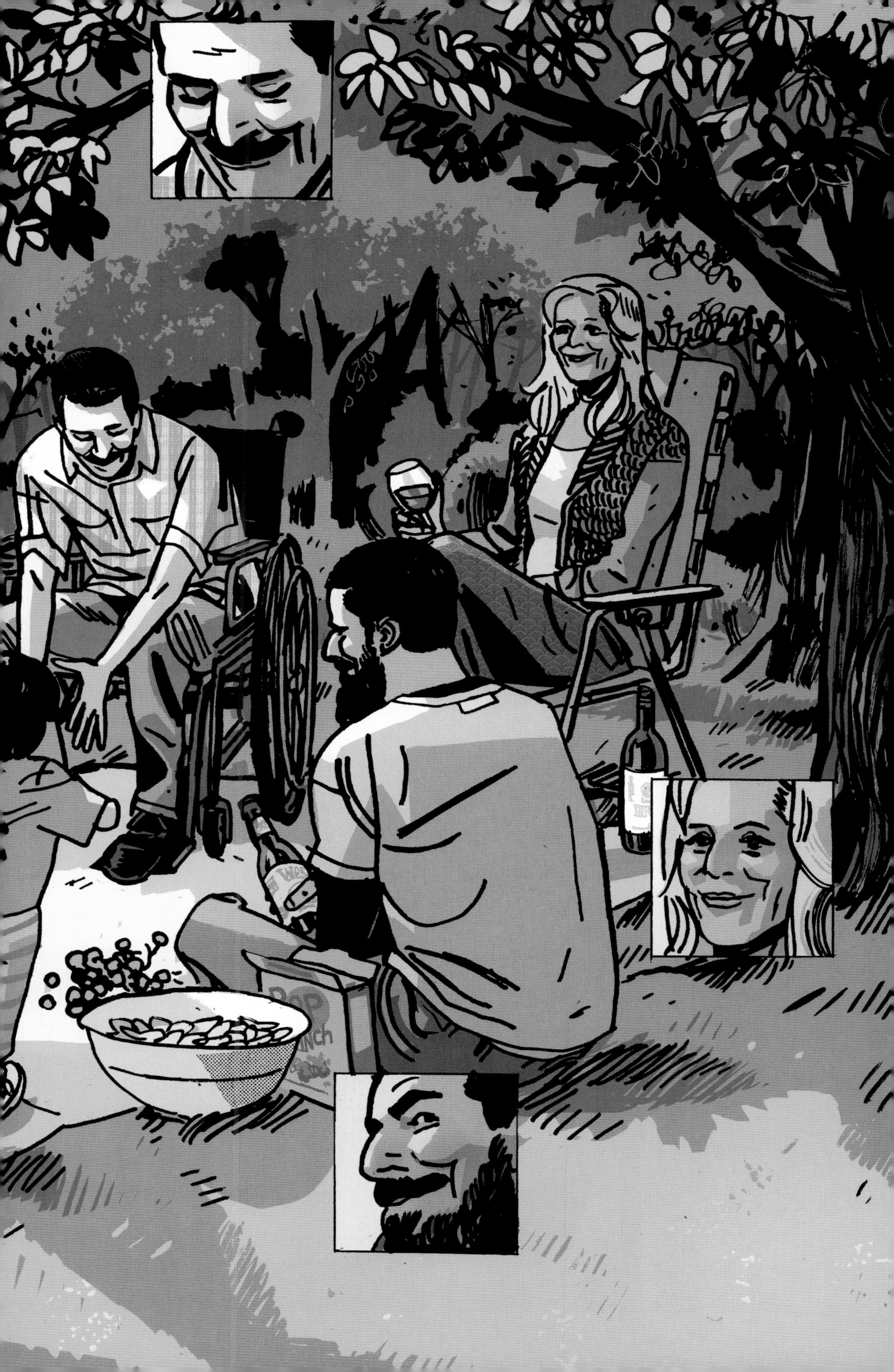

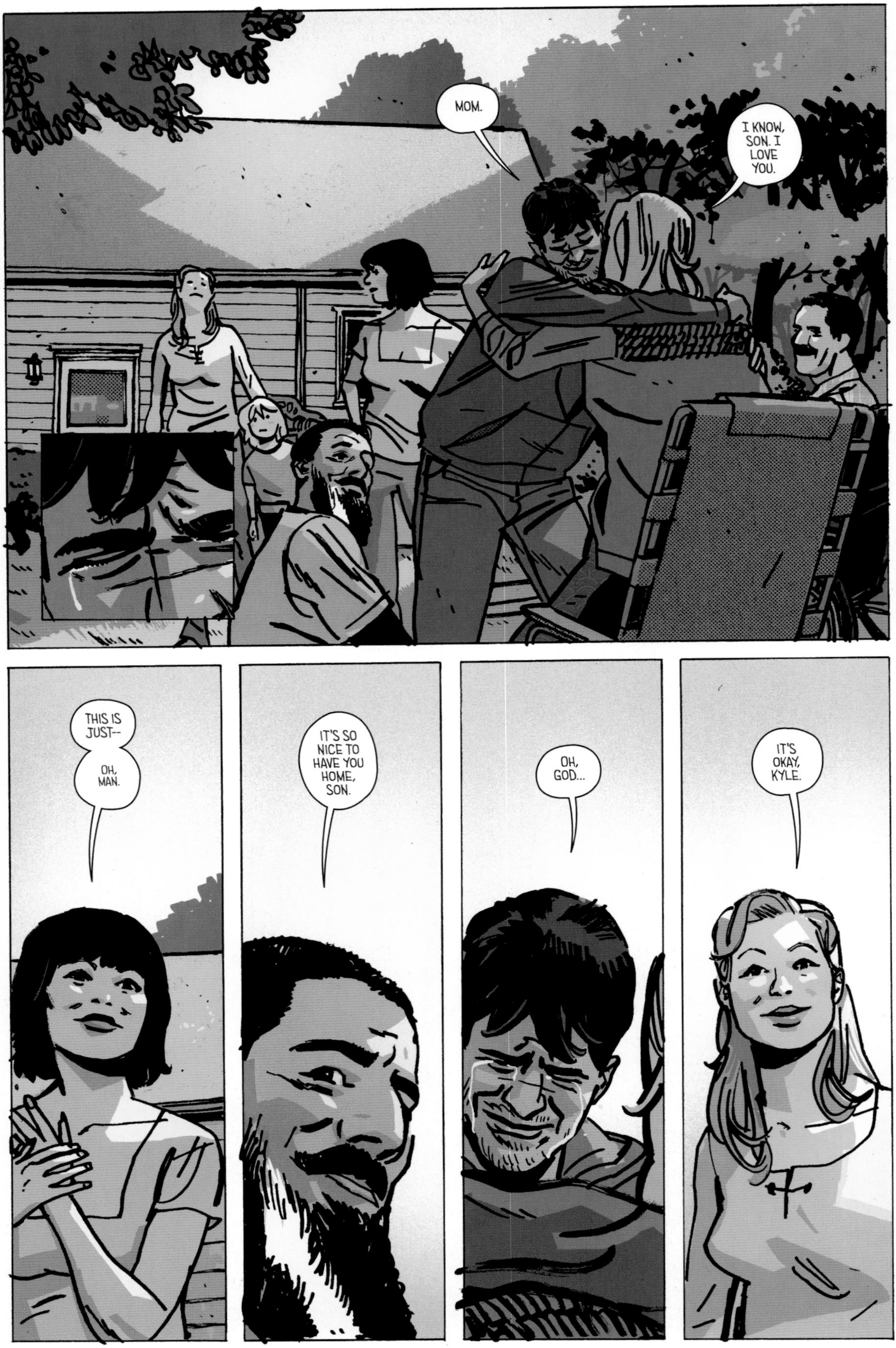
MOM.
I KNOW, SON. I LOVE YOU.
THIS IS JUST--
OH, MAN.
IT'S SO NICE TO HAVE YOU HOME, SON.
OH, GOD...
IT'S OKAY, KYLE.

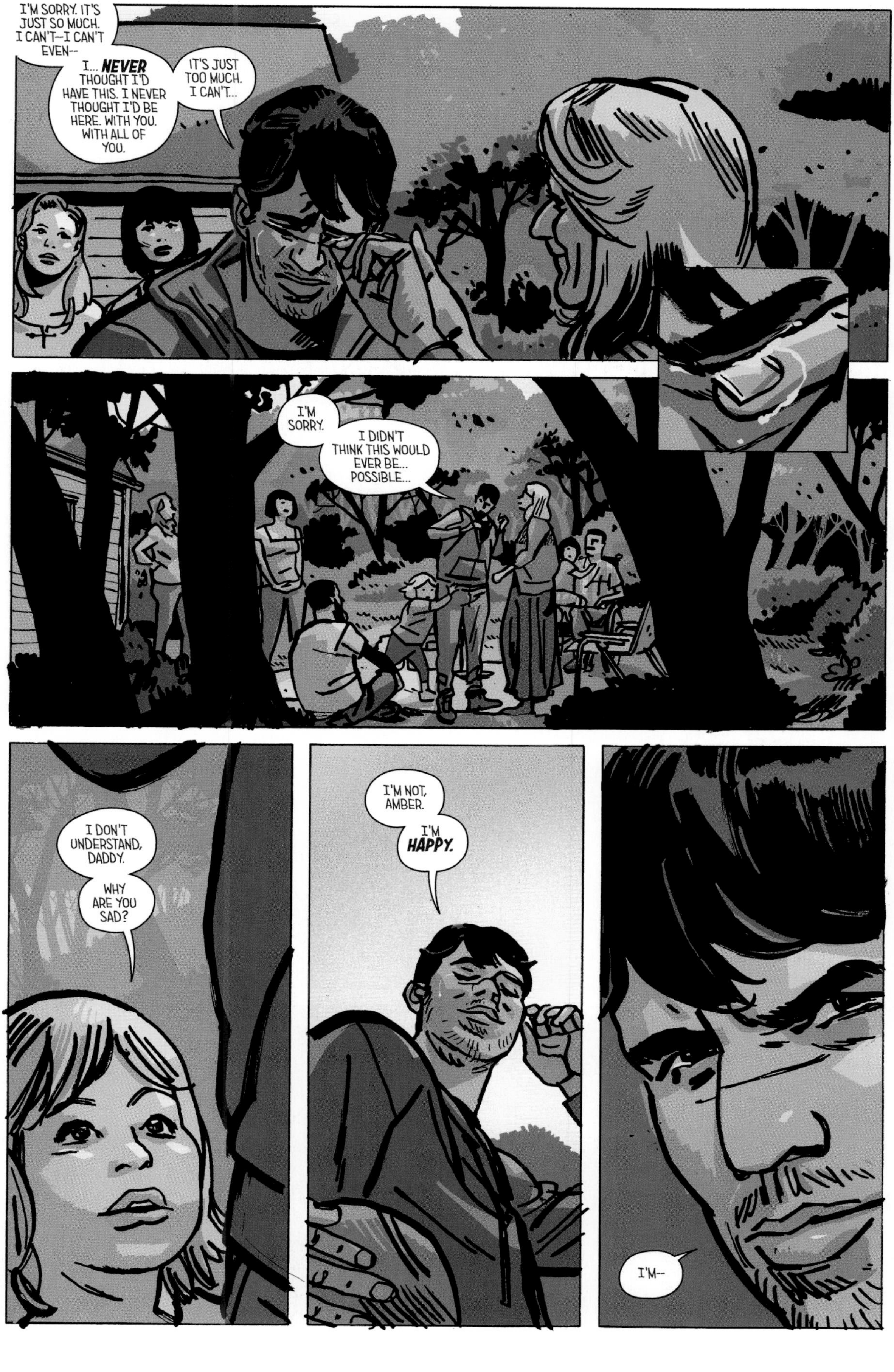
I'M SORRY. IT'S JUST SO MUCH. I CAN'T--I CAN'T EVEN--
I... NEVER THOUGHT I'D HAVE THIS. I NEVER THOUGHT I'D BE HERE. WITH YOU. WITH ALL OF YOU.
IT'S JUST TOO MUCH. I CAN'T...
I'M SORRY.
I DIDN'T THINK THIS WOULD EVER BE... POSSIBLE...
I DON'T UNDERSTAND, DADDY.
WHY ARE YOU SAD?
I'M NOT, AMBER.
I'M HAPPY.
I'M--

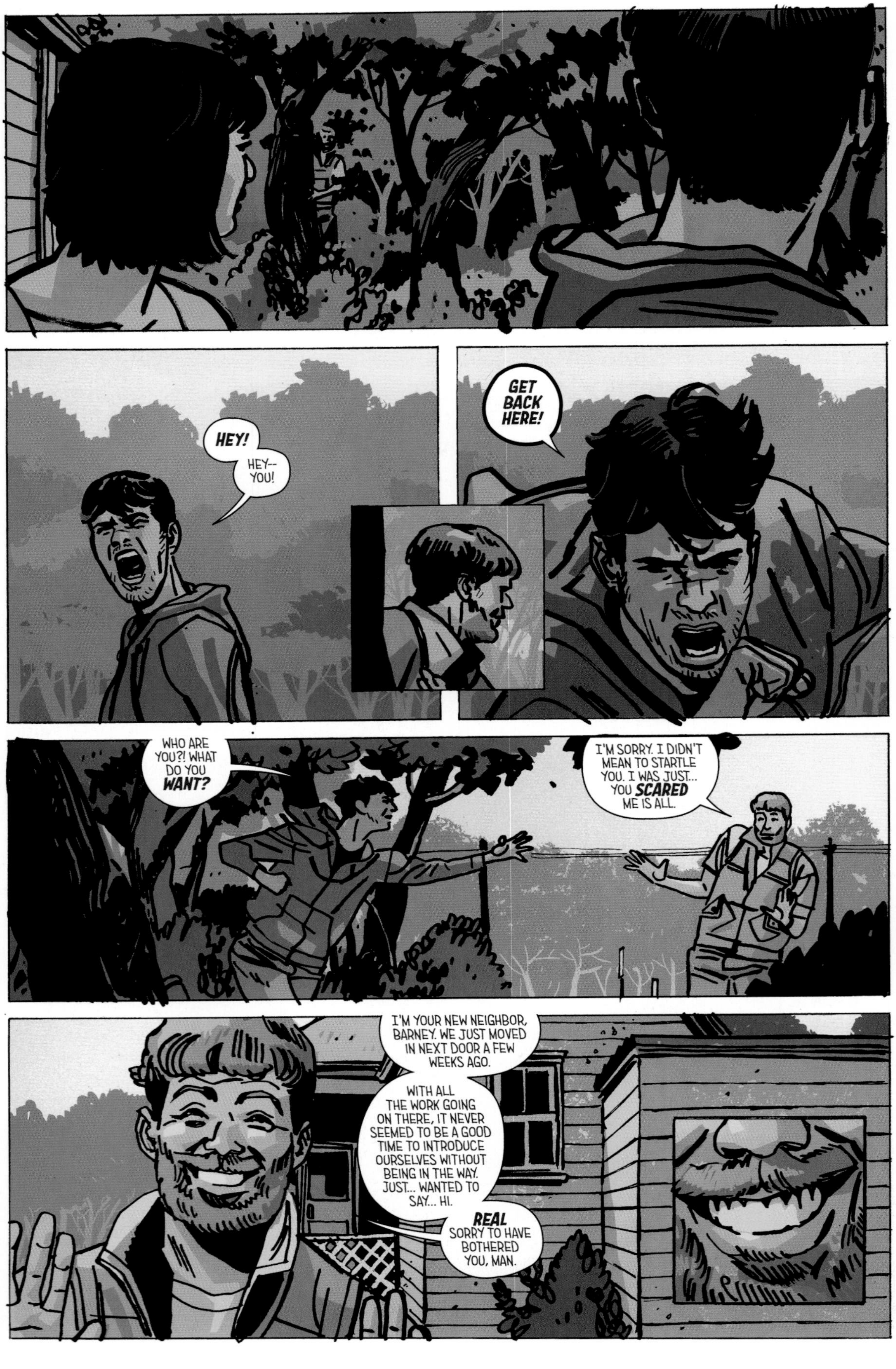
HEY!
HEY-- YOU!
GET BACK HERE!
WHO ARE YOU?! WHAT DO YOU WANT?
I'M SORRY. I DIDN'T MEAN TO STARTLE YOU. I WAS JUST... YOU SCARED ME IS ALL.
I'M YOUR NEW NEIGHBOR, BARNEY. WE JUST MOVED IN NEXT DOOR A FEW WEEKS AGO.
WITH ALL THE WORK GOING ON THERE, IT NEVER SEEMED TO BE A GOOD TIME TO INTRODUCE OURSELVES WITHOUT BEING IN THE WAY. JUST... WANTED TO SAY... HI.
REAL SORRY TO HAVE BOTHERED YOU, MAN.

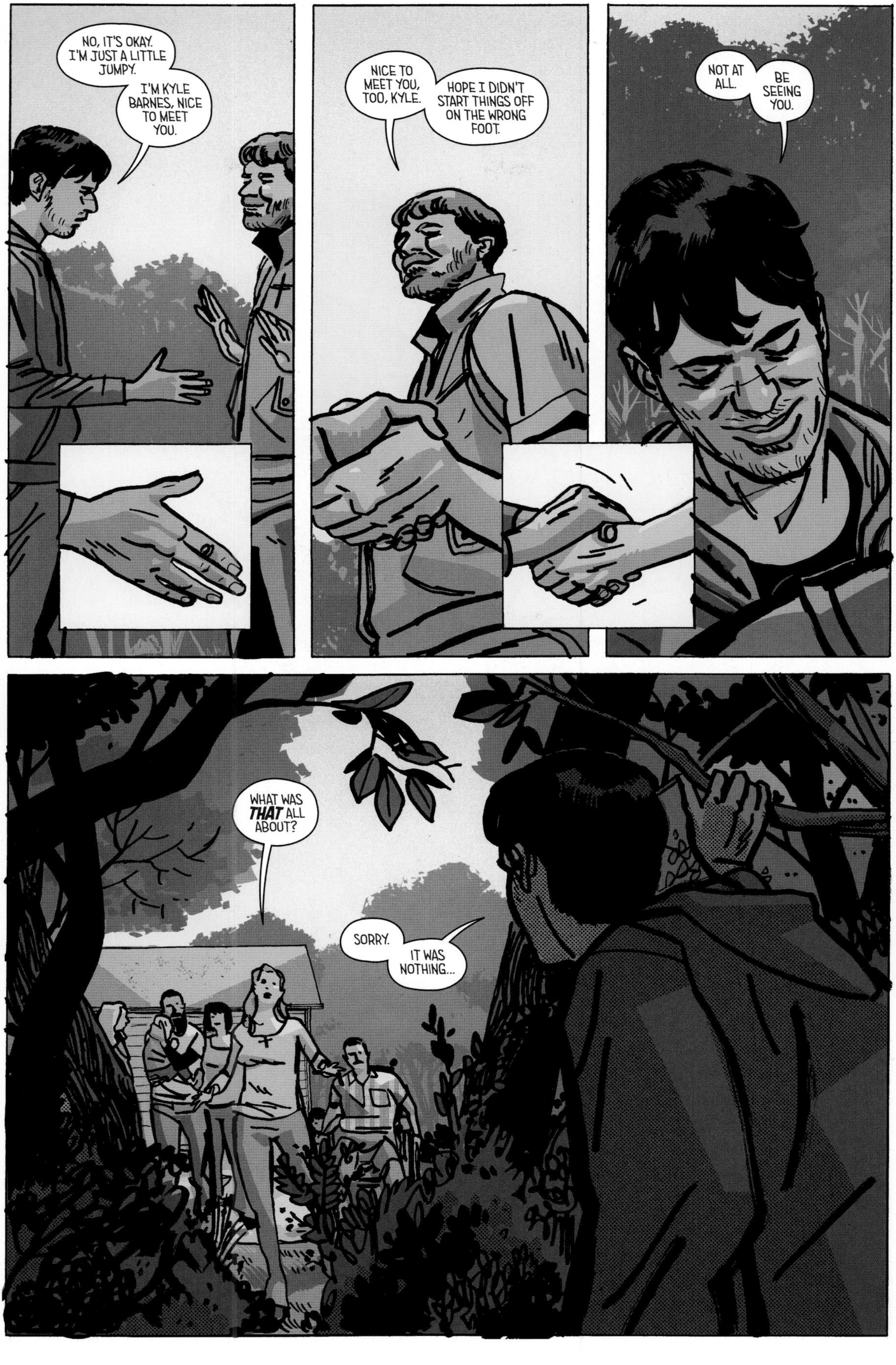
NO, IT'S OKAY. I'M JUST A LITTLE JUMPY.
I'M KYLE BARNES, NICE TO MEET YOU.
NICE TO MEET YOU, TOO, KYLE.
HOPE I DIDN'T START THINGS OFF ON THE WRONG FOOT.
NOT AT ALL.
BE SEEING YOU.
WHAT WAS **THAT** ALL ABOUT?
SORRY.
IT WAS NOTHING...

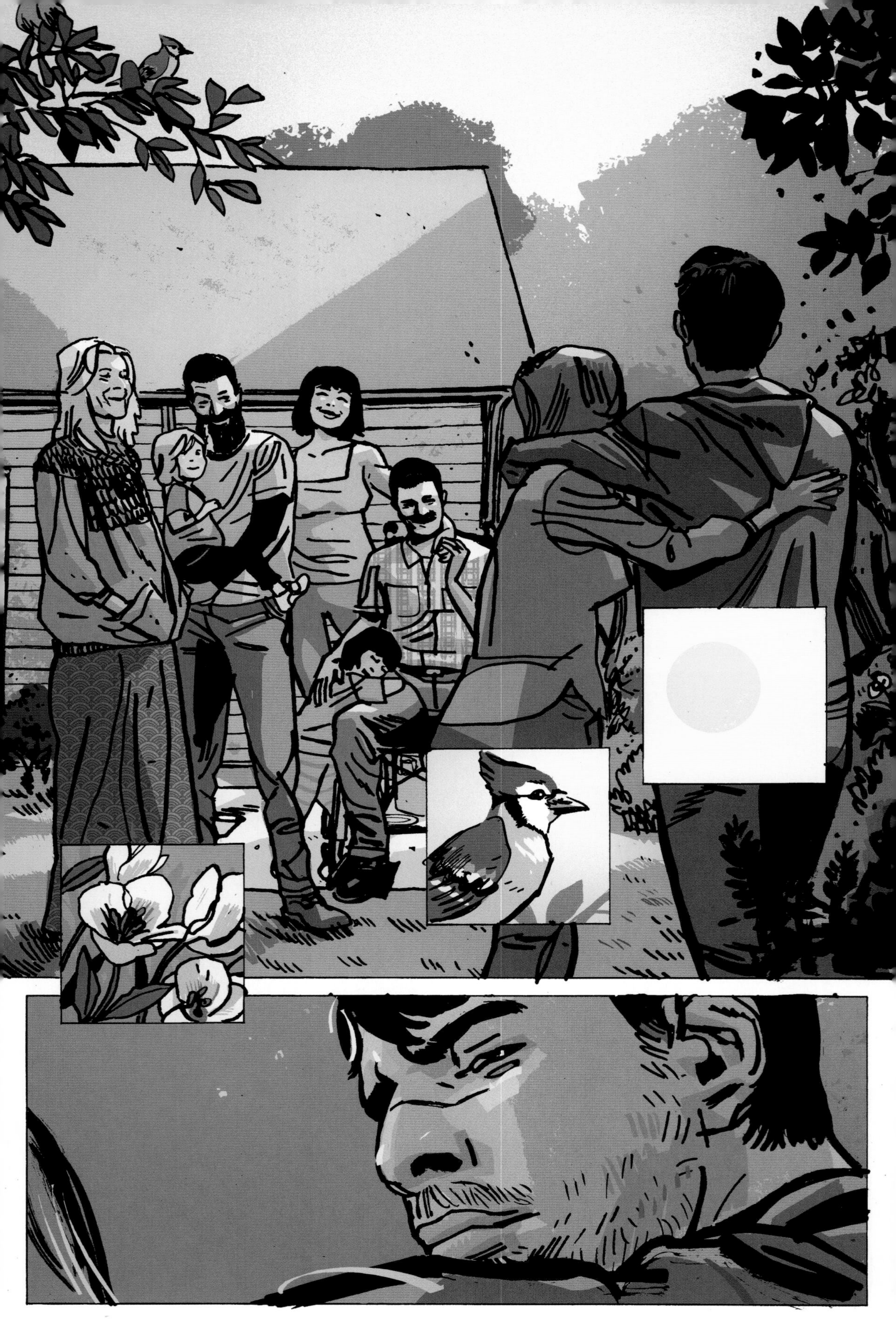

THE END

"Take care of yourself,

...Kyle Barnes"

It ends with a picnic.

When I was promoting the launch of this series, I said in interviews that this was the first series I'd ever launched where I knew the ending as I was starting. To be clear, it was super vague. I knew the merge would happen, that the merge would actually close the rift between dimensions and that everyone would live happily ever after. If you've read this series as well as THE WALKING DEAD and INVINCIBLE you might get the idea that I'm a sucker for happy endings. I guess that's true. I knew it would end with a family reunited... at a picnic. Can't get much happier than that.

There was a lot I didn't know.

I didn't know Allison would be "possessed" by an angel. I didn't know the outcasts would stand in that spiral formation to strengthen their powers to use them against the, for lack of a better name, evil entities. (Man... I really should have named them at some point.) I certainly didn't know poor Reverend Anderson would end up serving a life sentence in prison at the end of the series... and be HAPPY about it. Yeesh.

I did know Kyle's mother Sarah would wake up from her catatonic state in the end. When we were doing the OUTCAST TV show for Cinemax (two seasons still available, check them out maybe one day on HBO Max... but not yet, sadly) the showrunner, Chris Black, wanted to wake Sarah up nearly every episode of that show. It just KEPT coming up. Mostly because Julia Crockett, who played Sarah, was amazing and it was a shame to keep her mostly just lying in a bed during her scenes.

I can't really talk about OUTCAST the comic without talking about Outcast the TV show. Once *The Walking Dead* became a hit on television, there was a fair bit of interest in what I might do next. Most of my projects were vastly different than *The Walking Dead*. I do strive to break some kind of new ground with everything I do. But while it was clear I could probably get another TV project off the ground because of the heat around *The Walking Dead*... it was also clear that it needed to be a project somewhat similar to The Walking Dead. At the very least, it needed to be horror.

So I sat down and came up with the concepts that became OUTCAST. I drew upon my childhood growing up religion-adjacent and used those ideas to build the world of Kyle Barnes. I kind of sold the show by accident. I've told the story before, but I don't think I ever pinpointed it to the 2010 AFI Top 10 luncheon at the Four Seasons Hotel in Beverly Hills. They were celebrating the top 10 movies and top 10 TV shows of 2009. *Walking Dead* was somehow on that list. I was at a table with Sharon Tal Yguado who headed up FOX International, who handled *The Walking Dead* internationally. AMC only handles the show in the US. We'd gotten to know each other on the set of season 1, and she just casually asked me what I was doing next. So I told her about OUTCAST and rambled off a little about Kyle Barnes and his life surrounded by possessed people. She responded with, "That sounds cool. Let's make it." My representatives were receiving calls from Fox International the following Monday wanting to option the rights to OUTCAST.

The only problem is OUTCAST... didn't really exist yet.

I've stated publicly that the comic book series and the TV show were developed side-by-side, but in a lot of ways, the TV show almost came first. I wrote the pilot for the TV show myself... and that was the first thing that was completely written on OUTCAST. I had a bunch of notes for the comic series and I knew where I wanted things to go. So, the series was definitely based on the comics, but I hadn't quite written those ideas down in a complete form until I wrote the pilot script for the show.

So in some ways, the first comic script was actually adapting the pilot script of the show, which is super weird. I'd conceived the scenes as comic book scenes, wrote them to be shot as a TV show, then had to retroactively fit them back into comic scenes. Those little inset panels that run through the entire series? I came up with those because of this process. There were all kinds of little silent looks and nods and little moments that work in a TV script that I was going to have to lose for the comic version because they take up so much space. I really didn't want to lose them though, so I came up with the idea of adding tiny little panels on the page to keep these tiny moments intact.

And that brings us to Paul Azaceta.

Paul and I had known each other for years before we started OUTCAST, although I'll admit we didn't know each other all that well. Paul and I were in the same social circle at conventions, but had never really had a long conversation. That said, I was VERY familiar with his work. I'd loved Paul's art since he debuted with *Grounded* with Mark Sable at Image Comics. When I was still at Marvel he even reached out to me wanting to do a Darkhawk comic. I believe I was winding things down over at that horrific place to work, otherwise I would have taken him up on that offer (I love Darkhawk almost as much as I love Paul).

I knew I needed someone who could draw things that were creepy and scary. There needed to be a darkness to this book that dwarfed even what Charlie Adlard was doing with THE WALKING DEAD. This book wasn't going to have that survival angle, this book was pure horror. Paul was someone I knew would be able to handle that with ease. More than that, though... this was a book about normal people. Scary, yes... but there wasn't going to be any swords or zombies or ninjas or anything cool. I needed someone who could make boring old normal people interesting... again, Paul was perfect for that.

As I sit here typing this for our final issue, I couldn't be more certain I chose the right guy. Just look back at the 48 issues of this series. Each one of them is glorious to behold. This was a very emotional series and Paul did the heavy lifting needed to sell every moment. More than that, he was able to achieve a level of creepiness I'd thought impossible in comics. There are panels that I still have trouble looking at. This book was downright disturbing at times. I've always been amazed at what Paul was able to do with this series.

Elizabeth Breitweiser was someone I'd wanted to work with since I saw her work with Chris Samnee on *Captain America & Bucky*. She's someone who has long been at the top of every artist's list when you ask them who they'd like to work with. She was hand-picked by Paul to color OUTCAST and has been an essential part of the team since day one. Her color choice is second-to-none, and I couldn't imagine the world of OUTCAST seen through the lens of any other colorist.

Rus Wooton is the only letterer I've worked with since I stopped lettering my comics myself. He also just happens to be the premiere letterer in creator-owned comics. Rus's strength is that he can give every single book he does a completely unique flavor with his font choice and balloon design. I absolutely love what he did with OUTCAST, it's one of my favorite lettering jobs from him.

I also want to give a shoutout to our editorial staff. Sean Mackiewicz, Jon Moisan, Helen Leigh and Arielle Basich. They're so good I take them for granted. We certainly wouldn't have made it to this final issue without them.

And yet, here we are, at the final issue. Looking back, I'm very proud that we've had a consistent team for every single issue of this run. This team has been able to grow and evolve our talents along with the characters in this series. This series ran for nearly seven years... and a lot has happened in that time. I mean... who'd have thought we'd have a global pandemic during the run of this series? Certainly not me.

So this is the end, and it ends with a picnic. In the end this series, like everything I've ever written, is about family. I do think OUTCAST is different in that it didn't start that way. It started with a very fractured family, with seemingly no hope of ever repairing those fractures and reuniting. Kyle Barnes only ever wanted to reconcile with his wife and get his daughter back. His mother and father were lost to him. But through his actions, somehow, they all found themselves enjoying that picnic together.

I can't help but think about this last year and how apart we've all been, and I don't know about you, but there have definitely been times when I worried it would never end. It's still not over (despite so many people acting like it is) but there's at least a light at the end of the tunnel.

I, for one, am looking forward to a big family picnic. And thankfully, I probably won't be looking over my shoulder the whole time.

Thank you for taking this journey with us. I hope to see you all on the next one.

Robert Kirkman
Backwoods, CA
April 2021

I remember where I was when Robert first emailed me about OUTCAST. I didn't know it was about OUTCAST and I didn't realize the journey I was about to agree to, but there it was: a horror comic, a long run, and the chance to do something that I could really put myself into. I'd been working steady in comics for a few years at that point and I was not happy with the jobs I was being offered. Don't get me wrong, they were fun, but there wasn't anything I could sink my teeth into. An arc here or there, a fill-in, isn't enough time to develop and grow with a story. One of my proudest parts of the book is being the only artist to draw these characters. Kyle. The Reverend. Sidney. They are the way they live in my head. It's not all the time in this industry you get to do the things I was fortunate enough to have the opportunity to do on OUTCAST. It'll stay as a highlight of my career and a standard for everything that follows. It's something I'll always be grateful to Robert for, even if for him it was a simple email about a fun book to do. So thank you to Mr. Kirkman, Sean, Bettie, Rus, Jon and everyone at Skybound for such a unique and special gift.

Paul Azaceta
April 2021

FOR MORE TALES FROM **ROBERT KIRKMAN** AND **SKYBOUND**

ROBERT KIRKMAN CHARLIE ADLARD STEFANO GAUDIANO CLIFF RATHBURN
THE WALKING DEAD
VOLUME 32
REST IN PEACE

VOL. 1: DAYS GONE BYE TP
ISBN: 978-1-58240-672-5
$14.99

VOL. 2: MILES BEHIND US TP
ISBN: 978-1-58240-775-3
$14.99

VOL. 3: SAFETY BEHIND BARS TP
ISBN: 978-1-58240-805-7
$14.99

VOL. 4: THE HEART'S DESIRE TP
ISBN: 978-1-58240-530-8
$14.99

VOL. 5: THE BEST DEFENSE TP
ISBN: 978-1-58240-612-1
$14.99

VOL. 6: THIS SORROWFUL LIFE TP
ISBN: 978-1-58240-684-8
$14.99

VOL. 7: THE CALM BEFORE TP
ISBN: 978-1-58240-828-6
$14.99

VOL. 8: MADE TO SUFFER TP
ISBN: 978-1-58240-883-5
$14.99

VOL. 9: HERE WE REMAIN TP
ISBN: 978-1-60706-022-2
$14.99

VOL. 10: WHAT WE BECOME TP
ISBN: 978-1-60706-075-8
$14.99

VOL. 11: FEAR THE HUNTERS TP
ISBN: 978-1-60706-181-6
$14.99

VOL. 12: LIFE AMONG THEM TP
ISBN: 978-1-60706-254-7
$14.99

VOL. 13: TOO FAR GONE TP
ISBN: 978-1-60706-329-2
$14.99

VOL. 14: NO WAY OUT TP
ISBN: 978-1-60706-392-6
$14.99

VOL. 15: WE FIND OURSELVES TP
ISBN: 978-1-60706-440-4
$14.99

VOL. 16: A LARGER WORLD TP
ISBN: 978-1-60706-559-3
$14.99

VOL. 17: SOMETHING TO FEAR TP
ISBN: 978-1-60706-615-6
$14.99

VOL. 18: WHAT COMES AFTER TP
ISBN: 978-1-60706-687-3
$14.99

VOL. 19: MARCH TO WAR TP
ISBN: 978-1-60706-818-1
$14.99

VOL. 20: ALL OUT WAR PART ONE TP
ISBN: 978-1-60706-882-2
$14.99

VOL. 21: ALL OUT WAR PART TWO TP
ISBN: 978-1-63215-030-1
$14.99

VOL. 22: A NEW BEGINNING TP
ISBN: 978-1-63215-041-7
$14.99

VOL. 23: WHISPERS INTO SCREAMS TP
ISBN: 978-1-63215-258-9
$14.99

VOL. 24: LIFE AND DEATH TP
ISBN: 978-1-63215-402-6
$14.99

VOL. 25: NO TURNING BACK TP
ISBN: 978-1-63215-659-4
$14.99

VOL. 26: CALL TO ARMS TP
ISBN: 978-1-63215-917-5
$14.99

VOL. 27: THE WHISPERER WAR TP
ISBN: 978-1-5343-0052-1
$14.99

VOL. 28: A CERTAIN DOOM TP
ISBN: 978-1-5343-0244-0
$14.99

VOL. 29: LINES WE CROSS TP
ISBN: 978-1-5343-0497-0
$16.99

VOL. 30: NEW WORLD ORDER TP
ISBN: 978-1-5343-0884-8
$16.99

VOL. 31: THE ROTTEN CORE TP
ISBN: 978-1-5343-1052-0
$16.99

VOL. 32: REST IN PEACE TP
ISBN: 978-1-5343-1241-8
$16.99

BOOK ONE HC
ISBN: 978-1-58240-619-0
$34.99

BOOK TWO HC
ISBN: 978-1-58240-698-5
$34.99

BOOK THREE HC
ISBN: 978-1-58240-825-5
$34.99

BOOK FOUR HC
ISBN: 978-1-60706-000-0
$34.99

BOOK FIVE HC
ISBN: 978-1-60706-171-7
$34.99

BOOK SIX HC
ISBN: 978-1-60706-327-8
$34.99

BOOK SEVEN HC
ISBN: 978-1-60706-439-8
$34.99

BOOK EIGHT HC
ISBN: 978-1-60706-593-7
$34.99

BOOK NINE HC
ISBN: 978-1-60706-798-6
$34.99

BOOK TEN HC
ISBN: 978-1-63215-034-9
$34.99

BOOK ELEVEN HC
ISBN: 978-1-63215-271-8
$34.99

BOOK TWELVE HC
ISBN: 978-1-63215-451-4
$34.99

BOOK THIRTEEN HC
ISBN: 978-1-63215-916-8
$34.99

BOOK FOURTEEN HC
ISBN: 978-1-5343-0329-4
$34.99

BOOK FIFTEEN HC
ISBN: 978-1-5343-0850-3
$34.99

BOOK SIXTEEN HC
ISBN: 978-1-5343-1325-5
$34.99

ROBERT KIRKMAN
SCOTT M. GIMPLE
CHRIS BURNHAM
NATHAN FAIRBAIRN
2ND VOLUME

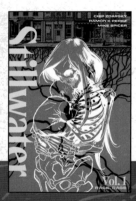

VOL. 1
ISBN: 978-1-5343-1214-2
$19.99

VOL. 2
ISBN: 978-1-5343-1707-9
$16.99

ROBERT KIRKMAN
CHRIS SAMNEE
FIRE POWER
VOLUME 2 HOME FIRE

VOL. 1: PRELUDE
ISBN: 978-1-5343-1214-2
$19.99

VOL. 2: HOME FIRE
ISBN: 978-1-5343-1718-5
$16.99

OBLIVION SONG
CHAPTER FIVE

CHAPTER ONE
ISBN: 978-1-5343-0642-4
$9.99

CHAPTER TWO
ISBN: 978-1-5343-1057-5
$16.99

CHAPTER THREE
ISBN: 978-1-5343-1326-2
$16.99

CHAPTER FOUR
ISBN: 978-1-5343-1517-4
$16.99

CHAPTER FIVE
ISBN: 978-1-5343-1728-4
$16.99

CHIP ZDARSKY
RAMON K PEREZ
MIKE SPICER
Stillwater
Vol. 1
RAGE, RAGE

VOL. 1: RAGE RAGE
ISBN: 978-1-5343-1837-3
$16.99